MISS MINCHIN DIES

Recent Titles by Betty Rowlands from Severn House

A FOOL THERE WAS
ALPHA, BETA, GAMMA . . . DEAD
COPYCAT
DEADLY OBSESSION
DEATH AT DEARLY MANOR
DIRTY WORK
A HIVE OF BEES
AN INCONSIDERATE DEATH
MISS MINCHIN DIES
PARTY TO MURDER
SMOKESCREEN
TOUCH ME NOT

MISS MINCHIN DIES

A Sukey Reynolds Mystery

Betty Rowlands

severn
House

This first world edition published 2010
in Great Britain and in 2011 in the USA by
SEVERN HOUSE PUBLISHERS LTD of
9–15 High Street, Sutton, Surrey, England, SM1 1DF.
Trade paperback edition first published
in Great Britain and the USA 2011 by
SEVERN HOUSE PUBLISHERS LTD.

British Library Cataloguing in Publication Data

Rowlands, Betty.
  Miss Minchin Dies. – (A Sukey Reynolds mystery)
  1. Reynolds, Sukey (Fictitious character)–Fiction.
  2. Policewomen–Great Britain–Fiction. 3. Serial murder
  investigation–Fiction. 4. Detective and mystery stories.
  I. Title II. Series
  823.9'14-dc22

ISBN-13: 978-0-7278-6990-6 (cased)
ISBN-13: 978-1-84751-322-9 (trade paper)

All Severn House titles are printed on acid-free paper.

Severn House Publishers support The Forest Stewardship Council [FSC],
the leading international forest certification organisation. All our titles that
are printed on Greenpeace-approved FSC-certified paper carry the FSC logo.

MIX
Paper from
responsible sources
FSC
www.fsc.org   FSC® C018575

Typeset by Palimpsest Book Production Ltd.,
Falkirk, Stirlingshire, Scotland.
Printed and bound in Great Britain by
MPG Books Ltd., Bodmin, Cornwall.

PROLOGUE

I t was Joe Atwood from the dairy who found Adelaide Minchin's body. When he called at her cottage on Saturday morning he found the pint of milk he had left on her doorstep two days before still standing there. He picked it up; the bottle was warm to the touch, the contents evidently curdled. He frowned. She hadn't said anything about not wanting a delivery on Thursday.

He gave his customary rat-a-tat on the door. When there was no answer he knocked again, a bit harder, but there was still no response. She was normally up and dressed at this time and would have his money ready on the window sill just inside the front door. He bent down and peered through the letterbox, but could see nothing. He became uneasy, sensing that something was wrong. He happened to know that she kept a key under a flowerpot beside the back door. He found it and let himself in.

He called her name, but there was no answer. Having checked the kitchen, the dining room and the lounge he went upstairs, tapped on several doors at random, repeatedly calling her name. After a moment he cautiously pushed one of the doors open. It was obviously a bedroom and the bed appeared to have been slept in. There was a door opposite the bed. *Must be the en suite bathroom*, he thought. The door was ajar; his gaze travelled to the floor, where an outstretched hand was just visible. He called again; there was no reply and the hand did not move. His mouth dry with apprehension, he crossed the room and bent down to touch it. It was stone cold.

ONE

'Feeling a bit better now, sir?' Sergeant Murray put a hand on Joe Atwood's shoulder as he sat slumped in a chair in the late Adelaide Minchin's kitchen. Having examined the scene and satisfied himself that there was no evidence of forced entry and no open window where an intruder might have entered, and after receiving the doctor's assurance that there was nothing to suggest that the dead woman had been the victim of physical violence, he gave permission for the body to be removed to the mortuary. He then returned to the kitchen to question the only witness.

Joe, who was staring with a dazed expression at the wall and appeared unaware of the sergeant's presence, gave a violent start at the touch of his hand. The face that he turned up to Murray was drained of colour. 'Who are you?' he asked shakily.

'I told you a moment ago, sir. I'm Sergeant Murray from Over Hampton police station.'

'Why are you here?'

'There seems to have been an accident,' said Murray patiently. 'A lady was found lying apparently unconscious on the bathroom floor and someone called for an ambulance. Was that you, sir?'

'That's right. I found her when I came for my money, you see. Thursday's milk was still on the doorstep . . . she didn't answer my knock . . . so I went in. Gave me a fair turn it did, seeing her like that.' Joe's voice was hoarse and unsteady and he passed a hand across his eyes as if trying to erase the memory.

'That's quite understandable, sir. Maybe a cup of tea would help?'

'The milk's off.' Joe pointed to the bottle that had somehow found its way on to the table.

'There's still a drop left in the fridge.' The sergeant held up a small glass jug and sniffed the contents. 'I reckon it's OK.' He filled a kettle, switched it on and rummaged around until he found everything he needed. He filled two mugs with strong tea, put them on the table, sat down opposite Joe and took out his notebook. 'I just need to ask a few questions to complete my report, sir.'

'Is Miss Adelaide all right? She was out cold when I found her.'

'I'll come to that in a moment, sir. Now, you are Joseph Atwood and you are a roundsman for Over Hampton Dairies. Is that correct?'

Joe took a deep draught of tea, coughed and wiped his mouth with the back of his hand. 'That's right officer. I've worked for them for five years and nothing like this happened to me before – that's to say, not since I came out of the army.' He drank some more tea and the colour began to return to his face. He glanced up at the clock on the kitchen wall; it was nearly eleven. 'I'm way behind with my round, the customers will be complaining.'

'That's all right, we've informed the dairy and they've sent a relief to pick up your float.'

'But it's Saturday – I have to collect the money.' Joe showed signs of agitation.

'I'm sure there won't be a problem.' Recognizing that the man was still in a state of shock, Murray spoke in as soothing a tone as possible. 'I have to ask you a few questions – it shouldn't take long and then I can drop you off at the dairy, or wherever you want.'

Joe put down the empty mug and exhaled noisily. 'That's better,' he grunted. 'So what do you want to know?'

'You asked about Miss Adelaide. Is she the lady who lives here?'

'That's right, Miss Adelaide Minchin.'

'Thank you.' Murray made a note. 'You were concerned because last Thursday's delivery of milk was still on the doorstep when you called this morning and there was no response to your knock?'

Joe nodded. 'I knocked two or three times and called through the letterbox, but she didn't answer. It wasn't like her; she's normally what you'd call an early bird.'

'Do I take it you don't deliver to her house every day?'

'Just three days a week – Tuesdays and Thursdays when she has one pint of semi-skimmed, and Saturdays when she has two pints and half a dozen eggs. My boss once said it's hardly worth coming out here for such a small order, but she's been a good customer in the past, that's before she started worrying about her weight. She used to take . . .'

'Let's just stick to this morning if you don't mind, sir,' Murray broke in. 'There was no answer to your knock so you went into the house to investigate?' Joe nodded. 'How did you manage that, sir? Did you find a door open – or perhaps a window?'

'No, I used the key.'

'Miss Minchin gave you her key? That's a little unusual, isn't it?'

The question brought a flush to Joe's face. 'Here, what're you suggesting?' he asked angrily.

'Sorry sir, no offence. If she didn't give you a key, where did you get it?'

'She always keeps a key under a flower pot by the back door because she's got this thing about getting locked out.'

'She told you this?'

'It came up in conversation one morning when I called for the money. I can't remember how. She quite likely told other people – she's a very chatty lady, quite different to Miss Muriel.'

'Miss Muriel?'

'Her cousin. She lived here for twenty years or more, so they say. Miss Adelaide moved in after she died. Seems Miss Muriel left it to her in her will. They say in the village that it caused trouble with some of her other relations. I don't know for sure, mind. It could be just gossip.'

'I see.' Murray made a note to make further enquiries on this point. 'So you went and found the key and entered by that door over there.' He indicated the glazed door that looked out over a well tended back garden, bounded on three sides by a low wall of red brick.

'That's right.'

'Was the door locked?'

'Of course it was – why else would I need a key?'

'I just need to get all the details right,' said Murray. 'So you let yourself in and found Miss Minchin lying on her bathroom floor. Did you touch anything?'

'Her hand was all I could see of her and I touched that. Very cold, it was.' Joe shuddered and passed a hand over his forehead. 'I asked her if she was all right, but she didn't answer.'

'Did you go into the bathroom?'

Joe shook his head indignantly. 'Certainly not, it wouldn't have been decent. I could tell she needed help so I called for an ambulance.'

'And then what did you do?'

'I waited in the front room until the ambulance came. There were two paramedics. I let them in, showed them where to go and then came and sat down in here.'

'You didn't speak to them?'

'No.'

'Did you speak to anyone else?'

'No.'

'What about the doctor?'

'What doctor?'

'The paramedics sent for a doctor. You're saying you didn't see him?'

Joe shook his head. 'I only saw the ambulance people – a man and a woman I think. I heard a lot of talk but I didn't catch what they were saying. I don't remember much else until you turned up.' He suddenly looked anxious. 'How is she? Is she all right?'

'I'm afraid not,' said Murray soberly.

'You mean she's dead?' Joe's mouth fell open. 'I can't believe it,' he whispered. 'She was such a lovely lady. What happened?'

'We don't know yet. Have you been sitting here all that time?'

'That's right. I thought I'd better keep out of the way and let the ambulance people look after her . . . and that's all I can tell you.'

'Thank you sir, you've been very helpful.'

Joe stood up. 'Is it all right if I get on with the round now?'

'Someone else is looking after it, remember?'

Joe sat down again. 'Oh yes, I forgot.'

'I'll be getting back to the station in a moment so we can leave together,' said Murray. He wrote in his notebook, closed it and put it in his pocket. 'Right, there's just one more thing – will you show me where Miss Minchin used to keep her key as we go out?'

'Sure.' Outside the back door, Joe pointed to an earthenware pot of brightly coloured geraniums. 'Under there. She was so proud of her flowers,' he added sadly.

'Did you put the key back?'

'No, I've got it here.' Joe took the key from his pocket. 'D'you want me to . . .?'

He made a move towards the geranium pot, but Murray said quickly, 'Thank you, I'll take charge of it.' With apparent reluctance, Joe handed it over. Murray noticed that it was still warm, as if he had been holding it tightly from the moment he entered the house.

The news of Adelaide's death spread like wildfire throughout the village. In the bar of the Red Lion that evening Joe Atwood, apparently recovered from the shock of his tragic discovery, had been kept well supplied with the local ale by residents hungry for details. Various theories as to how she came to be lying on the floor were put forward, from a sudden seizure caused by an unsuspected heart condition to slipping on a wet floor, losing her balance and sustaining a fatal blow on the head as she fell. During a gap in the conversation Miss Pryor, who worked in the public library, was known to have a weakness for mysteries and made a hobby of going to murder weekends, suggested – somewhat diffidently – that one of the disinherited relatives might have taken a belated revenge.

The inquest on the death of Adelaide Minchin opened in the parish hall in Over Hampton on the Wednesday following the discovery of her body. The hall was packed; Adelaide had been a popular and active member of the community, a regular worshipper at Saint Peter's church and a member of several local societies and social groups. She also had a wide circle of friends of both sexes. Her sudden death had sent shock waves through the village.

Her cousin Henry Minchin gave evidence of identification. He was a smartly dressed man of about seventy with neatly trimmed grey hair and a thin moustache. He gave his answers to the coroner's questions in a somewhat officious manner that one member of the public who managed to get into the hall was later heard to describe as 'sort of sneering, like he thought he was superior to Doctor Freeborne'. Once he had given his evidence, the coroner announced that pending the result of the post-mortem the proceedings would be adjourned until a date to be announced.

Henry Minchin's presence at the inquest caused a stir for another reason. Many local people recalled the strange developments that followed the news that his late sister Muriel had bequeathed Parson's Acre to their cousin Adelaide instead, as had generally been expected, of including it with the rest of her estate. The residue, after various charitable bequests, had been divided equally between her siblings – her brothers Henry and Jarvis Minchin and her sister Mavis Kellaway. After Muriel's funeral these three had been observed engaged in what appeared to be somewhat ill-natured exchanges with Adelaide. They had subsequently put in the briefest of appearances at the buffet meal at the Hampton Hotel following the interment and according to some highly coloured and possibly exaggerated reports from one or two of the other guests there had even been threats of legal proceedings. Rumour also had it that the house represented the greater part of Muriel's estate, which would have added fuel to their resentment.

Inevitably, a wave of further conjecture followed the coroner's decision to adjourn the proceedings. Since no one yet knew the cause of death, some people began to wonder if there was something in Ivy Pryor's theory after all. Opinion was divided on this point, but it was generally agreed in the bar that evening that if Henry Minchin's brother and surviving sister were anything like him it was no wonder that Muriel left her house to Adelaide.

'Never showed a spark of regret at the death of his own sister, let alone his cousin,' commented Ben Bridges, the landlord of the Red Lion. 'I reckon he can't wait to get his greedy hands on Parson's Acre. Assuming she's left it to him . . . or maybe one of the others, of course.'

The proviso gave rise to another series of speculations about the possible contents of Adelaide's will. It was suggested, not without a certain degree of malicious optimism, that there might be a resurgence of internecine warfare if she had followed Muriel's example and left it to another relation – if there was one, which seemed unlikely – or even to some person no one knew about. It would, someone said gleefully, serve her cousins right if she'd left her entire fortune – which was thought, judging from her lifestyle, to be considerable – to a cats' home. And the consensus was that a cats' home would be preferable to having any of the Minchin siblings living in the village.

Parson's Acre lay in an isolated position on the edge of the village and was overlooked by no other houses. However, Adelaide never made any secret of her movements and when she was expecting visitors she would occasionally invite members of her wide circle of friends in the village to meet them. In fact, anyone who called at the cottage for whatever purpose was sure of a cordial welcome and more often than not an offer of refreshment. What everyone agreed on was that she never even mentioned her relations, let alone spoke of plans to entertain or visit any of them. No one could believe she would have left the house to any of her unpleasant cousins.

'She loved that house,' remarked Jack Appleby, who with his wife Florence ran the village store and post office. 'Had plans for it too, so she was telling the wife only the other day.'

'What plans were they?' asked Ben.

'I'm not exactly sure, but Flo said she was very taken by an advertisement she'd seen in some country house magazine for an extension – what she called a garden room – at the back of the house. She said she might show it to Tom Hubbard and ask him for an estimate. Is that right, Tom?' Jack leaned forward and called to a man standing at the bar a short distance away. He had to repeat the question as Tom and his companion were carrying out a post-mortem of their own on the disastrous defeat of the local football team.

'Ay, she did say something,' Tom replied. 'I said I'd have a look at it.'

'And did you?'

Tom shook his head. 'Never got around to it,' he said and returned to his earlier discussion.

TWO

After studying the post-mortem report the coroner reconvened the inquest on the death of Adelaide Minchin. After all the evidence had been heard he had no hesitation in announcing a verdict of accidental death and the body was released for burial.

A few days later, DCI Leach of the Avon and Somerset Constabulary received a telephone call from the coroner, Doctor Freeborne. He immediately summoned DS Greg Rathbone to his office and gave him a brief report of the call.

'It appears the deceased's GP thinks there's something fishy about Adelaide Minchin's death,' he explained. 'Freeborne's inclined to think the man is making something out of nothing, but says he's pretty insistent so he's agreed to have a word with us just to keep him quiet.'

'Why didn't he speak up at the inquest, sir?'

'He's been out of the country attending a conference in the States and then stayed on for a couple of weeks' holiday, so he didn't get back till the day after the funeral.'

'Do you want me to go and see him, sir?'

Leach shook his head. 'No need for that at this stage – you've got enough on your plate anyway. Send one of your DCs to hear what the bloke's got to say and report back. We can decide then if he's made out a case for further investigation. You'll find all the details here.' He handed Rathbone a folder. 'Now, about this missing girl – Daisy Hewett.' Leach referred to his file on a fifteen-year-old girl who had left home for school some three weeks previously and had not been seen since. 'Have there been any sightings?'

Rathbone shook his head moodily. 'No, sir. It's almost a carbon copy of the Valerie Deacon case. I've looked it up and there's reason to believe the same person's responsible.'

Leach frowned. 'That was long before I came here, but I heard about it of course. Were there no leads at all?'

'Nothing concrete, sir. Several suspects were interviewed but we had to let them go for lack of evidence.'

Leach sighed heavily. 'And now we have another frantic family demanding action. What are you planning to do next?'

'We've set up an incident room in the local nick and we're making the usual house to house enquiries, but we haven't come up with any leads so far.'

They spent some time discussing the case and Rathbone went back to the CID office to brief his team. The discovery that numbers were reduced as three officers had reported sick did nothing to lighten his mood. He beckoned to DC Sukey Reynolds, who was sitting at her computer checking emails.

'Looks like you've drawn the short straw this morning, Sukey,' he informed her. 'A milkman found a woman apparently unconscious in her bungalow in Over Hampton a couple of Saturdays ago. He called an ambulance, but when it arrived the paramedics said she was dead and sent for a doctor. He was from the emergency services so wasn't her regular GP, but he confirmed she was dead and had her taken to the morgue. The inquest was adjourned pending further enquiries. There's been a post-mortem and everything seems to point to accidental death but for some reason her GP has told the coroner he isn't happy about the verdict. From what DCI Leach said he sounds an awkward bugger, but just the same we have to take him seriously. So you're to get on to him and find out what's worrying him. All the details are here.' He handed her the folder Leach had given him. 'Off you go.'

'Right, Sarge,' said Sukey. Without waiting to hear what plans Rathbone had for the rest of the team she called the number Rathbone had given her and asked for Doctor Hogan.

A receptionist at the Over Hampton medical practice answered 'He doesn't deal with patients' phone calls until after surgery,' she said. 'If you'd like to leave your number—'

'I'm not a patient,' Sukey interposed. 'I'm Detective Constable Reynolds of Avon and Somerset CID and I understand Doctor Hogan wants to speak to one of our officers.'

'Oh, I see.' The woman sounded taken aback, but quickly pulled herself together and said, 'He's with a patient at the moment but I don't think he'll be long. If you leave your number I'll ask him to call you as soon as he's . . . oh, the patient is just leaving; I'll try and catch him before the next one goes in. Please hold the line.'

There was a pause; then a man's voice came on the line. 'Doctor Hogan speaking. I'm told you're a constable from the CID, is that right?'

He spoke briskly, with a distinctly authoritarian note in his voice. *A man who doesn't suffer fools gladly*, Sukey thought to herself. Aloud she said, 'Yes, Doctor Hogan, that's right. It's about the post-mortem on Miss Adelaide Minchin who was found dead in her home recently. We understand you have some doubts about the verdict.'

'I have certain doubts about the case which lead me to believe further investigation is necessary, but I'm not prepared to discuss the matter over the phone.'

'That's not a problem, sir. Would you like me to come to your surgery?'

'I'd prefer a more senior officer.'

'I understand, sir, but I'm afraid we have a number of absentees through sickness and . . .'

'Flu, I suppose,' he cut in. 'All right, I suppose you'll do for now. The sooner the better.'

'I can come this morning, if that's convenient.'

'I see my last patient at eleven. Be here at eleven fifteen.' Without waiting for a response, he hung up.

The village of Over Hampton lay off the A4 a short distance from Keynsham, about fifteen miles from police headquarters. Despite being caught behind some slow moving traffic for a large part of the drive, Sukey reached the building where Doctor Hogan had his practice with nearly half an hour to spare. A short distance away was a row of shops, including a post office and general stores, where she asked for directions to Parson's Acre. The woman behind the counter was small and softly spoken, but she had sharp, beady eyes that seemed to take in every detail of Sukey's appearance at a glance.

'If you're thinking of visiting Miss Minchin, I'm afraid you've come on a wasted journey,' she said, almost apologetically.

'This isn't a social call.' Sukey held up her ID and the woman gave a nod of comprehension.

'Ah, I wondered when one of you would be turning up, although I can't think why you've been sent for. Sergeant Murray said at the inquest that there was no sign of a break-in or that she'd been attacked. It was that Doctor Hogan, I suppose – they say he's been complaining because none of your people were called in right away to investigate. Between you and me, miss, he can be a right old—' She broke off and cleared her throat as if she had been on the point of saying something critical. 'Still, whatever else they say about him, he's a good doctor. I suppose if he has his doubts it's right they should be cleared up.'

'Of course,' Sukey agreed. 'That's why I'm here.'

'Just the same,' the woman went on, 'everyone's sure it was a dreadful accident. I mean why on earth would anyone want to do away with a nice lady like Miss Minchin?'

'Is that what Doctor Hogan is suggesting?'

'Well, why else would he want further enquiries made?'

'That's what I'm here to find out,' said Sukey. 'Had Miss Minchin lived here long?'

'Getting on for five years now. She inherited the cottage

from her cousin – that was Miss Muriel Minchin. She died of a heart attack over six years ago, poor lady. Miss Adelaide was only in her fifties. It was such a lovely funeral; the vicar spoke so movingly.' For a moment Sukey feared the woman was about to enlarge on the vicar's eulogy, but she checked herself and said, 'Oh, sorry, I do let my tongue run away with me. My husband's always saying, "Flo Appleby, you do talk a lot".' She made a playful pretence of slapping her own wrist. 'You'll want to see the cottage for yourself of course – go straight along the village street, take the first turning on the left and it's the last house on the right. And if I can help in any way, you only have to ask,' she added eagerly.

Reflecting that if there was any foundation for Doctor Hogan's suspicions, there was at least one person in the village who would be only too ready to help the police with their enquiries, Sukey thanked her warmly and returned to her car.

Parson's Acre was a neat, brick-built cottage that Sukey guessed probably dated from the first half of the twentieth century. Outwardly well maintained, it was set back from the lane and separated from its nearest neighbour by a wide field populated by peacefully grazing cows. The ground floor windows were partially hidden by a screen of flowering trees and shrubs, and Sukey's first impression was of the average town dweller's dream of an idyllic rural retreat. Her second thought was that its air of modest prosperity and the isolated situation made it a potential target for thieves. But according to the statements Rathbone had given her, there was no sign of forced entry on the day of her death. She made a note to enquire if there had previously been such an incident.

A uniformed police constable with grey hair and a ruddy complexion was lounging in the sun on a bench beside the front door. He stood up as she opened the gate and strolled up the path to meet her, introduced himself as Constable Gleed and cast a cursory glance at her ID. 'Thought you'd have a look at the scene of the crime?' he said. It was plain from his whimsical tone and tilted eyebrows that the remark was not intended to be taken seriously.

'I've come to see Doctor Hogan, but I've got a bit of time in hand,' she explained. 'Do I gather you don't regard the death as suspicious?'

He pursed his lips and shook his head. 'No sign of a break

in, no reports of strangers acting suspiciously, nothing in the house disturbed – everything seems to point to an accident.'

'You attended the scene?'

'No, that was Sergeant Murray. I wasn't on duty that day and I only heard about it on the Tuesday morning from Joe the milkman. He said he found Miss Minchin lying out cold on the floor in her bathroom when he went to collect his money. It seems she'd fallen over backwards and knocked herself out banging her head on the radiator.'

'That was a week ago last Saturday, I understand?'

'That's right, Saturday the twelfth. Joe called the ambulance and the paramedics said she was dead. It being the weekend they called the emergency doctor and he confirmed what they said and notified us. As I'm sure you know, it's routine in the case of an unexpected death, although there was no reason to suspect foul play. Anyway, Sergeant Murray said it was OK to send her off to the morgue, but of course the doctor couldn't sign a death certificate. He was just a locum; Doctor Hogan – he's in charge of the practice in the village – was away and didn't get back until the day after the funeral. He called my inspector asking us to check Miss Minchin's house a second time for any sign of an intruder. Like I said, we came up here again, found nothing suspicious, but it seems he's still got some bee in his bonnet. He plays golf with the Chief Constable so I guess he managed to twist his arm.' From his slightly apologetic tone, it was clear that Gleed considered the whole exercise was a waste of both his own and Sukey's time.

'Did he say why?'

Gleed gave a hoarse chuckle. 'It's obvious you don't know Doctor Hogan. He doesn't give reasons, just says what he wants done. He can be very, shall we say, insistent. According to my inspector all he said was that there should have been a more thorough investigation at the time.'

'I see.' Sukey was beginning to sense that the impression she had gained from speaking to Doctor Hogan over the phone was fairly close to the mark. She glanced at her watch. 'Well, I'm due to see him in ten minutes so I'd better be going.'

Gleed grinned. 'Make sure you arrive on the dot. He used to be in the army and he runs that surgery like a military base. He'll have you on a charge if you turn up late!'

* * *

Shortly before eleven fifteen, Sukey presented herself at the reception desk in the Over Hampton Medical Centre and asked for Doctor Hogan. The receptionist picked up a phone, announced her arrival and said, 'Yes, Doctor Hogan', before leading her along a short passage and knocking on a door. A voice barked, 'Come!' and the receptionist scuttled away leaving Sukey to obey the command.

A man of about fifty was seated in his shirtsleeves at a desk in front of a computer. Without taking his eyes off the screen he pointed to the chair at his side. She sat down and waited. It was a couple of minutes before he switched off the computer and swivelled his chair round to face her. For the second time that morning she found herself the object of a rapid but intense scrutiny.

'ID?' he said in the same peremptory tone in which he had responded to the receptionist's knock. He took it from her, scrutinized the photograph and compared it with her face before handing it back. 'As I said, I'd have preferred a more senior officer. How long have you been in the CID?'

'Just over three years, sir,' Sukey replied, 'but before that I had several years experience attending crime scenes as a CSI – crime scene investigator.'

He gave a dismissive sniff. 'I know – used to be called SOCOs. Another example of this obsession with changing names for no good reason. Well, young lady, I'll assume for the moment that you're up to the job. I take it that you visited the house before coming here?'

'I went to Parson's Acre about twenty minutes ago and spoke to Constable Gleed,' said Sukey. 'He stated that the officer who attended on the day Miss Minchin's body was discovered found no evidence of an intruder or other suggestion of foul play.'

'Did you go in and have a look for yourself?'

'No sir, there wasn't time, but I intend to do so after we finish our discussion.'

'Do that,' he said. 'Now, about the circumstances of Miss Minchin's death, I take it you've been briefed?'

Before leaving headquarters Sukey had prepared a résumé of the information in the folder. With Hogan's eyes staring fixedly into hers, conscious that he was listening intently and certain that he would pounce on any omission or inaccuracy,

she read out what she had written, ending with: 'We do not
have full details of the pathologist's report on the post-mortem,
but we understand that death was caused by injuries consist-
ent with a fall.' For the moment she decided to avoid using
the word 'accidental'.

She waited in some trepidation for his reaction. To her relief,
he said crisply, 'Correct as far as it goes. Death was caused by
a heavy blow to the right side of the neck and was apparently
due to the victim having fallen sideways against the edge of
the hand basin.' He broke off for a moment and raised an
eyebrow. 'I wonder if you have come across a similar case?'

'Not personally,' Sukey admitted, 'but I have heard of what
is known as a "commando punch" when a victim is struck on
one of the arteries – I think they're called carotid arteries –
at the side of the neck. It can cause immediate loss of
consciousness, and be fatal if sufficient force is used.'

'Hmm, you're better informed than I expected.' There was
a hint of grudging respect in Hogan's voice. 'In Adelaide's
case death was instantaneous,' he continued, 'and she would
have collapsed to the floor. From the position in which I understand the body was found, it appears she then rolled over on
to her back, striking her head against the radiator. This caused
a contusion which, had she not been already dead, might have
resulted in mild concussion but hardly even temporary loss
of consciousness.' He fixed her with another piercing stare.
'We are still left with an important question unanswered.'

'What caused her to fall?' said Sukey.

'Precisely. Had I not been away when all this happened, more
attention would have been paid to that question at the time.'

She waited for him to say more, but he remained silent. 'Doctor
Hogan,' she said tentatively, 'Detective Sergeant Rathbone
informed me this morning that you wish the CID to investigate
further, but declined to give your reasons on the telephone. Could
I now ask why you have doubts over Miss Minchin's death?'

Doctor Hogan sat back in his chair and stared fixedly at the
blank computer screen. 'I was Adelaide Minchin's doctor, but
I was also her friend,' he began. 'I met her some years before
she moved into Parson's Acre. She used to stay there from
time to time with her cousin Muriel, who bought the property
about twenty-five years ago. The cousins were very different
in temperament but they were none the less very fond of

one another. Adelaide spent an increasing amount of time with Muriel when her health began to fail.'

'So you first met Miss Adelaide during your professional visits to her cousin?' said Sukey as Hogan fell silent for a moment, staring down at the desk.

He raised his head with a start, as if he had been deep in thought. 'Yes, that's right,' he said. 'When Muriel died it was discovered that she'd left the house and everything in it to Adelaide. It caused a bit of a rumpus in the family because everyone had assumed it would go to one of her siblings, who more or less accused Adelaide of persuading their sister to alter her will while she was in a vulnerable state because of her failing health.'

'I imagine that led to a lot of ill feeling,' said Sukey.

'Henry Minchin, Muriel's elder brother, threatened to contest the will, but I understand it was made shortly after Muriel bought Parson's Acre and long before she became ill, so he had little chance of success.'

'Which suggests that there wasn't much love lost between Muriel and her siblings.'

'Exactly.' Hogan sat back in his chair and began drumming his fingers on the desk. 'To my knowledge, there was never any communication between Adelaide and her cousins from that time on.' He directed a penetrating gaze at Sukey. 'Next question?'

'You say you and Adelaide were friends. Were you also Muriel's friend?'

He shook his head. 'Doctor yes, friend no. The cousins were chalk and cheese; Muriel was very reserved while Adelaide was very outgoing. In fact, it wasn't until after Muriel died and Adelaide moved into Parson's Acre and chummed up with my wife – they played bridge together – that we became part of her circle.'

'She had a wide circle of friends?'

'Of course; she had so many different interests.'

'But you were her doctor as well?'

'Oh yes. Not that I had occasion to see her very often – just a routine check-up from time to time, the usual thing for women of her age. The latest was just after her fiftieth birthday a couple of years ago. I told her she was as fit as a fiddle and would live to be a hundred. And that's what's worrying me.' He leaned forward until, as Sukey reported to her colleague Vicky later, they were "practically eyeball to eyeball". 'What caused a woman in excellent health to fall in her own bathroom and strike her neck with sufficient violence to kill her?'

Sukey referred to her notes and drew a deep breath. 'There was some reference in the milkman's statement to a reduction in her weekly order. Would that be because she was dieting?'

He shook his head. 'Her latest blood test showed a slight rise in her cholesterol level and I advised her to cut down on dairy fats and increase her intake of certain other foods. She had no reason to diet; her weight was ideal for her age and build.'

'So there was no reason to think she might have suffered a dizzy spell?'

'None whatsoever.' Hogan thumped his desk in a sudden flash of anger. 'Can't you get it into your skull that there was absolutely no medical reason why she should have fallen?'

Realizing that she had pushed him too far, Sukey hastily backtracked. 'Forgive me, Doctor Hogan, I just wanted to be sure . . .'

'All right, all right!' He made an impatient gesture. 'The plain fact is that, based on the results of the post-mortem, the verdict was accidental death. I do not accept that verdict.'

'May I ask why not?'

Hogan spread his hands in what seemed to Sukey an uncharacteristically helpless gesture for a man who seemed so sure of himself. 'Since Adelaide's death my mind keeps going back to something that happened when Muriel was thinking of selling Parson's Acre. Nothing came of it at the time because her situation changed, but now I have this gut feeling that something's wrong. The more time goes by before the house is thoroughly checked, the less chance there is of finding any useful evidence.'

'Evidence of what?' asked Sukey.

'Of murder,' he replied.

THREE

There was a long silence. Then Sukey said, 'Doctor Hogan, it's obvious you feel very strongly about this, but nothing you've told me so far is sufficient to justify treating Miss Minchin's death as a murder enquiry. I've had "gut feelings" of my own,' she went on when he did not immediately respond, 'and more often than not they've been justified, but they've never been enough on their own to convince my superiors. I've had to come up with something more concrete before they'd take me seriously.'

'Yes, I take your point,' Hogan agreed, 'and I'm prepared to be greeted with a certain amount of scepticism, but I'm as certain as I can be without positive proof that Adelaide Minchin's death was no accident.'

'So what is it that makes you so certain?'

'It was something Muriel told me after she had her first stroke. It wasn't a very severe one and she recovered remarkably quickly, but living alone in a somewhat isolated environment made her very conscious of her vulnerability and she said she was thinking of selling Parson's Acre and moving into sheltered accommodation. She had gone so far as to invite a couple of estate agents to value the property. They came on successive days and very shortly after the second visit she had a phone call from someone wanting to buy it.'

'Without inspecting it first?' said Sukey in surprise.

Hogan nodded. 'That struck me as odd too, but what came next was even odder. This man claimed to be the managing director of a property developer. He said he'd put in a planning application to build houses on land adjoining hers. It would, he told her, adversely affect the value of her property, but because he had always admired it – in fact he said he'd tried to buy it the last time it came on the market – he was prepared to give her a fair price. He did, however, mention a figure considerably lower than both the estate agents' valuations.'

'Can I take it that "the last time it came on the market" was when Muriel bought it?' said Sukey.

'That's right. The previous owner had died and it was sold at auction. Several people were interested as well as Muriel, but hers was the successful bid.'

'Do you think this man was one of the unsuccessful bidders?'

'It seems feasible, but as we don't know his name there's no way of telling.'

'How did she respond to him?'

'Very sensibly, she told him she had not yet made a firm decision to move, and that if and when she did she would instruct an estate agent who would consider his and any other offers.'

'She seems to have been a very businesslike lady,' Sukey commented.

'She was. I understand her family owned some sort of company so maybe she'd had some business experience. She didn't tell me that herself,' Hogan added. 'As I said earlier, she was a very private person. I learned more about her from Adelaide after she came to live in Parson's Acre.'

'But she did tell you about these telephone calls?'

'When she brought up the subject of sheltered accommodation she asked if there was somewhere locally that I could recommend. I knew of several places that might have suited her and promised to let her have details. It was when I went to see her with some brochures that she told me about the calls.'

'Did she get the man's name, or the name of his company?'

'If she did, she never mentioned it to me.'

'Did she ask the agents whether either of them had released details of the property before receiving her instructions?'

'She did, and they both stated emphatically that they had not. Nor could they explain how this unknown person came to know the property might shortly come on to the market.'

'Did this person call again?'

'He did and she gave him the same answer. In reply, he said something to the effect that his offer would come down considerably once planning consent was received.'

'He was certainly piling on the pressure,' said Sukey. 'Whoever he was, he seems to have been very anxious to acquire the property at the lowest possible price.'

'Obviously,' Hogan agreed. 'It wouldn't surprise me if he intended to sell it on at a profit. I suppose property developers are no less avaricious than other business people.'

Sukey, who had been taking careful notes, thought for a moment. 'If we could just go back for a moment to Muriel's plans to go into sheltered housing,' she said. 'Before she became ill, had she taken things a stage further, such as visiting one of the places you recommended?'

'I'm afraid not; there wasn't time. Not long after this happened she had a second stroke. Again, it wasn't a very severe one – she was actually able to call the surgery herself and ask for help. It was during this period that Adelaide began spending more time with her.'

'Doctor Hogan, forgive me if this question sounds a little out of order,' said Sukey, 'but can I take it you had no doubts about the cause of Muriel's death?'

To her relief, he showed no sign of offence at the question, 'None whatsoever. She was hospitalized after the final attack and never regained consciousness.'

'Were there any more phone calls from this unknown man?'

'I never heard of any.'

'How about when Adelaide moved in after Muriel's death?'

'She never said anything. I'm sure she'd have told me if there had been.'

'Did she know about them at the time?'

'I don't know – Muriel might have told her, I suppose, but she didn't mention them to me.'

'And she never received any such calls herself?'

'I'm quite sure she didn't.'

There was a silence. At last Sukey said, 'Doctor Hogan, I will of course make a full report of our conversation to my SIO, but nothing you have told me so far suggests any connection between those telephone calls and Adelaide Minchin's death.'

He made the same gesture with his hands as before. For a moment he appeared less sure of himself, but quickly recovered. 'We know that six or seven years ago someone wanted that house pretty badly,' he said adamantly. 'I believe that for some unknown reason he now wants it so urgently that he's prepared to kill to get it. I tell you, there was nothing physically wrong with Addie, nothing that would cause her to fall like that. Doesn't that strike you as suspicious?'

'There couldn't have been any hitherto unsuspected heart condition, for example?'

'Nothing showed up in the post-mortem.' Hogan banged a clenched fist on the desk. 'No!' he shouted, 'I'm convinced there was another person in the house, someone who threatened her or gave her such a fright that she staggered backwards, lost her balance and had that fatal fall.'

'But there was nothing to indicate that there'd been another person in the house,' Sukey reminded him.

'Lots of people knew where she kept her key – anyone

could have entered and taken her by surprise and then left without anyone being any the wiser.'

'Are you suggesting that whoever it was entered the house intending to kill Adelaide and that by sheer chance that person's presence gave her such a shock that it effectively did his dirty work for him?'

'Something like that.'

'About what time of day did she die?'

'The pathologist wasn't able to give an exact answer to that question, but as she was naked in the bathroom it was most likely she was about to take a bath.'

'Do you happen to know what time she normally took her bath?'

'My wife Joan tells me she thinks it was normally before breakfast.'

'Quite early, in fact,' said Sukey. 'Perhaps she had someone staying in the house as a guest?'

'Joan and some others played bridge with her earlier in the week and she's sure Addie would have mentioned it. We both believe it was someone who had no business there.'

'But is it really likely that anyone would have been prowling around at that hour?' Sukey persisted. 'It would have been broad daylight.'

'You've seen the place yourself. It's not overlooked from any direction. Look –' Hogan passed a hand over his eyes; for the second time his attitude momentarily seemed to soften – 'I can see you aren't convinced and I suppose I can't blame you. It probably wouldn't have occurred to me to ask questions if it hadn't been for those phone calls to Muriel.'

Sukey did her best to conceal her rising feeling of exasperation. 'But how do you suppose killing Adelaide would suddenly make it available to this unknown person?' she asked.

'That's what I want your people to find out,' he said, with a sudden return to his earlier, authoritative manner. He glanced at his watch, stood up and opened the door. 'You'll have to go now, I've got patients to visit.'

Sukey went back to her car and spent a few minutes writing up her notes of the interview. She had just finished when she saw Hogan come out of the building and stride across the car park. He was carrying his bag and he had a light coloured jacket over one arm. He tossed both on the back seat of a silver grey

Mercedes, climbed in and drove towards the exit, clipping on his seat belt with one hand while steering the car with the other. His whole demeanour was that of a man with a purpose. She felt that as a doctor he would inspire both respect and confidence. She recalled Flo Appleby's hint that he could be difficult and reflected that would be no bad thing in cases where he believed the authorities were not giving proper consideration to the needs of his patients. By the same token, he would be unlikely to have much sympathy with any he suspected of malingering. His manner throughout their conversation had at times been brusque to the point of rudeness, yet there had been moments when behind the mask she had caught glimpses of warmth, humanity and even vulnerability. It was evident that Adelaide Minchin's death had affected him personally, yet there had been nothing to suggest that the relationship between them had been other than simple friendship.

Sukey put her notebook away and turned on the ignition. Having given an undertaking to return to Parson's Acre she felt obliged to do so, although she could not help feeling that it would be a wasted journey. She parked a short distance before reaching the house and approached it on foot. As she opened the gate she noticed that there was a different officer on duty, a somewhat younger man who was basking in the sunshine on a wooden seat by the front door. On seeing her, he hastily stuffed his iPod into his pocket and hurried down the path to greet her. His cordial manner suggested that her arrival was a welcome diversion.

'Nice to meet you, Sukey,' he said after a glance at her ID. 'Constable Gleed said you'd be back to have a look round the house, although what you expect to find we can't imagine. I'm PC Jeff Griffiths, by the way. Would you like a coffee? There's plenty left in the flask.'

'Thanks, that'd be very welcome.'

'Come this way.' He led her round the house to the back door.

'This is the door the milkman used the day he found the dead woman, I suppose?' she said.

'That's right. From what we hear, half the village knew she kept a key under that pot of geraniums. They need dead-heading,' he commented and bent down to remove a few spent flower heads. 'She loved her garden.'

'Yes, I can see that.' Sukey paused for a moment before

following him indoors to admire the well tended plot, with its velvet lawn, colourful herbaceous borders framed by flowering shrubs and a few small, graceful trees. 'So she wasn't worried about burglars?'

'Not a bit. A few months ago we had a security drive in Over Hampton and several neighbouring villages. A team of us went round calling at houses and dishing out leaflets with advice on security locks and alarm systems and so on and she was one of the people I called on. I remember her saying she was more scared of locking herself out than being burgled, and couldn't get her head round electronics. Anyway she was sure none of the nice people in the village would rob her and strangers wouldn't know where she kept her spare key.'

'That sounds a little naive,' Sukey commented.

'Well there you go. All we can do is give advice; it's up to people whether or not they follow it.' He pulled a chair from under the table. 'Have a seat.' He unscrewed the cap of a large flask and poured steaming coffee into two mugs. 'There's sugar if you want it, and biscuits.' He waved a hand at some packets lying on the table. 'Help yourself.'

'Thanks.' She glanced round the kitchen while sipping her coffee and munching a biscuit. It was a bright, colourful room with a wood block floor, patterned tiles on the walls, cream counter tops and cupboards with doors finished in a soft shade of apricot.

'It's just as well the milkman knew where to look for her key I suppose,' she said after swallowing a few sips of coffee. 'It's surprising, when you come to think of it,' she went on after a moment's thought, 'that no one noticed she hadn't taken her milk in – the postman for example.'

'It just happened there were no letters for her on Thursday or Friday.'

'But from what I've heard, she had plenty of friends. You'd have thought someone would have noticed she wasn't around, or answering her phone, for example.'

He shrugged. 'One or two people mentioned calling her and getting no answer, but they left messages and assumed she'd get back to them when she had a moment. It isn't as though she was missing for a week or more and you know how it is . . . people have their own affairs to deal with.'

'Yes, of course,' Sukey agreed.

'In any case,' he went on, 'from what we hear there wouldn't have been anything anyone could do. The pathologist's report made it clear that the blow on the neck killed her outright.' He hesitated for a moment, turning his coffee mug between his hands. 'To be honest, we can't understand why your lot have been called in. There was never any reason to treat it as a suspicious death. Sergeant Murray had a good look round the house at the time; his report said quite definitely that nothing had been disturbed and there was no sign of forced entry. It was a tragic accident – that was the official verdict and that's the only possible explanation.'

Sukey finished her biscuit and took another. 'I've just been interviewing a person who thinks differently,' she said.

He gave a knowing grin. 'That'll be Doc Hogan, I guess,' he said. 'He had a bit of a run in with Inspector Watson, saying he hadn't ordered a proper search at the time. I suppose he's the one behind all this – if he gets his teeth into something he's like a dog with a bone.'

'That was my impression as well,' Sukey agreed. 'His concern dates from some rather strange telephone calls that Miss Muriel Minchin received while she was still living here.' She referred to her notes and gave him the salient points from her interview with Hogan. 'Did she ever report those calls to the police?'

'I don't know. That would be before I joined the force.'

'Perhaps you could check for me?'

'Will do.' He made a note. 'There's one thing I am pretty sure of,' he added, 'and that is there's never been a planning application to develop any of the land round this house. My dad's on the planning committee and I'm certain he'd have mentioned it – but I'll check anyway.'

'That's very interesting,' said Sukey. 'It rather looks as if this man, whoever he was, might have been spinning a yarn in an attempt to get hold of the house at a knock down price.' It crossed her mind to wonder why Doctor Hogan hadn't followed up this point at the time. She finished her coffee, pushed back her chair and stood up. 'Could I have a look round the house now?'

After her tour of the house and grounds, during which she made careful notes, Sukey drove back to the village. It was almost two o'clock, she was feeling hungry and the menu board outside the Red Lion Hotel caught her eye as she drove slowly past. It struck her that if she called in there for some lunch she might find an opportunity to talk to a few people about Adelaide Minchin. She found a space in the car park and went into the bar, noting as she entered that a sign above the door announced that the name of the licensee was Benjamin Bridges.

There were a number of people in the bar and only two people serving, one a girl whose size Sukey calculated to be no more than eight, and the other a plump man of about fifty with a polished skull fringed with curly grey hair, a round, good-humoured face and a paunch to match. The girl had long, straight blonde hair falling in curtains on either side of a small, heart-shaped face; she wore a low cut black top and it was noticeable that when taking orders she paid particular attention to the younger male customers.

Although it was well past the normal lunchtime period, business was brisk and it was several minutes before the man caught her eye and came to take her order. He served her with chilled apple juice, offered her a menu and went to attend to another customer. When he returned she ordered a ham sandwich with a side salad; as she handed over the money she said, 'Are you Mr Bridges?'

He gave a friendly smile and nodded. 'That's me. Who wants to know?' His voice was a warm baritone with a musical quality that made her think of a church choir. She held up her ID and the smile faded. 'You're here about the death of Miss Minchin, I suppose. Why they can't let the poor lady rest in peace I can't imagine.'

'So you know someone's been expressing doubts about the verdict?'

'I heard someone – they say it's Doctor Hogan – has been rattling a few cages, but I'd no idea he'd called in the CID.' His tone made it clear that he considered the doctor's interference uncalled for, to say the least.

'Actually, it was the coroner who asked us to make a few enquiries,' Sukey explained, 'although there's no secret that it was at Doctor Hogan's behest. In fact, I had an interview with him this morning.'

His eyebrows shot up. 'With Hogan?' Sukey nodded. 'So what's his problem?'

'Mr Bridges, were you here when Miss Muriel Minchin was alive?'

'I certainly was – I've been the licensee here for over twenty years. Why do you ask?'

'Do you remember the time when she was first taken ill?'

He thought for a moment, 'I heard about it, of course. She had a stroke and was in hospital – twice, I believe. Then she had a bad one some while later and that killed her.'

'Did you ever hear that after the first stroke she was thinking of putting her house on the market and moving into sheltered accommodation?'

He frowned and slowly shook his head. 'Can't say as I did. Anything like that would have got around very quickly, but I never heard mention of it. I never met the lady, or knew much about her,' he went on. 'She kept herself to herself by all accounts and she certainly wasn't the sort to drink in pubs. Now Miss Adelaide, she was a different kettle of fish altogether. She often had her lunch here, especially while she was having her kitchen refitted. She even had the odd go on the fruit machine over there.' He nodded towards the far corner of the room. 'A very jolly, friendly lady she was. It's hard to believe she's gone.'

'Yes, I've heard she was very popular in the village,' said Sukey. 'I imagine you hear about pretty well everything that goes on round here,' she added.

He appeared gratified at the suggestion. 'Most of it, I guess. This is a popular meeting place and of course all the regulars know one another and exchange local news and so on.'

'Do you remember any talk of a planning application to build houses on land next to Parson's Acre?'

He shook his head. 'I'm pretty sure there's never been one and if there was I doubt it would be granted anyway. The entire population of the village would be up in arms. Nick Granger's the one to ask; he owns most of the land that side of the village but I can't see him selling any of it.'

'Is he here, by any chance?'

Bridges glanced round the bar. 'I don't see him. He doesn't come in much during the week.'

'You mentioned Miss Adelaide had her kitchen refitted. Do you happen to know who did it?'

'I've got a feeling it was the Hubbards. It's a local family firm; father and son do the work and Bessie – that's the mother – does the books.' Bridges glanced round the bar. 'Tom and Jerry – yes, those are their real names,' he added in response to Sukey's raised eyebrows, 'sometimes drop in around this time for a pie and a pint but we haven't seen them today; they're probably working in another village. You'll find them in the phone book. Now, if there's no more questions I see a thirsty customer over there.' As he spoke he acknowledged the gestures of an elderly man at the other end of the bar who was impatiently waving an empty tankard.

Sukey sat down at a corner table and made a note of her conversation with Ben Bridges while waiting for her sandwich. When she had eaten it she drove back to headquarters. DS Rathbone had just returned from interviewing a witness who claimed to have seen the missing girl at a railway station fifty miles away. He was not in the best of moods.

'Waste of time – the woman's just an attention seeker,' he grumbled. 'I hope you're not going to tell me the same thing about Doctor Hogan,' he added morosely.

'He's certainly not an attention seeker,' Sukey assured him, 'but I'm not convinced he's made a case for opening an investigation.'

'So what was he on about?'

'He believes very strongly that there's something suspicious about the fall that caused Adelaide Minchin's death. He says she didn't suffer from any medical condition that might have made her keel over. He insists that someone was directly responsible and that a proper search should have been made at the time to check for signs of an intruder.'

'Did you go to the house and look for yourself?'

'Yes, Sarge, I had a good look round and in particular in the bathroom where the dead woman was found. I found nothing to suggest that the local police had failed to carry out a proper check at the time.'

'So he can't produce any evidence to support his claim?'

'Not exactly, Sarge.'

'What do you mean by that?'

'He says the previous owner had some suspicious phone calls suggesting that someone has such strong reasons for wanting to get his hands on Parson's Acre that he's prepared to kill for it.'

Rathbone's eyebrows lifted in surprise. 'When was this?'

'A year or so before she died.'

'Who was the previous owner?'

'A Miss Muriel Minchin – the cousin of the woman who's

just died. I understand she left it to her in her will, rather to the annoyance of other members of the family.'

Rathbone frowned. 'From what you tell me it doesn't seem as if there's much mileage in Doctor Hogan's assumption. Anyway, let me have a full report some time and I'll pass it to DCI Leach. I doubt if he'll be inclined to pursue it.'

'Will do, Sarge.' At that moment Rathbone's phone rang. He picked it up, listened for a few seconds and made a note on his desk pad before saying, 'Right, we're on our way.' He put down the phone. His face was grim. 'Someone's reported seeing a human hand sticking out from under a heap of builder's rubble that's been dumped in a lay-by. Uniformed are on their way.' He got up and grabbed his jacket. 'Let's join them.'

FOUR

The lay-by was on a road that ran from Over Hampton through an area of woodland before joining the main road. When Rathbone and Sukey arrived several police cars were already at the scene. The lay-by and a considerable stretch of road at either end were cordoned off with blue and white tape and officers were setting up a temporary system of traffic control. One of them directed Sukey to the rendezvous point that had already been designated under the direction of the uniformed inspector in charge of the team.

Rathbone approached him and said, 'DS Rathbone and DC Reynolds, sir.'

He nodded. 'Inspector Callow.' He gestured in the direction of two uniformed constables, a man and a woman, who were bending down beside a heap of broken bricks that someone had dumped in a ditch beside the lay-by. 'It's a human hand all right – what's left of it, that is – and we think it's still attached to the arm, but we don't know yet if the arm is attached to the body. We're waiting for the CSIs to do their stuff before we can establish whether we're dealing with a complete corpse or a disembodied limb. Go and see for yourselves.' He turned his attention back to the traffic controllers, who had reduced the carriageway to a single lane and with shouts and gestures were urging forward drivers who were slowing to a crawl in an attempt to see what was going on.

The two constables straightened up as Rathbone and Sukey approached. They immediately recognized the woman as PC Annie Darby, with whom they'd worked on a previous case. Her normally healthy colour had taken on a greenish tinge and she had a hand over her mouth. 'It's gruesome, isn't it Archie,' she said shakily, turning to her colleague.

'Not a pretty sight,' he agreed. He appeared equally affected by what he had just seen. 'PC Gill, Sarge,' he added. 'We're not sure yet if there's the remains of a complete body under that lot but we've been told not to touch anything until the CSIs get here.'

'Not that we're likely to,' said Annie with a shudder.

'Quite right,' said Rathbone, 'and stay where you are. Moving about can destroy evidence.' He cautiously stepped forward and squatted down, with Sukey beside him. 'Are you thinking what I'm thinking?' he said in a low voice.

Sukey felt tears welling up in her eyes at the sight of the pathetic remains of a once warm and living human hand reaching out of the pile of rubble as if in a mute appeal for help. A few shreds of shrivelled, greenish flesh still clung to the slender bones and she hastily looked away, swallowing hard. 'It's . . . it was . . . a very small hand, Sarge,' she said, 'and at a guess it's female.' She turned to meet his gaze. 'Daisy Hewett?'

He nodded. 'I reckon so. I'm not sure about the ring on the middle finger, though. The parents never mentioned it. We can't see it properly at the moment; we'll have to wait till we can get a closer look, but if they confirm it's one belonging to her then it almost certainly is Daisy's body. He stood up and beckoned to Annie. 'Where's the man who reported it?'

'He didn't wait for us to arrive, Sarge; he just made the 999 call and drove off.'

'He spotted it when he stopped in the lay-by and went over to have a pee in the ditch,' Archie added. 'He sounded pretty shaken – in fact he was almost gibbering. We tried to get him to sit in his car and wait for us till he'd calmed down, but he couldn't get away fast enough.'

'Understandable,' said Rathbone. He showed no outward sign of emotion, but Sukey knew instinctively that as the father of a young son he would have some idea of what Daisy's parents were going through.

'We thought at first it might be a hoax,' said Annie. 'You know, someone planting a joke skeleton.'

'A pretty sick sort of joke,' Archie commented.

'It wouldn't be the first time some moron's played that sort of trick on us,' said Rathbone. 'They're in the same league as the pond life who get their kicks calling out the fire brigade when there's no fire or pretending to have planted a bomb. Anything to waste police time,' he added. For the first time his tone betrayed some feeling.

'Like I said, the man sounded genuinely scared,' Archie repeated. 'It was almost as if he thought a killer might be lurking in the bushes. Anyway, here's his mobile number.' He tore a slip from his notebook and handed it to Rathbone, who passed it to Sukey.

'You can catch up with him and take a statement later,' he said tersely.

'Here come the CSIs now,' said Annie as a couple of vans slowed down and were directed to the rendezvous point. Men and women in white overalls climbed out and began unloading equipment.

Rathbone walked back to speak to them while they donned the rest of their kit. After a few minutes he returned and waited with Sukey and the two uniformed officers while the CSIs marked out a common approach path and made their initial assessment of the scene. 'It looks as if we'll be here for some time,' he said after a further consultation. He took out his mobile. 'I'll alert Doc Hanley and put the SIO in the picture.'

When Rathbone and Sukey returned to headquarters some hours later they were immediately summoned to DCI Leach's office.

'Right,' he said. 'I gather from your last message that the CSIs have succeeded in exposing the complete body and you think it's that of Daisy Hewett.'

'That's right, sir,' said Rathbone. 'Arrangements are being made to take the remains to the mortuary. They're in a pretty bad state of decomposition plus there's some crush damage to the features. If the parents identify the ring as one belonging to their daughter it should be pretty conclusive, but obviously, it would be too distressing to ask them to identify her so we may have to rely on dental or other records for confirmation.'

'I take it the parents have been warned to expect the worst?'

'Yes, sir. Vicky – DC Armstrong – went to see them straight away and of course a Family Liaison Officer has been with them from the beginning. All we've told them for the moment is that we've found the body of a young girl and we've called off the search for Daisy for the time being. They're naturally very distressed but they're bearing up well in the circumstances.'

Leach nodded. 'I can confirm that. I've been in to see them a couple of times to update them on our search. I think maybe I should call in again tomorrow, after I've spoken to Doc Hanley. Has he any idea how long she's been dead?'

'From a preliminary examination, assuming it is Daisy then he thinks she was probably killed not long after she disappeared. We'll have to wait for his PM report, of course, before we know exactly how she died and whether she'd been sexually assaulted.'

'Quite so. Have you found out how long that load of rubble's been there?'

'Not yet, sir. As far as we can tell, no one's reported it but that doesn't mean much. People only bother to report fly-tipping if it happens to be on their land. And it's possible that no one noticed it. It's a fairly busy road, but the heap of bricks is in a ditch and not really visible from the carriageway. This guy only spotted it because he pulled into the lay-by and got out of his car.'

'Maybe that's why the killer chose it, sir,' Sukey suggested.

'Possibly,' Leach agreed, 'although we have to keep an open mind – the girl's body might have been already lying in the ditch and a fly-tipper simply dumped his load on top without noticing it.'

'We'll need to trace it to its source,' said Rathbone. 'It looked like a heap of broken bricks so it could be part of a demolition job.'

'Get on to that right away, and get a statement from the guy who reported it as soon as possible. We'll tell the press we've found a body and as soon as the ID is confirmed we'll give them more information and ask them to put out an appeal for witnesses. Now,' Leach referred to the open file on his desk. 'I see there's a reference here to the disappearance of

Valerie Deacon twenty-odd years ago. You suspect a link between the two cases, Greg?'

'Only because the circumstances of the disappearance were similar, sir – both girls set off for Over Hampton Comprehensive School and never arrived. Valerie's body has never been found but a couple of textbooks she would have needed for that day's lessons turned up during a search in some long grass by the side of the footpath she sometimes used. We think they probably fell out of her school bag as she was snatched. The bag has never been found.'

Leach frowned. 'You say you interviewed some possible suspects but had to let them go. Was that because they had alibis?'

'In only one case did the man have a cast iron alibi. We didn't have any reason to hold either of the others but that doesn't mean we've eliminated them. Incidentally, one of them is a builder.'

Leach made a note. 'That could be significant. Anyway, I take it you'll be having another word with them about Daisy?'

'Naturally, sir.'

'Right, I'll leave you to get on with it.'

As the two detectives stood up to leave, Leach signalled to Sukey to remain behind. 'I understand you've had a word with this Doctor Hogan about his suspicions concerning the death of Adelaide Minchin in Over Hampton,' he said. 'Do you think there's any substance in them?'

'He gave me some information that he claims is enough to justify his demand that we make further enquiries, sir,' she replied.

'Do you think he's got a case?'

'I think his argument is a little far-fetched, sir.' She gave him a brief summary of Hogan's account of the mysterious telephone calls made to Muriel Minchin. 'I've spoken to several people in the village and I've learned quite a lot about Adelaide Minchin, but so far nothing to suggest she had any enemies – on the contrary, she seems to have been universally popular. In any case the calls to Muriel were made over six years ago.'

'Was she any relation to the dead woman?'

'They were cousins, sir. Muriel left Parson's Acre to Adelaide, rather than to one of her brothers or her sister. It gave rise to a lot of gossip in the village and I understand it caused ill feeling in the family. I imagine they'll be wondering who will inherit now.'

Leach thought for a moment. 'Is Hogan suggesting that one of the aggrieved relatives might have caused Adelaide's death to get their hands on a property they considered rightfully theirs?'

'He didn't say anything to that effect sir.'

There was a short silence before Leach said, 'I have a feeling you're not dismissing this out of hand?'

'It does seem a rather strange coincidence that there should be so many deaths and disappearances in the same village,' she said.

'There's hardly any similarity between odd phone calls to an elderly woman, the accidental death of another and the disappearance of two schoolgirls twenty years apart,' he pointed out.

'That's true, sir,' she said, 'but . . .' For a moment she was tempted to mention the sympathetic chord Doctor Hogan's mention of a 'hunch' had struck with her, but decided to keep the notion to herself for the time being.

To her surprise, it was as if Leach had read her mind. 'Another of your famous hunches, I suppose?' he said, with a familiar twinkle in his sharp blue eyes. 'Well, as I said before, it's best to keep an open mind. I'd like a detailed report some time, but needless to say the hunt for Daisy Hewett's killer has priority.'

Back in the CID office, Sukey found DS Rathbone sitting in front of his computer with his notebook open on the desk. When she appeared he swung his chair round to face her. 'I've just been mapping out a plan of action for tomorrow,' he said.

'What's my first assignment, Sarge?'

He closed his notebook and switched off the computer. 'It can wait till the morning. What did the boss want?'

'He wanted to know about my interview with Doctor Hogan,' she said, sinking a little wearily into her own chair. 'I told him about the iffy phone calls and so on and he's asked for a detailed report. It shouldn't take long so unless you're dead keen to have all the details right away . . .'

He made a dismissive gesture. 'I'm not holding my breath,' he said with a faint grin. 'We've got more important things to think about now.'

'That's what DCI Leach said. Just the same, I'd like to get

this out of the way while it's still fresh in my mind. I'll try and find time to do it before I go to bed – if I can stay awake, that is.' She gave an involuntary yawn. 'Sorry Sarge, it's been a long day.'

'You're dead right. I'm feeling pretty knackered too – and I could use a drink. Finding a goner is always depressing – when it's a kid it's even worse. Would you care to join me?'

'Thanks for the offer, Sarge, but all I had at lunchtime was a sandwich and I'd like to get home and have something to eat.'

'That's not a bad idea,' he said. 'Maybe I'll do the same.' He pushed back his chair and stood up. 'See you tomorrow.'

FIVE

The following morning Rathbone assembled his team – DCs Mike Haskins, Tom Pringle, Penny Osborne, Vicky Armstrong and Sukey Reynolds.

'As you all know,' he began, 'we're just a few of the foot-soldiers in the major investigation team that's been set up to investigate Daisy Hewett's disappearance. We're ninety per cent sure the body found yesterday is Daisy's, but because of the state of decomposition we can't ask the parents to identify her so we have to wait for dental records to be checked.'

'Have we had the CSIs' report, Sarge?' asked Mike.

'I was coming to that.' Rathbone took a sheet from his file. 'They still have quite a lot of work to do collecting samples and collating data and so on. They've been in touch with the council and have established there are no plans to fill in the ditch, so either the rubble was dumped by a fly-tipper who didn't see the girl's body, or her killer dumped her body and found a handy way of concealing it. The ditch is quite shallow and the quantity of rubble is comparatively small.'

'Isn't it possible, Sarge,' said Penny, 'that whoever dumped it might have spotted the body but didn't report it because he knew he'd be fined for fly-tipping?'

Rathbone nodded and made a note. 'There's some who'll stoop to anything rather than get involved,' he said contemptuously. 'Good point, Penny. We'll bear that in mind once

we've found the source. Meanwhile there's plenty more
spade work to be done. Vicky and Sukey, you're to talk to
the man who reported seeing the hand; he didn't leave his
name but Sukey's got his mobile number. Take him back
to the scene if you think it'll help jog his memory.'

'Right, Sarge.'

'And when you've done that, go and check on the builder in
Over Hampton that Sukey mentioned in her report on Adelaide
Minchin. Find out what job he's working on at the moment and
if it involves demolition get back to me right away. All right,
get going.' As Sukey and Vicky got up to leave he turned to the
remaining members of the team. 'The rest of you will be paying
return visits to the suspects in the Valerie Deacon case.'

'Ellery Computing Services, Malcolm Ellery speaking.' The
voice was a light tenor with a rising note on the final
syllable.

'Mr Ellery, this is Detective Constable Sukey Reynolds of
the Avon and Somerset police,' Sukey began.

There was an audible intake of breath at the end of the line
before the man spoke again. 'I was expecting to hear from
you,' he said. 'I apologize,' he hurried on, a little breathlessly,
'I know I should have remained at the scene, but it was so
awful . . . I just had to get away.'

'I understand, sir,' said Sukey. 'It was a very distressing
sight and you weren't the only one to be affected.'

'Thank you. I suppose you want to ask me some questions.
I'm not sure I can be much help, but I'll do my best. Do I
have to come to the police station?'

'That won't be necessary sir. Perhaps I and my colleague
DC Vicky Armstrong could call on you?'

'By all means. I work from home; come now if you like.'
He gave them an address in Portishead.

'Excellent,' said Sukey. 'We can be with you in fifteen
minutes.'

Ellery lived in the penthouse of a block of flats overlooking
the marina.

'He can't be doing too badly,' Vicky commented as she
pressed the button next to the card bearing his name. 'Chris
and I looked at a flat near here a couple of years or so ago.

It wasn't such a high-class development as this, but it was still way out of our price range. It would have been very convenient for me,' she added as they waited for a response from Ellery, 'but Chris would have had to change his job. That wouldn't have been a problem, not with his reputation, but he's happy where he is.' Vicky's partner was the head chef at a hotel on the outskirts of Bristol.

After a few seconds a voice on the intercom said, 'Come on up.' A buzzer sounded and the door lock was released.

'This is pretty posh,' Sukey commented as they crossed the entrance hall, which was furnished like the reception area of a hotel with fitted carpets, good quality pictures on the walls, comfortable chairs, magazines on a glass-topped table and a bowl of fresh flowers on a shelf. The lift to the penthouse glided smoothly upwards and came almost imperceptibly to a stop. The doors slid silently apart; a youngish, slightly built man in jeans and T-shirt awaited them with a welcoming but slightly nervous smile. He had a thin, colourless face, short fair hair and pale blue eyes behind wire-framed glasses.

'Malcolm Ellery,' he said. His right hand made a jerky movement as if he was about to extend it in a greeting before deciding it might not be appropriate. 'Do come in.' He led them through a spacious hallway into a large room with wide windows commanding an extensive view over the Bristol Channel. One wall was taken up with a computer workstation comprising an array of what was evidently state of the art equipment and a bank of shelving stacked with neatly labelled box files. 'This is my office,' he said, as if some explanation was called for. With a slight flourish he produced a card on which the words, 'Ellery Computing Services' were woven into a colourful abstract design and presented it to Sukey. 'Websites a speciality,' he added.

'Thank you, I'll bear that in mind,' she said, slipping the card into her pocket. 'Now, we don't want to take up too much of your time, so perhaps . . .'

'Of course, and your time must be precious too,' he said hurriedly. 'Do sit down.' He pulled up a couple of chairs with curved steel frames and bright orange cushions. 'Would you care for some coffee or tea?'

Sukey sensed that he was trying to postpone the necessity to answer questions for as long as possible. 'No thank you,'

she said firmly. She and Vicky sat down and Ellery did the
same. 'Now, according to our records,' she went on, consulting
her notebook, 'you made a 999 call at twelve thirty p.m. on
Tuesday the twenty-ninth of July to report seeing what
appeared to be a human hand protruding from the bottom of
a pile of rubble in a lay-by on the road to Over Hampton.'

Ellery nodded and swallowed hard, as if the memory still
had the power to turn his stomach. 'It was . . . dreadful. I'd
just had a . . . I mean, I'd just relieved myself and I turned
round to come back to the car . . . and I saw it. For a moment
I thought it moved . . . and then it was obvious it couldn't.'
He put a trembling hand to his mouth.

'Take a few deep breaths and you'll be OK,' said Sukey.

He nodded dumbly. After taking a few seconds to follow
her advice he swallowed hard and said, 'Sorry about that. It
was really horrid . . .'

'Don't worry about it; I'd quite likely have thrown up if
I'd been there,' Vicky said reassuringly, receiving a weak
smile in return. 'Now, just try and remember exactly what
you did next.'

'I rushed back to the car. I was shaking so much I was
afraid to drive off straight away . . . and then I realized it was
my duty to report it, so I made that call on my mobile. They
– the police – asked me to stay and wait for them, but I just
couldn't sit there with that . . . that . . . thing a few feet away.'

'Yes, we know you were too upset,' Sukey broke in, trying
not to show her exasperation. 'What we want you to do now
– and we know this will be a bit painful for you, but it really
is very important – is to try and relive the scene before you
saw the hand. You pulled over into the lay-by and turned off
the ignition. Were there any other cars parked there?'

'No, I was the only one.'

'So what did you do then?'

'I got out of the car, locked it, and walked across the lay-
by. There's a shallow ditch and some woodland on the other
side. I stepped over the ditch and went behind a tree to . . .
you know.'

'Yes, we understand why you were there,' said Vicky
patiently. 'Now, think about the pile of rubble; when did you
first notice it?'

Ellery closed his eyes for a moment. 'I saw it as I walked

across the lay-by, but I didn't pay much attention. If I thought about it at all I suppose I assumed it was there to fill in the ditch. Anyway I crossed the ditch and did what I had to do and I started to walk back to the car . . . and then I saw this hand, this dreadful, skeletal hand, sticking out from . . .' He put his hands over his eyes. 'Dear God, will I ever forget it?'

'I'm sure you will in time,' said Sukey. 'Did you touch anything?'

Ellery shuddered at the thought. 'I . . . I just stood there for a moment and stared. It was like something out of a horror movie . . . and then I ran back to the car and jumped in and locked the door.' He gave a weak, mirthless laugh. 'Stupid, isn't it? As if a dead hand could hurt you.'

'It's quite natural . . . you were in a state of shock,' said Vicky. 'Now, try and forget the hand and think about the pile of rubble. Did you notice anything special about it?'

'It looked like a load of broken bricks – and as I said, I assumed they'd been dumped there deliberately to fill in the ditch. Of course, it could have been some cowboy builder trying to avoid paying for disposal. Hang on a minute!' he exclaimed suddenly, showing for the first time a spark of animation, 'I remember noticing a lorry taking away some bricks from a place I passed a couple of weeks or so ago. I somehow got the impression that the remains of an old tumble-down outbuilding were being demolished . . . now where was it?' The two detectives held their breath and waited. With a slightly theatrical gesture he closed his eyes, leaned forward and put a clenched fist to his forehead. 'Yes, I remember, it was somewhere further along the Keynsham Road. I was on my way to visit a client.'

'Do you happen to know the date?' asked Vicky.

'Not offhand, but it'll be in the diary.' He went to the computer, called up a file and scrolled down the screen. 'Here we are, it was the second of July. I had an appointment with Jade Kingsley at eleven o'clock so it would have been some time around half-past ten. Jade lives just this side of Keynsham; she's the famous romantic writer, you know. I built her website and there were one or two things she wasn't happy about, so I thought it best to call on her so that she could explain exactly what she wanted. She's a charming lady, but very particular and—'

'I'm sure you did a splendid job for her,' said Vicky. 'I

don't suppose you can remember exactly where you saw that lorry?'

Ellery shook his head. 'I'm afraid not. I'm sorry. Is it important?'

'It might be. Thank you anyway for answering our questions so fully. We won't take up any more of your time.' By mutual consent, the two detectives stood up to leave.

'And if you should remember anything else that might be relevant,' Sukey added, 'perhaps you'd be kind enough to give us a call on this number.' She handed him one of her cards. As she did so her eye fell on a framed photograph on the desk. It was of two men in swimming trunks on a sunlit beach. One she recognized as Ellery; the other appeared about the same age but had stronger features and was of a more muscular build. They had their arms round each other and were smiling happily at the camera.

Ellery followed her gaze. 'That's me and my partner, on holiday in Ibiza,' he said. He picked up the picture and gently caressed it with his fingers before putting it down again.

'Nice-looking chap,' said Sukey.

He gave a fond smile. 'Yes, isn't he?'

'Is he in IT as well?'

'Oh no, he's in a different line of business altogether. We met when his company commissioned me to build their website. As soon as we met, we just . . . well, you know how it is.'

'What d'you reckon?' asked Vicky as she and Sukey returned to their car. 'Bit of a drama queen, don't you think?'

'It's understandable that he was upset at the time, but he did go a bit OTT with the emotional stuff,' Sukey agreed. 'I think he's on the level, though.'

'My impression as well,' said Vicky. 'I had a job to keep a straight face when he did his "Thinker" pose, though,' she added and the two chuckled at the recollection.

'At least, he's given us something useful to go on,' said Sukey.

'True,' Vicky agreed. 'The second of July was three days after Daisy disappeared. It might be a coincidence, of course, but it could be a breakthrough.'

'D'you think we should report it to the Sarge?' said Sukey.

'Let's see if we can find that demolition site first,' said Vicky, 'and we'd better make a note to check the date with the charming romantic novelist, although there's no reason to suppose he was mistaken. We can contact her through the website she was so fussy about.'

Sukey took a book of road maps from the glove pocket and studied it. 'He said it was somewhere on the Keynsham Road. Why don't we stop off at the lay-by and ask the CSIs to let us have a sample piece of brick?'

'Good thinking,' said Vicky.

Half an hour later they were heading for Keynsham with a few lumps of broken brick in a plastic bag on the back seat. 'With luck there'll be a board outside the site Ellery spotted,' said Sukey. 'It should have the name of the contractors, so if there's no one actually working on the site we'll know how to get in touch.'

They reached the outskirts of the town without success. 'We must have gone past it,' Vicky said impatiently. 'We'd better turn round and have a closer look. I'll drive a bit more slowly on the way back.'

They had retraced their route for about two miles when a large white van ahead of them signalled that it was about to turn left. Unable to overtake it because of oncoming traffic, Vicky slowed down and Sukey caught sight of the lettering on the side of the van as it drove through the entrance to a private drive.

'Find a convenient place to park,' she said urgently. 'I think we may be on to something.'

SIX

'What is it?' asked Vicky as she pulled into the side of the road.

'That van . . . it belongs to the Kozywarm Double Glazing Company,' said Sukey.

'So?'

'There's just a chance that there's been some kind of renovation or rebuilding work going on back there,' said Sukey. 'Maybe an extension or something and there had to be a bit of demolition first.'

'It's more likely to be replacement windows,' Vicky said doubtfully.

'It's worth a look, surely,' Sukey insisted. 'We haven't seen anything remotely promising so far.'

Vicky shrugged and switched off the ignition. 'OK, might as well.'

They got out of the car and walked back to where the van had turned in. A wooden gate that had fallen off its hinges and lay propped up against a post bore the name Cedar Cottage carved into the top bar. The drive, which was rutted and uneven, curved away to the right and led to a medium sized detached house that was obscured from the road by a tall hedge. A concrete base surrounded by a low brick wall abutted one end of the building.

'Looks like they're going to put up a conservatory,' said Sukey.

'Which is what those guys appear to be delivering,' Vicky agreed.

The white van was backed up by the front door; two men were unloading a number of double-glazed sections of varying shapes and sizes, which they stacked carefully against the front wall of the house. A bronzed, stocky man of about fifty was giving them directions; he was naked from the waist up, with brawny, heavily tattooed arms and gold studs in both ears. A luxuriant beard and a thick, dark brown tangle on his barrel chest more than compensated for the lack of hair on his glistening bronzed scalp. Catching sight of the two women, he strode towards them.

'Good morning ladies, can I help you?' he said. His manner was brisk but not unpleasant. The two showed their IDs.

'Police?' His tone indicated surprise but not disquiet. 'Is it me or one of those lads you want to talk to?'

'Can you tell us who owns this property?' asked Sukey.

'It belongs to me and my brother Dave,' he said. 'We bought it at auction about three months ago. It's our main business – we buy run down properties, do them up and either let or sell them on, hopefully at a profit. This is who we are.' He fished in the pocket of his jeans, produced a slightly dog-eared business card and waved it under their noses, giving them just enough time to read the words 'Don and Dave Keegan, House Extensions and Renovations' before putting it back in his pocket. 'We've had to do a lot to this place,' he went on. 'The main part of the interior work's almost done. We also had to knock down a dilapidated lean-to.' He waved a hand towards the end wall, where marks on the brickwork showed traces of the original structure. 'As you can see we're putting up a conservatory in its place. The deal was all above board,' he added, 'you can check with the agents who handled the sale – Weaver and Morris – if you want confirmation. Their office is in Keynsham. We've got nothing to hide.'

'That isn't what we've come about,' said Vicky. 'That fact is, we've had complaints about some illegal dumping of builders' rubble in this area and we're investigating local building sites.'

'There's been no illegal dumping from this site,' Keegan said firmly. 'All our stuff was properly disposed of.'

'Like where?' asked Sukey.

Keegan shrugged. 'What happened to it after it left the site isn't our problem. You'd have to ask the contractor who collected it. One thing I'm sure of is that it's a reputable outfit; they've been in business for years and it wouldn't do them any good to be caught fly-tipping.'

'Of course it wouldn't, sir, but perhaps you wouldn't mind giving us the name of the company and the date when they cleared the site.'

'They call themselves Premier Demolition Services. You'll find them in the phone book. I can't remember the exact date offhand – you'd have to check with them.'

'That's fine, sir. Now, we'd just like to have a quick look round the site before we leave, if you don't mind.'

He shrugged. 'Please yourselves, but I can't think what you expect to find.' He turned on his heel and went back to talk to the two men, who had finished unloading and were closing the back doors of their van.

The area round the foundations for the new conservatory might once have been part of a well-tended garden, but was now a virtual waste of compacted earth through which a few blades of grass and weeds had somehow struggled into the light. It was evident the site had been thoroughly cleared, but there were enough fragments of brick scattered around to send Vicky scurrying back to the car to collect a couple of fresh plastic bags in which they put half a dozen samples.

'What have you got there?' Unnoticed, Keegan came up

behind them just as they were sealing and labelling the bags.
They turned to face him.

'We're just taking these few bits of brick, sir,' Vicky
explained, holding up the bags for him to see. 'We found them
there.' She pointed at the ground close to where they were
standing. 'We'll give you a receipt for them if you wish.'

He gave a short laugh. 'You're more than welcome to them,'
he said, 'but I can't for the life of me think what good they'll
do you.'

'We need them for comparison with samples of the illegally dumped bricks,' Sukey explained.

'I've already told you there's been no illegal dumping from
this site,' said Keegan, a trifle impatiently, 'and I'd have
thought the CID had enough serious crime to deal with without
wasting their resources on a few trivial complaints.'

'I'm afraid there are times when we have to take even
apparently trivial complaints seriously,' said Sukey. 'It's
possible we may need to speak to you again, sir. Perhaps
you'd let us have the card you showed me a moment ago?'

For a moment he appeared to be about to make an objection, but evidently thought better of it, took out the card and
handed it over.

'Sorry it's a bit tatty,' he said.

'Thank you very much, Mr Keegan,' said Sukey.

'We appreciate your cooperation,' Vicky assured him. 'Do
you reckon he's on the level?' she said as they walked back
to their car.

'He didn't seem at all fazed by our questions,' said Sukey,
'and he was very definite all the rubble was disposed of legally.
Anyway, we've got his card and we can check on his firm
with the estate agents.'

'Right,' said Vicky, 'and we'd better talk to Premier
Demolitions and get them to give us a list of the sites they've
cleared since Daisy went missing.' Back in the car they studied
the bags of samples. 'What d'you reckon?' said Vicky. 'It
looks like a match to me.'

'They certainly look very similar,' Sukey agreed. 'Let's
hand them over to the CSIs and then report to the Sarge.'

There was evidence of a considerable amount of activity
in and around the site where Malcolm Ellery had made his
gruesome discovery, but when Sukey and Vicky arrived two

of the CSIs were taking a break, perched on the rear sill of one of the vans. One was munching a bacon sandwich and the other had a mug of tea in one hand and a cigarette in the other. They showed them the samples from Cedar Cottage and explained their background.

The smoker ground the butt of his cigarette beneath his heel and scrutinized one of the bags. 'Looks much the same colour and texture as the stuff we're finding here,' he commented. 'What d'you think, Dean?'

His companion swallowed the last of his sandwich and wiped his mouth with the back of his hand before taking the second bag. 'It looks interesting,' he agreed. 'Of course, only forensics can tell for sure; we'll send these off for comparison.'

'OK, thanks,' said Sukey. She got out her mobile. 'Better bring the Sarge up to date.'

DS Rathbone showed no sign of being overexcited by their report. 'OK,' he said wearily after listening to her account of their visit to Cedar Cottage, 'it doesn't sound too promising but we'll wait for the report from forensics before we eliminate the Keegans. For what it's worth you'd better have a word with the agents and the demolition people. And while you're at it, check on any other demolition contractors that cover this area.'

'Will do, Sarge.'

'Has he got anywhere with his enquiries?' asked Vicky as Sukey ended the call.

Sukey grimaced. 'I didn't like to ask, but from his tone I'd say probably not.' She put the mobile back in her pocket. 'So where shall we go first?'

'Let's try the estate agent,' Vicky suggested.

They drove into Keynsham, parked their car and were directed to the offices of Weaver and Morris by a Police Community Support Officer. A middle-aged woman seated at a desk in the reception area looked somewhat perturbed at being confronted by two members of the CID and asked them to kindly wait a moment while she spoke to her manager. She returned a few minutes later accompanied by a well-built man whom they immediately recognized as the original of the photograph on Malcolm Ellery's desk. 'This is our manager, Mr Baker,' she said.

He greeted them courteously and carefully scrutinized their IDs before saying, 'Perhaps you'd like to come into my office?' He ushered them into a small, unpretentious room, took his seat behind the plain, uncluttered desk and invited them to sit down. 'Before we go any further,' he said pleasantly, 'from your somewhat surprised expressions you appear to recognize me – or think you do. I assure you I haven't a criminal record,' he added, with a smile that revealed a perfect set of teeth.

'We're quite sure you haven't, Mr Baker,' said Sukey. 'We noticed your photograph in Malcolm Ellery's flat. He's been helping us with our enquiries.'

Baker's regular, clean-shaven features registered deep concern and he gave a slightly theatrical sigh. 'Ah yes, poor Mal. He's so distressed, poor love, he's hardly had a moment's peace since he made that awful discovery. But why have you come to see me?' he went on. 'I can't add anything to what he's told you.'

'No, we quite understand that,' said Vicky. 'We're here on another matter.' She quickly outlined the reason for their visit.

'Well, I can certainly confirm that Don and Dave Keegan bought Cedar Cottage at auction,' said Baker. 'In fact, they've picked up several properties through us over the years. I know of Premier Demolitions and so far as I'm aware they're a perfectly reputable outfit.'

'Thank you, sir, that's all we needed to know. We won't take up any more of your time.'

The two detectives stood up to leave when a thought occurred to Sukey. 'By the way,' she said, 'do you handle properties in Over Hampton?'

'Certainly,' said Baker. 'Are you interested in buying one?'

'I wish!' said Sukey. 'The reason I'm asking is that six or seven years ago a Miss Muriel Minchin was considering selling her house there and invited one or two agents to give a valuation. Was your firm one of them?'

'We might well have been, but that would be before my time,' said Baker. 'I could check for you. Did the lady put her property on the market, do you know?'

'As it happens she didn't, because unfortunately she died shortly after.'

'Could I ask what your interest is?'

'It's a long shot, but it might have a connection to another enquiry,' Sukey said cautiously. She took out one of her cards and handed it to him. 'If you could possibly check your records and let us know if your firm was asked to do a valuation on Parson's Acre in Over Hampton we'd be very appreciative.'

'I'll certainly do that. I might even be able to put you in touch with whoever handled the valuation – if it was anyone from our firm, of course.'

'Thank you, that would be great.'

'So what was all that about?' asked Vicky as they went back to the car. 'You're surely not still hoping to prove Adelaide Minchin's death was suspicious?'

'Let's say that in my book the verdict is still open,' said Sukey. She checked her watch. 'It's nearly one o'clock and I'm hungry. Why don't we go back to Over Hampton and grab some lunch in the Red Lion? With a bit of luck we might find the Hubbards there.'

'The Hubbards?'

'Tom and Jerry Hubbard. They're builders – father and son – and they sometimes call in for a bite at lunchtime.'

Vicky chuckled. 'I'm not sure I'd have much confidence in workers called Tom and Jerry,' she commented. 'Hang on a moment, though – didn't our Sarge say one of the suspects questioned over the Valerie Deacon case was a builder?'

'Exactly,' said Sukey.

SEVEN

The car park was almost full, but Vicky found a space at the far end. The way to the bar entrance was through a garden that was bordered on one side by a narrow stream. People in colourful summer clothing were enjoying the sunshine while eating their lunch seated at rustic picnic tables set out on the grass. A small flotilla of ducks paddled to and fro in the stream; now and then they plunged their heads into the water in search of food, upturned tails quivering and the wet feathers on their bellies sparkling in the sunlight. Two of the more adventurous had climbed up the bank and were waddling hopefully among the tables, competing with a small flock of sparrows for possible titbits.

As the two detectives approached, the girl who had been serving behind the bar on Sukey's previous visit emerged from the house with plates of food, which she placed in front of two men who were seated at the table nearest to them. They wore open-necked shirts with the sleeves rolled up and their heavy boots were powdered with dust. Each held a pint glass of beer in one hand.

Vicky gently elbowed Sukey in the ribs. 'Would you say they were father and son?' she said quietly out of the corner of her mouth.

'There's certainly a likeness,' Sukey whispered back. 'I wonder . . .'

The girl, apparently in no hurry to go back indoors, was exchanging banter with the two men. Sukey went over to her. 'Excuse me,' she said, 'do you take orders out here or do we have to go to the bar?'

'Order and pay at the bar,' the girl replied, a trifle tersely as if irritated at having her conversation interrupted. 'If you want to sit out here I'll bring it to your table,' she added in a slightly softer tone. She glanced round and added, 'we're pretty full at the moment but you might find a couple of seats in a minute or two.' She turned back to the two men. 'So long, guys! Enjoy your food!' With a jaunty wave she went back indoors.

The younger man smiled and gestured with his glass at two empty seats at their table. 'Sit there,' he said.

'Thank you, that's very kind of you,' said Vicky.

'No problem. We'll keep the seats free.'

They went into the bar. Business was obviously brisk. There were now three people serving – the girl, the licensee Ben Bridges whom Sukey had met on her previous visit, and a second, older woman – but they still had to wait several minutes while customers in front of them gave orders for drinks and food. Meanwhile they studied the printed bar menu and compared it with the list of 'Specials' written in chalk on a blackboard behind the bar. They were trying to choose between chilli con carne and paella when Bridges, who had approached without their noticing, said in his hearty baritone, 'Back again, constable? How are your enquiries going? We heard you'd found a body. Is it Daisy Hewitt?'

His voice carried round the bar. Silence fell. Heads swiv-elled. One or two people who were making for the door to the garden with drinks in their hands stopped in their tracks and turned round. 'This lady's a detective,' Bridges explained.

He raised an inquisitive eyebrow at Vicky. 'What about your friend? Is she . . .?'

'This is Detective Constable Armstrong,' said Sukey. 'The answer to your question is yes, we have found a body but it has not yet been identified.'

'What kind of body?' asked a smartly dressed man, who was clutching a foaming pint tankard in each hand. 'I mean,' he hurried on, 'is it a young girl? Do you think it could be Daisy Hewitt?'

'We're all so worried about her,' said a slim woman in a checked shirt, jodhpurs and riding boots. She had dark, cropped hair and finely cut features, and was sipping red wine from a glass held delicately in a beautifully manicured hand. 'We've all been hoping she'd turn up, but when we heard the news . . .' She pressed her lips together; a sad shake of the head indicated that in her opinion the hope was a faint one.

'We've had prayers in church for her and her family,' added a grey-haired, rosy-cheeked woman in a blue linen dress. 'She was . . . oh dear, it's awful to say "was", isn't it, but we're all so afraid for her. Such a lovely girl . . . we do so hope . . .' Her face crumpled and she dabbed her eyes with a handkerchief.

'We are working on the Daisy Hewitt case, but I'm afraid we can't answer any questions,' said Sukey. 'Our Superintendent has promised to issue a statement as soon as we have further information.' She turned back to the bar. 'Now if we could just give our order?'

'Yes, yes, of course.' Bridges wrote down their choice of food, poured their drinks and took their money. 'You're sitting outside? Right, Josie will bring it out when it's ready.'

'I need the loo before I eat,' said Vicky.

'Me too,' said Sukey. 'Over there,' she added, pointing to a door marked 'Toilets'.

When they emerged and went out into the garden they met Josie coming back indoors. 'I've just taken your orders outside,' she told them. 'You're sitting with the Hubbards, right?'

'Thank you,' said Sukey. 'I thought it must be them,' she whispered to Vicky. 'Maybe they can give us a bit more information about rubble disposal.'

They had barely sat down when the elder of the two men said, 'So you ladies are from the police? You never said.'

'You didn't ask us,' Sukey pointed out.

'Josie told us. She said you'd been in here before and you've found Daisy Hewitt's body.'

'Josie shouldn't have said that,' said Vicky firmly as she unwound her paper napkin and extricated the cutlery. 'Like we said in there, we've found a body, but it hasn't yet been identified.' She took a long drink from her glass of apple juice and plunged her fork into her dish of chilli con carne. 'We can't answer any more questions.'

'We know there's something going on in a lay-by on the Keynsham Road. Is that where you found it?'

'Look,' said Sukey, 'I thought we made it clear that we aren't authorized to give any information apart from confirming what's already been made public by our press officer. It so happens,' she went on, after swallowing a mouthful of paella and with the object of forestalling a further question, 'we are also making some inquiries about the illegal dumping of builders' rubble in this area. Josie said your name was Hubbard and Mr Bridges told me last time I was here that there's a family firm of builders in this village by that name. Would that be you two by any chance?'

'That's right,' said the older man. 'I'm Thomas Hubbard and this is my son Jeremy. We're otherwise known, as no doubt you'll be told if you're here long, as Tom and Jerry. We get our legs pulled about that, as you can imagine.'

'You and Mum should have thought of it before you named me,' his son said with a snigger. He turned back to Sukey. 'You've been here before, then? What about?'

'That was a different matter.'

'It was about Miss Adelaide Minchin, wasn't it?' said Tom. 'You were in here yesterday lunchtime and Ben Bridges mentioned it when I dropped in that evening. You remember, Jerry – I told you about it.'

Jerry nodded. 'That's right, I'd forgotten.'

'So what was it about Miss Adelaide?' said Tom curiously. 'You don't reckon there's anything dodgy about her death, do you?'

'No comment,' said Sukey firmly.

'She was a nice lady,' Tom went on. 'She was asking me about some work she wanted done to her house and I said I'd give her a quote, but I never got around to it and then I heard she'd died. Sad, that was.'

'We're asking about illegal dumping,' Sukey reminded him. 'Fly-tipping, I think you call it.'

He nodded. 'That's right. We'd never do that, would we Jerry?'

''Course not,' his son said emphatically, 'if we have stuff to get rid of we do it proper.'

'Like how?' asked Sukey.

'Depends on what it is,' said Tom. 'If it's something that can be reused – a fireplace, for example, or some crazy paving – we take it to a reclamation centre.'

'Sorry, I'm not with you,' said Sukey. 'What use is an old fireplace?'

'You'd be surprised. Some of them can be quite valuable. People having an old property renovated sometimes want what they call a "feature" – something that fits in with their idea of a period home.' Tom's intonation indicated that in his opinion there was no accounting for taste. 'And then again, people modernizing an old property usually want them ripped out,' he added.

'I suppose there are times when you have an opportunity to pass them on through the trade?' Vicky remarked.

Father and son exchanged glances. 'Look, you said a moment ago it was fly-tipping you two were interested in,' said Tom after a moment's hesitation.

'You're right, that is what we're investigating,' said Vicky, 'but it's bricks and rubble we're interested in, not old fireplaces. We're checking on all the builders and building sites in this area. Apart from you, we've only spoken to one other firm so far. It belongs to two brothers called Don and Dave Keegan. Maybe you know them?'

'Sure we do,' said Tom. 'They buy properties at auction and do them up.'

'So we understand,' said Sukey. 'I suppose they're the kind of firm that might be looking for feature fireplaces or crazy paving, or have something reusable they want to get rid of?'

'It so happens we took an old oak door off them a few weeks back,' Tom admitted. 'It was just the thing one of our customers wanted for the cottage we were doing up for him. Look, there's nothing iffy about that sort of arrangement – it's all above board.'

'We aren't suggesting it isn't,' Vicky assured them. 'It's just that we don't know anything about the building trade and . . .'

'OK, we take your point,' said Tom. 'So is there anything else we can help you with?'

'If you hadn't been able to take that door off them, would they have taken it to the . . . what did you call it . . . a reclamation centre?'

'Probably.'

'Suppose there are broken bricks and stuff to get rid of – what happens to that?'

'It's normally dumped in a quarry. The nearest one is about ten miles from here.'

'I see.' Vicky nodded and turned her attention back to her food.

'Is that where you take your stuff?' asked Sukey.

Both men shook their heads. 'Look,' said Tom, 'if you're talking about a demolition job, that's not our line – there are specialists with heavy equipment to handle that sort of work.'

'Like Premier Demolitions?'

Tom nodded. 'Ah, you've heard of them? They're the chief outfit round here. We do mostly construction work – extensions, renovations and so on. Now and again we have to knock something down – an old brick wall for example. If it's no use to us we hire a skip and get rid of it that way. Occasionally there's a small amount of stuff we think we might reuse. In that case we put it in the dumper truck and take it to the yard, but it doesn't happen very often.' He checked his heavy wristwatch, pushed aside his empty plate, drained his glass and stood up. 'Well, there's no rest for the wicked. It's back to work for us. Come on, son, the Wilsons' extension won't build itself and they're planning to move in soon.'

A little reluctantly Sukey thought, Jerry got to his feet. 'Best of luck, ladies,' he said with an engaging smile.

The minute they were gone, Vicky remarked with a chuckle, 'They probably think we're a pair of simpletons, trying to get our heads round the mystique of their highly specialized world.'

Sukey nodded and swallowed the last of her paella before commenting, 'I hope we didn't overdo "simple". It wouldn't do much for the CID's reputation, would it?'

'I don't think we came across as being that ignorant,' said Vicky. 'Anyway, they were pretty helpful and they didn't show any sign of being fazed by our questions – although I noticed the father did most of the talking.'

'They were a bit hesitant about admitting that reclaimed

materials get passed on through the trade,' Sukey pointed out. 'I imagine a few bob change hands now and again without appearing in the books, but I don't feel inclined to suggest an investigation.'

'Nor I,' Vicky agreed. 'Just the same,' she added, 'it'd be interesting to know if either of them was the builder who was interviewed when Valerie Deacon disappeared.' She finished her drink and pulled out her cell phone. 'I suppose we'd better report back to the Sarge. We wouldn't want him to think we've been wasting our precious time, would we?'

EIGHT

D S Rathbone's only comment in response to Vicky's report was to say that one possible suspect had been eliminated from the Daisy Hewitt enquiry. He then ordered her and Sukey to return to headquarters and, in conjunction with the remainder of the team, make a list of every firm of builders of whatever size listed in the Yellow Pages and divide them up between themselves. 'And if you don't get any joy there,' he ended, 'look under bricklayers, suppliers of building materials, aggregates . . . any bloody thing you can think of that's remotely connected with the building trade.'

'He didn't exactly enthuse over our efforts so far,' said Vicky, 'but it's probably frustration at the lack of progress. The only positive fact to emerge so far is that we can probably eliminate the builder who was interviewed in the Valerie Deacon case. He was a suspect then because he'd been seen chatting to Valerie the day before she disappeared and he didn't have an alibi for the time she disappeared, but he claims to have been on holiday with his family in Florida on the date of Daisy's disappearance. His statement will be checked as a matter of routine, but at the moment it seems he's in the clear as far as this case is concerned.'

For the rest of the afternoon and during the following day, the team worked systematically through the firms listed under 'Builders' in the directory. In every case they were met with emphatic denials of the offence of fly-tipping and, despite patient and painstaking questioning, none of the officers managed to elicit a single reason – subject to verification of statements where applicable – to justify further enquiries. It wasn't until late afternoon on Thursday, when they were on their way back to headquarters with only half the names on their list ticked off, that Sukey and Vicky struck what eventually turned out to be gold. They spotted a cement mixer and an open trailer parked on the drive of an end of terrace house on the outskirts of Portishead. A metal toolbox lay open on the ground and a man in overalls was tinkering with the mixer. Vicky pulled in and they consulted their list.

'There's no mention of a building firm at this address,' said Vicky.

'Maybe he doesn't advertise in the Yellow Pages,' Sukey suggested. 'If that's all the equipment he's got he's probably only in a small way of business.'

'D'you think it's worth having a word?'

'Might as well.'

The man straightened up and turned round as they approached. He appeared to be in his early sixties and had the weathered complexion of someone who has spent most of his working life in the open air.

'Excuse me,' said Sukey. 'We noticed your machinery – are you by any chance a builder?'

The man dropped the spanner he was holding into the toolbox and wiped his hands on a piece of oily rag. 'In a small way,' he said. 'Have you got a job for me?'

'Not exactly,' said Vicky. 'We're looking into reports of illegal dumping of builder's rubble. Would you mind answering a few routine questions, Mister . . .?'

His bushy grey eyebrows lifted at the sight of their IDs. 'The name's Phelps, Bob Phelps,' he said. 'I've no objection to answering questions and I've nothing to hide. I don't handle rubble – I haven't got the equipment for one thing, and for another, like I said, I only do small jobs these days.'

'You mean, you used to do larger jobs?' said Vicky.

'I used to work for a big construction company that went bust about five years ago,' he explained. 'I was too old to be taken on by another firm but I wasn't ready to retire, so I set up my own one-man business working from home. I can prove

I got permission to park this lot here,' he added, indicating the trailer and the mixer.

'That's not a problem,' Sukey assured him. 'It's just that someone has been fly-tipping their rubble and we're trying to find out who it is.'

'Well, I can assure you it wasn't me,' said Phelps. 'All I do these days is small jobs like replacing weather boards, repairing sills and gutters, laying concrete paths, that sort of thing. I keep a record of every job; you can check my books.'

'That really won't be necessary, thank you,' said Vicky. 'We apologize for the interruption.'

'No problem.' He picked up the spanner and resumed his work on the mixer. They were about to get back in their car when he gave a shout. 'Hang on a minute, I've just remembered something.'

They hurried back. 'What is it?' said Sukey.

'We reckoned kids had pinched the truck for a joy ride,' Phelps began, 'but now I come to think of it . . .'

'What truck was this?' asked Vicky.

'My mate's truck.'

'Your mate had his truck stolen?'

'That's right – with a load of old bricks on it.'

Sukey and Vicky exchanged glances. Could this be the breakthrough they had been hoping for? 'Can you give us some details?' said Sukey.

'It was a couple of weeks or so ago.' He paused to roll a cigarette, put it in his mouth, lit it, took a deep draw and blew out smoke before continuing. 'I'd been asked to do a job for a gent who had an old brick shed in his back garden. It was damp and the roof had fallen in so he and his son knocked it down to make room for a new wooden shed. They came round and asked me to quote for the shed and at the same time get rid of the broken bricks for them.'

'And were you able to help him?' asked Sukey.

'The shed was no problem. I gave him a quote; he was happy with it so I ordered it from a supplier.' There was a pause while Phelps re-lit his cigarette and took several more draws while the detectives did their best to contain their impatience. 'The rubble was another matter,' he went on. 'I couldn't handle it on my own – there was too much of it and in any case it would've been too heavy for the trailer. I've got a mate, Wally, who retired about the same time as I was laid off. He wasn't ready to sit around doing nothing all day so he bought some power tools and a motor mower and set up as a jobbing gardener. We help each other out, see? If one of his customers wants a path laid he refers them to me.'

'So it was his truck – the one he carries his machinery around in – that was used to take away the old bricks and stuff?' Vicky prompted, as there was yet another pause.

'Apart from a small quantity I kept back to use in the base for the new shed,' Phelps explained. 'Always ready to lend a hand is Wally,' he went on. 'If I need the cement mixer for a job he'll take it to the site for me. Nothing's too much trouble—'

'That sounds an ideal arrangement,' Sukey interposed, as he seemed on the point of adding to the catalogue of Wally's virtues. 'You said something about kids and joy riding,' she reminded him.

'Ah yes, that's what we thought at the time. Wally had been working till quite late on a gardening job that day so he picked me up after supper and we went to this gentleman's place and loaded the old bricks on the truck. By the time we finished it was getting dark so Wally decided to take it home and dump the load in the quarry first thing in the morning. He left the truck outside his place overnight and next morning it had gone.'

'Did he report it to the police?' asked Sukey.

'Of course he did – right away. They sent PC Plod round with a notebook and he gave Wally an incident number and went away again. Luckily all his tools and stuff was locked up in the garage. Not that he'd have left it on the truck overnight,' he added. 'He's very security conscious, but who'd have thought anyone would nick a load of old bricks?'

'When exactly did this happen?' asked Vicky.

Phelps shrugged. 'Can't remember exactly – two or three weeks ago, maybe more, maybe less.'

'Did Wally get his truck back?'

'Oh yes, your boys found it a couple of days later. Whoever pinched it left it in a field about fifteen miles away, minus the load. We thought it must have been kids, but on second thoughts maybe someone needed some old bricks for aggregate and decided to help themselves.'

'It's quite possible,' Sukey agreed, although privately she

hoped for a different explanation. 'I don't suppose you happen to know the incident number?'

Phelps shook his head. 'You'd have to ask him that. He lives in Dunford Road, number fifteen.'

'And would you mind giving us the name and address of the person who wanted the bricks taken away?'

'The address is twenty-eight Poplar Avenue. The name's Laurence. I think the father's ex-army – he did most of the talking but the son lent us a hand loading up the bricks. That reminds me, the shed hasn't been delivered yet. I must chase the supplier.' He took a ballpoint pen from a pocket in his overalls and made a note on the back of his hand.

Vicky jotted the addresses in her notebook. 'Thank you very much, Mr Phelps, you've been really helpful.'

'Any time.' Phelps nodded, dropped his cigarette, ground it under his heel and resumed his work on the cement mixer.

Back in their car, Sukey and Vicky had a brief discussion. There seemed little point in interviewing Wally before they had a chance to check on the incident report. On the other hand, it was possible that some traces of the brickwork had been left behind when the old brick shed was demolished. After locating Poplar Avenue in their street guide and finding it less than a mile away, they decided to call on Mr Laurence.

Number twenty-eight was a substantial, brick-built house with a detached garage and a neat front garden with a square patch of lawn surrounded by rose bushes. A red-faced, perspiring man of about seventy in khaki shorts, shirtsleeves and a Panama hat was pushing a lawnmower to and fro while a woman of about the same age in a flowery summer dress was dead-heading the roses. Vicky and Sukey got out of the car and opened the gate. Immediately, the man abandoned the mower and strode towards them.

'Look, if you're Jehovah's Witnesses, I've told your lot before – we're not interested,' he said with more than a hint of aggression.

'Mr Laurence?' said Vicky.

'Brigadier Laurence,' he corrected. 'Who wants to know?' The two detectives held up their IDs and he frowned. 'What do you want with me? I haven't reported any crime.'

'We understand that a quantity of rubble was removed from your property a few weeks ago by a Mr Robert Phelps.'

'So what? Nothing illegal in that, is there?' said Laurence.
'Not if it was done with your permission, sir,' said Sukey.
'Of course it was. There was an old brick shed in my back garden. My son and I knocked it down and we commissioned that chap Phelps to cart away the rubble and quote for a new wooden shed. He's put down a concrete base but we're still waiting for the shed. It's about time the blighter got on with it,' he added testily. 'It's damned inconvenient having to store all the garden stuff in the garage.'

'We spoke to Mr Phelps a few minutes ago and we can assure you he's doing his best to hasten delivery of your shed,' Vicky assured him.

Laurence gave a non-committal grunt. 'I still don't see what all this has got to do with the police,' he said irritably. 'Now if that's all you want . . .'

'Not quite,' said Sukey. 'The fact is that after the rubble was removed from your property it was dumped illegally instead of being taken to a recognized site for disposal.'

'You mean fly-tipping?' He gave them a shrewd glance. 'Not the sort of thing I'd expect the CID to be interested in – unless of course something more serious is involved.'

'You're right, sir,' said Vicky. 'The bricks were loaded on to a truck which was subsequently stolen and later recovered minus its load. We believe there may be a connection with a very serious crime.'

'Why the hell didn't you say so?' Laurence's manner underwent a noticeable change. 'After forty years serving Her Majesty all over the world I think I know my duty. How can I help you?'

'What we would like, sir, is to look at the site where the old shed stood to see if any fragments of brick are still there.'

Laurence nodded. 'For comparison, I suppose. Let's go and see. You carry on with your snipping, Lucy,' he said to the woman – presumably his wife – who had been standing motionless, secateurs in hand, during the conversation. 'This way.' He opened a side gate leading to a paved path between the house and the garage.

Sukey had expected an ornamental back garden with a well-planned arrangement of shrubs and herbaceous borders, with possibly a water feature and an arbour. Instead, apart from a patio with a table and chairs set out under a canvas awning and a patch of lawn surrounded by a low lavender hedge, almost the entire area was given over to fruit and vegetables. Along one boundary was a cage where a variety of red berries were ripening in the sun, and beyond it an apple tree laden with glossy fruit. The remainder was planted with every kind of vegetable, all planted in straight lines and looking, as Vicky commented later, like soldiers drawn up on a parade ground.

'I can see you're surprised,' Laurence remarked over his shoulder as he led the way towards the far left hand corner of the plot. 'Lucy and I try to be self-sufficient. We grow all our own fruit and veg – or most of it anyway. Can't grow oranges and lemons here of course, ha ha!' His laugh was a deep rumble from somewhere in his chest. 'Environmentally friendly too,' too, he went on, 'that's why I use a hand mower instead of one of those noisy petrol driven monstrosities.' He continued in a similar vein until they reached their destination. 'Here you are, that's where the old shed stood.' He pointed to a rectangular area of concrete surrounded by wooden boards. 'We haven't touched anything since the rubble was cleared and the base put down. We expect Phelps to deal with that when he puts up the shed.' He squatted down and peered at the ground. 'You should be able to find a few bits there by the looks of things.'

He stood aside while Sukey and Vicky examined the area surrounding the base. There were indeed a number of useful-sized pieces of broken brick scattered around and it took only a few minutes for them to store and label samples in the plastic bags they had brought with them.

'Reckon you've got anything?' asked Laurence as they returned to the front garden.

'We hope so, but we can't be sure until forensics have examined them,' said Sukey.

'No, of course not. Well, best of luck – and don't forget, if there's anything else we can do . . .'

They thanked Brigadier Laurence, politely declined his wife's offer of tea and took their leave in a state of suppressed excitement. On returning to headquarters they made straight for the CID office where they found the rest of the team standing round DS Rathbone's desk. They handed him their bags of samples. He gave them a brief glance and laid them on the table without comment. His face was expressionless.

He cleared his throat and said, 'There's been a significant new development. Now you're all here we're to report to the SIO immediately.'

NINE

The moment the door closed behind his team, DCI Leach dropped his bombshell.

'We have received a further report from Doc Hanley on the remains found under rubble in the lay-by,' he began. 'His findings, together with the comparison with Daisy Hewitt's dental records, make it clear beyond doubt that those remains are not hers.' There was a shocked silence as the significance of his words sank in. 'You don't need me to tell you what this means,' he continued.

Sukey was the first to speak. 'The body of the girl under the rubble can't be Valerie Deacon's because she's only been dead just over three weeks and Valerie disappeared twenty odd years ago,' she said slowly, 'so if it isn't Daisy's we're looking at a third murder.'

'Which has never been reported,' Vicky added.

'Exactly,' said Leach. 'There are other discrepancies as well. Samples from Daisy's hairbrush, although similar in colour to those of the dead girl, don't match hairs recovered from the body, which are naturally black. Daisy's hair was light brown but she'd had it darkened. And there's one other significant factor: the mystery girl was nearly three months pregnant. DS Rathbone and I have already discussed some of the possible implications and now I'd like your reactions.' He sat back in his chair and waited.

'Perhaps she wanted to keep the baby and put pressure on the father to support the two of them, and he killed her to avoid the pregnancy – or even the relationship – being known?' said DC Penny Osborne. 'If he was married he'd be terrified his wife would find out.'

'That wouldn't explain why no one, not even her family, reported her disappearance,' DC Tim Pringle pointed out.

'She might have run away from home after a row with her

parents,' suggested DC Mike Haskins. 'Maybe she was seeing someone they thought unsuitable. If he'd been stringing her along with promises of marriage she would have expected him to do just that when she found she was pregnant.'

'Instead of which he probably wanted her to have an abortion,' said Pringle, 'and when she refused – or possibly threatened to tell his wife – he killed her. Do we know how she died, by the way?'

'Strangled,' said Leach.

'She might have been a victim of people traffickers,' Penny suggested. 'If she'd been kept in a brothel, being pregnant would have been a liability so the obvious solution would have been to get rid of her. That could explain why no one reported her missing.'

'Unlikely,' said Leach. 'Those people take good care that their sex-slaves don't get pregnant – they'd be no more use to them if they did.' His tone held a hint of despair at the depths to which human beings could sink.

There was a silence while everyone tried to think of other possible explanations for the girl's anonymity. 'Suppose it was an honour killing?' said Sukey suddenly. 'There've been several cases within the past few years where girls who refused to go through with arranged marriages, or found a boyfriend of a different faith, have been killed because according to their culture she'd brought disgrace on the family.'

'That's true,' said Leach, 'and in such families getting pregnant by an unsuitable man would compound the felony.' He referred to an open file on his desk. 'There is a reference here to skin pigmentation that could possibly indicate Asian or Middle Eastern origin. Just the same,' he went on, it doesn't explain why the girl wasn't reported missing. Obviously, in such circumstances her family wouldn't have done it, but this girl was of school age so her absence should have been treated as truancy and enquiries made.'

'Maybe someone visited the family and were told she was on holiday with an aunt – in India or Pakistan, for example,' said Mike. 'I'm told it happens quite often in perfectly genuine circumstances so the story might have been accepted without too many questions being asked. In which case, of course, we're looking for two killers.'

'At least,' Leach corrected. 'It's possible – in fact, I'd say more than likely – that Valerie and Daisy were victims of the same killer, but we can't take it for granted.'

'There's one thing that no one's mentioned,' said Vicky. 'The ring the girl in the lay-by was wearing has been identified as the one Daisy's parents admitted she might have had on when she went missing. Since the body in the lay-by wasn't hers, there could be at least one other ring of that design.'

'That particular ring might have become a kind of must-have fashion accessory, so there could be plenty of other girls wearing them,' said Penny.

'Or maybe Daisy lent hers to the girl in the lay-by,' Sukey suggested, 'in which case they could have been at the same school – or possibly belonged to the same youth club.'

'Good points, all of them.' Leach added a further note to the ones he had been writing during the discussion. 'Well, we've got plenty of lines of enquiry to follow up. No doubt Chief Superintendent Baird will shortly be summoning the full team for a conference. Meanwhile I'll try and get forensics to get a move on with the tests on the brick samples Sukey and Vicky have brought in. Does anyone else have anything to say?'

'I'm thinking of Daisy's parents,' said Sukey with a sigh. 'They must be devastated. It was bad enough thinking their daughter had met such a ghastly end but the ring must have made them reasonably sure her body had been found. And now they're . . .' Her voice trailed away as she tried to imagine the probable effect of this latest cruel development.

'Back in limbo,' said Leach sombrely. 'Right everyone, I'll be speaking to Chief Superintendent Baird shortly, but time's getting on and we can only authorize overtime in urgent cases. Be here first thing in the morning for instructions. Good night everyone.'

He shut his notebook and put it in a drawer in his desk. With a chorus of, 'Good night, sir,' the team filed out of his office.

Sukey's mood as she drove home was despondent. Her mind went back to the day when, after some five years as a civilian Scenes of Crime Officer, she had been accepted for intensive training with the aim of joining the CID. She had passed the demanding course with flying colours and her first posting was to the headquarters of the Avon and Somerset Constabulary, where she had been ever since. The change of career had necessitated a move from the home in Gloucester where she had lived with her son Fergus after her divorce from Paul. So much had happened since then, not least the ending of her relationship with DCI Jim Castle. That had hurt at first, but with hindsight she realized that it could never have worked. When he told her he was back with the wife who had divorced him it had, surprisingly, come as a relief.

She had thrown herself with enthusiasm and dedication into her work as a detective, receiving both reprimand and commendation (the latter unofficial) and forming rewarding relationships with colleagues and neighbours. There had been some frightening experiences, and some moving ones as well when she had been touched and saddened by the effects on the innocent of the crimes she had been called on to investigate. But she had never before experienced such a feeling of desolation as now seemed to overwhelm her at the thought of the three young girls whose lives had been brutally cut short, and of the families grieving over their loss.

The traffic was heavy and it was nearly seven o'clock when she got home. Wearily, she climbed the stairs to the flat in Clifton where she had lived since moving to Bristol. She threw her bag on the floor, went into the kitchen and poured a glass of wine. It was a fine evening and she went out on to what she thought of as her roof garden and stood for some time contemplating the view across the city while sipping her drink. After a while, conscious that she was hungry, she went into the kitchen to prepare her evening meal. She peeled some potatoes, put them in a saucepan on the stove and took a packet of parsley sauce mix from her store cupboard before going to the refrigerator for the piece of fresh fish that she had taken from the freezer that morning. It was then that she realized she was out of milk. With a muttered exclamation she slammed the refrigerator door, grabbed her purse and her keys and headed for the convenience store round the corner.

She had just paid for her milk and was putting her change in her purse when a voice behind her said, 'Hi Sukey! Haven't seen you in ages. How are you?'

She swung round and found herself face to face with Harry Matthews, the son of her neighbour, Major George Matthews. 'Oh, hello Harry,' she said, and after a moment added, 'Yes, I suppose it has been quite a while.' She moved away from the till and headed for the door. 'Sorry, I have to get back, I left some potatoes on the stove.'

'Hang on a sec and I'll walk back with you.' Harry paid for the few items on the counter, put them in a bag and pocketed his change. 'Something tells me you haven't had the best of days,' he said as he took her arm.

At his touch, Sukey felt her depression lift a little. 'Does it show?' she said.

'Well, your face didn't exactly light up at the sight of me,' he said. His tone was flippant, but his look held concern. 'Nothing wrong with Gus, I hope?'

'Oh no, nothing like that. It's just . . .' They had almost reached her front door. On an impulse, she said, 'If you're not in a hurry to get back, why don't you come in for a quick drink?'

'I'm in no hurry at all,' he assured her. 'Dad's gone away for a few days with Lady Freddie. They're visiting war graves in France. Dad's brother – my Uncle Donald – was killed during the D-Day landings. I never knew him of course; that was before I was born.'

'There's so much sorrow in the world,' said Sukey. 'It makes you wonder sometimes . . .' To her surprise and embarrassment her voice died away in a wave of emotion.

'Hey, what's all this?' He put an arm round her and gave her shoulders a squeeze. 'Here, let's have your key.' She handed it over without a word and he juggled with the key and his bag of shopping while he opened her door. Back in the kitchen, she dumped the milk on the table and sank into a chair with her hands over her eyes. He stood at her side, gently patting her arm, until she pulled herself together.

'Sorry about that,' she said feebly, scrubbing her eyes with a tissue.

'Want to talk about it?' Harry asked. He grabbed a chair and sat down beside her with his face close to hers.

'It's just . . . all these young lives cut short when they've hardly begun, and we don't seem to be getting any nearer finding who killed them,' she began. 'First Valerie Deacon, then Daisy Hewitt, and now . . .' She broke off suddenly, realizing she had said too much.

'And now . . . what?' There was a new note in Harry's voice that Sukey immediately recognized. He was a sympathetic friend, but he was also a journalist and it was plain he scented a story. 'Are you saying another girl's gone missing?'

'You know I can't give you any information that hasn't
been officially released,' she protested. She moved away from
him and stood up. 'What about that drink I promised you?'
She took a second glass from the cupboard and put it beside
her own. 'Help yourself and give me a top up while I check
my potatoes.'

'Never mind the potatoes.' He pushed her gently back into
her chair, poured the wine and sat down again. 'It so happened
that just before I left the office a call came through telling us
there's going to be a special press briefing first thing in the
morning because something big is about to break. You've
already as good as said it's not an arrest, so could it be another
teenage girl gone missing?'

'Who made that call?' she countered.

Harry grinned. 'You know we never reveal our sources.
Come on Sukey, you can trust me. It's too late to get anything
into the evening edition anyway.'

'But you'd like to see it on your front page first thing
tomorrow before any of your rivals,' she countered. A combi-
nation of red wine and Harry's charm was restoring her spirits
by the minute. She was also conscious that it was having the
effect of lowering her guard.

'How well you know me,' he said disarmingly. His smile
deepened and Sukey felt her pulse rate rise a little. 'Look, I
promise not to jump the gun, but it would be nice if I could
have my story all ready to print the moment the police make
their statement in the morning,' he coaxed.

Despite herself, Sukey was beginning to waver. 'You'll have
to give me your solemn promise,' she began, 'that you won't
...' At that moment, the alarm over her cooker suddenly
emitted an ear-piercing whistle. Smoke was pouring from the
saucepan; the potatoes had boiled dry. The problem was dealt
with swiftly and with no permanent damage to either the
saucepan or its contents, but it was enough to stiffen Sukey's
resolve. 'Sorry,' she said firmly, 'you'll have to wait till the
morning.' She picked up her drink and raised her glass. With
a resigned shrug he did the same.

'OK, have it your way,' he said, 'and just to show there's
no ill feeling, how about lunch on Saturday?'

'That would be great,' she said warmly. A thought struck
her. 'Do you know the Red Lion Hotel at Over Hampton?'

He thought for a moment. 'I can't say I do, but the name of the village rings a bell. Has it been in the news lately?'

'A woman named Adelaide Minchin was found dead in her bathroom a few weeks ago. There was an inquest and the verdict was accidental death.'

Harry nodded. 'Yes, I remember now. One of my colleagues attended the inquest. What about it?'

'The woman's doctor wasn't happy with the verdict and he had enough clout with the Chief Constable to get us to look further into the death. I was the one to get the short straw.'

Harry paused with his glass halfway to his lips. 'And?'

'I spoke to the officers who attended when the death was discovered and they were positive there were no suspicious circumstances. I also interviewed the doctor. I listened to what he had to say and told him I'd report back to my superiors, but I had to tell him that in my opinion there was nothing to justify any further investigation.'

'So how did he react to that?'

'He more or less admitted that he had very little concrete evidence, but he still had a hunch that there was something suspicious about the woman's death.'

At the word 'hunch', Harry's face lit up. 'I get it!' he exclaimed. 'You too have a hunch all is not right – is that it?'

'Well, yes,' Sukey admitted. 'I've actually made a few tentative enquiries among the locals. That's why I suggested we go to the pub where I had lunch after talking to Doctor Hogan. I had to put the whole thing on the back burner when a girl's body was found in the lay-by, but when you mentioned lunch on Saturday it suddenly occurred to me that . . .'

'I was just the person to do a bit of ferreting around?' he said eagerly.

'Partly – I mean, I'd like to be involved as well, although it will have to be off the record as far as I'm concerned.'

'You're on!' he said, 'but I'll need some background information.'

'Of course; I'll dig out all my notes,' she said. 'Look, I'd like my supper and I take it you've got something to eat planned?' He nodded. 'Right, why don't you drink up and go home, and come back later – say about half-past eight?'

He drained his glass and stood up. 'Will do. See you later.'

TEN

At the press briefing the following morning the chair was taken by Superintendent Baird.

'From a detailed forensic examination of the remains found in the lay-by near Over Hampton,' he began, 'we now know that they are not, as we originally thought, those of the missing teenager Daisy Hewitt, but of an as yet unidentified girl of similar age and build.' He waited for a further few seconds for his audience to absorb this startling information before continuing. 'Further tests are being carried out; at present the cause of death appears to have been strangulation and because all her clothing is missing we cannot rule out the possibility that she was sexually assaulted. We also think she may be from a non-European background.'

There was an immediate babble of questions. Baird put up his hand for silence before continuing. 'We have no reports of any other missing girl and we are therefore appealing for information from members of the public, especially anyone who knows of a girl of about fifteen or sixteen years of age who has not been seen recently. We would particularly like to talk to girls of similar age who have been trying during the past three to four weeks to contact a friend – for example by text message or calls to her mobile phone – and have had no response. We ask any teacher who has reported the persistent non-attendance of a student with no history of truancy to get in touch with us. We should also like to hear from youth club organizers who have noted the unexplained absence of a member – in fact, anyone who thinks they have information that may help us identify this girl. And if any person is withholding information because of fear or intimidation, we urge them to call us anonymously on our Crimestoppers number. Any such calls will be treated with the utmost discretion. All right, I'll take questions now.'

A forest of hands shot up. Baird took the first question from a young woman reporter from one of the national dailies. 'Yes?'

'You said "non-European"; can you be a little more specific?' Sukey, seated with Vicky and the other members of Rathbone's team in a corner of the room, detected a hint of aggression in the woman's tone. 'And can you tell us what effect this will have on your line of enquiry?' she continued before Baird had a chance to speak.

'From a close examination of the few remaining fragments of skin our forensic experts have noticed traces of pigmentation that could possibly indicate non-European origins,' he replied. 'The dead girl also had naturally black hair, although that in itself is of no particular significance other than to eliminate girls of different colouring.'

'Can you be certain that she wasn't African or Asian?' the woman persisted.

'The skeletal remains give no such indication, but every scrap of information we find will be taken into account,' Baird said tersely, 'and I can assure you that these are merely factors that we have to consider; they do not mean that our enquiries will be concentrated in any one direction.' Sukey noticed that he was beginning to show signs of impatience. 'Next question?'

'Do you believe Daisy and the unidentified girl were victims of the same killer?' asked a reporter from the *Wiltshire Post*.

'Until we find a body we cannot know for certain that a missing person is dead,' Baird pointed out. 'There are similarities between the circumstances of the disappearance of Daisy Hewitt and another teenager, Valerie Deacon, who vanished some twenty years ago. The latter case remains open, although we have had no new leads recently. Our hopes of finding either Valerie or Daisy alive are fading, but we have as yet no concrete evidence that the cases are connected.'

'What about the ring on the dead girl's finger?' asked a reporter from the *Avon News*. 'We were told it had been identified as belonging to Daisy.'

'It was the ring that led us to believe initially that the dead girl was probably Daisy,' Baird acknowledged. 'It is of course possible that Daisy knew her and lent or gave her the ring.'

'So you'll be questioning her friends?'

'We shall be speaking to anyone we believe may have useful information.'

'Perhaps there are other rings of the same or similar design knocking around?'

'That is another line of enquiry we are pursuing. Next question?'

Harry Matthews raised his hand. Sukey had naturally expected him to be there. She had earlier caught his eye for a second and looked hastily away, thankful she had resisted his efforts to worm advance information out of her.

'This development must have had a devastating effect on Daisy's parents,' he said. 'Can you tell us how they are coping?'

'You are right, it has been very distressing for them,' said Baird, 'but they are a strong couple and we are giving them as much support as we can. Needless to say, they are appealing for their privacy to be respected.' Baird stood up. 'No further questions on this case. One of my colleagues will continue with the regular briefing.' Ignoring the chorus of pleas for more information he picked up his papers and left the room, followed by DCI Leach and his team.

'Grab yourselves a coffee and meet in my office in fifteen minutes,' said Leach as they returned to the CID offices.

'I wonder why that woman kept harping on about race?' said Sukey as she and Vicky drank their coffee.

'She probably wanted to spice up the story,' said Vicky with a touch of scorn. 'A headline hinting at racial prejudice would give circulation a lift.'

'It wouldn't be the first time we've been accused of racism,' said Sukey.

'True,' Vicky agreed, then added, 'I notice your boyfriend didn't have much to say, except to express sympathy with the family. Or had you already briefed him?' she added, her eyes twinkling mischievously above the rim of her plastic cup.

'As if I would!' said Sukey with mock indignation, 'and by the way, he's not my boyfriend.'

'If you say so.' Vicky was plainly unconvinced, but to Sukey's relief she did not press the point. 'I noticed the Super didn't reveal the fact that the girl was pregnant,' she said thoughtfully.

Sukey nodded. 'Yes, I was wondering about that. Maybe DCI Leach will give us their reasons.' She finished her coffee and dropped the cup in the waste bin. 'Ready?'

'No doubt you observed that we made no mention of the girl's pregnancy,' Leach began as soon as the team was assembled.

'The reason is simple: not so long ago we had a case of an honour killing involving a Middle Eastern family. When the story broke it aroused a great deal of hostile feeling among the neighbours on both race and religious grounds and there were some very ugly scenes with innocent families being victimized. We have to face the possibility that this is another such case, but Superintendent Baird sees no reason at this stage to release information that might cause people to jump to conclusions.' His gaze swept round the room. 'You will, of course, bear this in mind when making your enquiries,' he said, and everyone nodded agreement.

'Right,' he said, 'let's get down to business. Our appeal for information will be going out in the midday editions and on the radio and TV. In the meantime DS Rathbone and I have drawn up a list of schools where the dead girl may have been a student. He will divide them up between you according to area. As you'll see, there are quite a few and we want to be seen to be getting on with it, so for the time being you'll have to work singly. Use your own cars if necessary but try and keep the mileage down. That's all for now. Good hunting!'

Back in the CID office, Rathbone sent them to the canteen for an early lunch while he got out maps. By the time they returned he had prepared individual lists of schools and handed one to each member of his team. Sukey was the last to receive her list. As he gave it to her he said, 'I'm afraid you've drawn the most tricky part of the assignment, Sukey.'

'Sarge?'

'Daisy Hewitt's school is at the top of your list, but before going there I want you to have a word with her parents. They're not the easiest people to deal with and it will call for a certain amount of diplomacy. DCI Leach and I agree that you're the best person to talk to them. We're paying you a compliment,' he added, evidently noting her look of concern.

'Thank you, Sarge,' she said without conviction.

'The mother has confirmed that Daisy had a ring like the one found on the dead girl's finger, but said her father had told her not to wear it,' said Rathbone. 'It's an unusual design, and I think it's unlikely there are others exactly like it. You may have to probe quite deeply into Daisy's life outside her home to find out how another girl came to be wearing it. There may

be sensitive areas we don't know of that her parents might not
want to talk about. For example, she may have mixed with
people they don't approve of. All they've said so far is the
usual stuff about what a lovely, normal, popular teenager she
is and how her disappearance is completely out of character.'

'Yes, I remember the appeal they put out on the television,'
said Sukey. 'They were obviously desperately worried but
they put on a brave show.'

Rathbone gave a slightly dismissive grunt. 'The stiff upper
lip syndrome,' he said with a faint note of scorn in his voice.
'They're in the public eye quite a lot – the father's a district
councillor and the mother's on the committees of various char-
ities. I seem to remember he made a great thing during his
election campaign about having sent his daughter to the local
comprehensive when one of his opponents educated his children privately.'

Sukey made a note. 'Right Sarge, I'll bear that in mind.
By the way, any news from forensics about the bricks?'

'The first two samples you and Vicky brought in have been
eliminated – wrong sort of stone and the soil clinging to them
didn't match. The last lot looks more promising but they've
got a few more tests to do. Fingers crossed!'

Before setting out, Sukey spoke to the Family Liaison Officer
who was staying at the house. Having briefly put her in the
picture and received an assurance that Daisy's parents had
taken the news bravely and had promised to help the police
in every way possible, she drove to the detached house in Over
Hampton where the Hewitt family lived. A woman of about
fifty dressed in well-cut blue trousers and a white T-shirt opened
the door in response to her knock.

Sukey held up her ID card. 'Mrs Hewitt?'

The woman gave a faint smile as she stood aside for Sukey
to enter. 'No, I'm Mrs Prescott, the housekeeper. Mr and Mrs
Hewitt are expecting you. They're in the lounge; this way, please.'
She led the way into a spacious, comfortably furnished room
where a couple in their early forties were seated side by side on
a couch, together with Shirley Patton, the Family Liaison Officer
who had been supporting the couple throughout their ordeal.
Sukey noticed that while Mrs Hewitt was clutching Shirley's
hand there was no physical contact between her and her husband.

Patrick Hewitt half rose to his feet as she entered. He waved her to a chair and sat down again. 'I hope you'll keep this interview as brief as possible,' he began. 'I have business to attend to. You can imagine what a shock this has been to us,' he added. A sideways tilt of the head included his wife in the latter remark.

'Indeed I can,' Sukey said gently. 'It was bad enough believing your daughter was dead, but at least you felt you knew what had happened to her and you could start to grieve.'

'Quite so,' said Hewitt. His wife said nothing; her mouth was compressed in an apparent effort to hold back tears and with her free hand she toyed with the rope of pearls round her neck. Despite her distress, she had evidently taken pains with her appearance: her sage green dress was the latest fashion, her face carefully made up and her hair immaculate.

'First of all,' said Sukey, 'I want to assure you that there will be no let-up in the search for your daughter.' Hewitt nodded; his wife's lips framed a silent 'thank you'.

'Meanwhile,' Sukey continued, 'we are investigating the murder of an unknown girl who was wearing a ring that you identified as one Daisy used to wear. Did you give it to her?'

'Certainly not,' said Hewitt curtly.

'Do you happen to know how she came by it?'

The parents exchanged glances; there was a pause of several seconds before Mrs Hewitt said, 'We saw it for the first time one evening at dinner. As you've no doubt noticed, it's a rather unusual design . . .'

'It's a cheap, trumpery thing,' her husband interrupted. 'I ordered her to take it off.'

'And did she?' Sukey ventured to ask after a longer period of silence.

'Not there and then, I'm afraid,' Mrs Hewitt admitted. 'There was a . . . well, we had a bit of an argument . . . but she was . . . she is . . . fifteen's such a difficult age . . .' The words, uttered in a series of staccato jerks, died away as they were drowned in muffled sobs. Shirley offered her a glass of water, but she waved it away.

'It was nothing serious,' Hewitt insisted. 'Just a teenage tantrum. It was all over very quickly.'

'So that was the end of the matter?'

'Naturally. Once she calmed down she admitted I was right.'

Hewitt glanced at his watch and stood up. 'Look, I have a meeting in half an hour so I'm afraid I have to leave you. I'm sure my wife can answer any further questions, but you have my office number so you can contact my secretary to make another appointment if you want to speak to me again.' He bent down to plant a perfunctory kiss on his wife's forehead. As he did so, he appeared to whisper something in her ear before straightening up and saying more audibly, 'See you later, darling,' before leaving the room.

Sukey waited for a short while before saying, 'Do you feel up to answering one or two more questions, Mrs Hewitt?'

'I'll try.' She straightened up and patted her hair. 'What else do you want to know?'

'Did Daisy tell you where she got the ring?'

'She said something about buying it off a stall in some craft market.'

'And you're sure she stopped wearing it after her father had told her not to?'

There was yet another hesitation before the mother said, with evident reluctance, 'She stopped wearing it in the house, but I can't be certain she didn't wear it at school. She may have got rid of it I suppose, knowing her father disapproved of it. It was a terrible shock when we were asked to identify it. In fact, it's come as quite a relief to know she's not the girl who was wearing it. It seems she decided after all to obey her father's wishes.'

'It would seem so,' Sukey agreed, although privately she was unconvinced. 'I take it then, that apart from the odd teenage disagreements, you and your husband had a good relationship with your daughter?'

'*Of course we did!*' Sukey was startled by the degree of emphasis on the reply. 'She wanted for nothing . . . she had all the things girls of that age want and more . . . we took her on luxury holidays . . . we gave her *everything*.'

'You told us in an earlier interview that she has plenty of friends. Did she bring any of them home?'

'She knew . . . knows . . . she was free to bring home any friends that we approved of. We had to be a little careful, you see – after all, there is a certain undesirable element at her school, but there are plenty of nice girls as well.'

'Did you meet any of them?'

'Well, of course, now and again.'

'There is a possibility,' said Sukey, choosing her next words carefully, 'that the dead girl came from a non-European family – for example, one from the Indian subcontinent. Did Daisy have a friend who might answer that description?'

'I'm quite sure she didn't!' said Mrs Hewitt frostily.

'But if she did have a, shall we say, non-English friend, would you have welcomed her in your home?'

'I can assure you Daisy had several friends from other countries.' Sukey noted an immediate change of tone. 'There was a very sweet French girl called Huguette; she stayed with us under an exchange system after Daisy had spent a month with her family to improve her French. And I seem to remember a German girl . . . or was she Swedish? Anyway, she was a pen friend of one of her classmates and she came several times. I can't always be here, but Mrs Prescott – my housekeeper – would have looked after them, given them tea and so on. Does that answer your question?'

'Yes, thank you,' Sukey assured her, privately thinking that Daisy's parents had given her far more information than they were aware of. 'I think perhaps we'll leave it at that for now,' she said.

'I'm afraid we haven't been very much help.'

'On the contrary, you have helped a great deal,' Sukey assured her, hoping that she would not be asked to enlarge on that statement. 'It's very good of you to see me at such a painful time,' she added.

'Thank you so much for being so sympathetic.' Mrs Hewitt's mouth began to quiver; the defensive attitude of the past few minutes had slipped away. 'You won't give up searching for our little girl, will you?' she added brokenly, her hands covering her face.

'Of course not,' Sukey replied gently.

'If only she'd listened to us . . . we never liked her using that footpath . . . one of us would always take her to school . . . or Mrs Prescott if we can't be there . . . it's the age, you see . . . they get rebellious . . .'

'I promise you we'll never give up looking for her,' Sukey repeated. She quietly left the room, leaving Shirley doing her best to comfort the grieving mother. As she closed the door behind her and crossed the hall, the housekeeper appeared.

'Could I possibly have a private word with you some time?' she said in a low voice.

Nothing could have suited Sukey better. She took out one of her business cards and handed it over. 'Call me any time on this number,' she said.

ELEVEN

James Bradley was appointed head teacher of Over Hampton comprehensive school after it received an unsatisfactory report from a team of inspectors. Within two years he had brought about improvements in both discipline and academic results, while morale in the staff room was higher than it had been for years.

Having made a brief check on his background, which included a spell in the army during which he rose to the rank of major, Sukey was prepared to meet someone with a similar, rather overbearing manner to that of Doctor Hogan. She was pleasantly surprised when he rose from behind his desk to greet her with a smiling, 'Good afternoon,' and a friendly handshake before inviting her to take a seat.

'As you can imagine, we are all very shocked to learn of the mistaken identity of the remains found in the lay-by,' he began. 'The news has caused further distress among Daisy's class-mates and some of them may need further counselling. Now,' he continued with a glance at a notepad, 'I understand from your telephone call that you have reason to believe the dead girl knew Daisy on account of a ring that was found on her finger?'

'We know Daisy had such a ring,' Sukey agreed, 'but her father disapproved of it and according to him she stopped wearing it. We're considering the possibility that she lent or gave it to a friend, but we have to take all possible explanations into account, such as there being other rings of similar design in circulation.'

Bradley nodded. 'Yes, you mentioned that and I have asked Daisy's class teacher to make enquiries among her students.'

'That wasn't what we had in mind,' Sukey began, 'I mean,

we have our own specially trained staff to interview under-
eighteen-year-olds when necessary.'

'Yes, I remember such people being called in to talk to
Daisy's friends when she was first reported missing,' Bradley
agreed, 'but we couldn't conceal this latest development from
them; it was in the midday edition of the *Echo,* they all have
mobile phones and the news got around very quickly. I didn't
see any harm in their teacher asking if anyone had seen another
ring like Daisy's,' he added with a frown.

'I'm sure there wasn't,' Sukey replied. 'In the circumstances,
it quite likely made them feel they could do something to help.'

'That was my feeling when Mrs Kitson came to tell me they
were all talking about the ring and begging her to find out more.
She will be free in a couple of minutes and I have asked her
to join us,' he said. At that moment there was a knock at the
door. Bradley called 'Come!' and a woman of about forty with
neatly cut blonde hair and bright blue eyes entered. 'Ah, Mrs
Kitson, please sit down. This is Detective Constable Reynolds.
She would like to ask you a few questions.'

'I understand you're interested in the ring found on the
dead girl's finger,' said Mrs Kitson. 'The one Daisy's parents
identified as one they'd seen her wearing,' she added.

Sukey nodded. 'Yes, that's one of the reasons why I'm here.'

'Well, none of my students knows of any such ring other
than the one Daisy wore. They think she bought it off a craft
stall somewhere so it's quite possible there are others like it.
I couldn't question them further, they're too upset.'

'That's all right, we're not asking you to question them.'

'They were all in tears,' the teacher went on. 'I can't tell you
how much this latest development has upset them. They're desperately worried about Daisy. They're having counselling . . .'

'Yes, yes, we've been through all that.' There was a hint
of impatience in Bradley's voice. He turned to Sukey. 'You
have other questions, I think?'

'Thank you, yes. Mrs Kitson, we understand that Daisy had
a wide circle of friends.'

'Oh yes, she was a very popular girl,' said the teacher
earnestly.

'Did she have a particular friend, would you say?'

'If I had to single one out, I'd say her best friend was Zareen
Hussein. Incidentally,' she turned to the headmaster, 'I've had

a further chat with Social Services. They're not entirely satisfied with the explanation Mr Hussein has given for Zareen's
continued absence from school.'

'I see.' Bradley made a note. 'I'll have a word with them.
Right, Ms Reynolds, have you any more questions for Mrs
Kitson?'

'Actually, she's just answered a most important question.
About Zareen – the girl's who's been absent – are her family
by any chance Muslims?'

'I believe so, although I'm not sure how strict they are. She
certainly wears a head scarf, but this is a mixed-sex school
so they're obviously not so worried about segregation as some
families.'

'Does she have much to do with boys?'

'I don't think so.'

'But you think she and Daisy are best friends?'

'Yes, I'd say so.'

'Thank you.' Sukey made a note. 'Now, about Daisy's parents
– do they keep in close touch with the school? I mean, do they
attend school functions, parent-teacher meetings and so on?'

The teacher hesitated for a moment before replying. 'I understand they are both very busy people,' she said carefully, 'but
yes, they do turn up on such occasions from time to time.'

'You've met them?'

'Once or twice. They always expressed themselves satisfied
with Daisy's academic progress, but I had the impression . . .'
Mrs Kitson's colour deepened slightly and she broke off in
apparent confusion.

'Come on, speak up,' said Bradley sharply. 'The police are
conducting a murder enquiry and nothing relevant should be
withheld.'

'Perhaps I can help you,' said Sukey, who sensed what lay
behind the teacher's hesitation. 'I'm told that Daisy's parents
are in a position to educate her privately, but chose not to do
so for what one might call political reasons. Did either of
them say anything to you, or in your hearing, to suggest they
might be concerned about her choice of friends?'

'Yes, indeed,' Mrs Kitson replied eagerly, evidently relieved
at this opportunity to express her misgivings. 'Mrs Hewitt
mentioned at our first meeting something about there being
what she called "all sorts" at the school and that she trusted

the staff to let her and her husband know if we considered their daughter was mixing with what she called "undesirables".'

'And what did you understand by the question?'

'Well, as you can imagine, we have a pretty wide social mix among our students. There are certainly some I am sure Daisy's parents would not approve of, but I was able to reassure them.'

'So Daisy's friends were, generally speaking, what her parents would have considered "the right type"?'

'Oh yes,' said Mrs Kitson emphatically. 'They might not come from such privileged backgrounds, but they're all from decent, hard-working families who are keen for them to do well at school.'

'What about Zareen?'

'Mr Hussein is a very well educated man, a lawyer I believe, and he takes a great deal of interest in Zareen's progress. I can't think of any reason why the Hewitts would object to their daughter being friendly with his.' Mrs Kitson glanced at her watch. 'Will that be all? I have another class in ten minutes.'

'Just one more question.' Sukey checked her notes. 'You say Zareen hasn't been at school for a while and there is some doubt about the cause of her absence. Can you give me a little more information?'

'The story is that she went with her parents to a wedding – in one of the North African countries, Egypt I believe – and was taken ill while she was there. Mr Hussein says she was in hospital for a couple of weeks and still isn't well enough to come home.'

'And the social workers aren't satisfied with this explanation? Why not?'

'They suspect the wedding may have been the girl's own – in other words, that she's been the victim of a forced marriage.'

'Have they any evidence to support their suspicions?'

'Not that I know of,' said Mrs Kitson after an enquiring glance at Bradley, who shook his head. 'But I do remember,' she went on, 'one or two of her friends telling me they thought something was bothering her, although when I asked her she said she was all right. It occurred to me she might have been worrying about her exam results.'

'How long has she been absent from school?'

'About three weeks,' Bradley interposed. 'If you want the exact date I can check the register.'

'Thank you, that would be a help,' said Sukey.

Mrs Kitson stood up, straightened her skirt and went to the door. 'I hope I've been of some help, but if there's anything else you can always reach me here.'

'You've been a great help,' Sukey said warmly, receiving a shy smile in return.

'Anything else you want to ask me?' asked Bradley when they were alone again.

'If I could have Zareen's address?'

'Of course.' He referred to his computer, wrote something in his notebook, tore out the sheet and gave it to her.

'Thank you.' She put the slip of paper in her bag. 'We may want to talk to some of Zareen's other friends, but that will be a matter for the Senior Investigating Officer to decide. Perhaps I could leave this with you.' She handed him one of her business cards. 'Thank you very much for your time, Mr Bradley. If anything else occurs to you, please call this number.'

'Thank you.' Bradley took the card and put it in a drawer. 'I have no doubt that unless Mr Hussein's story can be veri-fied, we're faced with another, even uglier reason for Zareen's absence,' he said gravely. 'I was afraid for a moment that the possibility would occur to Mrs Kitson and we'd have had more tears. She's an excellent teacher, but inclined to be emotional as you may have noticed.'

Sukey nodded. 'We can't exclude anything at this stage.'

'Indeed not,' he agreed. 'Needless to say, we're still hoping Daisy will turn up safe and well. But it doesn't look very hopeful, does it?'

'We are extremely worried about her,' Sukey agreed.

She stood up. Bradley moved towards the door and grasped the handle, but instead of opening it he said quietly, 'Strictly between you and me, I'm pretty sure Daisy's parents would not approve of her friendship with Zareen – for reasons they would perhaps not wish to admit.'

Sukey nodded. 'I take your point. I gained that impression myself from talking to Mrs Hewitt.'

'Mrs Kitson is completely colour-blind,' said Bradley, 'which is a very laudable quality in this multiracial school, but in some respects she is also a little . . . shall we say, naive?'

*   *   *

Back at headquarters DCI Leach was debriefing his team. So far none of the schools visited, other than Over Hampton comprehensive, had been able to give any significant information. Vicky, however, had spoken to a youth club leader who recalled a member – a girl of about the right age – who had stopped going to meetings a few weeks ago. 'He couldn't give an exact date and he had no idea of the reason,' she said. 'He couldn't remember seeing her wearing a ring like the one we found on the dead girl's finger either. He gave me her name and address. I called at the house but there was no one in.'

'So try again,' said Leach. 'Right, Sukey, I've left you till last as I understand from DS Rathbone that you've learned something positive, so let's hear it.'

Sukey gave a concise account of her conversation with Daisy Hewitt's parents and her subsequent interview with Daisy's headmaster and class teacher. As she spoke, DCI Leach made notes.

When she had finished he said, 'There's obviously plenty there that needs following up. Greg, you and Sukey will go and see Mr Hussein. If Zareen still hasn't returned home, ask what evidence he can show to support his story. You could also find out if he knows what was troubling her earlier. Any thoughts on that Sukey?'

'I think Mrs Kitson might have had a point about her exam results, sir. She said Zareen's father takes a lot of interest in her progress. Maybe he's been putting pressure on her to do well and she's afraid of disappointing him.'

Leach nodded. 'That does happen, so bear it in mind. And of course we need to know if he's seen Zareen wearing Daisy's ring, or one like it. And get flight details for the trip to the supposed wedding, ask to see photographs, medical certificates . . . you know the drill.' He glanced at the calendar on his desk. 'You say they're from Egypt and most likely a Muslim family. Today's Friday so in that case a visit wouldn't be appropriate. Greg, you've had a further report from Doc Hanley?'

'It's about the DNA samples, sir. Two types have been isolated – one from the girl's body and one from the foetus, which could help if we ever manage to trace the father.'

Leach grunted. 'We're a long way from needing that information, but with luck it will come in useful one day.' He made a further note and put down his pen. 'I'll have a word with the SIO and bring him up to date. Right, everyone, do your written reports and we'll call it a day. We start again on Monday. You still have plenty of schools to check on, plus we've had any amount of possible leads reported by members of the public: neighbours who've noticed a face missing from local families, that sort of thing. Some we can put on hold for the time being because they're from people who've previously claimed to have seen Daisy and been recognized as probable attention seekers. We've got enough on our plates without dealing with a load of time-wasters.'

Back in the CID office, Sukey switched on her computer. After a few minutes' consultation with the rest of the team, DS Rathbone came over and perched on the edge of her desk. 'Reading between the lines, it sounds as if Daisy had a rebellious streak,' he said. 'She probably knew her parents would disapprove of her friendship with Zareen so she wouldn't have been able to invite her to the house.'

'Unless her parents were absent, which it's obvious they are quite often,' Sukey agreed. 'I have a feeling Mrs Prescott, the housekeeper, might be able to fill in one or two gaps there. She wants a word with me.'

At that moment her mobile rang. The caller was Mrs Prescott.

TWELVE

'Constable Reynolds, I need to speak to you in confidence. Is it possible for us to meet this evening? Say about half past six?'

'Yes, I can manage that,' said Sukey after a quick glance at her watch. 'Have you any particular place in mind?'

'I have a free evening and I've arranged to meet a friend for dinner at the fish restaurant on Whiteladies Road – do you know it?'

'I know it well; it so happens I live in Clifton.'

'We're due to meet at seven o'clock, but if I get there half an hour early we could have a talk over a drink before he arrives. Would that be possible for you?'

'No problem. I'll be there,' Sukey assured her.

'Excellent. I'll see you shortly then.' Sukey gave a thumbs-up sign to Rathbone as she ended the call.

'Good news?' he asked.

'I hope so, Sarge. I've a feeling I'm about to learn something that Mrs Prescott's employers wouldn't want known. Or maybe they're not even aware of,' she added.

'Sounds promising,' he said, 'but before you get too carried away, don't bank on overtime. The purse-strings are pretty tight these days.'

'Don't worry, the restaurant's on my way home.'

When Sukey reached the restaurant shortly before half past six there were still only a handful of customers. Mrs Prescott was already seated in a corner, with empty tables on either side. She had changed into a pale green linen suit and wore a jade necklace and matching earrings. She leaned forward and Sukey caught a whiff of expensive perfume. 'This isn't the table my friend has booked, but I asked if I could wait here so that no one would overhear us,' she explained. 'Would you like something to drink?'

'Just an orange juice, thank you,' said Sukey.

Mrs Prescott gave the order and waited without speaking until it was delivered. Then she said in a low voice, 'I don't want to give the impression that I don't have every sympathy for Mr and Mrs Hewitt – they are genuinely desperate to know what's happened to their daughter – and I don't want to appear disloyal, but there are things I'm sure they won't tell you that I feel the police should know. If they – the Hewitts – knew I was saying these things they'd probably sack me on the spot without a reference,' she added with a wry smile, 'so please, if you use any of the information I give you, I hope you can keep my name out of it.'

'I think I can promise you that,' said Sukey. 'Please go on.'

'As I'm sure you know, both Mr and Mrs Hewitt are very well thought of in the community and there's no doubt they do a lot of valuable work, in her case much of it voluntary. However, they do have certain . . . prejudices, shall we say?'

'You mean they're snobbish and racist?' suggested Sukey, as Mrs Prescott appeared reluctant to go into details.

The housekeeper gave a slight nod of agreement. 'Well, yes, I'm afraid so,' she admitted, 'particularly as regards Daisy's friends. There was one in particular I'm sure they would not have approved of – and certainly not have allowed in the house.'

'Do you mean Zareen Hussein?' Sukey prompted.

Mrs Prescott gave a little start of surprise. 'You know about her?'

'I called at Daisy's school after speaking to the Hewitts and Mrs Kitson, her class teacher, seemed positive that Zareen is her best friend. She obviously has no idea that Mr and Mrs Hewitt would object to the friendship on grounds of race – on the contrary, she is sure they would welcome it because the girl's father is a professional, educated man and by implication in the same social class as they are. However, the head teacher told me privately that he did not share her opinion. Now perhaps,' Sukey went on while Mrs Prescott took a sip from her glass of white wine, 'you'll tell me what you know about Daisy's relationship with Zareen.'

'Daisy confides in me a lot,' the housekeeper said, 'and I soon realized that her friendship with Zareen meant a great deal to her. She knew her mother wouldn't approve so she started bringing her to the house after school only when she knew her parents wouldn't be there. They would go up to her room and chat or play games on the computer. I'd give them tea and make sure Zareen left well before either Mr or Mrs Hewitt was expected back.' Mrs Prescott gave a slightly mischievous smile as if she took a certain amount of pleasure in the conspiracy to thwart her employers' wishes. 'Of course,' she hurried on, 'I always knew they wouldn't approve, but Daisy pleaded with me and . . . oh, I've always felt so sorry for the child. To me she's the typical poor little rich girl, showered with material goodies, all the latest gizmos, money no object and so on, but with parents too busy with their good works to give her much of their valuable time.' The smile became very close to a sneer of contempt.

Sukey gave a sympathetic nod. 'I rather thought that was the situation,' she said dryly.

'I pray constantly that she'll come back safe and sound,' Mrs Prescott said sadly, 'but in my heart I know she's dead, even though it's not her body that's been found.'

'Yes, I'm afraid a lot of us feel that way,' said Sukey, 'but we're not giving up the search for her. Now, can you tell me

about the ring? You no doubt know Daisy's father objected
to it. Did she go on wearing it after he told her not to?'

Mrs Prescott shook her head. 'She had a few disrespectful
things to say about her father at the time,' she said with another
wry smile, 'but I never saw her wearing it again. Of course,
when that body was found I assumed – we all did – that she
must have gone on wearing it behind his back and that it must
be her.'

'Do you think she might have given it away?' Sukey
suggested. 'To Zareen, for example?'

Mrs Prescott's eyes widened in horror at the implication
and she put a hand to her mouth. 'Oh, no!' she gasped, 'you
don't think . . . it never occurred to me that . . . but it's possible
I suppose. I don't remember seeing Zareen wearing it, though.'
She thought for a moment, frowning. 'In fact,' she went on,
'I don't remember her wearing any kind of jewellery. Now I
come to think of it, I don't think she took much notice of it
when Daisy started wearing it.' The thought seemed to reassure her.

'What's your opinion of Zareen? I assume you consider her
to be a suitable friend for Daisy – apart from knowing her
parents would object on the grounds of race – or you wouldn't
have encouraged her visits?'

'Certainly.' The tone was emphatic. 'Zareen is a very nice
girl. A little on the serious side for her age, and quite studious,
which is no bad thing of course. Daisy teases her sometimes,
calls her a swot, but she takes it in good part. They really were
. . . are . . . the best of friends. I took this picture of them in the
garden one day.' She took a snapshot from her purse and showed
it to Sukey. It was of two girls with their arms round one another's
shoulders, one fair skinned and slender, with short, curly hair,
the other plump, olive skinned and wearing a head scarf. 'They
make quite a contrast, don't they? Daisy was . . . is . . . very diet
conscious and she once asked me if I thought she should tell
Zareen she ought to watch her weight – as you can see she is
on the chubby side. Daisy dyed her hair shortly after I took
this,' she went on. 'That caused another dust-up with her father.'

'What about Daisy's other friends?' asked Sukey as she
handed back the picture. 'Does she bring any of them home,
and have either of her parents met them?'

'Oh yes, there are a few. Mostly they come when Daisy's

mother collects her from school. Not Zareen, of course, just the ones she considers "suitable".' Mrs Prescott made quotation marks with her fingers.

'I understand that one of your duties is to drive Daisy to school and bring her home when her mother isn't able to do it.'

'Yes, if the weather's bad, but very often she insists on walking. I think it gives her a sense of freedom.'

'You'd say she has a rebellious streak?'

'Definitely. I was due to drive her to school the day she disappeared, but she said, "Don't bother, I'm going to walk" and ran out of the house before I could stop her. And that was the last time any of us saw her,' she finished sadly. 'I can't help blaming myself for letting her go off alone like that, although her parents have both assured me it wasn't my fault.'

'Well, thank you very much for your time,' said Sukey. 'You've given me some very useful information.'

'I'm so glad,' Mrs Prescott said. 'I felt it was my duty to speak out, but you will keep my name out of it, won't you?' As she spoke her eyes slid past Sukey to the door, where a distinguished looking man with iron-grey hair and moustache had just entered. Her eyes lit up in a smile of pleasure that transformed her slightly nondescript features. 'There's my friend!' She waved and he came over to the table. 'Ms Reynolds, may I introduce Thomas Elliott?'

'How do you do,' said Sukey. She stood up and offered him her hand.

'Delighted,' he said with a courtly little bow. 'Please don't leave on my account.'

'That's all right. We've finished our chat and I really must be going,' said Sukey. 'I wish you both a pleasant evening.' She left the restaurant and returned to her car. As soon as she reached home, she called Rathbone and told him of the conversation.

'From what Mrs Prescott said about her attitude to the ring, it seems doubtful that the dead girl is Zareen,' he said. 'We can't rule anything out, of course, but I'm more inclined to think there's something in the forced marriage theory. Just the same, we'd better do a DNA check before talking to Social Services. You and I have already been briefed to call at the girl's address first thing on Monday. It'll be interesting to see how the family react when we ask for samples.'

'Right, Sarge. Have a good weekend.'

'Thanks. Same to you.' She thought he sounded less than enthusiastic.

Half an hour later Harry Matthews rang. 'Just checking we have a date for lunch and a spot of sleuthing tomorrow,' he said breezily. 'I'll pick you up at twelve, OK?'

'That'll be fine, thank you.'

'I thought you might like to know I'm already on the case,' he went on. 'I popped into the Red Lion this afternoon and—'

'Hang on a minute!' she interrupted in alarm. 'This is my case and you're my right-hand man but you're not supposed to go ferreting around without telling me what you're up to.'

'What a nasty suspicious mind you've got,' he said reproachfully.

'I'm reminded of a poem by Wendy Cope called "How to Deal with the Press",' she retorted.

'Oh really? What does she have to say about the fourth estate? Something disrespectful, no doubt.'

'Her advice is "Never trust a journalist".'

'And you're applying that advice to me?' She thought he sounded genuinely hurt. 'Sukey, don't you trust me? I thought we were friends.'

'Yes, of course we are, which is why I want your help, but . . .'

'So who said anything about ferreting around? If you'd just let me finish what I was going to say . . .'

'All right, I'm listening.'

'I think perhaps I'll save it until tomorrow. I'll tell you on the way to the Red Lion.'

He was being deliberately provocative, but she refused to bite. 'All right,' she agreed after a moment's hesitation, 'I'll see you at twelve.'

He was at the door on the stroke of twelve. He leapt out of the car, held the passenger door open while she settled into her seat, fed her safety belt over her shoulder and waited while she clipped it into place before closing the door and getting into his own seat. It was only their second date; the previous time he had ordered a taxi rather than hunt for parking in the city centre. For a moment or two Sukey found her thoughts going back to the times when Jim Castle had taken her out.

He would sit behind the wheel with the engine running while she climbed in beside him. In those days, besides being lovers, they were colleagues and in such situations he treated her like an equal. Was that the only difference, she asked herself?

'Penny for them,' said Harry as he turned into Whiteladies Road and headed for the Downs. 'You aren't mad at me?' he added anxiously before she had time to answer.

'Mad at you? Why should I be?'

'You sounded a bit tetchy on the phone – as good as accused me of trying to pull a fast one.'

'Oh, that. I'm sorry; I was tired. It's all a bit much at the moment. One teenage girl missing, believed murdered, and a second very definitely murdered.'

'To say nothing of a middle aged lady also definitely dead – possibly as a result of foul play,' he said. 'Yes, I can understand your getting depressed.'

'Not exactly depressed – more frustrated,' she sighed. 'Never mind that now. What did you mean by saying you were "on the case" if you haven't been ferreting around?'

'It's like this,' said Harry. 'It so happens I had to cover a story in Keynsham yesterday and on the way back I did a quick detour and dropped in at the Red Lion – purely out of curiosity. I promise you I didn't . . . I mean, it wasn't far out of my way and I just thought I'd get a feel for the place.'

'The journalist doth protest too much, methinks,' Sukey misquoted dryly. 'All right, I accept your motives were impeccable. Do go on.'

'Thank you. Anyway, there was a bunch of people very exercised over something so I kept my ears open. And guess what . . . there's a rumour that Miss Adelaide Minchin has pulled the rug from under her relations' feet by leaving her house to some woman that no one's ever heard of. Needless to say, the entire village is dying with curiosity.'

'Gosh, if it's true it will really put the cat among the pigeons,' said Sukey. 'Did you get any details?'

'Not really – I mean, no names were mentioned and no one's exactly sure what happened, but someone called Frank who I gathered is a local postman was telling the assembled company that when delivering to the offices of Howland and Walker, Solicitors, who have an office in Over Hampton, he overheard a man in Mr Walker's office saying, "Who is this woman anyway?" and a moment or two later, "Well, we shall of course contest the will," and "It's obvious she wasn't in her right mind". It seems this chap was so steamed up he wasn't bothered about being overheard and as you can imagine, the two girls in the outer office were sitting there with their ears flapping.'

'I'll bet they were. Did I tell you that the previous owner's siblings – there are two brothers and a sister – assumed their late sister Muriel had left her entire estate to them, but instead she left most of it to their cousin Adelaide. She spent a lot of time with Muriel towards the end of her life and they claimed she'd somehow persuaded their sister to make a new will in her favour. Cousin Adelaide inherited her house – it's called Parson's Acre and I was told it represented a pretty large slice of the estate – so they got a lot less than they hoped for. There was a suggestion then that they might contest the will, but apparently they were advised there were no grounds; Muriel Minchin was in good health and in her right mind when she made it.'

Harry gave a soft whistle. 'That's quite a story,' he said. 'Murder has been committed for less,' he added soberly. 'I gather you and your doctor friend are thinking on the same lines – that if Adelaide were to die as well the property would almost certainly come to them.'

'More or less,' said Sukey, 'and now it seems they've once again been pipped at the post. I don't suppose you got any hint about the new owner's identity?'

He shook his head. 'Afraid not.'

'So that's it?'

Harry nodded. 'That's it. Any idea where we go from here?'

Sukey's thoughts were racing, but all she said in reply was, 'Maybe.'

THIRTEEN

The bar of the Red Lion was comparatively quiet when Sukey and Harry arrived. A small group of people, one or two of whom Sukey recalled seeing on previous visits, stood at the counter chatting to Ben Bridges. He broke off the conversation and came to greet them.

'Welcome back, sir,' he said to Harry. 'Nice to see you again, Miss,' he added to Sukey. 'Any news of Daisy Hewitt? And what about the dead girl? Any idea who she is? That must have been a slap in the face for your people, finding it was a different girl altogether.'

'Yes it was,' Sukey agreed, 'but I'm afraid I can't add anything to the official statements.'

'I understand,' he said affably, 'so what can I get you?'

They ordered their drinks and took them to a table by the window. 'I'll bet he doesn't miss much,' said Harry, with a jerk of his head in Bridges' direction. 'I wonder if he's learned a bit more about the new owner of Parson's Acre since yesterday.' He took a pull from his drink before saying, 'Any objection if I pump him a little? I promise to be very discreet and not show my press pass.' His eyes twinkled at her over the rim of his glass.

Sukey thought for a moment. 'The first time I was here it was to ask him about Adelaide, and the official police line is that there was nothing suspicious about her death so no ongoing enquiry. If you start asking him about Parson's Acre he's sure to think I've put you up to it and jump to the opposite conclusion.'

'OK, but if I'm going to do any ferreting around I'm going to have to start asking questions sooner or later.'

'Yes, but pumping mine host isn't what I had in mind. I'll explain later, but for the moment let's just keep our eyes and ears open.'

'As you say.' Harry took a menu from a stand on the table. 'Let's see what's on offer in the way of food.'

Sukey noticed that Harry's attention was divided between the choice of dishes on offer and the steady trickle of people entering the bar. 'Looking for anyone in particular?' she asked.

He grinned. 'You don't miss much either, do you?' he said.

'It's my job not to,' she retorted. 'I'm going to have the steak and ale pie,' she added, returning to the menu. 'What about you?'

'I'll have the same. I'll go and order.' As he returned to his seat he happened to glance at the door and said in a low voice, 'See that chap in postman's uniform who's just come in? That's Frank, the one I was telling you about.'

'The one who overheard . . .?' Sukey got no further as the new arrival marched up to the bar and announced, 'Guess who

I saw earlier on, folks! Mr Walker, of Howland and Walker, being driven through the village by a lady in a red sports car! They were going in the direction of Parson's Acre. What's the betting she's the new owner?'

He immediately became the focus of attention. Observing the customers, Sukey mentally divided them into casual passers-by who had called in for a drink and a meal, and regular drinkers who knew exactly what Frank was referring to and began bombarding him with questions. What did the woman look like? What sort of age was she? Was there a family resemblance? To universal disappointment, which seemed to be shared by regulars and visitors alike, Frank could add very little to his dramatic opening announcement.

'I only got a quick glimpse as they drove by,' he explained. 'She had long hair blowing round her face and she was wearing sunglasses, that's all I can tell you.'

'When was this?' someone asked.

Frank glanced at his watch. 'About forty-five minutes ago,' he said after a moment during which his lips moved as he made mental calculations.

'Mr Walker sometimes brings a client in for lunch,' said Bridges. 'Maybe they'll come in here for a drink or something to eat on the way back.'

At that moment Josie, one of the bar assistants whom Sukey had met on her previous visits, gave a little squeal of excitement. 'I do believe . . . yes, there's a red sports car just turned in . . . the driver's a lady and she's got Mr Walker with her.'

'Looks like we might be in luck, Sukey,' said Harry. From their secluded corner, the two were able to observe both the entrance to the bar and the group of drinkers, who had fallen silent, heads turned towards the door, the moment Josie made her announcement.

'You can almost feel the excitement,' Sukey said gleefully.

Harry chuckled. 'They're like a clutch of fans awaiting the arrival of a star.'

They had only moments to wait before the door opened and a man of about fifty entered, escorting a woman who appeared to be at least ten years younger. He was dressed in an undistinguished grey suit, in sharp contrast to his companion, who wore an emerald green silk shirt with matching sandals and black silk trousers. Her straight, reddish-brown hair was parted in the centre and held back with silver filigree clips on either side of her face. Silver bracelets circled her wrists, silver hoops dangled from her ears and several graded rows of silvery chains cascaded over her breasts.

'An artist, would you say – or something else creative?' said Harry.

Sukey nodded. 'Could be, I suppose.'

'Interesting face,' he went on, 'good bone structure – and amazing eyes.'

'You're quite a connoisseur.' He smiled as if she had paid him a compliment. Her tone had been light but she was aware of a twinge of something – surely not jealousy? – at his evident appreciation of the newcomer's appearance. She pushed the thought to the back of her mind and said, 'I wonder if Frank's right and she's the mystery heiress?'

The woman stood and looked appraisingly round her for a moment as if absorbing the atmosphere before glancing up at the beamed ceiling. 'This is perfect – I love it!' she intoned in a vibrant contralto. She treated her companion to a brilliant smile. 'How old did you say this place was, Mr Walker?'

'Parts of it date back to the seventeenth century,' he said. 'There have been later additions, of course – and if you're thinking of staying here tonight I assure you the plumbing is modern,' he added.

'If there's a room free I'll certainly stay.' She went to the bar where Ben Bridges was waiting to greet her, a jovial smile on his round, rosy face. She seemed oblivious to the fact that she was the focus of everyone's attention. 'Good afternoon,' she said, 'are you the landlord?'

'That's right, madam. Do I understand you're wanting a room for the night?'

'Yes, if you have one available. My name's Leonora Farrell and I'd like a single with en suite facilities, please.'

'I'll have to check with the wife.' He went to a telephone behind the bar, spoke a few words and came back. 'That'll be fine,' he said. 'Do you want to see the room right away or would you like to order something first?'

His glance took in Walker, who said hastily, 'Which would you prefer, Miss Farrell?'

'Oh a drink – a white wine spritzer please – and something

to eat, I'm starving,' she said. 'It's the excitement; it's given
me an appetite. I can see the room later.'

Walker ordered the spritzer and a half of bitter for himself
and picked up a menu from the counter. 'Shall we go and sit
down while we have a look at this?'

'Oh, let's choose first and then sit down.' She took from
her shoulder bag a pair of glasses with a sparking diamanté-
studded frame, put them on and started to read. 'Oh look,
they do toad in the hole! I haven't had that for ages.'

'I can recommend it,' said Walker. 'I'll join you.'

As he was giving the order to Josie, Frank the postman
cleared his throat, edged along the counter and said, 'This
your first visit to these parts, Miss Farrell?'

For a moment she appeared surprised at the question, but
she replied with only a slight hesitation, 'Oh no, I used to
come with my mother to visit Auntie Muriel.'

'You mean Miss Muriel Minchin?'

'That's right? Did you know her?'

'I delivered her letters for more than twenty years,' he said
with obvious pride before adding, 'you're a member of the
family then?'

'Not exactly. Muriel wasn't really a relation, but when I
was a child I used to call her Auntie because my grandmother
was her nanny.'

'I really think we should find somewhere to sit,' said Walker
firmly, taking her by the arm. 'The tables are filling up fast,
but there's a free one over there.' He steered her towards a
table by the window, but was intercepted by Josie on her way
to deliver plates of food. 'I'm sorry sir, that table's reserved,'
she informed him.

Harry was on his feet in a moment. 'There are two seats
free at our table. Please join us,' he said.

'That's very kind, thank you.' As they settled into their seats
Walker lowered his voice and said to Leonora, 'Frank's a good
sort, but as you may have noticed, he's a bit of a nosy parker.'

She gave a soft, musical chuckle. 'I gathered that. I'm a
bit that way myself. I'm Leonora Farrell, by the way,' she
added, turning to Sukey and Harry, 'and this gentleman is Mr
Walker, my legal adviser. I'm going to be living in Over
Hampton soon. I've just inherited a property here. There's
some boring legal stuff to be got through before I can move

in, but I hope it won't take too long. Do tell me your names,'
she hurried on without waiting for any response, 'I like to
know who I'm talking to.' They introduced themselves and
Leonora's bracelets jingled as they all shook hands. 'I paint,'
she told them. 'Flower studies, mostly for calendars and
greeting cards, run of the mill stuff actually, but I've sold a
few privately. Now I'm going to be living in the country I've
a mind to try my hand at landscapes. What do you do?'

'I work on the *Bristol Evening Echo*,' said Harry. 'Once
you're settled perhaps we could talk about doing a feature on
you and your work.'

'That would be *marvellous*!' Leonora's eyes, which – Sukey
privately had to agree – were strikingly beautiful, glowed with
enthusiasm. 'I've never had that sort of publicity. Living in
London, I'm just a little fish in a big pond; no one's ever
heard of me.' She turned to Sukey. 'What about you? Are you
a journalist too?'

'I'm in the CID.'

'A detective – how exciting! Are you on a case today?'
Leonora's smile suddenly faded and she put a hand to her
mouth. 'But of course! I was forgetting, how awful of me!
That poor girl, the one whose body's been found . . . they said
on the news last night that it wasn't who your people thought
it was, the one who lived . . . lives here I mean. So who do
you think it was, and what's happened to the other girl?'

'Look,' said Sukey quietly, 'I'm off duty and if you don't
mind, I'd rather we talked about something else. That case is
still under investigation so in any case I'm not at liberty to
discuss it.'

'Of course you're not – how silly of me! Oh goodie, here's
our food,' she exclaimed as Josie appeared with a laden tray.
'Am I ready for this?'

They ate in silence for several minutes until Leonora put
down her fork, took a mouthful from her glass and said, 'Harry,
are you what people call an investigative journalist?'

'If there's something important to investigate,' he replied,
evidently surprised at the question. 'Why do you ask?'

'Because if you are, I'd like you to do a little investigating
for me.'

'What sort of investigating?'

Leonora gave Walker a sidelong glance before saying in a low voice, 'I want to find out why Muriel left Parson's Acre to Adelaide. She never married, but she had two brothers and a sister and some of them have probably got kids, so why did she leave everything to her cousin instead of to one of them? I asked my mother about it once but she went all cagey and said it was none of our business. I was only ten when my mother died and I've always supposed there was some family scandal that she thought I was too young to know about. And on top of that, why on earth has Adelaide left everything to me? I hardly knew her.'

'Miss Farrell,' said Walker, who had been listening with evident concern, 'are you sure you want the press involved in your private affairs? You may find yourself the subject of some very unwelcome publicity.'

'Who says it would be unwelcome?' she retorted. 'If Harry can get a really juicy story and publish it at the same time as I have an exhibition, just think – I might become famous and make lots of money!'

FOURTEEN

'I don't think Mr Walker is exactly thrilled with his new client,' said Harry.

'You're right,' Sukey agreed. 'I think he's going to find her a bit of a handful. His face when she asked you to dig into the past history of the Minchin clan was a study.'

Harry gave a gleeful chuckle. 'Wasn't it just? You could almost see him wondering what she was going to come out with next, and he looked even more disapproving when she offered to pay my expenses.'

'Maybe he's had experience of dealing with the Minchins over Muriel's will,' Sukey suggested. 'From what I heard on the grapevine they're not noted for their charm.'

'I imagine most solicitors have at least one difficult client so I'm sure he'll cope,' said Harry. 'By the way, you haven't told me yet what you think of Leonora's idea. I noticed you kept very quiet while all this was going on.'

'That was because I didn't want to give the impression that I had any interest in the affair. Probing into the reasons why

Muriel had apparently fallen out with her family wasn't part of my plan, but it's no bad thing now I come to think of it. I notice you didn't actually commit yourself,' she added. 'Does that mean you have reservations?'

'None on my own account; on the contrary it could, as Leonora said, have the makings of what is euphemistically known as a human interest story. A good family feud is guaranteed to sell papers.'

Sukey frowned. 'That's a bit mercenary, isn't it?'

He shrugged. 'I'm afraid so, but we have to live in the real world. Anyway, to get back to your question, the reason I kept my options open is that I wanted a chance to find out how you feel about it. I didn't want to risk scuppering any plans you've got for me.'

'That's very considerate. Thank you.'

'We're a team, aren't we?'

'I like to think so.'

After lunch Leonora had insisted that Walker accompany her back to Parson's Acre, 'So's I can give a bit more thought to how I'm going to arrange things,' she had said enthusiastically. 'I've already decided which room will be my studio; the light is just perfect.' Before leaving she had given Harry her card and begged him, with a blatantly seductive use of her expressive eyes, to *please* let her have his decision *as soon as possible*. Harry had politely accepted the card and slid it into his pocket.

By mutual consent, he and Sukey took a short walk before returning home. They followed a footpath leading from the garden of the Red Lion, through a spinney and across a stream. After half an hour, having described a circle, the path led back to a point where the stream was spanned by a little rustic bridge. They stopped for a few minutes leaning on the handrail and looking down at the clear water flowing gently beneath their feet. Harry took out Leonora's card and they studied it together. The words 'Leonora Farrell, Artist' were printed in an elaborate cursive script against an intricate background of brightly coloured flowers. The reverse, in addition to a telephone number and email address, bore the claim, 'Commissions of all kinds accepted'.

'That's a rather ambitious undertaking for someone who specializes in flower studies,' he commented. 'I wonder what sort of a fist she'd make of a portrait.'

'Are you thinking of asking her to paint yours?' said Sukey.

He laughed. 'Perish the thought! Having to sit for an hour listening to her rabbiting on about whatever bee was currently buzzing around in her bonnet would be my idea of torture.'

'Does that mean you're having second thoughts?' Sukey found herself torn between disappointment at the prospect of losing what she was fast beginning to think might be an important lead in her unofficial enquiry into the possible murder of Adelaide Minchin, and a mischievous feeling of satisfaction at Harry's less than complimentary assessment of Leonora's personality. She was also pleasurably aware that as the two of them studied the card his head had moved closer to hers.

'You mean about digging into the family history? Far from it!' he said emphatically. 'I recall a reference in the notes you gave me about the unpleasantness between Adelaide and the Minchin siblings at Muriel's funeral. They threatened to contest her will and we now know that they're threatening to contest Adelaide's – that's probably the boring old legal stuff Leonora was talking about. There was no justification for contesting Muriel's will. Were they perhaps so desperate to get their hands on Parson's Acre that they were prepared to commit murder for it?'

'I don't see how they could imagine killing Adelaide would do them any good,' Sukey objected. 'If their own sister cut them out of her will, they could hardly expect Cousin Adelaide to include them in hers.'

'I suppose not,' he admitted. 'Maybe it was just losing the money that got up their noses. Unless,' he broke off and thought for a moment, 'I wonder – could there be something significant about the place that we don't know about?'

'Like what?'

'I don't know,' Harry said vaguely. 'Buried treasure in the garden perhaps? A skeleton mouldering away in the attic? How old is the place, by the way?'

'I don't think it's that old but it would be easy to find out.'

'It might be worth checking. I wonder if one of the family found out that Muriel was thinking of selling the property.'

'You're thinking he might have been the mystery caller? Or someone they'd instructed to act on their behalf?'

'They'd know she wouldn't consider selling it to one of them so maybe they instructed a third party to approach her.'

'There's obviously a lot of ill feeling that goes back a long way,' Sukey said thoughtfully, 'so much so that Adelaide decided to leave the property to someone she hardly knew rather than let it go back to any of Muriel's siblings.'

'And since Leonora has no connection with the family they probably think they're on stronger ground this time,' said Harry. He turned to her with a gleam in his eyes, which the afternoon sun seemed to change from brown to a warm shade of amber that made a perfect foil for his clear, lightly tanned skin. He put an arm round her shoulders and gave her a squeeze. 'If they should win their case,' he said with a chuckle, 'Over Hampton will be denied the pleasure of welcoming a famous artist to its bosom! Anyway, that's not our problem. Let's go home and decide what to do next.' As they returned to the car park Sukey felt a twinge of anticipation that was not entirely due to the challenge that lay ahead of them.

It was after four o'clock by the time they returned to Clifton. Harry pulled up outside Sukey's front door and said, 'I take it you've got some ideas you want me to follow up?'

'Several, and today's encounter has added to them. Why don't you come in for a cup of tea and we can talk about them?'

'Fine. I'll put the car away and be back in five minutes.'

Sukey went indoors, filled the kettle and got out a folder marked 'Adelaide Minchin'. Inside were copies of the reports she had filed on her first visit to Over Hampton at the request of Doctor Hogan, including her conversations with Flo Appleby in the Post Office, Sergeant Murray and PC Griffith, and on her subsequent visit with Vicky to Malcolm Ellery following his discovery of the mystery girl's body in the lay-by. On a separate sheet was a duplicate list of questions to which she now added a pencilled note: *Minchin family – financial situation?*

By the time Harry returned, bringing the notes she had given him earlier, she had made a pot of tea and put it on the kitchen table with milk, sugar and a plate of biscuits. She filled two mugs and gave him one with a copy of the list. She waited, quietly sipping her tea, while he studied them. After a few moments he put them down, picked up his mug, drank a mouthful of tea and said, 'Well, there's plenty to go on here. Where do you want me to start?'

'Those points aren't listed in order of preference,' she said after a moment's thought. 'I realize assignments from your editor take you to various destinations and I suppose I imagined you'd fit them in as and when you could. On the way home I was thinking some more about the mysterious caller who tried to get Muriel to sell Parson's Acre to him.'

'You're still thinking it might have been one of them?'

'I think it's possible, but whoever it was had advance notice that it might be coming on the market. Did someone in the estate agent's office make the call or maybe pass the info to someone else they thought might be interested? Or did the family have a contact in the village who heard of Muriel's plans to go into sheltered accommodation.'

'It sounds unlikely,' he said. 'From what you told me Muriel wasn't given to taking people into her confidence.'

'She told her doctor,' Sukey reminded him. 'Perhaps he mentioned it to his secretary, or she or someone else in the practice office read it in her notes.'

'You're suggesting there might be a Minchin family spy?'

Sukey gave a self-conscious laugh. 'I know it sounds fantastic,' she admitted, 'but I've come across far more bizarre examples of human behaviour. And this is a kind of brainstorming session so we have to consider every possibility, however far-fetched.'

'OK,' he said. 'We know Muriel didn't confide in her neighbours and appears to have been on bad terms with her family.'

'Except for Cousin Adelaide,' Sukey pointed out.

'Except for Cousin Adelaide,' he agreed. 'That being the case it's likely that, if they heard about her plans, they might have suspected she wouldn't sell Parson's Acre to any of them – out of spite, for example – and decided to try by devious means to get their hands on it for less than its true value. If they could afford to buy the place, they weren't that hard up so maybe it was just greed on their part. Then she died and left the house to Adelaide so they thought of contesting the will, but were advised they didn't have a case.'

'But now that the property's gone to Leonora, who by all accounts has no connection with the family, they may feel they're on firmer ground.'

'So would you like me to see what I can find out about the Minchins? Presumably one of the family identified her body and gave evidence at the inquest, so there should be something in our records to give me a lead.'

'That would be a start,' she said, 'and while you're at it, maybe you can find out why Muriel fell out with them.'

He made a note. 'That would be interesting,' he agreed.

Sukey referred back to her list. 'I asked Mr Baker of the estate agents Weaver and Morris whether his was one of the firms Muriel instructed to value Parson's Acre. He couldn't tell me – said it was before his time – but he'd find out and let me know. So far I haven't heard from him. If it wasn't his firm, then maybe he can suggest others Muriel might have approached.'

Harry made more notes and said, 'OK, I'll follow that one up, but I'm not sure how it will help.'

'Whoever made those phone calls was very keen to get his hands on it before it was officially advertised. So keen that he told Muriel a string of porkies to try and con her into selling at a knock-down price.'

'That was a shabby trick,' he agreed, 'but as a possible link to a subsequent death that's been officially described as accidental it doesn't seem to me to hold much water. Sukey, is this really all you've got to go on?'

She made a helpless gesture with her hands. 'I know it sounds flimsy, even to me,' she agreed, 'but Doctor Hogan was so insistent – he kept saying he had a hunch that the verdict at the inquest was unsound and I suppose it was catching, a bit like flu. I somehow feel it's important to know who made those calls and why. If we can't find a link with the family, at least we can eliminate them as possible suspects. Look, Harry, if you're having second thoughts, or if you think it's all going to be a waste of your time, then don't feel under any obligation . . .'

Harry reached across the table and put a hand over one of hers. Its warmth sent a glow along her arm. 'I have to admit I don't normally suffer from hunches,' he said gently, 'but I have enough faith in you to respect yours. It so happens I'm beginning to think up a few questions of my own.'

'Yes?'

'It occurs to me that we know very little about Adelaide, apart from the fact that she had lots of friends, played bridge, was very extrovert, in excellent health, watched her diet and so on. But we don't know anything about her daily life when she was at home on her own. Did she have any particular likes or dislikes? Did she have a computer? Did she perhaps have a cleaning lady she used to chat to?'

Sukey thought for a moment. 'I'm pretty sure she didn't have a computer. I remember one of the local police telling me she refused to have an alarm system installed because "she couldn't get her head round technology". It's a fairly big house so she probably did have a cleaning lady. And another thing, why didn't the postman notice that she hadn't taken her milk in? You're right, there is quite a lot we don't know.'

'I'll see what I can dig up.' Harry carefully folded the list of questions, put it and his pen in his pocket and sat back. 'I'd say that was enough to be going on with,' he said. He glanced at his watch. 'It's gone five. Have you any plans for this evening?'

Sukey shook her head. 'Nothing special. I know I don't want anything much to eat after that super lunch. Thank you once again.'

'My pleasure; we must do it again soon. I'm not going to be hungry for hours yet either. Why don't we have a quiet drink and watch a film? If we do feel peckish later on, I make a mean Spanish omelette.'

'That sounds a good idea. What film shall we watch?'

They spent a companionable few minutes discussing the latest releases before Harry went out to fetch a DVD and call at the grocery store. While waiting for his return, Sukey found her thoughts running ahead. She wondered if he would suggest staying a while after the film ended and they had eaten the omelette and drunk the wine. She knew she wanted him and she believed he wanted her. But she was not yet sure that she was ready for a new commitment.

FIFTEEN

A feeling of well-being that Sukey enjoyed throughout Sunday was still with her when she awoke on Monday morning. She pressed the snooze button on the alarm and lay quietly in bed for a few minutes, recalling with quiet pleasure her evening with Harry on Saturday.

After they had watched a film, Harry had as promised whipped up a delicious omelette and they carried it back into the sitting room to watch the late news while eating it and finishing the bottle of wine he had opened earlier. When the programme ended, Sukey picked up the remote and switched off the television. There was a long silence. Then Harry put an arm round her shoulders and with his free hand gently turned her face towards him.

'You know what's happening, don't you?' he said.

His breath brushed her cheek and she had the odd sensation that if she were standing she would go weak at the knees. 'I think so.' Her voice sounded faint, almost unsteady in her own ears. She made no attempt to pull away from him, conscious only that the ripple of desire she had been trying to suppress was flowing more strongly by the minute. His mouth closed over hers; his kiss was gentle but searching and the ripple became a surge. Her instinct was to yield unconditionally, but something held her back.

After a moment he drew away, looked into her eyes and said, 'I have a feeling you're not ready for this.'

'You're right.' She felt her face burn and she hid it against his shoulder. She realized to her dismay that she was very close to tears. Words came out in a series of staccato jerks. 'It probably sounds stupid, but . . . I was married to Gus's father . . . and that went sour . . . but I got over it and after a while I started to rebuild my life with Gus. Then I began a new relationship . . . we never got around to talking about marriage . . . but it was good for both of us and looked like becoming permanent . . . until I came to live here. After a while we began to see less and less of each other until . . . well, it ended. It didn't hurt as much as I thought it would, but the fact is . . .'

'You're afraid of another disappointment?' he finished as her voice trailed off.

'I guess that's it.'

'I understand.' He was still holding her close to him, but she sensed that he too had drawn back. 'Something similar happened to me a few years ago,' he said, 'and I told myself I'd stay clear of relationships. There were a few brief affairs, but nothing serious on either side. And then I met you at that drinks party and something told me . . . anyway, I wanted to call you, but I chickened out. And then our work threw us together and we got involved in the Delta case and I knew . . . or at least I hoped . . . that sooner or later . . .'

It was his turn to trail off and Sukey, who had been surreptitiously dabbing her eyes, suddenly burst out laughing. 'A journalist lost for words!' she chortled. 'I'd never have believed it.'

'See the effect you've had on me!' he said as he joined in her laughter. Then he became serious again. 'It's too early to say I love you, Sukey, but I haven't felt like this for a long, long time. I promise not to rush you . . . and,' here the slightly impish smile that she was beginning to find endearing crinkled the corners of his mouth, 'in spite of what the lady poet says about journalists, I'd never let you down.'

'No, I don't believe you would,' she said. After that he kissed her again, very gently, said good night and left.

The alarm sounded again, more insistently. Reluctantly, Sukey got up, showered, dressed and had breakfast. A few minutes before nine o'clock she and the rest of DS Rathbone's team reassembled in the incident room for instructions.

Vicky greeted her with a keen glance of appraisal. 'I can see you've had a good weekend,' she said knowingly. 'Want to tell?'

'Maybe later,' she replied. Vicky knew of her continuing interest in the death of Adelaide Minchin and there was no reason not to tell her that she had asked Harry to investigate certain aspects of the case. At the same time, she resolved not to allow herself to be drawn into a discussion of her personal feelings towards him.

'Right,' Rathbone began, 'you've all got plenty of leads to follow up. Vicky, have another shot at contacting the absentee from the youth club before you check any more schools on your list. Anyone who comes across anything that looks promising is to report straight away. Meanwhile Sukey and I are calling on Zareen Hussein's parents. If we're looking at an honour killing – and personally I have my doubts about that – then she could be the dead girl, but if she's still alive and we can find out where she is there's an outside chance she may be able to give us a bit more information about the ring.'

'Supposing the Social Services are right and she's been spirited away to get married, Sarge?' said Vicky.

'Or supposing the girl is genuinely ill?' Rathbone countered. 'We don't know what checks they've made, but as her father's a lawyer we presume he'd know how British courts view that kind of practice. All right, on your way everyone.'

The previous twenty years had seen considerable development in Over Hampton. The address James Bradley had given Sukey was in a quiet street of modern houses and bungalows about a quarter of a mile from the historic centre of the village and further still from the more exclusive area where the Hewitts lived. Mr Hussein himself opened the door in response to their knock. He was tall, clean-shaven, with regular features, olive skin and neatly trimmed black hair ending in a widow's peak. As Rathbone had previously telephoned to make the appointment he gave only a cursory glance at the IDs that he and Sukey held up before standing aside to admit them. His greeting was courteous, but unsmiling.

'Before we go any further, Sergeant,' he said, 'there are two people I should like you to meet.' He showed them into a sitting room. Seated on a couch were a woman and a girl of about fifteen, both wearing head scarves. They rose to their feet as the detectives entered. 'Allow me to present my wife, Selina, and my daughter Zareen.' He waited for a moment while formal greetings were exchanged before saying, 'Please sit down.'

There was no doubt in Sukey's mind that Zareen's father had been telling the truth. The contrast between the plump, round-faced girl in the photograph Mrs Prescott had taken and his thin, hollow-eyed daughter was sufficient on its own to confirm his story.

'I imagine you are here at the instigation of the Social Services,' said Hussein. His voice was cultured, well modulated and with very little trace of accent. 'I accept that if they ask you to investigate a particular case you are in duty bound to comply, but I wish to make it clear that I intend to make a formal complaint about the way my wife and I have been harassed during a period when we have been extremely worried about our daughter's health.'

'Mr Hussein,' said Rathbone, 'it so happens that we have not come here in response to a request from the Social Services, although we are aware there has been concern over your daughter's absence from school.' He paused for a moment before saying, 'I wonder if we could have a word with you in private, sir?'

There was an exchange of glances between Hussein and his wife before he replied, 'If you wish.' He led them upstairs to a spacious room that appeared to be used as an office. 'I do a lot of my work from home,' he explained. He neither offered them a seat nor sat down himself. 'What do you wish to say?'

'Mr Hussein, it is obvious from her appearance that your daughter has been seriously ill,' said Rathbone, 'and for this reason I am particularly anxious not to cause her any distress, but the fact is she may have information that will help us in the investigation of a serious crime. Perhaps you can guess what I'm talking about?'

Hussein nodded. 'It will be the disappearance of her friend Daisy, I imagine?'

'Does she know about it?'

'She left for Cairo with my wife and myself the day before it happened. We attended the wedding of my brother's daughter the day after our arrival and our intention was to return a couple of days later. Zareen was struck down by a mysterious virus and as I have repeatedly told the social worker, she was extremely ill for over a fortnight. Once she was out of danger my wife and I came home and her aunt – my sister-in-law – visited her daily until she was discharged from hospital. Only then was she told about Daisy's disappearance. She was deeply distressed by the news, as she had constantly been saying how much she was looking forward to seeing her friend again. We have not, however, told her that Daisy's body has been found, although I fear we cannot keep that from her much longer.'

'Exactly when did your daughter return home, sir?'

'My wife and I flew to Cairo on Friday and we returned with her yesterday morning. Due to administrative delays we have only just been able to obtain medical certificates and I was met with nothing but suspicion when I explained this to the social worker.' His exasperation over his difficulties with officialdom on all sides was becoming increasingly apparent.

'I assure you, sir,' said Rathbone, 'that we are not acting on behalf of the Social Services, and it is not primarily about Daisy Hewitt's disappearance that we would like to speak to your daughter. You are obviously not aware that the girl whose body was found recently is not Daisy.'

Hussein's eyebrows lifted in astonishment. 'Not Daisy?' he exclaimed. 'Then who . . .?'

'The victim has not yet been identified,' said Rathbone. 'She was about the same age as Zareen and we have reason to believe she can help us. It's obvious that her illness has considerably weakened her, but with your permission we should like to ask her a few questions.'

Hussein hesitated for a moment. 'In what way do you think she can help?' he asked doubtfully. 'As you say, her illness has left her quite weak.'

Rathbone showed him a picture of the ring found on the dead girl's finger. 'We know Daisy had such a ring, which is why we thought at first it was her body that was found. It was only on Friday that we learned of our mistake. One possibility that we considered was that as her father had forbidden her to wear it she had either lent or given it to a friend. We were told by their teacher that Zareen was her best friend, and . . .'

'And as she had been missing from school for three weeks you put two and two together and made five!' Hussein interrupted angrily. 'You thought we had been telling lies, you thought because of the ring it must be Zareen's body and you suspected me and my wife of killing our own child, didn't you? I can hear you all saying amongst yourselves, "Oh yes, people who follow these outlandish religions put family honour before human life". Well, I admit that there are a few like that, but let me assure you most of us have moved out of the dark ages.'

'DC Reynolds and I came here with completely open minds, sir,' said Rathbone earnestly, 'but please understand that it is our job to consider every possibility.' He turned to Sukey with a slightly desperate look that said, '*you talk to him.*'

'Mr Hussein,' she said quietly, 'both DS Rathbone and I have children of our own and we know what it is to suffer anxiety on their behalf, whether through illness or other problems. It's obvious you and your wife have been through an extremely worrying time and we have no wish to put additional pressure on you. However, the fact is we are faced with two very distressing cases: the disappearance of one teenage girl and the murder of another. We have very little to go on and we have to pursue every possible lead, however slender.' She waited for a moment in the hope of some response, but none came. 'We believe your daughter may be able to give us a clue to the identity of the dead girl,' she went on. 'Because she and Daisy were very close friends we are hoping she might have some idea what happened to the ring.'

Hussein frowned and folded his arms. His attitude suggested that he was considering her words; encouraged, she pressed on. 'Zareen appears to be on the mend, for which we must all be thankful. Sadly, there is no end in sight to the anguish of Daisy's parents, and somewhere another family is frantic for news of their missing child. We need all the help we can get and that's why we're here. Any scrap of information, however small, may be valuable.'

Hussein appeared to think deeply for a moment. Then he said, 'Wait here.' He went out of the room, closing the door behind him.

'D'you reckon you got through to him?' said Rathbone.

'I'd like to think so,' she said. They waited in silence as the minutes ticked by. Eventually Hussein returned.

'I have spoken to Zareen and she is most anxious to help in your search for her friend,' he said. 'I will allow this lady,' he indicated Sukey while addressing Rathbone, 'to speak to her for a few minutes in the presence of my wife and myself, but if Zareen shows any sign of distress I shall insist you both leave at once.'

'Thank you very much, sir,' said Rathbone. He turned to Sukey. 'I'll wait for you in the car.'

Fifteen minutes later she joined him. 'Any luck?' he asked.

'I think so.'

He listened intently as she gave a brief account of her conversation with Zareen. 'Right,' he said, 'Straight back to the station. The SIO must know immediately.'

SIXTEEN

As soon as they were back in the incident room, Sukey made a telephone call. She then wrote a hasty report of her conversation with Zareen, which, on Rathbone's instructions she despatched to DCI Leach by email, flagged as urgent. After reading it, he immediately instructed Rathbone to recall his team and by noon they were reassembled.

'We have made significant progress,' Leach announced. 'First of all, DS Rathbone and Sukey have established that the reason given by Mr Hussein for his daughter's absence from school is genuine. The girl is now recuperating at home from a serious illness contracted abroad and this morning Sukey was allowed a brief interview with her. Sukey, please tell everyone what you learned.'

'The poor kid is obviously still pretty frail,' she began, 'and her father had his beady eye on her all the time, watching for signs of distress, so I had to be very careful what I said. I spent several minutes tiptoeing around, assuring her that we were continuing to look for Daisy and hadn't given up hope of finding her. She actually said at one point –' here Sukey read from her notes – '"Daisy did once say something about running away to teach her parents a lesson, but I never believed she'd do it, or that she'd hide away from them for so long." She said Daisy loved her parents but got upset because they spent so little time with her.'

'Is there any mileage in that suggestion d'you think, Greg?' said Leach.

Rathbone shook his head. 'We know from what the house-keeper told Sukey that the parents didn't spend as much time with their daughter as she would have liked, and that the girl was inclined to be rebellious, but I doubt if she'd have stayed away all this time without letting her parents know she was all right.'

Leach nodded. 'I agree it seems unlikely. Go on, Sukey.'

'I brought up the subject of the ring in a roundabout way by asking if Daisy ever gave presents – such as jewellery – to her friends. Without any further prompting from me she started talking about a ring Daisy bought at a craft fair. I asked her what it looked like and it was obvious to me that it was the one found on the dead girl's hand. She said Daisy wore it a few times until her Dad said it looked "cheap and nasty" and told her to take it off. It seems she carried on wearing it at school for a few days as an act of defiance, although she took it off before going home. Then she seemed to get tired of it and offered it to Zareen, who declined it because she didn't like it very much. This was at the end of a school day

when the kids were packing up to go home, and on impulse
she gave it to another girl who happened to be hanging around
at the time and showed an interest.'

'Does Zareen remember when this happened?' asked Leach.

'She couldn't remember exactly but she thinks it was maybe
a couple of weeks before Daisy disappeared. She said the
girl's absent quite a lot and she doesn't know her very well,
but she thinks her name is Sharon.'

'Wow!' said Penny Osborne excitedly. 'It sounds as if you
struck gold there, Sukey.'

Leach frowned at the interruption. 'There's more, I think?'

'Yes, sir. I've since spoken to Mr Bradley, the head teacher
at Over Hampton Comprehensive. He identified the girl at
once – she's Sharon Swann and apparently she's a regular
truant. Her last attendance was shortly before Daisy disappeared, but as she was just short of her sixteenth birthday and
anyway there were only a few weeks left till the end of term,
the truancy officer decided it would be a waste of time chasing
her. She comes from a somewhat dysfunctional family; the
mother suffers from depression after a series of broken relationships and can't hold down a job so she's dependent on
social security benefits. There are three children, all with
different fathers. Sharon is the eldest and Mr Bradley thinks
she's of mixed race. He added that she's a bright, attractive
girl who could do well if she attended school regularly and
had a more settled home life.'

Leach made a note. 'Thank you, Sukey, very well done.
On the face of it, it looks as if we might have an ID for the
body in the lay-by. I take it you have Sharon's address?'

'Yes, sir.'

'Good. I'd like you and Vicky to call there, talk to Sharon's
mother and see if you can get anything useful out of her. Bear
her state of health in mind; you'd better check with her social
worker first for some advice about the best way to approach
her. The rest of you can take a break from the case for the
moment; no doubt you've got plenty of other stuff to deal
with. Yes, Yvonne, what is it?' he said as his PA entered with
a note in her hand.

Leach scanned it briefly and said, 'Forget that last bit
everyone. This is a report from forensics about the brick fragments that Sukey and Vicky found in the garden in Portishead.

They match the samples taken from the scene where Sharon's body – if it is Sharon of course – was found.'

It took Sukey nearly half an hour to contact the appropriate department and speak to an official who was able to access the file of Jessie Swann. After a brief conversation, during which she made several notes, she turned to Vicky and said, 'Well, that was worth doing. The person I spoke to was floundering a bit as she's not been doing the job long and it took her a while to access the right database. Anyway, she confirmed that Jessie receives various benefits for herself and the children and has a doctor's certificate to say she's unfit to work. And guess who her doctor is?'

'Not the one who's got a fixation about Adelaide Minchin being murdered?' said Vicky resignedly.

'The same. If the mother's registered with him it's odds on the whole family is, so he may be able to give us some useful information about Sharon.'

'You mean, if he diagnosed her pregnancy and has he any idea who the father is?'

'Exactly. Unless, of course, he feels he can't tell us anything because of patient confidentiality.' Sukey reached for the phone again. 'I'll call the surgery right away. He's probably on his rounds, but I can leave a message.' After a few minutes' conversation with the receptionist she said, 'Right, they've asked him to call me on my mobile. He's probably somewhere in the Over Hampton area so I suggest we head for the Red Lion and have some lunch while we wait to hear from him.'

'You realize what you're letting yourself in for, don't you?' Vicky warned her. 'He's going to want to know if you're on the track of Adelaide's killer.'

'That's all right,' said Sukey cheerfully as they headed for the car park. 'I'll tell him I'm on the case.'

'Meaning what?'

'I'll tell you on the way.'

'So you've been dating Harry Matthews,' said Vicky when Sukey came to the end of her story. 'Good for you; it's time you had a man in your life. You must bring him round for supper one evening. I'll get Chris to cook something special.'

'Hey, not so fast!' said Sukey. 'We're not an item yet and I don't want him to get ideas.'

'Too soon after Jim?'

'Something like that.'

They had reached the Red Lion. Sukey found a space in the car park and switched off the engine. They were about to leave the car when her mobile rang. Doctor Hogan was on the line.

'DC Reynolds? Have you got something to report?'

'If you mean about Miss Minchin's death, nothing concrete at the moment but I am following up one or two possible leads,' she said guardedly before hurrying on. 'At the moment we need your help on another serious case. Is it possible for my colleague and me to make an appointment?'

'Where are you?' he asked. Sukey told him. 'Excellent! I'm on my way there myself for a quick bite. With you in about ten minutes.'

It was barely five minutes later when Hogan's car turned into the car park. The two detectives walked across to greet him. Sukey introduced Vicky and at Hogan's suggestion the three of them sat together in the back seat of the Mercedes to ensure privacy. Sukey sensed that he was in a more amenable mood than during the previous encounter. 'All right ladies, how can I help you?' he said.

Sukey explained the background to their enquiry. 'I heard of course that a girl's body had been found and there was speculation that it was the Hewitts' daughter, but that's all I know,' he said. 'They aren't registered with my practice and I don't know them personally.'

'But we understand that a Mrs Swann and her family at this address –' Vicky showed him her notebook – 'are your patients?'

'That's right. What about them?'

'Is there a teenage daughter called Sharon?'

'Yes.' Hogan's features, which up to that moment had appeared relaxed, suddenly tensed. He gave Vicky a sharp look. 'Has something happened to her?'

'Is she giving you cause for concern, Doctor?'

'I'm concerned for all my patients,' he retorted.

Sukey sensed that he was prevaricating and said quickly, 'We'd like to talk to Sharon because we understand she's in the same class as Daisy Hewitt, the girl who's disappeared.

We think she may know something about a ring that Daisy was seen wearing and is known to have given to Sharon some time before she disappeared. Knowing the way girls barter and give away odds and ends, we'd like to ask Sharon if she still has the ring or whether she gave it to someone else.'

'Why are you asking me?'

Sukey explained about the advice she had received from an employee in the social services department. 'She told me Mrs Swann has a medical certificate from you to prove she is unfit to work on account of depression, so we thought it advisable to speak to you first. It's really important that we see Sharon, but we don't want to upset her mother.'

Hogan sighed. 'Poor Jessie, she's had a really raw deal,' he said. 'Her family refused to have anything to do with her when she married Sharon's father – he's from the West Indies, and a nice enough chap but he couldn't cope when she went into depression after the birth so he left her.'

'There are other children, I believe?' said Vicky.

'Yes, two. After a while Jessie managed to pull herself together and get a job. Noah – Sharon's father – sends money fairly regularly and she was doing quite well. Then she took up with another man, got pregnant again and the same thing happened, but that didn't stop her making the same mistake a couple of years later. So now she has three kids with little or no support from two of the fathers.'

'We really do need to speak to Sharon,' said Sukey. 'Can you give us some advice on how to approach her mother?'

Hogan shrugged. 'Be gentle, don't rush her . . . that's all I can say. Basically, she's a nice woman, but she finds life a struggle. She does her best for her kids; most of the time they get enough to eat and they're clean and fairly well dressed. I'm afraid Sharon's been a bit of a handful, though. Sixteen's an awkward age and her mother finds it difficult to keep tabs on her a lot of the time.'

'Difficult in what way?'

Hogan made a vague gesture with his hands and shook his head. 'She's a very bright kid – I suspect she takes after her father – but I'm afraid she often bunks off school and we can only guess what she gets up to.'

'Can you remember the last time you saw her – either at home or in your consulting room?'

'I haven't called at the house for several months. Sharon came to see me fairly recently, but you'll appreciate I can't tell you what it was about.' He glanced at his watch. 'If there's nothing else, I would like to have something to eat before—'

'Doctor Hogan,' said Sukey quickly, 'I'm afraid we haven't been entirely frank with you. We are trying to identify the girl whose body was found in the lay-by. We originally believed it was that of Daisy Hewitt because of a ring she was wearing. We know now that Daisy gave that ring to Sharon although we don't know whether she still has it. The forensic pathologist advises us that the dead girl was about sixteen years old, had black hair, was possibly of mixed race and –' Sukey paused for a moment – for effect, as she admitted to Vicky afterwards – 'was about three months pregnant. Does that description fit anyone you know?'

There was a long silence. Then Hogan said, 'Let's have some lunch and then we'll go back to the surgery.'

'In the light of what you have told me, I feel I have no alternative but to break the patient confidentiality rule,' Hogan began when they were settled in his consulting room. 'Sharon came to me recently and said she wanted to have sex with her boyfriend. I gave her a prescription for the contraceptive pill but as it turned out the damage was already done; about four weeks later she came back and I found she was about eight weeks pregnant. I advised her to tell her mother, but she got very upset at the idea.'

'Was anything said about an abortion?'

'I suggested she consider it, but she didn't want to do that either. She said she'd go to the father and "sort him out", as she put it.'

'About how long ago was this, Doctor Hogan?' asked Sukey.

He thought for a moment. 'At a guess I'd say it was about five weeks ago.'

'That would make her about three months pregnant now?'

He nodded. 'About that.' He made a movement as if to switch on his computer. 'Do you want the precise date?'

Sukey shook her head. 'Not for the moment. This boyfriend she was having sex with – did she tell you anything about him? Is he a student at her school?'

Hogan gave a half-smile. 'As I said, Sharon didn't spend

a lot of time at school. Now I come to think of it she did say something that indicated it was an older man. She said he had a good job – now what was it? Something to do with computers maybe – I can't be sure.'

Vicky showed him a photograph of the ring. 'Do you remember seeing her wearing this?'

He shook his head. 'I'm afraid not. Is it important?'

'It's the one that was on the finger of the dead girl. Surely you saw the publicity in the media?'

He gave a slightly apologetic shrug. 'I don't have much time to read the papers – there's too much medical stuff to keep up with.' He took a closer look at the picture. 'If she was wearing it, I'm afraid I didn't notice. I'm sorry.' He looked from one to the other and said, 'I take it your next move will be to call on Jessie Swann? If so, I'd like to come with you. She's going be devastated when she hears your news and she may need medical support.'

'Doctor Hogan,' said Vicky, 'until we can get DNA samples for comparison and have them checked by forensics we can't be a hundred per cent sure that it's Sharon's body we found in the lay-by, so there's no question today of telling her mother about our suspicions. We need to ask her some questions, but we don't want to frighten her if it turns out we're on the wrong track.'

Hogan looked puzzled. 'How are you planning to get DNA samples without telling her why you want them?'

'We have our methods,' said Sukey, smiling, 'and we'll be very glad of your company because it will be reassuring for Jessie. Shall we go?'

SEVENTEEN

Jessie Swann was small and pale with straight dark hair falling limply from a centre parting. In response to Hogan's knock she opened the door a fraction and peered through the gap with a fearful expression in her eyes until recognition dawned at the sight of him and her heart-shaped face lit up in a smile.

'Doctor Hogan! How nice of you to call!' She held the door open to admit him, but her expression darkened again as she caught sight of the two detectives standing discreetly behind him. 'Who are these people?' she asked. 'They're not the usual social workers.'

'They're friends of mine,' said Hogan. 'May we come in?'

Somewhat reluctantly, she made room for the three of them to enter the narrow hallway and closed the door behind them. 'You'd better go through,' she said.

Sukey and Vicky exchanged glances. 'Nervous,' Vicky mouthed as they followed Jessie and Hogan into an untidy living room where the remains of what looked like breakfast were still scattered on the table. The air was stale and smelt of burned toast. 'You'd better have a seat.' Jessie indicated some chairs and they sat down and waited while she aimlessly moved plates and mugs around in a pretence of clearing up. 'The kids'll be home from school soon. They'll be wanting their tea,' she mumbled, almost to herself. 'If only Sharon was here . . . she shouldn't stay away so long . . . I need her help.' She sank into a chair and put her head in her hands.

'So she's still not come back?' said Hogan. She shook her head. 'These two ladies are detectives,' he explained, 'they'd like to speak to her about a ring a girl at school gave her.'

Jessie lifted her head and looked at him. 'What ring was that?'

Vicky showed her the photograph. 'It was this one,' she said.

Jessie gave it a brief glance. 'Yes, I've seen her wearing one like that. She didn't say where it came from. You say she got it off a girl at school?'

'That's what one of her friends said.'

Jessie shrugged. 'More like she got it off some feller she's been seeing. What about it?'

'She's been seeing a man?' asked Vicky. 'Have you any idea who he is?'

'She never tells me anything these days. I just wish she'd come home and give me a hand. It all gets too much, what with the kids and everything.' Her voice quavered and tears spilled from her eyes, which were a striking shade of blue. It wasn't difficult, thought Sukey, to understand how a certain kind of man would be attracted to her and quite likely see her as an easy lay.

'You say Sharon hasn't been home lately?' she said gently. 'Do you know where she is?' Jessie, scrubbing at her eyes with a soggy-looking paper tissue, shook her head. 'How long has she been away?'

Jessie gulped, dropped the tissue on the floor and reached for another from a box on the table. 'Dunno,' she said vaguely. 'One day's like any other. Pattie might know, she'll be home from school soon.'

'Pattie is Jessie's second daughter,' Hogan explained. 'She's just turned ten. She's a great help to her mother.'

'Jessie,' said Sukey, 'I wonder if we could have a look in Sharon's room? There might be something there that would give us an idea where she might be.'

Jessie shrugged. 'Help yourselves. It's the one over the front door.' She stood up. 'I'll show you . . .'

'I'm sure the ladies can find it,' said Hogan. He pushed her gently back into her seat. 'Why don't I give you a quick check-up while I'm here?' Very pointedly he held the door open for Sukey and Vicky, closing it behind them.

They found the room without difficulty. It was a typical teenager's room. The air smelt of stale perfume, the walls were covered with pictures of pop stars, the bed covers untidily thrown back, garments scattered over the floor or draped over the one rather rickety looking chair. On top of a chest of drawers were a comb, a small hairbrush and an assortment of half-used items of make-up. Sukey slipped the brush and comb into a sterile bag and put it in the capacious pocket of her denim jacket.

Beside the bed was a small cabinet on which lay a romantic paperback novel, face down and open about halfway through. 'It looks as though she meant to carry on reading that,' Vicky commented. She opened the single drawer in the cabinet. 'Aha, what have we here?' She held up a small book with a bright purple plastic cover and a pencil tucked into a pocket in the spine. 'Eureka! She keeps a diary!' Sukey peered over her shoulder while she flipped through the pages. The last entry was dated two days before Daisy Hewitt's disappearance. In a round, childish hand it read, '*Seeing Gordie tomorrow to sort things out.*'

'Methinks we're getting warmer,' said Vicky.

They went back downstairs. Recalling the ruse by which Hogan had persuaded Jessie not to follow them, Sukey tapped on the living room door.

'Just a moment.' They waited a minute before he called, 'You can come in now.' When they entered, Jessie was doing up the buttons on her shirt and Hogan was putting his stethoscope back in his bag. His eye fell on the diary. 'Found something useful?'

'Could be.' Vicky showed it to Jessie. 'This was in a drawer in Sharon's room. Have you seen it before?'

Jessie shook her head. 'I never go in there. What is it?'

'It looks like her diary.' Vicky opened the book at random. 'Is this Sharon's writing?'

'Let me see.' Jessie glanced at the open page and nodded. 'Yes, that's her writing. Good, isn't it?' she said with an unexpected burst of animation and pride. 'She's a bright kid, is Sharon. I keep telling her, if you spent more time in school instead of bunking off so much and getting me into trouble with the social, you could make something of yourself. But all she says is, "Yeah, yeah, Mum, don't keep going on about it". And then for a week or two she'll be good. Until next time.'

'Has she ever mentioned someone called Gordie?'

Jessie thought for a moment. 'Not that I remember. D'you think it's a boyfriend?'

'It might be but she doesn't say. She just refers to seeing someone of that name,' Vicky explained. 'Have you any idea who he or she might be?' Jessie shook her head. 'There might be something in here to give us a clue where to look for her. Is it all right if we take it with us? We'll bring it back as soon as we've finished with it.'

Jessie looked dubious. 'Sharon'll be livid with me when she finds out.'

'Then you can tell her we wouldn't have come looking for her if she hadn't stayed away so long,' said Sukey.

Jessie shrugged. 'All right then, take it. You'd better go now, the kids'll be in any minute, asking questions.'

'Thank you very much for your help,' said Sukey. A sudden thought occurred to her. 'Is Sharon interested in computers?'

Jessie looked blank. 'She might be – I suppose they have them at school.'

'There isn't one here?'

Jessie gave a bitter laugh. 'Where would we get the money?'

'I'm sorry, it was just a thought,' said Sukey.

'I'll pop in again soon, Jessie,' said Hogan. 'Remember to ask Mrs Ingram to get that prescription made up for you, and be sure to take it.' Back in the car he said, 'I'll drop you two off at the Red Lion before I go to my next patient.'

'That'll be fine, thank you,' said Vicky.

'By the way, did you find anything else besides the diary?'

'A hairbrush and comb.' Sukey produced the bag from her pocket. 'For obvious reasons I had to smuggle them out. Forensics should be able to get DNA samples from them.'

'I imagine your next step will be to find this chap Gordie?'

'If it is a chap, which seems likely,' Vicky agreed.

As they were getting out of his car in the Red Lion car park he said soberly, 'It doesn't look very good for Sharon, does it?'

'I'm afraid not,' Sukey sighed. 'Once we know for certain she's dead we'll have to break it to her mother, but we'll get a Family Liaison Officer to look after her and the kids for a while. She'll need a lot of support.'

'Indeed she will.'

'Do you know if Sharon ever sees her father?'

'I doubt it. I believe he went back to Jamaica when Sharon was a few months old, although as I said he sends money from time to time. I suppose you'll need to contact him as well?'

'It looks like it.'

As Hogan drove away, Vicky called Rathbone and reported their findings. 'Well, thank heaven for something positive!' he said. 'I'm back at HQ. You and Sukey join me here and I'll alert the SIO.'

When they reached headquarters they were immediately summoned to Superintendent Baird's office, together with DS Rathbone.

'I hear these two members of your team have got something of interest to report, Sergeant,' he said.

'They haven't had time to give me a full report, but they have found certain evidence that looks promising and I thought you should know right away, sir,' said Rathbone.

'Quite right,' said Baird. 'I understand they've been to the home of a girl you think might be the lay-by victim? All right, Sukey, you go first. Who is this girl?'

'Her name is Sharon Swann, sir, and I've spoken to a witness who saw Daisy Hewitt give her the ring the lay-by victim was wearing. The mother confirms having seen her daughter wearing it. Mother and daughter relations aren't good. The girl has a bad attendance record at school and frequently goes AWOL for extended periods, never says where she's been but until now has always come back in her own good time.'

Baird nodded. 'Which presumably is why she hasn't been reported missing.'

'That and the fact that the mother is taking medication for depression, which means she's not always sure what day of the week it is, let alone how long it is since she last saw her daughter.'

'A very sad situation,' Baird observed. 'Right, go on.'

'We found these items in her bedroom.' Sukey handed him the bag containing the hairbrush and comb.

He scrutinized the contents and nodded. 'Forensics should be able to get some DNA from those. I'll get them fast-tracked and with luck we'll soon have an ID for the lay-by victim. Now you, Vicky. What have you got for me?'

'A possible clue to a man Sharon was seeing, sir.' Vicky handed him the diary. 'Her mother confirmed it's her daughter's handwriting and there are several references to someone called Gordie. Sharon's mother didn't recognize the name, but she referred earlier to "some feller Sharon was seeing".'

'Presumably Gordie is short for Gordon,' said Baird. 'It could be either a surname or a given name. Any ideas?'

'Doctor Hogan said that when Sharon told him she was having sex and asked for the pill he thinks she said the man did something in IT, but he couldn't be sure.'

'The mother told us there's no computer in the house so it's unlikely she met him at home,' said Sukey. 'There are sure to be computers at school for the students to use – he might be a visiting technician, or possibly a teacher.'

'Well, there's a starting point, so get on with it,' said Baird brusquely. He turned to Rathbone. 'I gather you've found the source of the bricks, Sergeant. Any further joy there?'

'The house-to-house enquiries haven't yielded anything so far, sir.'

'Well, keep at it.'

Back in the CID office, Sukey called Over Hampton School, only to be told that neither Mr Bradley nor Mrs Kitson was available. 'They left early because there's a PTA meeting this evening,' said Sukey as she put down the phone.

'Good, that means we can leave early as well,' said Vicky.

'We'd better make the most of it,' said Sukey. 'Now we've got what looks like a breakthrough I've a feeling we're going to be working all hours.'

'Any news from Harry?' asked Vicky as they cleared their desks.

'No, but it's early days yet.'

As if the question had flicked a switch, there was a buzz from Sukey's mobile. There was a pause while her thumb moved rapidly over the keys. 'Well, would you believe?' she said excitedly, 'he's just sent me a text saying "something to report".' She put the phone back in her pocket and made for the door.

'Aren't you going to call him?' said Vicky.

'I will when I get home. Don't worry, I'll keep you posted.'

EIGHTEEN

Before leaving for work that morning Sukey had taken a fish pie from the freezer for her supper. When she reached home she was tempted to contact Harry straight away but, conscious that she was feeling tired and empty, having had nothing but a sandwich for lunch, she put the pie in the oven and prepared some vegetables before making the call.

'I got your text,' she said. 'Have you come up with something?'

'Haven't I just!' Harry's tone was gleeful. 'It so happens I've got some leave due to me so I thought I'd use some of it to work on our project. I've already dug up some very interesting stuff. Is it OK if I pop round?'

'Can it wait for an hour while I have something to eat?'

'I guess so. See you about eight.'

He arrived with a notebook in one hand and a bottle of red wine in the other. Sukey looked at the bottle with raised eyebrows. 'What are we celebrating? Don't tell me you've found Adelaide's killer already.'

Harry grinned. 'Not quite, but I think I may have found the reason why Cousin Muriel left Parson's Acre to her instead of to one of her siblings.' He marched into the kitchen, put the notebook on the table, took an opener from his pocket and pulled the cork from the bottle before she could stop him. 'How about some glasses?'

'I had wine with my supper and I'm not sure I want any more.'

'I think you'll find this is worth another snifter.'

She took an extra glass from a cupboard. 'OK, let's hear it.'

'It's been so easy, I can hardly believe my luck,' he said as he poured the wine. 'I know why Adelaide left the property to Leonora Farrell, who isn't even a member of the family.'

'Well, that was pretty obvious,' said Sukey. 'There was some sort of family feud.'

'It didn't take a genius to figure that one out,' he agreed, 'but that's just for starters – wait till you hear the details. Shall we sit down?'

She led the way into the sitting room. 'This had better be good. I've had a pretty stressful day.'

For once, he made no attempt to worm information out of her. 'I promise you won't be disappointed.' Treating her to his most engaging smile, he raised his glass. 'Cheers!'

For once the smile failed to strike the customary spark. Instead, she glared at him over the rim of her glass. 'Will you take that smug grin off your face and get on with it,' she said with a touch of exasperation.

'Was I looking smug?' he said.

'You were.'

'When you hear what I've uncovered maybe you'll forgive me.' He put down his glass and opened his notebook. 'The first task was to track down the aggrieved relatives. You may recall that Henry Minchin gave evidence of identification at the inquest into Adelaide's death, so I checked the records and found his address. And guess what else I found.'

'That he'd given a false address?' Sukey suggested.

'Something far more interesting,' said Harry. 'It was genuine all right, but it also happens to be his business address. The name of the business is Minchin Brothers and Kellaway Limited, and they describe themselves as property developers.'

Sukey gave a low whistle. 'Gosh, that means the joker who tried to get hold of Parson's Acre on the cheap when Muriel was thinking of selling could have been one of her brothers.'

'I thought that'd make you sit up.'

'It's certainly something to think about. How does the name Kellaway fit in, by the way?'

'Philip Kellaway is an architect who married Mavis, one of the Minchin sisters, the other being Muriel, who bought Parson's Acre. Philip was kicked off the board five years ago after a rather acrimonious divorce. When the dust had settled, Mavis was made a director in his place. And that's where it gets even more interesting.' He topped up their wine glasses. 'How about some crisps?'

'You really want to make a meal of this story, don't you?' She went into the kitchen, took a packet from a cupboard and threw it at him. 'Just get to the point, will you?'

'The point,' he said, opening the packet and helping himself, 'is that I had a very revealing conversation with the vicar who married Philip Kellaway to Mavis Minchin.'

Sukey felt her jaw drop. 'How in the world did you manage that?'

'As I'm sure you know, there's very little you can't find out nowadays, courtesy of the inventor of the worldwide web. Now there *is* a genius,' he said, raising his glass with one hand and reaching for the crisps with the other.

Sukey grabbed the packet and held it out of reach. 'Just get on with it!' she said through gritted teeth.

'All right, here's the story in a nutshell. The company was started up by one Joseph Minchin back in the nineteen thirties. He'd inherited some capital and used it to buy up half-finished houses where the builder had gone bust, finish them, sell them at a profit and buy up more. He had four children; Muriel was the eldest, then came Henry, Jarvis and finally Mavis. His wife died when Henry was about sixteen and still at public school. Eighteen-year-old Muriel found herself acting as housekeeper and mother to her younger siblings. When Joseph died, some time in the seventies, the sons took over the business and as I've explained, sister Mavis became a director after the divorce. She'd shown some aptitude for business and the boys had sent her on some sort of management course.' Harry took a mouthful of wine and gave Sukey a penetrating look. 'I can almost hear your synapses clicking,' he said. 'Any questions?'

While he was speaking, Sukey had made a few notes. 'The situation at present is that the business is currently owned by Henry and Jarvis Minchin and their divorced sister Mavis Kellaway,' she said. 'Can I assume that when the father died, Muriel was expected to continue acting as housekeeper to the others and that at some time she decided she'd had enough of the Cinderella role, walked out and left them to get on with it?'

'Exactly.'

She thought for a moment, frowning. 'Does that mean the brothers didn't marry and set up homes of their own?'

'They both married quite late.'

'After Muriel left them having to manage without a cheap housekeeper, I suppose,' said Sukey scornfully.

'Probably,' Harry agreed.

'But where did Muriel get the money to buy Parson's Acre? As far as we know she never married.'

'That's in a way the saddest part of the story,' he said. 'The Reverend Carew – he's retired but he still takes services at St Andrew's Church now and again – remembers the family very well. All four of them attended church while he was vicar, but he believes Muriel was the only one who was really sincere in her faith. He says she was a quiet, reserved young woman and it was obvious she was very much under the thumb of the other three, who were much stronger characters. She was very attractive and there were several young men in the congregation who showed an interest in her. One in particular was more persistent than the others and made several attempts to invite her out but somehow or other her siblings made a kind of defensive wall round her.'

'And she didn't show any sign of rebellion at this stage?'

'Apparently not. The young man – his name was Raymond Hickson – was evidently very serious about Muriel and he asked the vicar's advice. He suggested that he write to her, which he did, several times, but never received an answer. It seems doubtful if she ever received his letters.'

'You think they destroyed Muriel's letters?'

'That's what Mr Carew thinks.'

'That's appalling!' Sukey exclaimed. 'That can't be the end of the story, though?'

'Of course not. Maybe on reflection Raymond decided he wasn't considered good enough for Muriel, but whatever the reason he appears to have given up trying. The rest of it is pure Somerset Maugham. He went to somewhere out East, made a pile of money and after a few years told his friends he was going back to England to marry the girl of his dreams. Then he went down with malaria, was very ill and eventually died. But before the end he was able to dictate a letter to Muriel saying he'd never ceased to love her and when he died they found he'd made a will leaving his entire fortune to her.'

'So Cinderella is suddenly transformed into a fairy princess, but without a Prince Charming,' said Sukey. 'That's really sad.'

'In a way, yes,' Harry agreed, 'but wouldn't you have loved to be a fly on the wall when she broke it to the Ugly Siblings that they were losing their tame housekeeper?'

'I guess so.' Sukey drank the rest of her wine but waved the bottle away when Harry offered to refill her glass. 'At least we know why Muriel left Parson's Acre to Adelaide – and why Adelaide made sure it never got to any of Muriel's siblings. But we still don't have a motive for murder.'

'You still think Adelaide was murdered?'

'Let's say I'm not convinced she wasn't. We've been thinking up to now that it was purely for commercial reasons that someone found Parson's Acre such an attractive proposition – but was it? Thinking back to those dodgy phone calls to Muriel, I'm wondering . . . if it was one of her brothers, how did they know she was thinking of putting Parson's Acre on the market?'

'In their line of business they probably have all sorts of contacts,' said Harry.

'I suppose so,' Sukey agreed, 'and it's true the mysterious caller claimed to be a director of a property development company. But look at it this way: Muriel might not have been actively involved in the day to day running of the family company, but according to Doctor Hogan she was nobody's fool and she'd almost certainly have picked up enough knowledge of the business through hearing the others talk about it to see through the yarn he spun her.'

Harry frowned. 'I don't quite follow you.'

'Anyone with a knowledge of the planning laws would have known there was no application for development on the land adjoining Parson's Acre – and that in any case such an application would have little or no chance of success. No, I reckon her mystery caller concocted that story off the top of his head without knowing what kind of person he was dealing with. Muriel was a very private person and very few people knew her background.'

'Hmm, I see what you're getting at.' Harry thought for a moment. 'That means we're back to square one. We've no clue as to the identity of the mystery caller or why he was so keen to get his hands on Muriel's house.'

Sukey sat for a few moments absent-mindedly twisting the stem of her wine glass between her fingers. 'Penny for them?' said Harry.

'I can't help thinking we've missed something . . . and for some reason the term "planning application" keeps coming to mind. What kind of person would be likely to have knowledge of the procedure?'

Harry shrugged 'Another property developer? A solicitor? An estate agent?'

'How about a builder?'

'I suppose . . . yes, a builder might see scope for an improvement or extension to Parson's Acre. Muriel had lived there a long time and it could probably have been in need of a face lift of some kind.'

'And I remember now,' said Sukey, 'I heard some mention of Adelaide asking a local firm of builders – the Hubbards – to call and see her about building an extension. That would have needed planning permission, wouldn't it?'

Harry nodded. 'True.'

'And Adelaide, being a chatty sort, would have told her friends about it. But supposing Muriel had a similar idea for some improvement – say a conservatory – that would also need planning permission, and someone got to hear about it?'

'It's possible, I suppose,' said Harry, 'but I'm not sure how it would be relevant.'

Sukey gave a slightly despondent sigh. 'I suppose I'm clutching at straws, but we know Doctor Hogan is convinced there's a link between those phone calls and Adelaide's death and I'm beginning to think he's right. Harry, will you check on the planning records round about the relevant time?'

Harry opened his notebook. 'Which is, exactly?'

'Good point. I'm not exactly sure – I'll check with Doctor Hogan and let you know. Meanwhile, I suggest you have a word with Leonora and tell her you've solved the mystery of the Minchin wills. You might be able to wangle a few expenses,' she added mischievously.

NINETEEN

Sukey got ready for bed uncertain whether to feel relieved or disappointed that Harry had not so much as hinted at the possibility that he might stay a while longer after they had finished discussing the case. His goodnight kiss had been tender and affectionate rather than passionate. Was this out of respect for her earlier reluctance to start a new relationship? Did it mean that he really cared for her and was prepared to wait until she was ready? Supposing he was merely looking for an affair that would be mutually enjoyable but with no firm commitment on either side? If that were the case, might he now decide to look elsewhere? Or was he stringing her along because their project, as he called it, appealed to him as a journalist? Such an attitude was hard to reconcile with her belief in both his sincerity and his professional integrity.

Once in bed she tried to settle down with a book in the hope of focusing her thoughts elsewhere, but when she realized she had read the same page three times she put it away and turned out the light. Fretting over the conflicting possibilities kept her awake for a while, but before long exhaustion overcame uncertainty and she fell into a deep and dreamless sleep.

When she awoke next morning the air was still and heavy, the sky overcast. The first drops of rain began drumming on her car as she reached headquarters and she pulled the hood of her waterproof jacket over her head before making a quick dash from the car park to the main entrance. When she reached the CID office DS Rathbone was already at his desk drinking his first coffee of the day and within a few minutes the rest of his team had assembled.

'Needless to say,' he began, 'the SIO has a team of uniformed hard at work in search of a witness or witnesses who saw anyone acting suspiciously with a trailer, either near or in the lay-by, or in the area between the house in Dunford Avenue and the field where the empty trailer was found. It's unfortunate that it was used a number of times before we knew of its connection with the case. Forensics have been over it with a tooth comb. Naturally most of the prints they found belong to the owner, Wally Horner, but surprisingly, considering the length of time involved, they have managed to lift a few that aren't his. We need to know how many people other than Wally himself have handled that trailer during the past few weeks. I want the name and address of every one and their prints for elimination. Make a special note of anyone who refuses and refer them to me. Sukey and Vicky, your priority this morning is to track down this guy Sharon refers to in her diary as Gordie. With luck, the school may know him. Otherwise . . .'

'Something about needles and haystacks, Sarge?' suggested Vicky as he left the word hanging in the air.

His mouth crimped in a humourless smile. 'You said it.'

Back at her desk, Sukey called Over Hampton School and asked to speak to the head teacher. 'Mr Bradley, we're following up a new lead in the lay-by murder case and we think you may be able to help us,' she began. 'Could my colleague and I come and see you this morning?'

'Oh er, yes, I suppose so.' She thought he sounded harassed. 'We're rather busy . . . this is the last week of term, you know but . . . perhaps if you were to call around one o'clock I could spare a few minutes.'

'Thank you, Mr Bradley.' Sukey put the phone down and turned to Vicky. 'He can't see us till one o'clock. He's probably giving us part of his lunch hour.'

'That leaves us with the whole morning to fill,' Vicky grumbled. 'Any ideas?'

'We're assuming that Gordie is either an IT teacher or a technician and that Sharon met him at school, aren't we?' said Sukey.

Vicky nodded. 'So?'

'From what I remember of the time Fergus was at school, specialist teachers for subjects like music and art tend to be peripatetic. The same may apply to IT.'

'You're saying he may teach at other schools in the area?'

'It's a possibility. Or maybe in further education classes.'

'Good thinking. Maybe if we look back at earlier diary entries we might find a clue.'

They found several entries that read simply 'had a date with Gordie yesterday – it was wonderful!' but with no additional comment. It was not until they found an entry in the last week in April that they found the first, rather flimsy clue to Gordie's identity. Sharon had written, 'Oh boy! Am I glad I saved myself for a real man!'

'What does that suggest to you?' said Vicky.

'That some of the kids at Sharon's school who fancied their chances with her had been given the elbow but that she'd had it off with someone older and more experienced – and thoroughly enjoyed it,' said Sukey. 'Any other dates?'

'Several. And here,' Vicky was riffling through the later pages, 'we find the first reference to her pregnancy. Look.' She handed the diary back to Sukey and pointed to the entry that read, "Uh-oh, it looks like we slipped up. Never mind, I trust Gordie – he's always promised to look after me". And look at the date – it's just a week before the latest entry.'

'So, she started having unprotected sex with Gordie, hurried off to see Doctor Hogan for the pill, carried on having a wonderful time with him thinking she was safe and then found she was already pregnant—'

'—told him about it, expecting him to say, "No worries, we'll get married".'

'He tells her "nothing doing", she goes along to "sort him out" – according to what she told Doctor Hogan – which probably means she was going to make him at least look after her financially—'

'—and he's already married. She threatens to tell the wife so he kills her and dumps her body in the lay-by with Wally Horner's bricks on top of her.'

They sat looking at each other for a few moments. Then Sukey said, 'It's all conjecture of course, but it's been known to happen. Where do we go from here? There's still no clue to his identity other than that he's a man and not a boy.'

'We can always go back to our original idea – that he's an IT teacher or technician,' Vicky suggested.

'Right,' said Sukey, 'let's get Googling.'

They had been working in silence on their respective computers for half an hour when Vicky gave a squeak of excitement. 'There's a Brian Gordon who runs a course called "IT for Silver Surfers" at the College of Further Education in Keynsham.' She checked the time. 'We're in luck; he has a class from nine till eleven this morning. If we get a move on we can be there before his class ends.'

'Should we check first to make sure the class is still on?' said Sukey. 'Sometimes they get cancelled at short notice.'

Vicky shook her head. 'I vote we take a chance. If he's got anything to hide we don't want to give him advance warning.' She glanced out of the window. 'Thank goodness it's stopped raining.'

Brian Gordon was a man of about forty with nondescript features and thinning mousy hair. He wore shapeless corduroy trousers and a tweed jacket with a button missing. *Not exactly the sort to turn on a sixteen-year-old, but you never can tell,* Sukey thought to herself.

He glanced with mild curiosity as the detectives held up their IDs. 'How can I help you?' he asked. 'I'm not a witness to a crime, so far as I know.'

'We have no reason to think you are, sir,' said Sukey, 'but it's possible you may be able to help us with some enquiries. Do you by any chance teach IT at centres other than this college?'

'As it happens, I do,' he said. 'Why do you ask?'

'Do you teach at Over Hampton Comprehensive School?' asked Vicky. 'The school where the missing girl, Daisy Hewitt, is a student?' she added, as he appeared to hesitate.

'Yes, I do teach IT to the Business Studies students there,' he admitted. 'Why do you ask?'

'Is Daisy in your class?'

'Yes, she is. My God!' He put a hand to his mouth. 'You don't suspect me of having anything to do with her disappearance?'

'As it happens, it isn't about Daisy that we're here,' said Vicky. 'How long have you been teaching at that school, Mr Gordon?'

'I've been going there one full day a week for the past three years. Look, if this isn't about Daisy, will you please tell me . . .?'

'How do your students address you?'

'Mostly they call me "Sir" or "Mister Gordon", but I still don't understand . . .'

'Is there a student on the register called Sharon Swann?'

'Sharon Swann?' Gordon chewed his lower lip, frowning. 'Let me think. I take four separate classes . . . yes, there is a girl by that name on one of the registers. She's quite bright, very quick to grasp each new piece of information, but I don't recall seeing her lately.'

'She's been missing from home for several weeks,' said Sukey, 'and the last entry in her diary indicates that she was planning to meet a man she refers to as Gordie with the intention of "sorting things out".' She waited for a couple of seconds before asking, 'Could that be you, by any chance, Mr Gordon?'

'Me?' Gordon's scandalized expression was so comical that despite the seriousness of the situation Sukey found it hard not to smile. 'I'm a married man with two children and another on the way, Constable.'

'That doesn't answer my question, sir. Sharon Swann hasn't been home or attended school for several weeks and we are seriously concerned for her safety. Did you, on or about the twenty-eighth of June, arrange to meet her?'

'Certainly not!'

'Did she ever ask you for such a meeting?'

'No!' A few beads of sweat had appeared on his upper lip and he pulled a handkerchief from his pocket and dabbed at them with a shaking hand. 'You read about these things in the papers and you think "how terrible" but you never imagine it will happen to you,' he almost wailed.

'Things? What things, Mr Gordon?' asked Vicky.

'Girls getting attracted to teachers . . . especially older men . . . and then claiming they've behaved improperly and reporting them . . . and they lose their jobs, even if enquiries prove it's malicious and there's nothing in it, because there are always doubts. Look!' He glanced wildly from one to the other. 'Is this what it's all about? Sharon's made some kind of complaint about me and then gone off and hidden somewhere to make it look as if . . .' He put both hands over his eyes.

'Have you ever given her cause to make that kind of complaint?' Vicky continued relentlessly.

'Of course not, but who will believe me? My wife . . . she's expecting another baby very soon . . . she'll think I needed another woman when we . . . she . . .' His voice wavered and he appeared about to break down.

'Mr Gordon, to our knowledge no one has made a complaint about you,' Sukey interposed. 'The purpose of this interview is to find out whether you are the person referred to in Sharon Swann's diary as Gordie. Has she, or any other of your students, addressed you by that name?'

'Not to my face, no.' Gordon appeared almost affronted at the suggestion. 'I don't allow familiarity from the students, but I suppose some of them may use the name behind my back. I wouldn't know about that, would I?'

Vicky gave him a reassuring smile. 'Of course not, sir. Thank you for your time. Just one more thing; in case we need to speak to you again, would you be kind enough to give us a note of your address and phone number?'

'Speak to me again . . . but why?' Gordon passed a tongue over his lips.

'Just routine, sir,' she assured him. 'We have to fill in a form for every person we speak to.' She waited while he tore a piece of paper from his notebook, wrote on it and gave it to her. 'Thank you, sir, and, thank you for answering our questions so frankly.'

'I hope you're satisfied that I have never behaved improperly towards Sharon – or any other of my students,' he said, with what seemed to Sukey an almost pathetic eagerness.

'We have no reason at present to think so, sir,' said Vicky, but her tone was non-committal.

'What d'you reckon?' said Sukey as they returned to their car. 'From what we've gleaned about Sharon's character I wouldn't have thought Brian Gordon was her type, but you can't judge by appearances.'

'And we know of plenty of cases of teachers having sex with under-age students,' Vicky pointed out. 'With a wife in the late stages of pregnancy he could be suffering from sex starvation.'

'I notice you said we have no reason "at present" to suspect him,' said Sukey. 'Do I gather you have doubts?'

'Maybe having hunches is catching.' Vicky gave a half smile at the notion. 'I'm not sure how you feel, but I don't think we should tick the "eliminated from enquiries" box for the moment.' She glanced at her watch. 'It's gone half past eleven. It'll be nearly twelve by the time we reach Over Hampton. Why don't we grab a sandwich at your favourite watering hole before we tackle Mr Bradley?'

'Good idea, but I've just remembered I need to have a word with Doctor Hogan and with luck I'll catch him before he starts on his visits. I've asked Harry to check on some planning applications for Parson's Acre and I need some approximate dates,' she added in response to Vicky's unspoken but obvious curiosity. 'It's to do with our project.'

'Oh, that!' Her friend's tone was dismissive.

Doctor Hogan was still at the practice and was able to give Sukey the information she needed. 'Why do you want to know?' he demanded.

'It's a long story and I haven't much time now,' said Sukey. 'I've learned quite a lot about how Muriel Minchin came to Parson's Acre, but so far I'm unable to establish a link between the mystery calls and Adelaide's death. This information may help; I'll let you know immediately I have anything significant to report.'

'Do that,' he said.

'That's Harry's car!' Sukey exclaimed as they drove into the car park at the Red Lion. Glancing round, she spotted a bright red convertible in the far corner. 'If I'm not mistaken, that's Leonora's. I imagine he's arranged to meet her and tell her what he's found. Let's go inside.'

'Oh goody, you can introduce me!' said Vicky.

'Don't you dare say anything!' Sukey said in some alarm.

'Don't worry. I'm just curious to get a good look at him. Where is he?' Vicky's eyes searched the bar.

'Over there.' Sukey nodded in the direction of a corner table, where Harry Matthews and Leonora Farrell were seated, apparently deep in conversation.

'I admire your taste. He's dishy!' said Vicky. 'The woman with him, the one with all the silverware – is she the artist you were telling me about, the one who's inherited Parson's Acre?'

'That's the one.'

'She's fairly gobbling him up with those huge eyes. Are you sure he's safe to be let out when she's on the prowl?'

'Don't be daft!' Despite Harry's earlier dismissal of Leonora's charms, Sukey could not help a slight twinge of unease. 'I told you, she asked him to do some research for her and it so happens he's already uncovered some very interesting stuff.'

'Is that why you rang Doctor Hogan?'

'Right.'

'You can update me later. Meanwhile, how about an introduction?'

Harry's greeting as he shook hands with Vicky was cheerfully businesslike. Leonora appeared less than delighted at the interruption, but recovered sufficiently to express her admiration for Harry's efficiency in dealing with her request. 'He's absolutely brilliant!' she said earnestly, silver hoops swinging wildly as she switched her gaze from one to the other.

'Yes, he's pretty good at his job,' Sukey agreed.

'As I'm sure you and your friend are at yours,' Leonora said graciously before adding pointedly, 'I expect you're on a case and need to talk privately, so we mustn't keep you.'

Polite expressions of pleasure at the meeting were exchanged before Sukey and Vicky went to the bar to order their lunch.

'She looks as if she'd like to have him for breakfast,' Vicky remarked. Unexpectedly she put a hand on Sukey's arm. 'Do be careful,' she said in a low voice, 'I'd hate to see you hurt.'

Sukey patted the hand in appreciation. 'That's sweet of you, but I'm pretty sure Harry can see through her. That's the way she looks at all men, from the chap behind the bar to her rather boring solicitor.' She picked up the menu. 'What are we going to have?'

'We appreciate you're very busy, Mr Bradley,' said Vicky. 'We'll try not to take up too much of your time.'

'You said something about a new lead in the lay-by murder case,' said Bradley. 'Incidentally, I've had a call from Zareen Hussein's father. I understand the girl was genuinely ill and is now recuperating at home under the care of the family GP.' He gave a wry smile. 'Mr Hussein is not best pleased with

the way he's been treated. He even hinted at charging the
Social Services with racism. But you don't want to hear about
other people's problems,' he hurried on. 'You said something
about new information?'

'After talking to Zareen, my colleague and I called on Mrs
Jessie Swann,' said Sukey. 'Sharon's mother,' she added as
Bradley raised an eyebrow.

'Ah yes, Sharon Swann,' said Bradley. 'Her mother's far
from well, as I'm sure you realized when you saw her. What
is your interest in her?'

'Sharon has not been home for several weeks,' Sukey
explained. 'We found a diary in her room in which there is
an entry referring to a meeting with someone called "Gordie".
Does that name mean anything to you?'

Bradley frowned and shook his head. 'I don't think so.
Should it?'

'We understand an IT specialist called Brian Gordon teaches
one day a week at this school.'

'That's right.' His jaw dropped. 'Surely you're not
suggesting that the entry in Sharon's diary refers to him?' he
said in obvious disbelief.

'Did Sharon attend his IT classes?'

'I'll check.' Bradley consulted his computer. 'Brian Gordon
teaches four classes every Wednesday,' he said after a minute
or two. 'Sharon's on the register for the second period in the
morning and she has attended on a number of occasions . . .
but not for the past four weeks.'

'What about the weeks before that? Did she attend the IT
class regularly?'

Bradley manipulated the mouse. 'I wouldn't say regularly,
but considering Sharon's record it would seem to be one of
her favourite subjects. You know,' he said gravely and with
conviction, 'I find it impossible to believe that Brian would
enter into an improper relationship with a student.'

'We'll make a note of that, sir,' said Vicky. 'Now, regarding
the maintenance of your computer equipment. Do you employ
a full-time technician or do you have an arrangement with a
commercial firm?'

'I can answer that one straightaway. The caretaker looks
after general maintenance, but our computer equipment is regularly checked over and where necessary repaired by a young

man called Joshua Bennett. He's a former student at this school
and on leaving he got a job working on computers. After a
few years with a firm in Bristol he set up his own business
here in Over Hampton.'

'What name does he trade under?'

'He calls himself Bennett Computer Services.'

'Well, thank you very much Mr Bradley, you've been really
helpful.'

Back at headquarters they wrote up their reports and left them
in DS Rathbone's in-tray before heading to the canteen for a
cup of tea.

'Maybe Sharon saw him as a father figure,' said Vicky as
she spooned sugar into her cup.

'You mean Brian Gordon?'

'Who else? And then,' Vicky continued after further thought,
'things sort of got out of hand.'

Sukey sat cradling her cup in her hands. 'I'm beginning to
think your hunch may be right,' she said.

TWENTY

When Sukey and Vicky returned to the CID office
they found DS Rathbone speaking on the telephone. He glanced across the office and beckoned.
'They're here, sir. Do you want to speak to either of them?
No? Very good, I'll tell them.' He put the phone down. 'I've
just read your report to DCI Leach and we both see Brian
Gordon as very much in the frame for Sharon Swann's disappearance, if not her murder. Until we have the DNA reports
on the items you brought from her home we can't be a hundred
per cent certain that the lay-by victim is Sharon, but in the
meantime he wants us to pull Gordon in for further questioning under caution. You might as well get on with it right
away.' Without waiting for a response he swung his chair
round and began working on his computer.

'It's going to be a long day,' said Sukey resignedly as she
and Vicky picked up their jackets.

'At least we seem to be getting somewhere,' said Vicky. Back in the car, she opened Sukey's street atlas. 'Gordon lives in Farm Avenue, Portishead.' She ran a finger down the index. 'That's interesting!' she exclaimed after finding the relevant page. 'I've a feeling it was somewhere near here that we spotted Bob Phelps tinkering with his cement mixer. And we know the load of bricks that his mate Wally helped him load into the trailer are the ones dumped over the body in the lay-by!' Her voice rose in excitement. 'What's the name of the street where Wally lives? Is it Dunford Avenue?'

Sukey thought for a moment. 'I'm pretty sure it was Dunford something. What are you thinking?'

'Don't you see? Whoever pinched that trailer needed the bricks to cover the body. And it's a safe bet that it's someone living locally who happened to be passing, noticed what was in it and immediately thought . . .' Vicky checked the index again and then turned back to the same page. 'Ah, here we are . . . Dunford Road . . . it's just round the corner from where Brian Gordon lives. Sukey, he *has* to be Gordie!'

'Oh dear, I hope not!' said Sukey.

Her friend looked at her in astonishment. 'Don't you want to crack this case?'

'Yes, of course I do. I was thinking of his wife . . . and the kids and the new baby that's due any day.' Almost reluctantly, Sukey turned on the ignition and put the car in gear. 'I'm just not looking forward to this particular assignment, that's all.'

'You know your trouble,' said Vicky as she marked the page in the book and closed it before settling comfortably into her seat, 'You're too soft-hearted.'

The door of Number Thirty-Six Farm Avenue was opened by a woman in a loose floral blouse and shapeless skirt that did nothing to disguise her advanced stage of pregnancy. Her straight fair hair was tucked behind her ears and her clear complexion was innocent of make-up, giving her a fresh and youthful appearance. The little girl at her side sucked her thumb as she clung to her mother's skirt and peeped shyly up at the visitors. Upstairs, another child was wailing and a man whose voice the two detectives recognized was trying to soothe it.

'Mrs Gordon?' asked Vicky. The woman nodded. She held up her ID and Sukey did the same. 'Could we have a word with your husband, please?'

'Police?' Her expression was puzzled rather than alarmed. 'Yes, of course. I'll call him. Our son enjoys his bath so much he objects to being taken out of it,' she explained with an apologetic smile. 'If you'd like to come in . . .' She held the door open, they stepped inside and she closed it behind them. At the foot of the stairs she called, 'Brian! Can you come down? There's someone to see you.'

'Co . . . ooming!' The crying had ceased and Gordon appeared at the top of the stairs carrying a child swathed in a towel. His gaze travelled past his wife. His smile faded and he stiffened as though turned to stone. 'Will you come and take Peter, quickly please Miriam.'

'Yes, of course.' It was evident from her change of tone and anxious glance back at the detectives that she realized something was amiss. She plodded up the stairs, clinging to the banister with one hand.

Gordon handed her the child and whispered something in her ear. She nodded and vanished, followed by the little girl. A door closed as Gordon almost ran down the stairs.

'For God's sake, what is it now?' he said. 'You can see her condition . . . what am I supposed to tell her?'

'That's up to you, sir,' said Vicky. 'Our instructions are to request you to come with us to headquarters as there are some further questions we'd like to put to you.'

'What further questions? How long will it take?'

'That depends on your answers, sir.'

'But you must give me some idea . . . an hour, two hours? Supposing my wife needs me . . . you can see she's very near her time.'

'Perhaps there's a neighbour or a friend she can call on in an emergency?'

'I suppose . . . oh my God, what's happening to us?' He put a hand to his head in a gesture of utter despair.

Sukey's heart went out to him and she had to remind herself that she had a job to do. 'Mr Gordon, provided you have done nothing wrong and are prepared to give us frank answers to our questions, we're sure this can be cleared up very quickly,' she said, doing her best to give reassurance to a man who appeared to be at his wits' end. 'We'll wait for you down here while you go back upstairs and explain the situation to your wife. I suggest you tell her you are helping us with our enquiries into the persistent truancy of one of your students.'

'You think she won't see through that? This happened some years ago to one of our dearest friends . . . some snotty little kid brought a trumped up charge of indecent assault against him. He lost his job, his wife left him and in the end he killed himself.'

'Mr Gordon, please!' Vicky said sharply as he appeared on the verge of breaking down. 'We've already made it clear no one has made a complaint against you, but the fact is that a girl is missing and we have to question everyone who has had any contact with her recently. Now, do you wish to speak to your wife before you come with us or not?'

'Just give me a couple of minutes.' Without waiting for a response he bolted back up the stairs. Five minutes passed and Vicky was about to go up in search of him when he came running down again. 'Please, let's get this over quickly,' he begged as they escorted him to the car.

The formalities completed, Brian Gordon sat in the interview room, ashen-faced and visibly trembling. At his side was Mervyn Rafferty, the duty solicitor, with whom he had spent some twenty minutes in consultation before the interview. Opposite them, between DCs Sukey Reynolds and Vicky Armstrong, sat DS Rathbone.

'Now, Mr Gordon,' Rathbone began, 'as you know, we are very concerned for the safety of Sharon Swann, a student at Over Hampton Comprehensive School. It is true, is it not, that she is on the register of one of your IT classes at that school on Wednesday mornings?' Gordon nodded. 'Please answer aloud for the tape.'

'Yes.' The voice was barely audible.

'Louder, please.'

'Yes!' Gordon almost shouted. 'I've already told you . . .'

Rafferty laid a hand on his arm and said, 'Sergeant, my client has assured me that he has committed no offence and is willing to answer all reasonable questions. I ask you to bear in mind that he is extremely anxious about his wife, who as you know is liable to give birth at any time.'

'We are already aware of Mr Gordon's domestic situation, which is why we wish to proceed as quickly as possible,'

Rathbone said with a hint of impatience. 'All right, Mr Gordon, let's continue. Are you aware that Sharon Swann has a history of truancy?'

Gordon glanced nervously at Rafferty, who gave a reassuring nod. 'No, I didn't know that. As I'm not a full-time member of the staff I'm unfamiliar with the general attendance records of any of the students who come to my class.'

'What about her attendance in your class?'

'She attends fairly regularly. She enjoys IT and does well at it.'

'So although she's been in the habit of missing other classes – a habit of which you claim to be unaware – she has regularly attended yours?'

Again Gordon flicked a glance at the solicitor before saying, 'Until recently, yes.'

'When she started to miss classes, did you mention the matter to any of the other teachers?'

'Not being a full-time member of staff, I seldom had the opportunity.'

'She's a promising student, attending regularly, and yet you attached no particular importance to her sudden absence?'

'I simply mark the registers. It isn't my responsibility to check on reasons for absence,' Gordon pleaded. 'In any case, there's very little time between classes.'

'Ah yes, you teach four classes during the day. Generally speaking, how does Sharon compare with other students? You've already told us she's very bright.'

'Compared with most, I'd say she was, if not outstanding, certainly one who showed above average promise.' For the moment, Gordon appeared to forget the reality of the situation in his enthusiasm for his subject.

Rathbone pounced. 'Mr Gordon, why have you suddenly started using the past tense?'

'What?'

'You've just said, "She certainly *showed* above average promise".' The detective leaned forward, and looked Gordon straight in the eye. 'I suggest, Mr Gordon, that you *know* the reason for her absence.'

'What do you mean? How could I possibly know?'

'I put it to you that you know very well why Sharon Swann

has missed classes for several weeks. And that,' Rathbone continued with a dramatic lowering of tone and with his face inches away from Gordon's, 'is why you made the fatal mistake of using the past tense when speaking of her. It's the tense we use when speaking of the dead, isn't it?'

'No! It . . . it was a slip of the tongue. Are you saying she's dead? I have absolutely no reason to know . . .'

'Did she threaten to tell your wife about your relationship? Is that why you killed her?'

'What relationship?' Gordon cast a beseeching glance at Rafferty. 'I never . . . I swear I had nothing to do with this girl's disappearance.'

'Sergeant, unless you have some evidence to support such an accusation I must object to this line of questioning,' said Rafferty.

'All right, let's move on.' Rathbone sat back in his chair. 'As Sharon is such a bright student, you no doubt spend extra time with her during the lessons?'

Again Rafferty intervened. 'Sergeant, do you have specific grounds for making that assumption?'

'Let me put it another way. Do you sometimes spend extra time with her?'

'I may have done. I mean, she quite often wanted . . . wants . . . to learn some function that we haven't yet reached in the syllabus. I once had the impression,' here Gordon seemed to dredge up something from the back of his memory, 'that she had picked up some reference elsewhere – possibly on some TV programme or an article on computer technology – and wanted to find out more.'

'I suggest that she developed a special liking for you, was always looking for reasons to seek your attention, and that you found this flattering?'

As if he saw the trap that Rathbone was setting for him, Gordon flinched as if he had been stung. 'I assure you I was never aware of it.'

'It has been known to happen,' Rathbone said smoothly. 'As I'm sure you're aware,' he continued after a brief pause.

Gordon appeared to be on the verge of an indignant outburst, but a restraining hand on his arm made him hesitate before muttering, 'No comment.'

Rathbone waited a full minute before putting his next question. 'How long have you lived at your present address, Mr Gordon?'

Gordon blinked in apparent surprise. 'Just over three years. We moved in about six months before Libby – that's our little girl – was born.'

'So you've had time to get to know the neighbourhood fairly well?'

'I suppose so. We meet quite a few people at church, and my wife meets other mothers at the toddlers' group Libby goes to.'

'Do you know a man called Wally Horner?'

'You mean the jobbing gardener? Yes, I know him. He did some tree cutting for us when we first moved in.'

'He lives quite close to you, I believe.'

'That's right.'

'You probably know that from time to time he helps his friend, the builder Bob Phelps, to move heavy loads on his trailer.'

Gordon shook his head. 'I can't say I've heard about it, but it doesn't surprise me. Wally is a very helpful sort of chap.'

'Just under four weeks ago – shortly after the last time Sharon Swann was seen alive – Wally's trailer containing a load of rubble that he had helped Bob remove from a customer's garden was left overnight outside his house. It was Wally's intention to dispose of this rubble at a local quarry the following morning, but the trailer was stolen during the night. It was found abandoned a few days later, empty.'

During the last few exchanges, Sukey had kept a close watch on Gordon's face. It registered at first curiosity, then puzzlement, and finally wariness mingled with apprehension, as if he was expecting an attack to which he had no convincing defence. He sat motionless with his eyes fixed on the detective's face.

'The empty trailer was found in a field,' Rathbone continued relentlessly, 'but the contents, a quantity of builder's rubble, were subsequently found dumped in a lay-by close to Over Hampton. They concealed the remains of a sixteen-year-old girl who was wearing a ring last seen on the finger of Sharon Swann.'

*   *   *

'I've never seen anyone look more like the proverbial scared rabbit,' Sukey told Harry when she called him later that evening. 'I can't give you any details . . . I shouldn't be talking to you about it at all, but I just feel so churned up I have to talk to someone. There'll be a mention of the body in the lay-by case at tomorrow's briefing and you must swear not to let on that you've had advance notice.'

'Of course I won't; trust me. Who is this guy and do you reckon he did it?'

'He teaches IT,' she said. 'As to whether he did it or not, I don't know what to think. DS Rathbone gave him a really hard time and all but accused him of killing the girl whose body was found in the lay-by. He'd accepted the services of a duty solicitor and eventually his brief requested a break so they could confer. When they came back the Sarge went over the same ground again and we had a series of "no comments" from Gordon or "my client has already answered that question" from the brief.'

'So I take it you had to let him go?'

'I'm pretty sure Rathbone would have liked to hold him but after consulting the SIO he had to admit there were insufficient grounds so in the end we took him home to his pregnant wife with the order not to leave the district . . . the usual stuff.'

'And you still can't make up your mind about him?'

'He kept banging on about a friend who was falsely accused of assaulting a student and ended up topping himself and how he'd always had a secret terror of having the same thing happen to him. I can't decide whether he's using that as an excuse for the state of his nerves or whether he's on the verge of cracking because he's guilty.'

'I have a sneaking feeling that you rather hope he's innocent.'

'To be honest, I don't have a lot of sympathy for him. He seems such a wimp. It's his wife I feel sorry for. Harry, I really shouldn't have told you all this,' she hurried on. 'You won't . . .?'

'Don't worry; you know you can trust me. You know something else, Sukey.' His tone became gentler. 'I think you're a bit of a softie.'

She gave a weak, almost self-deprecating laugh. 'That's what Vicky tells me.'

'It's one of the things I love about you,' he said. 'Good night; sleep well.'

TWENTY-ONE

It was Friday afternoon before there were any further developments in the case that the media had come to refer to as 'the lay-by murder', despite the fact that the actual killing had undoubtedly taken place elsewhere. The news landed on DCI Leach's desk shortly before three o'clock in the form of a report from the fingerprint department, and it brought little cheer to the team of investigators. Matches had been found for two prints lifted from Wally Horner's trailer. Further investigation quickly eliminated the individuals concerned, both clients of Horner – one a woman and the other an active pensioner – who had assisted in the unloading of deliveries of garden supplies. A third print found on the underside of the ball-hitch did not, to Rathbone's intense frustration when Leach gave him the news, match those of Brian Gordon and remained unidentified.

Efforts to trace a witness, either to the actual theft of Horner's trailer or to a sighting of a trailer being towed along the route the thief would have taken to the lay-by during the crucial time, were still continuing but with little success. One resident in Dunford Road, who had left home earlier than usual on the day in question to catch a train to London, said he had noticed the trailer outside Horner's house when he went to bed at ten o'clock the previous evening. He recalled being surprised that it was no longer there at seven in the morning, but as rain was forecast for later that day he had assumed that Horner planned to do as much work as possible while it was still fine.

'Blank walls all round!' Rathbone thumped his desk in sheer frustration. 'Every scrap of circumstantial evidence we have so far points to Brian Gordon, right down to the fact that he has a caravan and his car is fitted with a tow-bar. His wife sleeps fitfully because of her pregnancy and she insists he never left their bed that night, but she would say that, wouldn't she?' He sat back in his chair and took a gulp of coffee from the mug that he kept almost permanently refilled whenever he was forced to spend time in the office. 'Now we've got another interminable wait for his DNA results to compare with the ones from the foetus. And we're still waiting for confirmation that Sharon is the lay-by victim. Why does everything have to take so long?' He drained the mug, got up and marched over to the coffee machine for a refill, leaving his team waiting for further instructions.

'He'll OD on caffeine if he's not careful,' said Vicky. 'I know how he feels, though – I think we all do. He was practically grinding his teeth when we had to let Brian Gordon off the hook. I agree with him; if we'd been allowed to keep him overnight he'd have cracked.'

'If he really is guilty,' Sukey said doubtfully.

'You saw the fuss he made when we took his prints and a DNA sample,' Vicky reminded her. 'Does that sound like innocence?'

'I think he feels he's living in some kind of nightmare where anything can happen. He couldn't have looked more terrified if we'd actually charged him and he almost cried with relief when we said he could go home. I felt really sorry for him.'

'Ooh, you're all heart!' said Vicky cheerfully.

Rathbone came marching back, taking swigs of coffee on the way. 'What are you all sitting around for?' he barked. 'There's plenty of other stuff waiting to be seen to, so get off your backsides and find something useful to do. Vicky and Sukey, get over to the incident room in Over Hampton and check on the Daisy Hewitt case and see if you can spot any avenue we haven't explored yet. The rest of you have a look at whatever's come in during the past few days and still awaiting attention.' He sat down at his computer, grabbed the mouse and began scrolling down the screen, while his team scattered to obey his instructions.

'Let's recap,' said Sukey as she and Vicky began a detailed examination of the hefty accumulation of reports in the Daisy Hewitt file. 'Daisy vanished without trace after leaving home for school at about eight thirty on the morning of Wednesday the thirtieth of June. It is believed that she intended to walk along a footpath a short distance from her home – a footpath her parents had forbidden her to take, but that she was in the habit of using whenever she could evade parental control.'

'The same path Valerie Deacon took the day she disappeared twenty years earlier,' Vicky continued as they leafed through the file. 'Valerie's school bag has never turned up but a couple of textbooks were found in the long grass by the same path. Her body has never been found and no arrest made.'

'So how does that compare with the Daisy Hewitt scenario?' Sukey mused as they continued their search. 'The field footpath was gone over with a toothcomb but there was no flattened grass or any other apparent sign of a struggle, which suggests Daisy was snatched while walking along a road. My guess is that she's more likely to have used Hampton Lane – that's the road leading to Parson's Acre – as it's quieter than Upper Keynsham Road, where the school is.'

'Which is the one the path leads to,' said Vicky. 'I see what you're driving at.'

Sukey nodded. 'Maybe she was lured into a car before she even reached the path.'

'No mobile phone, school bag or clothing has ever been traced,' Vicky went on as she turned a further page.

'When we checked the mobile it was switched off, but it's unlikely she left it at home,' Sukey reminded her.

'A mobile is like a third ear to most teenagers,' Vicky agreed. 'So what became of it? Has it been dumped along with her school bag?'

'Hang on a minute,' said Sukey. 'Supposing she wasn't snatched. Supposing,' she hurried on in pursuit of an idea that had suddenly sprung up in her mind, 'she never intended to go to school that day? Supposing she'd arranged to meet someone . . . maybe some man she'd met on an Internet chat line, for example?'

Vicky gave a soft whistle. 'Gosh, you could be right! There are a lot of pervs around, dirty old men who groom these kids by pretending to be about their own age or a bit older and email a picture of some handsome young guy, lure them to some quiet place and . . .'

The two stared at one another in mingled apprehension and excitement. 'Mrs Prescott said Daisy insisted on walking to school that morning, and I got the impression she went off in a bit of a hurry,' said Sukey. 'If she had given this man the impression that she was a bit older, she may have sneaked out in ordinary clothes instead of her school uniform without the housekeeper seeing her.'

Without further ado, Sukey called DS Rathbone, who was still at headquarters. 'We've had an idea, Sarge,' said Sukey. He listened attentively while she explained. 'It's certainly worth a try,' he said. While he did not respond with the same degree of enthusiasm as theirs, his spirits appeared to lift a little. 'Go back to the Hewitt's house right away and search the girl's room again.'

'Will do, Sarge.'

'I'll try and have a word with Mrs Prescott first. I've got her mobile number,' said Sukey. 'You know,' she went on, 'if we're right, and Daisy not only used the forbidden footpath but actually managed to sneak out of the house done up in a sexy outfit to meet a supposed boyfriend, it won't be long before the lady is looking for another job.'

Vicky shrugged. 'That's not our problem.'

Mrs Prescott was alone in the house as Daisy's parents were in London for the weekend. She showed considerable surprise at Sukey's request, but made no objection. It was a little before six when the two detectives arrived. 'I'm sure your people had a good look round Daisy's room when she first went missing,' she remarked as she led them upstairs. 'They took some of her things away – for testing, they said – but I've no idea what they were.'

'It's always possible they missed something,' Vicky explained.

'I suppose so,' Mrs Prescott admitted with a sigh.

'Just one thing before we start,' said Sukey when they reached the top of the stairs. 'Will you cast your mind back to the last time you saw Daisy? It would, of course, be the day she disappeared. I seem to remember that you said you'd drive her to school. Is that right?'

'Yes, but she said she'd rather walk. It was against her parents' orders, of course, but as I think I told you, she was . . . she is a very wilful girl.'

'Did you have breakfast together?'

'Yes.'

'Was she wearing her school clothes?'

'I suppose she must have . . . No, wait a moment. She came

down early for her breakfast and now you come to mention it, she was still in her dressing gown.'

'And it was during breakfast that you said you'd drive her to school?'

'That's right.'

'And her response was?'

'She said, "Don't bother, I'm going to walk". I reminded her not to use the footpath and she said, "Don't worry, I won't". But I suppose,' Mrs Prescott added with a sigh, 'she must have done.'

'This is something we don't know for certain,' said Sukey. 'Now, Mrs Prescott, this may be very important so will you please try and recall exactly what happened next.'

The housekeeper closed her eyes as if reliving the scene. 'When we'd finished breakfast she went upstairs to get dressed and ready for school,' she began, 'and I took the breakfast things into the kitchen and loaded them into the dishwasher. The next thing was I heard her call out "goodbye" and I heard the door bang.'

'Did you actually see her go?'

'Well, no, I didn't. I never even heard her come downstairs. As I said, I was in the kitchen and you can't see the stairs or the front door from there, even when the kitchen door's open.'

'Was it open that day?'

'I doubt if it would have been closed, but it may not have been wide open.'

'So it would have been possible for Daisy to run downstairs and out of the house without you actually seeing her.'

Mrs Prescott looked perplexed. 'Yes, obviously . . . but what difference does it make? The fact is, I heard her go out and that was the last time I saw her.' She looked first at Sukey and then at Vicky. 'Is that all you want to know?'

'For the moment, yes,' said Vicky. 'Perhaps we can see her room now?'

'Yes, of course. It's the one on the right at the top of the stairs. Do you want me to come with you?'

'Yes please.'

Daisy Hewitt's room and its contents echoed the housekeeper's description of her as 'a poor little rich girl'. The thick carpet, the suite of luxury furniture, the colour television mounted on an adjustable bracket, the computer station that had obviously been tailor-made in what looked like solid oak to fit into a niche, the hi-fi equipment and the heaps of albums of the latest pop groups – all testified to an unstinted outpouring of money. The built-in wardrobe with its full-length mirror was full of clothes and shoes that might have walked off the pages of the most expensive fashion catalogues. On the shelves in the en suite bathroom were a variety of perfumes and lotions, all of them top brands, most only partially used.

'As you mentioned to my colleague, it appears money was no object to her parents even if their time was at a premium,' said Vicky. 'Did her mother ever take an interest in her clothes and stuff?'

'Oh yes, sometimes,' the housekeeper acknowledged, a little grudgingly Sukey thought. 'Daisy used to buy all the teenage fashion magazines and when her mother had a moment she'd show her something that had taken her fancy and ask her advice. I know Mrs Hewitt liked to see her daughter looking nice, which is natural I suppose. I remember once or twice she talked her out of something she considered unsuitable, but mostly she let Daisy have her own way. She'd just say, "If you like it, darling, go ahead and order it and let Mummy have the bill".'

During this exchange, Sukey was searching through the racks of clothes. 'Where did she keep her school uniform?' she asked.

'In there with her other things I suppose,' the housekeeper said, indicating the wardrobe. 'I used to come in and make her bed and so on after she'd left for school, so obviously it wouldn't be here then.' She gave a puzzled frown. 'Why do you ask? She must have been wearing it when . . .' She broke off as Sukey reached into the back of the wardrobe and pulled out a small case of the type normally used as carry-on baggage by airline passengers. Like many of the garments, it bore the name of a top designer. 'That's the hand luggage she takes on holiday,' she said. 'She has a larger case of course, but that's stored in a cupboard with her parents' luggage. They normally take several large cases when they go away.'

'I can imagine,' said Vicky, a little scornfully.

Sukey lifted the case and put it on the bed. 'It's not empty, by the feel of it,' she said. She opened it, took out the contents one by one and laid them on the bed.

The three stared at them in silence for a second or two before Vicky said, 'It's pretty obvious that on the day she disappeared Daisy had no intention of going to school.'

TWENTY-TWO

'I don't understand,' said Mrs Prescott shakily. She stared as if mesmerized at the items on the bed: the white socks, the short black skirt, the white blouse, the blazer with the Over Hampton Comprehensive school badge on the pocket and the plain black shoes. In addition there was a school bag with its contents laid out beside it: a loose-leaf binder, a couple of textbooks, a pencil case and a diary. 'If she didn't go to school, where on earth did she go?'

'Good question,' said Sukey. She opened the diary and began turning over the pages with Vicky looking over her shoulder. 'Maybe this will tell us something. Yes, here we are. Sunday the twenty-ninth of June. *Meeting Jake tomorrow – at last!! Can't believe it's really happening. I know I won't sleep a wink tonight!* Well, that's a partial answer – and the start of a whole new line of enquiry. Mrs Prescott, has Daisy ever mentioned a person called Jake? A boy at school, for example?'

The housekeeper slowly shook her head. 'Not that I remember . . . I mean, I may have heard her and her friends talking about boys or teachers . . . when she brought them round after school and so on . . . but she never said anything about them to me. Do you think she was going to meet this boy the day she disappeared?'

'It certainly looks as if she was going to meet someone,' said Vicky, 'and from what she's written it was someone she hadn't actually seen before.'

'I don't understand,' Mrs Prescott repeated. 'Is she referring to a pen friend, do you think? She's never mentioned one.'

'Does she spend a lot of time on her computer?'

'I've really no idea. She certainly spends a lot of time in here playing her music. Sometimes she plays it rather loud and if her father's in the house he shouts at her to turn down the volume. I suppose she watches the television but I don't know about the computer. I wouldn't hear that, would I?'

'Not unless she plays noisy computer games,' Vicky agreed and received a vague nod in return. It appeared that Mrs Prescott was unfamiliar with that form of entertainment.

Sukey went back to the open wardrobe. 'According to her diary, this was obviously a very important, exciting meeting, so I think we can assume she'd have wanted to look her best. Will you have a look among these things and see if there's anything missing, such as a special outfit she was particularly fond of?'

Mrs Prescott spent some time rummaging through the garments on the rail. 'There's one she ordered quite recently from one of those,' she said, indicating an untidy heap of catalogues on the floor. 'She was so thrilled with it that she tried it on straight away and showed it to me. It looked absolutely lovely on her.' A sudden rush of tears made her grope blindly in her pocket for a handkerchief.

When she was calmer, Sukey said gently, 'Is it in the wardrobe?'

Mrs Prescott scrubbed her eyes and put the handkerchief away before saying in a hoarse whisper, 'That's what I've been looking for, and no, it isn't there. She must have been wearing it when . . . oh, dear God, what am I going to say to her parents? I let her get away with too much . . . I should have been firmer with her.' She clasped her head in both hands and began rocking to and fro in her distress.

'We need to talk some more,' said Vicky. 'Perhaps we could go downstairs and have a cup of tea?'

It was after eight o'clock when Sukey and Vicky, the latter having briefly reported the result of their visit to the Hewitts' house on her mobile phone, returned to headquarters. They were immediately summoned to DCI Leach's office, where DS Rathbone was also awaiting them.

'We've listed the items and bagged each one separately, sir,' Vicky explained, 'although we've no reason to suppose that the mysterious Jake ever even saw, let alone handled any of them. According to the diary, the planned meeting on the thirtieth of June was their first.'

'And almost certainly their last,' Leach commented grimly.

'The diary seems to point to something I've suspected for some time: some pervert's been grooming her through an Internet chat room. We have of course already taken her computer for examination by our experts and they should be able to find out who she's been exchanging information with. It's obvious from your previous reports that the poor kid, if not emotionally starved, was at least in need of some kind of support to compensate for the lack of attention from her parents.' He referred back to the list of items and picked up the fashion catalogue. 'I see the housekeeper has marked the outfit she thinks Daisy was probably wearing when she disappeared. That'll be a great help if the Super decides to set up a *Crimewatch* reconstruction.'

'That could be tricky, sir,' Sukey pointed out. 'We can't be sure which of two possible routes she took, although it seems almost certain she was picked up in a car so it's unlikely to have been the field path.'

'Which explains why there was no sign of a disturbance along that route,' said Leach. 'By the way, have Daisy's parents been informed of this new development?'

'Not yet, sir. They're away for the weekend but the housekeeper has a contact number. She asked us if she should tell them and we advised her to wait until we could check with you.'

Leach nodded. 'Quite right, but they should be put in the picture as soon as possible. I'll report to the Super and see if he wants to handle that himself.' He put the diary back in the bag, closed it and picked up the phone. 'You two might as well go home now,' he said as he pressed buttons. 'Report to me in the incident room first thing on Monday. Well done both of you,' he added, almost as an afterthought.

'I can't remember the last time I went so long without food,' Vicky complained as she and Sukey left the building and headed for the car park. 'Chris is on duty tonight – some rotary club dinner or other – but he's promised to leave me something I can put in the microwave.' Vicky's partner, who had been given cookery lessons from an early age by his Italian grandmother, was head chef at a five star hotel on the outskirts of Bristol.

'Lucky you!' said Sukey with feeling. 'Chris's food is to

die for. Still, I mustn't grumble; my dinner can go in the microwave as well, but it's only a supermarket special.'

'Well, *buon appetito* anyway,' said Vicky cheerfully. 'Enjoy the weekend.'

Traffic was light and Sukey reached home a little after nine o'clock. Despite feeling hungry, she felt almost too tired to eat and as soon as she had taken off her jacket and dumped her bag on the floor she sank into a comfortable chair and closed her eyes. She had almost dozed off when her telephone rang.

'Where have you been?' Harry demanded. 'I've called twice and left messages. Is everything all right?'

The concern in his voice gave her a feeling of comfort, like having a warm shawl thrown over her shoulders. 'Yes, I'm quite all right, thanks, just tired. Been working late, big things happening.'

'Which case?' he asked eagerly.

Sukey smiled to herself at the change in his tone. 'So now we know why you're so keen to contact me,' she teased him. 'And here was I thinking it was my safety you were concerned with.'

'You know it was. Why do you keep misjudging me?'

'Just kidding. Look Harry, I've only just got in, I'm flaked out and I haven't eaten since heaven knows when. Have you got anything special to tell me?'

'I just wanted to bring you up to date with my researches. I've come across a few interesting facts but nothing that can't wait. Will you be working tomorrow?'

'I sincerely hope not.'

'Then how about lunch?'

'That'd be great.'

'Right, I'll pick you up at twelve. Sleep well.'

'I intend to, once I've eaten. Good night Harry, see you tomorrow.' She put the phone down and went with a light heart into the kitchen to prepare her belated supper.

On Saturday morning Sukey awoke after a deep, refreshing sleep to find that the recent spell of unsettled weather had given way to blue sky and bright sunshine, with the temperature steadily climbing to the upper twenties Celsius. Dressed in jeans and a bright yellow T-shirt, she ate her breakfast on the terrace before going to her computer to work on her report

of the previous day's events. She had just finished it when
Harry rang her doorbell. 'I'll be down in a minute,' she told
him over the newly installed intercom.

'Make sure you bring a hat and some sun lotion, it's going
to be a scorcher,' he called back.

Ten minutes later they were on the M5 motorway, heading
south. 'I thought you might fancy a whiff of sea air,' he said.
'I've discovered a very nice Italian restaurant in Cleveden
with a view over the estuary. After lunch, I thought we might
take a boat trip. How does that grab you?'

'It sounds lovely.' Sukey sat back in her seat with a sigh
of contentment.

'So what sort of week have you had?' he asked. 'I guess
it was pretty gruelling if yesterday was anything to go by.'

'Yesterday was the first day we saw any real action. All I
can tell you is that we're following a new line of enquiry in
one case and waiting for the result of forensic tests in another.'

Harry gave a sigh of mock frustration. 'What's the use of
having a girlfriend in the police force if I can't get the occa-
sional scoop?' he lamented.

'You get the chance to do some off the record sleuthing for
me,' Sukey pointed out. 'What about those interesting facts
you were talking about last night?'

'I could of course do a *quid pro quo*,' he said without taking
his eyes off the road. 'Interesting facts in exchange for new
line of enquiry, for example.'

'That wasn't part of the bargain,' she protested, and he took
his left hand off the wheel for a moment and patted her knee.

'Just kidding. Well, first of all I managed to track down
one of the estate agents who valued Parson's Acre for Muriel
Minchin when she was thinking of moving into sheltered
accommodation.'

'Oh, well done! Was he able to help?'

'Possibly. That is, he remembers doing the valuation and
for what it's worth he gave me the figure he quoted. It was
several years ago so it's quite likely increased in value since
then, but that doesn't concern us for the moment. What is interesting is that this chap – his name's Burford and it so happens
he was working for Weaver and Morris at the time – is quite
definite that no details were ever made public because the firm
was never instructed to put the property on the market.'

Sukey frowned. 'That doesn't add anything to what we know already.'

'Ah, but there's a bit extra. Burford recalls that when he and the manager were discussing the property there was someone – a workman, he thinks – in the office at the time. It's just possible that this person overheard the conversation and passed the information on to someone he knew was interested in the property. Or used it himself, of course.'

'You reckon he might be a clue to the mystery caller?'

'It's possible, don't you think?'

'Any chance of tracking him down?'

'I had a chat with the secretary at W and M and she's promised to check her records and see if she can find out if they had any workmen in on the day in question and who they were working for.'

'What about the auction when Muriel bought the property? Did you find out who handled it?'

'I did, but they don't keep a record of unsuccessful bidders unless one of them asks to be notified if a similar property becomes available, and it appears that didn't apply in this case. Still, you never know, the secretary might come up with something.'

They had left the motorway and were heading for the seafront. Harry found a vacant parking bay. The tide was full and they sat quietly for a few moments enjoying the glittering reflection of the sun on the water. Sukey broke the silence. 'So is that all you have to tell me?' she asked.

'There is a bit more, but whether it helps I'm not too sure. I checked the planning records and as we suspected there were no applications for permission to develop any of the land adjacent to Parson's Acre, or for change of use from agricultural land to housing. So no joy there, I'm afraid.'

'And that's it?'

'Apart from Mrs Clutterbuck,' said Harry, rather smugly Sukey thought. 'She's a gem,' he went on in response to her quizzical look, 'the archetypal ancient retainer. Well, cleaning lady, actually, but she's "done" for every owner of Parson's Acre since the one before Muriel. It seems he died in an accident shortly after moving in, and when first Muriel and then Adelaide also popped their clogs unexpectedly she decided there must be a curse on the place. She's going to warn Leonora at the first opportunity.'

Sukey shook her head in disbelief. 'It's true Adelaide's death was entirely unexpected, but Muriel was pushing seventy and had more than one stroke, which isn't unusual at that age. Did you manage to find out what happened to the previous owner?'

'As it happens I did. He was a man called Edward Cox, a bachelor and by all accounts a bit of a lush, who was in the habit of wandering about in the garden during the night with his bottle of scotch. He moved in before the site was properly cleared and there was still some builders' rubble and stuff lying about. It seems he tripped over a heap of bricks in the dark, fell head first into the ornamental pond, cracked his head on the bottom and drowned. It was only half full, but the post-mortem revealed that he was so full of booze he probably passed out before he landed.'

'So there was nothing suspicious about his death?'

'Evidently not – unless you go along with Mrs Clutterbuck. She believes there's a prehistoric burial ground on the site and the dead are taking their revenge on whoever disturbs them. I checked with the president of the local history society but he just laughed and said it's a load of old codswallop and Mrs C is a bit batty anyway. Just the same, it is a bit of a coincidence, don't you think?'

'Coincidences do happen,' said Sukey. She gave a sudden chuckle. 'Does Leonora know about this all this? Should we advise her to heed these awful warnings?'

'Oh, I've already told Leonora about Mrs Clutterbuck,' said Harry gleefully. 'She can't wait to meet her.' He checked his watch. 'Come on, let's have some lunch.'

TWENTY-THREE

When Sukey awoke on Sunday morning she experienced the same contented glow that had lingered after her evening with Harry the previous Saturday. She lay in bed for a while, happily reliving their day together: the lunch at a table overlooking the Bristol Channel, the stroll along Clevedon pier where they lingered to chat to some anglers, the couple of hours spent wandering round the shops and strolling along the front to watch the miniature railway chugging round its circular track with crowds of excited children on board. In the evening they took a boat trip to Sharpness. With her eyes closed Sukey recalled the splendour of the sinking sun, the gentle splash of the vessel's wake against the bank, the warmth of Harry's arm round her shoulders and the softness of the breeze that fanned her cheek. His goodnight kiss after he dropped her at her door was slow and passionate. When at last it ended he murmured, 'Maybe soon?' and she had pressed her cheek against his and whispered, 'Maybe.'

She had dozed off again when her phone rang. 'How did you sleep?' he asked.

'Like a log,' she replied softly.

'Me too. What's your programme for today?'

'I thought I'd go to the gym for a workout and maybe a swim. How about you?'

'I'm off to cover a political rally down in Bridgewater.'

She gave a sympathetic chuckle. 'Have fun.'

'You too. Be in touch again soon. Bye.'

'Bye.' She put the phone down. A stab of disappointment that he hadn't asked for another date was tempered with an underlying sense of relief that he was respecting her reluctance to rush things.

'The DNA boys really went to town once the Assistant Chief Constable gave both our cases Category A rating,' DS Rathbone informed his team when they assembled in the incident room on Monday morning. 'We've now had the results of the DNA samples taken from the brush and comb belonging to Sharon Swann, and you will not be surprised to hear that they match those taken from the lay-by victim. So at last we've got an ID. Now we have to wait for the sample taken from Brian Gordon to be checked against the one from the foetus, but I don't have much doubt in that direction. In fact,' he put down the reports he had been referring to and rubbed his hands together in satisfaction, 'I think we can safely say we've got this case wrapped up.'

For once, Sukey was unable to share his understandable enthusiasm at what appeared to be the successful conclusion of a case. Her mind flew to the two women whose lives would be devastated – Jessie Swann and Miriam Gordon.

'Sharon's mother will have to be told right away,' Rathbone continued as if he read her thoughts. 'We know she's pretty fragile. The family GP has been very helpful and he should be asked for advice before we break the news as he might want to prescribe something to help her deal with the shock. She'll need the support of an FLO as well, of course; I'll organize that but in the meantime I'd like Sukey and Vicky to contact Doctor Hogan and then go and see Mrs Swann. It'll be doubly hard for her to learn her daughter was not only murdered but pregnant, but it's more important than ever that you get as much information as possible out of her about the girl's close contacts of either sex. If necessary, go back to the school. I'm in no doubt that Gordie is Sharon's pet name for Brian Gordon, but it would be good to find a witness who can confirm it.'

'We'll do our best, Sarge,' said Sukey.

'We'll pick him up the minute we've got the final bit of evidence in the bag,' Rathbone continued. 'Now, the rest of you are back on the Daisy Hewitt case and the hunt for Jake. We've managed to get hold of an outfit in the same style and colour as the one we believe Daisy was wearing the day she disappeared and this will be shown to the media later on this morning. I understand Superintendent Baird is already liaising with a TV channel with a view to setting up a reconstruction. The IT experts have been working over the weekend but so far they haven't found any leads. Facebook was their obvious first line of enquiry as it's what most of the kids seem to use. She has an account with them, but so far none of her contacts look in the least suspicious. There are some other chat lines and it'll take time to work through all of them.'

Doctor Hogan received their news without surprise. 'I was expecting this, and I believe Jessie is prepared for it,' he said. 'I'm reluctant to increase her medication and if, as you say, there will be one of your people giving her support, I suggest you give that person my number and tell her to call me if she has any concerns. In any case, I'd like to be kept informed.'

'We'll certainly do that,' Sukey assured him. 'We're on our way to see her now and the FLO will join us there.'

'Good.' He ended the call without giving her time to say anything further.

Sukey passed the message to Vicky and started the engine.
'Right, let's go.'

Jessie Swann's face was pale but her hand, as she closed
the door after admitting them, was steady. 'I know why you're
here,' she said in a toneless voice. She led the way into the
sitting room and sat down on the shabby sofa with Sukey and
Vicky on either side of her.

Sukey took her hand. 'We have to tell you that we recently
found the body of a teenage girl. She was wearing an unusual
ring; we showed you a photo of it and you said you'd seen
Sharon wearing it – or one like it. Do you remember?'

Jessie's mouth twisted in a sad hint of a smile. 'Of course
I remember. It was found on the body in the lay-by, the one
that's been on the TV news, wasn't it? And now you've come
to tell me it's Sharon's body, haven't you?'

'I'm afraid so,' Sukey said gently. 'We're so very sorry.'

'It's a relief to know for certain.' Jessie's voice, though flat,
was surprisingly steady. 'I've had a feeling all along she was
dead because she's never stayed away this long before, but I
just didn't want to believe it. Stupid, isn't it?'

'It's quite understandable,' said Vicky.

'You're probably expecting me to break down and cry
myself sick,' Jessie went on, 'but I've done that a hundred
times already in secret. I've always been afraid something
like this would happen . . . I used to tell her she'd come to a
bad end but she always laughed at me . . . said she could take
care of herself.' She waited for a moment, and then said softly,
'You will find the bastard who did it, won't you?'

'We intend to, but we need your help,' said Vicky. 'There
are one or two things we're concerned about. First, we don't
think you should be on your own for the time being so we've
arranged for someone – she's what we call a Family Liaison
Officer – to stay with you and give you some support until
you've had time to get over the shock. By the way, where are
your two other children?'

'They're spending the day with a friend. She's going to
take them to the pictures later on and then bring them back
here for tea.' She put a hand up to her eyes. 'What am I going
to tell them?'

'That's the sort of problem the FLO can help you with,' said
Sukey. 'She should be here fairly soon. She's very experienced

in sad situations like this. Now, do you feel up to answering a few more questions?' Jessie nodded. 'You remember we found Sharon's diary with a reference to someone called "Gordie". She was going to meet him – we assume it was a man – the day she disappeared. Are you sure you never heard her mention that name?'

'Quite sure.'

'When you told us you'd seen her wearing the ring, and we said we understood a girl at school had given it to her, you said –' here Vicky referred to her notebook – '"more like she got it off some feller she's been seeing". Apart from Gordie, do you remember her mentioning any other man's name?'

Jessie's mouth turned down at the corners and she shook her head. 'She stopped telling me things a long time ago,' she said dolefully.

'So what made you think she'd been seeing a man?'

'There was something different about her – a sort of sparkle, and she started wearing more sexy clothes. She used to do babysitting jobs so I suppose that's where she got the money for them.'

'Didn't you ever question her at all?'

'Once when she was getting ready to go out I said something like, "You're looking extra nice – are you meeting someone special?" and she went a bit red but she didn't give a proper answer.'

'And that was the only time you asked her about her friends or people she was meeting?'

'Just lately, yes. She used to chat away quite freely, until . . .'

'Until you noticed this change in her attitude?'

'Well, yes.'

'Did she have a mobile phone?' asked Sukey.

'Of course she did,' said Jessie, evidently surprised that anyone would ask such a question about a teenager. 'Spent half her time rabbiting away on it to her friends. At least, I suppose they were friends. She never told me who they were or what they were talking about.'

'Please, Jessie, think carefully,' said Sukey, 'and try to recall any name she might have used. For example, when her phone rang and she answered, maybe you heard her say something like "Hi Andy!" or "Hi Jackie!" Is there a name that you heard her use quite often?'

Jessie frowned and closed her eyes as if concentrating. After what seemed an age to the two detectives she said, 'Tel. She used to talk to someone she called Tel. Funny sort of name – short for something I suppose but I can't think what.'

'It might be Terry, which is sometimes short for Terence or Teresa,' said Vicky. 'Well done, Jessie.' She made a note of both names. 'Someone at school will probably know who he or she is, and they might help us track down "Gordie". Does any other name occur to you?'

'I don't think so. Most of the time when she answered her phone she just said "Hi".'

'Never mind, this is something to go on. Now, is there anything you want to ask us?'

Jessie closed her eyes and clenched her hands until the knuckles became white. 'How did she die?' she asked in a low voice.

'She was strangled.'

'I see.' She sat for a few seconds, apparently deep in thought. Then she said, 'Is that all you have to tell me?'

'There is one more thing,' said Sukey gently, 'and I'm afraid this is going to be very upsetting for you.'

'I think I can guess.' The next words were barely audible. 'She was pregnant, wasn't she?'

'You knew?'

'I recognized the signs.' A muscle twitched at the corner of Jessie's mouth. She took a deep breath. 'And that's why he killed her, isn't it?' Tears welled up in her eyes and flowed slowly down her cheeks, but her voice was devoid of expression. For a moment, it was as if she were talking in her sleep. 'So I've lost a daughter and a grandchild.' There was a long silence. Then, without warning, she made a grab at Sukey's hand and said brokenly, 'Please, please, don't let him get away with it.'

'We won't,' Sukey assured her.

There was a knock at the door. 'That'll be the FLO,' said Vicky. 'Shall I go?'

'It might not be easy tracking down Sharon's friend Tel,' Sukey remarked as, after leaving Jessie in the care of the Family Liaison Officer, they returned to the car. 'The term's finished and the kids and staff have all gone off on holiday.'

'Yes, I was thinking about that,' said Vicky. 'I doubt if she's one of Daisy's crowd so Mrs Prescott probably won't know her.'

'Zareen Hussein might know.' Sukey suggested. 'She put us on to Sharon – why don't we ask her?'

'It's worth a try,' Vicky agreed. 'Have you got her number?'

'Got it right here.' Sukey keyed it in and was answered almost immediately. After a brief conversation she said, 'Thank you so much, Mr Hussein,' ended the call and slipped the phone back into her bag. 'Well, that's OK,' she told Vicky. 'We can go to the house right away and I can see Zareen for a few minutes.'

'That's good,' said Vicky as she settled into her seat. 'I take it she's feeling better?'

'Yes, but he's still in protective mode – only one person is allowed to see her and I'm afraid that has to be me because she knows me.'

'No problem.'

As on the previous visit a week ago, both Zareen's parents remained in the room. The girl was sitting on the sofa beside her mother, who stood up to greet Sukey and invited her to sit on a chair facing them. 'I'm glad to see you looking so much better,' Sukey said warmly. It was true; Zareen's face had filled out, her eyes were bright and she had lost the fragile appearance of someone recently brought back from a severe illness. 'Your father tells me you still tire easily and I promise not to stay long.'

'Have you found Daisy?' Zareen asked anxiously.

'I'm afraid not, although of course we're still hoping for news of her,' said Sukey, 'but there is another girl we'd like to talk to. We don't know her full name, but we think it might be Terry or Teresa because at least one of her friends calls her "Tel". Does that . . .'

Before Sukey could finish, Zareen exclaimed, 'Terry Burden! All her friends call her "Tel".'

'You know her?'

'She's in my class . . . she's best friends with Sharon Swann. They spend ages together and they whisper and giggle a lot.' Zareen made no attempt to hide her disdain of such infantile behaviour.

'That's brilliant. Have you any idea where she lives?'

Zareen shook her head. 'Sorry.'

'Never mind, I'm sure we can find it.'

'What about the ring? Did you find out about that?'

'Yes, thanks to your help.' Anxious to avoid having to reveal possibly distressing details, Sukey hastily stood up to leave. Mr Hussein went to the door and opened it for her. 'I'm delighted to see Zareen looking so much better,' she said warmly. 'It's obvious you and your wife are taking great care of her.'

For the first time, something like a smile softened Hussein's impassive features. 'Thank you,' he said. 'She is very dear to us.'

When Sukey and Vicky returned to the incident room they learned that there was to be a press conference at headquarters at midday. In the half hour that remained they told DS Rathbone of their visit to Zareen and the information she had given them about Sharon's friend Terry Burdon. 'The school's closed for the summer holiday,' said Sukey. 'We'll need to get her address from the local authority.'

'So get on with it,' he said. 'Mind how you tackle her though. By the time you track her down she'll probably know her friend's dead. She could be a bit emotional, so be gentle with her. What we need is confirmation that Sharon was having it off with Brian Gordon. That should be enough for us to pull him in for more questioning while we wait for the DNA results.'

TWENTY-FOUR

It was Thursday by the time they were able to arrange a visit to the fourth floor flat where Terry Burdon lived with her mother, a faded blonde in her mid thirties, who peered short-sightedly at the IDs that Sukey and Vicky held up and said, 'I'm Rita Burdon, Terry's Mum, you'd better come in.' She led them into a cramped sitting room where the television was showing a repeat of an old cartoon comedy. She switched it off with the remote and indicated a pair of armchairs, each covered with the same shabby brown upholstery as the matching sofa. 'She's in her room,' she said. 'She's upset because they had a row and all this time she's been thinking Sharon was still mad at her and that was why she never answered her calls. When we heard the news on the telly on Monday evening she broke down and sobbed her heart out. She's hardly stopped crying since.'

'Do you know what the row was about?' asked Vicky.

'Something about a feller Sharon was seeing, I think. I don't know the details. She just keeps crying and saying she never meant the things she said.'

'They must have been very close friends,' said Sukey. 'I'm sure she'd want us to find out who killed Sharon. Do you think she feels up to answering a few questions?'

'I'll go and ask her.'

She went out of the room but left the door open. They heard her voice; the words were indistinct but they had the impression she was trying to coax her daughter to speak to them. Several minutes passed before they heard the sound of a toilet flushing and a door closing. Eventually Rita returned leading a red-eyed girl with long, untidy blonde hair. Her own eyes were wet and she brushed away the tears with the back of her hand.

'This is my daughter Terry,' she said. 'Her friends call her Tel,' she added with a faint, slightly apologetic smile. She guided the girl to the sofa and sat down next to her.

'Terry, we're so very sorry about your friend Sharon,' Sukey began. The girl nodded and choked back a sob. 'We're doing everything we can to find out who killed her and we think you may be able to help us. It will mean asking you one or two questions. Is that all right with you?'

'Yes.' The word was more a sigh than a whisper.

'Is it true that you and Sharon had a disagreement?' asked Vicky. There was the same barely audible reply. 'Can you tell us what it was about?'

Terry scrubbed her eyes with a sodden paper tissue, swallowed and said, 'She was seeing someone – a feller.'

'One of the boys at school?'

'Don't think so.'

'An older man, perhaps?' There was no reply. 'Anyone you know?'

After a long pause the girl said, 'She wouldn't say who it was. Said it was a secret – she'd promised not to tell.'

'Is that what upset you?'

'We were mates, we told each other everything. I couldn't understand . . . and then I thought . . . I was almost sure there was a problem. I thought maybe she was . . . you know . . .'

'Pregnant?' Sukey prompted. Terry nodded. More tears began to flow. Rita silently held out a box of tissues. She took one and used it vigorously for several seconds, ending by blowing her nose.

'I asked her about it and she said she was, but it was all right, he was going to look after her. I said she was a fool to let it happen and a fool to believe him. I reminded her what happened to Jilly Foster.'

'Another friend of theirs who got dumped when she told her boyfriend she was up the duff,' Rita explained.

'She got really mad at me then,' Terry went on, 'said it was none of my business and I was only jealous because I didn't have a boyfriend.' The girl became increasingly indignant as she relived her resentment at being excluded from her friend's confidence. 'I told her if she didn't trust me I wouldn't be her friend any more and all she said was "suit yourself" and walked off. And that was the last time I saw her. I kept calling her mobile to say I was sorry but she never answered.' Grief took hold once again and the last words were barely distinguishable.

'Didn't you wonder why she didn't come to school?' asked Sukey when she was calmer.

It was Rita who answered. 'You obviously didn't know Sharon. She only turned up when she felt like it. Her Mum was always in trouble over it.'

'Yes, we heard she had a record of truancy,' Vicky agreed.

When Terry was calmer, Sukey said, 'We found Sharon's diary. She mentioned going to see someone called "Gordie". Have you any idea who that might be?'

Terry looked blank. 'Never heard her mention anyone with that name. D'you reckon that's the feller she was seeing?'

'We're pretty sure it is. It's obviously a pet name of some kind – or possibly it's short for his real name.' Sukey waited for a moment for a sign of recognition, but none came. Then she said, 'Did you know that Sharon was very interested in computers?'

'Of course I did. She used to turn up for IT more often than not; she was best in class.'

'We understand the IT teacher at your school is a man called Brian Gordon.' Vicky laid extra emphasis on the surname.

For a moment Terry looked bemused. Then, despite her distress, she almost burst out laughing as she grasped the implication. 'You reckon Sharon might have been having it off with that boring old stick? You've gotta be joking!'

'Some girls fancy older men,' Vicky pointed out. 'I take it you were in the same IT class as Sharon?'

'Yes.'

'How was the class organized?'

Terry shrugged. 'We each had our own computer and we worked from a manual. If we had a problem we'd put up a hand and Mister G would come and help us get it sorted.'

'Please think very carefully, Terry,' said Vicky earnestly. 'Can you remember Mr Gordon spending any extra time with Sharon? Or Sharon making a particular habit of asking Mr Gordon for help?'

Terry's expression was scornful. 'If you think there was anything between them, you're out of your tree,' she said. 'Sharon enjoyed IT; that's the reason she went to the class. She hardly ever needed to ask for help – in fact she used to help me sometimes if he was busy.'

'Did Mr Gordon praise her for that?'

Terry shook her head. 'That's not his way. Never singles anyone out, not like some teachers.'

'He gave you a good end of term report though, didn't he?' Rita reminded her.

The girl shrugged. 'Yeah, well . . .' She lapsed into silence.

With a quick exchange of glances the two detectives agreed that there was nothing to be gained from further questioning. 'Thank you Terry, you've been really helpful,' said Sukey warmly. She received a tremulous half smile in return.

On the way home Vicky said, 'You're happy Terry didn't finger the boring old stick, aren't you?'

Sukey nodded. 'Yes, I am. I know everyone from the SIO downwards is convinced Brian Gordon is their man, but I've had my doubts all along.'

'He's not in the clear yet,' Vicky reminded her. 'There's still the DNA test result to come. Just the same, our Sarge is going to be very disappointed with us.'

Sukey chuckled. 'I know. So are a lot of people who thought the case was all but done and dusted.'

'There's no need to look so pleased with yourself,' said Vicky. 'Don't forget that if Gordon isn't Gordie we don't have much in the way of other leads. If he really is out of the frame we could do with one of your flashes of inspiration to make up for it!'

'I'll work on it,' Sukey promised.

There was more disappointment for the team the following day when the results of the test on Brian Gordon's DNA came in, proving beyond doubt that he was not the father of the child Sharon was carrying when she died.

Sukey set off for home on Friday evening in a somewhat pessimistic state of mind, despite the fact that she felt a sense of relief that the cloud had been lifted from Brian Gordon and his family. DCI Leach had given her the task of informing him that he was no longer under suspicion, and she decided to call at the house to deliver the news in person.

'He was over the moon when I told him,' she confided to Vicky on her return. 'He was just off to the hospital to fetch his wife home – she had a little girl yesterday. It was really touching. I felt a bid dewy eyed myself!'

'Like I've said before, you're all heart,' Vicky said affectionately.

'It's heads that are needed from now on,' she had replied disconsolately, foreseeing hours of painstaking sifting through witness statements in the hope of finding some clue that had somehow escaped the notice of countless pairs of eyes.

On reaching home she dumped her bag, took off her jacket and reached for the phone.

'Hi!' said Harry, 'Is this a social call or do you want my expert help in solving a tricky case?'

'Both in a way, I suppose,' she replied, 'at least, I need cheering up after a frustrating few days.'

'Then you've come to the right person. I was going to call you anyway. How about a drink and a bite at the Jersey Lily?'

'That sounds perfect. Just give me time to freshen up.'

'I'll call by in half an hour.'

The pub, named for a former royal mistress, was only a

short walk from their respective homes. They found seats in
a corner by the window; Harry bought two glasses of red wine
and carried them to the table. He sat down and their eyes met
as they raised their glasses before drinking.

'Sorry I haven't been in touch all week,' he said. 'I've been
covering this political scandal – maybe you've heard about
it. It's been making the headlines in the *Echo* all week.'

'I've hardly looked at the papers, apart from checking our
latest press release to make sure it's been quoted accurately,'
she confessed, 'and I don't suppose you've found time to read
about what we've been doing while you've been dabbling in
politics?'

'You mean about the Daisy Hewitt case?' said Harry. 'One
of my colleagues has been covering that. Any news of . . . oh,
excuse me.' He broke off as his mobile phone rang. 'Harry
Matthews . . . hello . . . what? Oh my Gordon Bennett! With
you in half an hour!' He switched off and said, 'Wow! There's
a turn up for the book!'

Sukey was staring at him with her glass halfway to her
mouth. 'What was that you said?'

'A turn up for the book? Surely you've heard that . . .'

'No, before that. Gordon something.'

'You mean "Oh my Gordon Bennett?" That's something my
Dad says when he hears something shocking. The story goes
that the guy in question was a lush who peed in the fireplace
in the house of his prospective in-laws during the engagement
party they were throwing for him and their daughter. Needless
to say, the wedding never took place,' he added with a chuckle.

Sukey's brain had suddenly gone into overdrive. 'So what
prompted it this time?'

'The MP at the centre of the scandal who's been denying
all the allegations against him has been arrested. Look,' he
went on with a glance at his watch, 'I'm sorry but I'm afraid
I'm going to have to cut this evening short. I simply have to
follow this up.' He picked up his glass and gulped the
remainder of his wine.

'There's no need to apologize – on the contrary,' Sukey
assured him. She finished her own drink and took out her mobile
phone. The sudden rise in her pulse rate had nothing to do with
either the wine or the company of the man she was falling in
love with. 'There's something I have to follow up as well.'

He gave her a questioning look. 'Was it something I said?'

The bar was filling and Sukey had noticed a couple on the next table apparently taking an interest in their conversation. She leaned forward and said in a low voice, 'It was, actually. Harry, it's just possible you've helped me solve a murder. I can't explain now, but . . .'

'Understood. Let's go.' Outside, he gave her a quick peck on the cheek and with a wave and a hasty, 'Bye, I'll be in touch,' he hurried up the road.

Sukey, with her phone to her ear, followed more slowly. At the end of the conversation she said, 'Thank you so much; that could be really important . . . yes, of course I'll let you know . . . goodbye.'

Next, Sukey called DS Rathbone.

TWENTY-FIVE

'I'm drowning my sorrows with a pint and a bag of crisps in the Jolly Sailor,' said Rathbone when he took Sukey's call. 'Is there any chance you've got something to cheer me up?'

'I'll let you be the best judge of that, Sarge.'

'All right,' he said without any noticeable hint of optimism in his tone, 'let's have it.'

'I've just heard something that might give us a new lead in the Sharon Swann case.'

He listened in silence while she gave him a brief account of her conversation with Harry. Then he said, 'Of course I've heard of that expression, but it's very old-fashioned.' There was a pause during which Sukey heard the sound of swallowing. 'I don't see how it helps us,' Rathbone resumed, 'unless . . . hang on a minute!' She could almost see him suddenly becoming alert. 'That computer technician the school uses – isn't his name Bennett?'

'Spot on, Sarge.'

'So maybe his given name's Gordon.'

'I'm pretty sure Mr Bradley said it was Joshua,' said Sukey. 'He's a former student at the school who's set up his own

business called Bennett Computer Services. He and Sharon
must surely have come into contact at some time when he
was servicing the school equipment; we know she made a
point of going to computer classes even though she skipped
most of the others. Supposing they started a relationship that
got out of hand and when she became pregnant he—'

Her excitement evidently communicated itself to Rathbone,
who said in a phlegmatic tone, 'Let's not get too carried away.
You obviously reckon it's a hot new lead but it could be
nothing but a coincidence.'

'But Sarge . . .'

'The expression "Oh my Gordon Bennett",' he continued,
in the somewhat patronizing way he had been in the habit of
using during her probationary period as a DC, 'is hardly the
sort of thing one of today's teenagers would use, is it? So
why would she think of calling anyone "Gordie"?'

'I thought of that, Sarge, but it occurred to me that it might
mean something to Jessie Swann.'

'OK,' he conceded after another short interval. 'I suppose
Sharon might have heard her mother use it. But there still
doesn't have to be a connection,' he went on. 'The kid may
have hit on the name Gordie for a totally different reason,'
there was the sound of another swallow before he added, 'but
have a word with the mother anyway.'

'I already have, Sarge,' she replied, trying not to sound
smug. 'I was a bit concerned that a call from me might give
the impression that we were about to make an arrest, but fortunately her FLO answered the phone so I was able to speak
to her first.'

'And?'

'Jessie admitted straight away that she uses the expression
quite often. She sounded a bit embarrassed actually. She said
she picked it up from her own mother, who used it a lot. Sharon
must have heard her say it plenty of times, but as far as Jessie
knows the girl never said it herself. In fact, she once made fun
of her mother for saying it. She said it was a stupid expression.'

'And Doctor Hogan told you he thought Sharon's boyfriend
worked in computers, didn't he?' said Rathbone. It was evident
from his change of tone that he was beginning to take the
new development seriously.

'Exactly, Sarge. It struck me straight away that when he

told her his name she might have thought of her mother's favourite saying. So if Josh Bennett is the man she was seeing she might have decided to call him Gordie as a kind of pet name, maybe as a joke. Or maybe so that anyone reading her diary wouldn't know who she was referring to.'

'It's certainly worth looking into,' said Rathbone. 'I'll have another pint while you find out as much as you can about Joshua Bennett of Bennett Computer Services and let me know what you come up with.'

'Will do, Sarge. And you have a nice weekend as well,' she muttered between her teeth after ending the call.

Back in her flat, she rummaged in her freezer for a prepared meal. She regarded it with some distaste as she put it in the microwave to defrost, thinking of the tasty supper she had been hoping to share with Harry. By way of consolation she treated herself to a second glass of red wine while looking for Joshua Bennett's company in the business section of the local telephone directory. The modest entry listed under the heading 'Computer Services' gave only a mobile number, which she called. The recorded message, spoken by a young-sounding female voice with a strong local accent, informed her that the office hours of Bennett Computer Services were from nine a.m. to five p.m. Monday to Friday and promised early attention to requests for assistance left outside those hours. She called Rathbone, found his phone was switched off and left a message asking for further instructions.

A call from Harry at around ten o'clock that evening went some way to raising her spirits. 'Sorry I had to dash off,' he said. 'I hope I didn't spoil your evening.'

'No problem,' she assured him. 'I had some dashing off to do myself.'

'So I gathered. I seem to have said something important. Did you make an arrest and am I going to get some of the credit?'

'You gave me what may turn out to be some crucial information, which I've passed on to my sergeant. I can't say more than that at the moment – but if anything comes of it I'll put in a word for you,' she added with mock condescension.

'Much obliged I'm sure. Look, I'm going to be tied up tomorrow, but I hope to be free on Sunday. Dad has invited the two of us out to lunch.'

'That's very kind of him. Will his lady friend be with us?' To Harry's great delight, Major Matthews had recently become friendly with a retired lawyer, Lady Frederica Sinclair.

'No, Freddie's visiting an aged relative in Scotland so he's at a loose end. He particularly asked me to bring you along. He often refers to that evening when you and Gus joined us for dinner. He was so impressed with Gus, said he'd obviously been well brought up and you must be very proud of him.'

'I am, and it's nice of your Dad to say so.'

'Anyway, he's promised to take us to his golf club. We'll pick you up soon after twelve.'

'That sounds lovely. One thing though, if there are any further developments I may have to cry off.'

'We'll keep our fingers crossed then. Sleep well darling – sweet dreams.' He ended the call without waiting for her to reply. The last few words lingered in her ear like a snatch of music.

'It's nice of you to come to an old man's rescue,' said Major Matthews as he escorted Sukey and Harry to a table by a window overlooking the Severn estuary. The air was crystal clear and the water sparkled in the early afternoon sunshine that picked out the white sails of a small flotilla of yachts scudding along in a brisk breeze. 'Freddie and I often come here on a fine Sunday for lunch and a few holes,' he went on. 'I'm a bit lost when she's away.'

'It's very kind of you to include me, Major Matthews,' said Sukey warmly.

He wagged an admonitory finger at her and said roguishly, 'My name's George, remember? I thought we'd agreed to drop the formalities.'

'So we did. Sorry, George.'

'Right, now what are we going to eat?' There was a brief discussion while they made their choice. 'And what about drinks? Red wine for you, Sukey? Good. I'll have a beer. What about you, Harry? Sit down lad, you're making the place untidy,' he said with a touch of impatience, seeing his son still on his feet.

'Half of bitter for me, Dad, but I've just realized I left my mobile in the car. I'll be back in a minute.'

'I wonder he doesn't have the thing taped to his ear,'

Matthews said with a chuckle. He signalled to the waiter and gave their order, then turned to Sukey. 'I hope I'm not speaking out of turn, but I've noticed a big change in Harry lately and I believe it has a lot to do with you.'

'I hope it's a change for the better,' Sukey replied, keeping her tone light but being careful not to sound facetious.

'Very much so,' said Matthews earnestly. 'He's sleeping better for one thing, and he's generally a lot perkier. You know,' he leaned forward and continued in a confidential tone, 'he had a relationship some while ago that ended disastrously. Can't go into details of course,' he cleared his throat and took a swig from his glass, 'but it quite broke him up for a while. I began to think it had . . . well, sort of, put him off women for good. Since he's met you he's been . . . well, let's say I'm beginning to be more hopeful. Except, of course, that I'd hate for him to have another . . .'

'Disappointment?' said Sukey as he broke off in embarrassment. He nodded. 'I understand what you're trying to say,' she said quietly. 'Harry did confide in me a little . . . and he knows I've had a similar experience. We both understand that neither of us is ready to rush into another relationship without feeling quite sure it's the right thing to do.'

'Well, that's a relief.' He took another deep draught of his drink before saying, 'I hope you don't mind . . .'

'No, of course I don't.' She glanced over his shoulder and waved. 'Here he comes now, complete with mobile.'

'That was silly of me,' said Harry as he slipped into a chair and picked up his drink. 'If I'd done that anywhere in town it would probably have been nicked the minute my back was turned.'

'That's because there are too many crooks around and not enough bobbies on the beat these days,' his father declared. 'I'm sure you agree, don't you Sukey?'

'That's not her department, Dad, so get off your soapbox,' said Harry. He turned to Sukey. 'By the way, you remember me telling you about the superstitious Mrs Clutterbuck?'

'Adelaide's cleaning lady?' said Sukey.

'Right. There's one thing I forgot to mention. Adelaide suffered from arachnophobia.'

'That sounds pretty serious,' said Matthews, frowning. 'What are the symptoms?'

'The sufferer goes berserk at the sight of a spider,' said Harry with an indulgent smile. 'To quote Mrs C's words, "Miss Adelaide couldn't abide having one near her". Not that I imagine it helps much in the scheme of things.'

'Probably not,' Sukey agreed, 'but you never know, sometimes even the smallest scrap of information can turn out to be important.'

'I don't recall your mentioning a Mrs Clutterbuck, or a lady called Adelaide,' said Matthews, with a hint of reproach. 'Is this something to do with a story you're working on, Harry?'

'In a manner of speaking, but it's *sub rosa* at present so I can't say any more,' said Harry.

At that moment, his father spotted a three-masted sailing ship heading majestically up river. He pulled a small pair of binoculars from his pocket and followed the vessel's progress for a few moments while giving his companions an enthusiastic commentary. Shortly afterwards their food arrived and the conversation turned to more general topics. They were on their way back to the car when Sukey's mobile rang. Rathbone was on the line.

'We've got an address for that number you gave me. Bennett lives in Over Hampton. Pick me up at seven thirty sharp tomorrow morning.'

'Right, Sarge.'

'Development?' whispered Harry as he opened the car door for her.

'Could be.'

TWENTY-SIX

'He seems to be doing quite well,' commented DS Rathbone with a nod at the brand new van with the legend 'Bennett's Computer Services' and the mobile telephone number painted on the side. 'I doubt if he could have used that to tow a trailer full of bricks, though – it's too light and anyway it hasn't got a tow-bar.'

'There are still unidentified prints on the trailer,' Sukey reminded him. 'He might have had an accomplice.'

'True. Right, let's hear what he has to say for himself.'

They walked up the short path to the front door of the neat but undistinguished semi-detached house and rang the bell. The door was opened after a short interval by a young man dressed entirely in black with a half-eaten slice of toast in one hand. 'If it's about a job . . .' he began.

'Joshua Bennett?'

'Who wants to know?'

Rathbone gave their names and they showed their IDs. Bennett's eyes, almost black behind fashionable dark-rimmed glasses, scanned the badges and then fixed the detectives in an almost hypnotic stare. With his closely trimmed black hair and tight jeans and T-shirt that seemed to cling to his lithe figure like a second skin, he reminded Sukey of a panther.

'Who is it, Josh?' A young woman in a dressing gown appeared behind him and peered at the detectives over his shoulder. Her face was pale and her tousled hair fell round her face in loose strands. 'You're running late. If it's about a job, I can take the details and make an appointment.'

Bennett jabbed her with his elbow. 'Go back to the kitchen,' he said without taking his eyes off Rathbone.

'But . . .'

'Do as you're told.' Reluctantly, she vanished. Bennett took a bite from his toast before stepping to one side and holding the door open. 'You might as well come in,' he said with his mouth full. He ushered the detectives into the front room and closed the door behind them. 'So what's this all about?' He sat down in an easy chair, crossed his legs, put the last of the toast into his mouth and brushed away some invisible crumbs. Sukey had the impression that he was working hard at appearing relaxed.

'I take it you've no objection if we sit down,' said Rathbone with studied politeness.

Bennett waved a hand at two upright chairs. 'Feel free.' He lit a cigarette from a packet he took from the pocket of his jeans.

They sat down and pulled the chairs closer to Bennett. 'We're making enquiries into the murder of Sharon Swann,' said Rathbone.

Bennett drew on the cigarette before saying languidly, 'Sharon who?'

'Sharon Swann. The girl whose body was found in a lay-by a couple of miles or so from here. I take it you see the papers or watch the news on TV?'

The eyes behind the glasses narrowed a fraction. 'Oh, that one. Yeah, I've heard about it of course. Poor kid.' He gave a sorrowful shake of the head. 'I don't see what it's got to do with me, though.'

'We have reason to believe you may be able to assist us in our enquiries.'

Bennett frowned. 'I don't see how. I didn't even know the girl.'

'She was a student at Over Hampton Comprehensive School.'

'So was I, about ten years ago. What of it?'

'We understand that you have a contract to service their computer equipment.'

For the first time Sukey noticed a flicker of concern disturb the man's hitherto studiously detached attitude and there was a momentary hesitation before he asked, in a tone suggesting mild curiosity, 'What've they been saying? I haven't had any complaints.'

'We're not suggesting you have,' said Rathbone, 'but we're interested in the logistics of the job. For example, I assume your duties mean you spend most of your time in the computer department?'

'Where else?'

'So your work brings you into contact with the students?'

'There may be a class going on while I'm working, but I don't touch a piece of equipment that's in use.'

'Do you ever talk to the students?'

'Why should I? They're supposed to be working or listening to the teacher.'

'What about between lessons?'

'It's more likely I speak to the teacher about the job. Sometimes I have to take something away with me or order a spare part. Look,' Bennett adopted a more aggressive atti-tude, 'just what is this leading up to?'

'Mr Bennett,' Rathbone's voice assumed a steely tone, 'we have reason to believe that you are not being entirely honest with us. We think that on one of the occasions while working at the school you found an opportunity to strike up a conversation with Sharon Swann, the sixteen-year-old girl whose body was discovered recently hidden under a pile of builder's rubble.'

Bennett shook his head slowly from side to side. To a detached observer his slightly puzzled expression might have appeared genuine, but it struck Sukey, as she commented later to Vicky, that he might well have been prepared for a situation such as this. 'I just explained,' he said with a hint of exasperation, 'I didn't know her. As far as I know, I never set eyes on her.'

'Never? Sharon was a very attractive girl.' Rathbone's slightly tilted head and raised eyebrow were almost the equivalent of a sly wink, but there was no response from Bennett. 'Maybe you caught her eye and she looked back at you in a way that made you think you might be in with a chance.' He leaned forward and fixed Bennett with a penetrating stare. His voice took on a soft, menacing quality that Sukey had often heard him use when questioning a suspect whose stubborn resistance he was trying to overcome. 'I suggest that is exactly what happened and that it led to a meeting – out of school hours, of course – a meeting that led to the start of a sexual relationship. Maybe you even led her on with hints of something permanent. No doubt it was a lot of fun at the time, but after a while you got bored with her and wanted to end it. She became very demanding, maybe found out you were married and threatened to tell your wife, so you decided to get rid of her.'

Bennett listened stony faced while Rathbone was speaking, but he met the detective's eye without flinching. 'That's a load of crap,' he said defiantly. 'I've got a wife so why would I want to have it off with a snotty kid?'

'Plenty of married men find teenage girls attractive.'

'That's their problem.'

Rathbone waited for a few seconds before saying, 'Have you ever heard anyone say, "Oh my Gordon Bennett"?'

'Can't say I have.' This time the puzzled frown struck Sukey as genuine. 'What's it mean?'

'It's a rather old-fashioned way of expressing surprise.' Rathbone waited a moment before adding, 'Sharon's mother uses it.'

The corners of Bennett's mouth lifted in a hint of a sneer.

'Don't tell me you're accusing me of trying to pull the kid's mum as well. Now I've heard it all.'

Rathbone ignored the taunt. 'We found a note in Sharon's diary, written the day before she disappeared. It refers to an appointment with someone she refers to as "Gordie". We think Gordie is short for Gordon and that because your name is Bennett she used it to refer to you. A kind of pet name, you could say. Perhaps she used to call you by it when you were alone together.'

Bennett uncrossed his legs, sat forward in his chair and clenched his fists, accidentally burning himself on his cigarette. He swore and stubbed it out in a conveniently placed ashtray. 'I keep telling you,' he said angrily while sucking the injured finger, 'I didn't know the girl. When I go to the school I do whatever's needed, fill in my worksheet and leave.'

'You're seriously asking us to believe that you regularly visit Over Hampton School during lesson time to service the computer equipment and yet you never have any contact with any of the students, never exchange a word with them or even know any of them by sight?'

'You can believe what you bloody well like. I have a job to do, I get on with it and when it's finished I go to the next one. I haven't got time to waste talking to kids.'

'Not even sexy teenagers?' There was no answer. After a moment, Rathbone sat back and said, almost casually, 'You are of course aware that Sharon Swann was pregnant?'

'So I heard, but it wasn't mine if that's what you're suggesting.' Bennett lit another cigarette. His hands shook slightly and the muscles round his mouth had tightened.

'But you are no doubt aware, since you admit having seen the reports of the discovery of Sharon's body, that it was discovered in a lay-by a couple of miles or so from Over Hampton, buried under a load of builder's rubble.'

'If you say so. I don't remember all the details.'

'Then let me refresh your memory. The bricks and rubble were in a trailer parked overnight outside a house in Portishead. The trailer was stolen during the night and recovered a few days later – empty – in a field a few miles away.'

'So whoever killed the girl dumped her body in the ditch

and emptied the bricks on top of her. It doesn't take a genius to work that out.' Bennett took a drag on the fresh cigarette, tilted his head back and exhaled smoke towards the ceiling. Sukey sensed that he considered directing it at them but thought better of it. 'I still don't know why you're telling me this,' he said.

'Our forensic experts have subjected the trailer to a very detailed examination. In addition to the fingerprints of the owner and one or two other people, all of whom have been eliminated from the enquiry, there are two that remain unidentified. Do you still maintain that you are not in any way involved in the case?'

'How many times do I have to say it?'

'Then I assume you won't have any objection to coming with us to the station to have your fingerprints taken so that we may eliminate you from our enquiries?'

For the first time Bennett's carefully maintained *sang-froid* showed signs of crumbling. 'You're trying to stitch me up,' he muttered.

'On the contrary, we are trying to get at the truth.'

'I've told you the truth.'

'Some of it, perhaps, but I suspect not all.'

'And if I refuse to allow you to take my prints?'

'In that case we have the power to arrest you on suspicion of being involved in the murder of Sharon Swann,' said Rathbone. As Bennett still appeared to hesitate, he added, 'If you have a solicitor you may wish to consult him or her; if not, we can arrange at the station for a duty solicitor to advise you.'

There was another short silence. Suddenly Bennett leapt from his chair like a spring suddenly uncoiled. 'Wait here,' he snapped. He opened the door and shouted, 'Holly!'

The young woman appeared within seconds. 'What is it, Josh?'

'These people are police officers. Something's cropped up and I have to go to the station with them.'

'Police?' Anxious, pale blue eyes darted from his face to the detectives and back again. 'Josh, what have you done?'

'I haven't done anything,' he said roughly, but Sukey noticed that he avoided her gaze. 'They think I may be able to help them on a case.'

'How long will you be away?' She turned to Rathbone. 'He's got clients who need their computers seeing to urgently.'

'Just shut up and ring round to cancel today's appointments,' said Bennett, as Rathbone remained silent.

'What do I tell people?'

'Say you'll get in touch to make another appointment. Don't argue, just do as you're told,' he went on as she opened her mouth as if to ask another question.

'All right, Josh,' she said hastily and scuttled away.

Bennett followed the detectives from the house and closed the door behind them. 'I take it I'll get a lift back,' he said as they escorted him to the car.

'Provided we have no reason to detain you,' Rathbone replied.

Bennett threw away the butt of his cigarette before climbing into the back seat with Rathbone beside him while Sukey took the wheel.

At the police station they handed their suspect over to a uniformed officer to have his fingerprints taken. They waited in the incident room until the officer came in with the forms in an acetate folder. 'Here you are Sarge.'

Rathbone passed them to Sukey, who placed the folder in her bag. 'Thanks. I take it he didn't give you any trouble?'

'No Sarge.'

'We're going back to HQ to get these checked,' he said. 'It shouldn't take long.'

'Do we let him go?'

'No, give him a cup of tea and keep him here till we get back. If he asks for a brief you know the drill. And put the cup in a sterile bag when he's drunk the tea so we can get a sample of his DNA.'

'We can get his DNA from this, Sarge,' said Sukey. She showed him a transparent envelope containing the stub of Bennett's second cigarette. 'I scooped it up while he was getting into the car.'

'That was a smart bit of work,' said Rathbone. 'He's a hard case and he's had plenty of time to decide what line he's going to take,' he added as they returned to the car. 'He'll take a bit of breaking, but I'm pretty sure we've got our man this time.'

'He walked right into the little trap you set him, Sarge.'

'Giving away he knew the girl was pregnant, you mean?' Rathbone allowed himself a hint of a smile. 'The Super knew what he was doing when he withheld that titbit from the press, didn't he? You noticed Holly has the remains of a black eye, of course, and the way she'd pulled her hair forward, thinking she was hiding it?'

'His body language tells us he's capable of violence,' said Sukey. 'I think Holly was scared he was going to hit her when she started asking questions. He probably would have done if we hadn't been there. I wonder if he beat Sharon before he killed her,' she added, half to herself.

'A wife-beater, a seducer and a killer?' Rathbone mused. 'If she is his wife – she wasn't wearing a ring. Not that that means much nowadays.'

Back at headquarters Sukey handed the folder to the finger-prints department for comparison with the prints found on Wally Horner's trailer. When she returned to the CID office Rathbone informed her that he had reported to DCI Leach and been told to await instructions before taking any further action. An hour later, having received confirmation that Bennett's prints matched one of those found on the trailer, Rathbone made a further call.

'Bennett's to be questioned under caution,' he said when he put the phone down. 'The press will be told an arrest has been made and a man is helping us with our enquiries. Sukey and Vicky, you are to go back to Bennett's house and talk to his wife. Get as much information as you can about his movements, acquaintances and so on – you know the kind of background information we need, I don't need to spell it out. We'll get forensics to give his van a going over and one of our experts will check his computer.'

'Any developments on the Daisy Hewitt case, Sarge?' asked Vicky.

Rathbone gave a weary smile. 'That's something else the Super has dropped in our laps. He doesn't want us sitting around on our backsides.'

TWENTY-SEVEN

'Regarding the Daisy Hewitt case,' Rathbone continued, 'the situation at present is that her computer has gone for examination. We haven't heard anything so far; in the meantime the techies have filmed a reconstruction of what we believe were Daisy's movements after leaving the house on the day she disappeared. It was a bit tricky because we can't be sure which route she took, but the outfit we believe she was wearing is quite striking so we're hoping that will jog someone's memory. The programme is to be screened on the box at nine o'clock tomorrow evening so you'll be on duty to deal with calls – and keep your fingers crossed that someone will come up with something that will give us a breakthrough. Meanwhile DCI Leach and I will tackle Bennett. First things first; I need a coffee,' he added wearily. He got up and marched across the office to the machine.

'I've been doing a load of boring paperwork while you've been having all the fun,' Vicky grumbled after his retreating figure.

'Sorry about that,' said Sukey. 'DCI Leach thought it too risky to send two women to interview Bennett in case he turned nasty. As I'm sure he could have done,' she added. 'If he'd tried to do a runner I wouldn't have fancied my chances at arresting him – or even catching him. He looks as if he can run like the wind. There's something almost feline about him.'

'D'you reckon he's the type Sharon would have gone for?'

'Definitely. He has a sort of animal magnetism that plenty of girls – and older women too, I imagine – would find attractive. Trendy black outfit, designer glasses, very good looking and no doubt able to turn on the charm, although needless to say we didn't see much of that.'

'Sounds intriguing.' Vicky checked the time. 'It's just gone twelve. Let's nip down to the canteen and grab a sandwich before we set off and you can fill me in with the details.'

They were on their way to the car park after their hurried

lunch when Sukey's mobile rang. 'Harry!' she exclaimed in surprise, 'you don't usually call me at work. Is it important?'

'I've just heard there's to be a press release later on today. Which case is it?'

'You'll have to wait and see.'

'I guessed you'd say that.'

'Then why the call?'

'I've got something really interesting to tell you. Have you got a moment?'

'What's it about?

'Muriel Minchin.'

Sukey glanced at Vicky, who was unashamedly listening. 'OK, go ahead.'

'You remember she was thinking of selling Parson's Acre shortly before her last illness?'

'Of course.'

'Well, my contact at Weaver and Morris, the estate agent who carried out the valuation, has found the name of the builders who were carrying out some work in their offices around the time when the possible sale was being discussed. According to her it was the Hubbards, although there's no way of checking which of them was actually doing the job. It could have been either or both, I suppose.'

'Thanks, Harry. I'm not sure how it helps, but I'll pass it on.'

'Fine. Is there any chance of seeing you this evening? It's been a long time – a whole day in fact.'

'Yes I know, but I can't talk now. I'll call you later, bye,' she said hurriedly, conscious of Vicky's appraising gaze. She ended the call before he could press her any further.

'Well, from your happy smile that was obviously good news,' said Vicky as they got into the car.

'It might be.' Sukey relayed the information Harry's contact had given him, conscious that her pleasure at the call was due as much to his eagerness to see her as to what he had to say.

'That means,' said Vicky, 'that if one of the Hubbards happened to overhear the conversation he might have assumed Parson's Acre was definitely coming on to the market at a certain price and passed the information on to someone he knew would be interested. And that person might have made the dodgy phone call.'

'It's certainly possible,' Sukey agreed.

'D'you reckon it's worth following up?'

'It was a long time ago and they may not remember, but I suppose it wouldn't do any harm to check. I'll tell the Sarge when I've got a moment, but I doubt if he'll think it's significant – he's never taken Doctor Hogan's theory seriously.'

'DCI Leach was more sympathetic,' Vicky reminded her.

'Sure, but like everyone else he's got more important things on his mind just now. I'll try and find time to follow it up when I'm off duty and I'll call Doctor Hogan just to let him know I haven't forgotten. Meanwhile, let's see what we can get out of Holly Bennett.'

As she drew up in front of the house, Sukey exclaimed, 'Bennett's van's gone. I hope that doesn't mean Holly's out.' They exchanged resigned glances at the possibility of a long wait.

'It could be forensics have got here before us and taken it,' Vicky suggested. 'Let's try the door anyway.'

When Holly opened the door she gave Sukey a nod of recognition and her eyes lit up momentarily as they slid past her to the car. Sukey guessed she was hoping to see her husband getting out of it. On seeing it was empty, her face fell. 'Where is he?' she asked anxiously. 'When's he coming home? Why did they take the van and the computer? We can't carry on the business without them. What's going on?' The questions rushed out with scarcely a breath between them.

'This is my colleague, DC Vicky Armstrong,' said Sukey. 'We need to talk to you; shall we go inside?'

Mutely she beckoned them in and closed the door behind them before leading them into the room in which Rathbone and Sukey had questioned her husband that morning. She invited them with a gesture to sit down and perched nervously on the edge of the chair where her husband had sat, apparently at his ease. 'Please tell me what this is all about,' she said piteously. She was plainly on the verge of tears. 'The people who took the van and the computer wouldn't tell me anything.' She looked from one to the other in bewilderment. 'Has Josh been arrested?'

'He's being questioned about a very serious crime,' said Sukey. 'Some of the information he gave Sergeant Rathbone and me this morning led us to believe that he may be able to help us with our enquiries into the case. Since then certain facts have come to light that make it necessary for us to detain him for further questioning.'

'What case . . . and what facts?' Holly's eyes were wide with apprehension.

'All we can tell you at the moment is that he has not so far been charged with any offence,' said Vicky. 'He is quite adamant that he knows nothing about the case and if he is able to establish his innocence than obviously we will release him and return his property without delay. What we need to do now is to ask you a few questions and it's possible that your answers may help him.'

'I'll do anything I can,' said Holly earnestly. 'If it's about tax, I keep all his accounts and I promise you everything's above board.'

'It isn't about tax.'

'Then what . . .?'

'We understand that his business is mainly repairing computers when they go wrong and also supplying new computers to order. Is that right?'

Holly nodded. 'Yes.'

'What can you tell us about his clients? Are they local businesses or private individuals? Does he have any clients he calls on at regular intervals? Or do people ring up to report a fault and ask him to come and fix it?'

'Sometimes it's that, but he has his regulars.'

'Perhaps you can tell us who they are.'

'Of course. I'll get the diary.'

As she left the room, the two detectives exchanged optimistic glances. 'I reckon she's going to be very helpful,' said Sukey.

By three o'clock, they were back in the incident room at Over Hampton police station. A little under an hour later, just as they finished writing their reports, the rest of the team appeared, followed shortly by DS Rathbone. He looked exhausted.

'How did it go, Sarge?' asked Sukey.

'Bennett's still denying he had anything to do with Sharon Swann and knows nothing about her death. When pressed to explain how he knew she was pregnant all he would say was he didn't know for sure but thought he'd overheard someone talking about the discovery of the body and supposed that's what they'd said.'

'That sounds pretty thin, Sarge,' said Vicky.

'No thinner than his explanation of how his prints came to be on the abandoned trailer,' said Rathbone. 'He says he "happened to come across it one day when he was out walking and played around with it out of curiosity," as he put it. And of course he couldn't remember exactly where or when it was – he says he often goes for short walks in between jobs "to stretch his legs and get some fresh air". He threw out a few locations where there's a bit of open space near where he's had jobs, none of which incidentally is anywhere near where the trailer was found.'

'It all seems a bit circumstantial, Sarge,' Tim commented.

'You're right,' he agreed, 'and to any question that looks the least bit tricky he falls back on our old friend "no comment". The Super's pretty confident that given time he'll have enough to build a case, but there's no doubt Bennett is going to be a tough nut to crack.'

'If there's a match between his DNA and the foetus in Sharon's body, "no comment" won't be much help, will it Sarge?' said Sukey.

'In that case he could hardly deny being the kid's father,' Rathbone agreed, 'but it wouldn't of itself prove he killed the mother. It's obvious he's not only devious but he's also got a very sharp brain. The Super reckons it wouldn't be beyond him to admit he'd had sex with Sharon but claim that she wasn't a virgin and in any case she was such an easy lay there were sure to have been others. The entry in her diary plus what Sukey learned from Doctor Hogan suggest otherwise, but if there is any truth in it – which we can neither prove nor disprove – she could have accused some other bloke of making her pregnant, one who was so desperate to keep the affair secret that he'd killed her. Whether it's an argument that would convince a jury would depend on how smart his lawyer was.'

'What about the diary reference to "Gordie"?' asked Vicky.

'There's no proof it refers to him.' Rathbone spread his hands in a slightly helpless gesture. 'No, the fact is that so far, unless more solid evidence turns up or we get a confession, we simply haven't enough to charge him.'

'So what's the order of play, Sarge?' asked Mike.

'That depends on whether Sukey and Vicky have come up with anything useful.' He jerked a head in their direction. 'The floor is yours.'

'Our reports are in your in-box and we've emailed copies to DCI Leach, Sarge,' said Sukey.

'OK, I'll read them later. Just tell me, have you come up with anything useful?'

'We think we may have done, Sarge. First of all, one of Josh Bennett's clients is a farmer whose land adjoins the field where Wally Horner's empty trailer was recovered. As no doubt you remember, it's been neglected by its owner and is overgrown in places, which is probably why the trailer was dumped there. We've taken Bennett's appointments book for detailed examination.'

'Good. Anything else?'

'We had a long chat with Holly Bennett. She absolutely adores Josh, won't hear or say a word against him and was pathetically keen to defend him. We didn't tell her he's being held on suspicion of murder, but we think she has a pretty shrewd idea that some sort of violence is involved because she went out of her way more than once to say what an easy-going chap he is, hardly ever loses his temper and so on.'

'How did she account for the bruise on her face?' asked Rathbone.

'The usual excuse – she walked into a door.'

'What about his movements? Does he come home during the day, say for lunch? What sort of hours does he keep?'

'It depends on where the jobs take him. He appears to cover quite a wide area. The farm I mentioned earlier is nearly ten miles away.'

'What about their social life? Do they go out together or does he sometimes go off on his own?'

'He has a married brother called Max who lives in Portishead and they quite often go out as a foursome, but now and again the two boys have a night out on their own or with some other lads.' Sukey glanced across at Vicky before continuing. 'We've already concluded that whoever stole the trailer-load of bricks and tipped them over Sharon's body must have had an accomplice. The brother seems a possible candidate. Holly gave us his address without our having to ask. She seemed pathetically anxious for us to get him to back up everything she told us.'

Rathbone grunted. 'She's not over bright by the sound of it. Good news for us, but if he gets sent down on the strength of her evidence then Heaven help her when he comes out. Well done, you two. We'll pull Max in without delay and get his prints.'

TWENTY-EIGHT

As Sukey anticipated, Rathbone merely shrugged when she mentioned the information Harry had given her. Doctor Hogan was more receptive when she called him after the meeting broke up. 'The Hubbards must have plenty of contacts in the trade so they might well know of someone who'd be interested in Parson's Acre,' he said. 'Go and have a word with them.'

'I'll try and find time, but it will have to be unofficial and when I'm off duty.' *And we do have a few really important cases to investigate,* she added mentally.

'The logistics are up to you.' He hung up. Sukey did the same, fighting back the temptation to tell him to do his own investigating for a change. She glanced at the clock. It was a little after five. On impulse, she picked up the phone and called the Hubbards' number.

A warm, friendly female voice with a strong West Country burr answered. 'Hubbard and Son, Bessie Hubbard speaking. How can I help you?' She listened without interruption while Sukey explained, as simply as possible, the purpose of her call. 'Ooh, I wouldn't know about that,' she said, 'you'll have to ask Tom. He's still out on a job but he's got his mobile with him.'

Sukey thanked her for her help and called the number Bessie had given her. When she put her question to Tom Hubbard there was a short silence before he said, 'I don't doubt there's several folk who'd have put in a bid for Parson's Acre if it came on the market.'

'Yes, I'm sure that's true,' said Sukey, 'but what I'd like

to know is, do you remember, while you were working in the offices of that estate agent, whether you happened to over-hear a conversation indicating that Miss Muriel Minchin was about to sell?'

'Look, that was a long time ago,' said Hubbard, after a further pause during which Sukey had a mental picture of him scratching his head in perplexity. 'I can't recall doing a job at – where did you say it was? Weaver and Morris in Keynsham? Maybe it was Jerry. He's on another job at the moment but we're meeting in the Red Lion in an hour or so. I'll ask him.'

'Thank you, I'd really appreciate your help. Maybe you'd be kind enough to call me and tell me what he says?' She dictated her number and gathered from a series of grunts that he was making a note of it.

'Is it important?' he said.

'It might be just the piece of information we need to clear up a very serious crime,' she said earnestly.

'All right. Like I said, I don't remember the job, but I'll see if Jerry can help.'

'Thank you very much.' Sukey ended the call and turned to Vicky, who was working at her computer. 'Tom Hubbard can't remember but he's promised to ask his son and call me back.'

'I wouldn't hold your breath,' said Vicky. 'Builders are notoriously bad at keeping promises.'

'Just what I was thinking,' said Sukey despondently. Then an idea struck her and she reached for the phone again. 'Harry? About this evening – can you meet me at the Red Lion in Over Hampton at around six o'clock?'

It was a little after six when Sukey reached the Red Lion. Harry's car was already there and she parked alongside him. He greeted her with a hug and a kiss that momentarily took her mind off the reason for the meeting. 'I sense that something's afoot,' he said as he released her. 'Was my bit of info useful after all?'

'It might be.' She told him of her conversation with Tom Hubbard. 'Of course, there's no guarantee they'll be here, but it's worth a try and just in case we pick up anything useful I thought you'd like to be in on it.'

'You're dead right,' he said with enthusiasm.

The bar was fairly full and it was several moments before they spied Tom and Jerry Hubbard sitting in a corner. Harry bought drinks and they went over to greet them.

'We were just talking about you, Miss,' Tom said to Sukey as they sat down. 'Jerry does remember doing a job at that estate agent you mentioned.' He turned to his son, who was munching crisps in between swigs of beer from a pint tankard. 'That's right, isn't it?'

'Can't recall exactly when,' said Jerry with his mouth full of crisps. 'It was only a replastering job so I did it on my own.' He took another swig from his tankard, wiped his mouth with the back of his hand and said, 'I didn't hear any talking though. Sorry I can't help.'

'Oh well, thanks anyway,' said Sukey. She was coming to the conclusion that there was nothing to be gained from the meeting and was trying to think of an excuse to move away from the Hubbards, who obviously had no interest in prolonging the conversation.

At that moment a penetrating female voice from the other end of the bar called, 'Harry and Sukey! How *lovely* to see you!' Leonora Farrell, a drink in one hand and the menu in the other, drifted across in a cloud of perfume to greet them. 'And Mother Hubbard's two lovely boys!' she gushed, treating them to a dazzling smile. 'Just the chaps I want to see,' she went on, apparently oblivious to their lukewarm response to her attempt at humour. 'Mr Walker has been going through dear Aunt Adelaide's papers and stuff and he's discovered that before she died she was planning to have some building work done. He says she made a note saying she was waiting for you to quote.'

Jerry drained his glass, stood up and pointed to his father's half-finished drink. 'Want a top-up, Dad?'

'Not just now, thanks,' said Tom. He turned back to Leonora. 'I recall Miss Adelaide did say something about a building job she wanted doing,' he said, 'but the poor lady died before I had a chance to go and have a look at it.'

'It looks really exciting and I want you boys to look at the plans and give me an estimate,' Leonora went on. 'Oh, thank you,' she said to Harry as she sat down in the chair he had pulled up for her. 'I'll have to get several estimates,

I suppose – Mr Walker will insist, he's such an old fusspot but he's so kind I feel I have to take his advice,' she paused for breath and to take a mouthful from her drink, 'but I'd really like you boys to do the job because people have told me how good you are.'

'Thank you, Miss Farrell,' said Tom. 'What kind of job is it?'

'It's an extension at the back of the house. Adelaide got an architect to draw up plans for what he called a garden room. It looks wonderful.'

'Well, we'll be happy to look at it, of course.'

'Oh goody!' Leonora beamed.

'When are you moving in?' asked Sukey.

Leonora sighed. 'Not for a while yet, I'm afraid. I managed to persuade Mr Walker to let me borrow the keys so I could measure up for curtains and think about decorating and how I'm going to arrange my furniture and so on – dear Auntie Addie had *terrible* taste in wallpaper – and I've spent lots of time finding my way around the village and making sketches of trees and flowers and other beautiful things.' The words tumbled out at breathless speed and she paused for a few more sips before continuing. 'He's talked Adelaide's family out of contesting the will so that will speed things up, but then there's something called probate that will take up more time.' She rolled her enormous eyes upwards in exasperation. 'I've been staying here for the past few days but I have to go back to London tomorrow. I'll be down at weekends as long as this lovely weather holds,' she rushed on, turning back to Tom. 'Perhaps you could meet me at Parson's Acre soon to talk about the garden room. We don't need to go into the house for that, do we?'

'That'd be fine; just give me a call,' said Tom.

'Oh *thank you!*' She finished her drink and stood up. 'Well, I must go and order my dinner. It's been *lovely* seeing you all! Bye bye!'

As she made her way back to the bar, Sukey caught Tom and Jerry exchanging meaningful glances. 'I don't think they're all that keen on their new client,' she remarked to Harry as a short while later they returned to their respective cars.

Harry chuckled. 'I've a feeling you're right. Didn't we say the same thing about her solicitor?'

TWENTY-NINE

Within minutes of the screening of the programme showing a reconstruction of Daisy Hewitt's last known movements and the possible routes she might have taken on her way to school, calls began coming in. Several were from people who had previously been interviewed during house to house enquiries, particularly those who lived on the route leading from her home to the footpath she was known to have taken on her way to school on previous occasions. None of them remembered seeing her – or any other girl in school uniform – but the programme reminded them that they had noticed a girl wearing an outfit similar to the one featured in the reconstruction walking in the direction of the point where the footpath joined the road leading out of the village. One woman claimed to have mentioned when interviewed that she had seen a girl of approximately the right age, although not in school uniform, but either it had not been recorded or not considered significant.

'She had a real spring in her step, as if she was feeling on top of the world,' the woman recollected, adding a trifle wistfully, 'I remember saying to myself, "She looks so happy, I wonder if she's going to meet her boyfriend". Oh dear, maybe that's exactly what happened . . . and maybe he's the one who killed her. Oh, how awful! I do hope you catch him.'

'It never occurred to any of them at the time that the girl they saw might have been Daisy,' DCI Leach remarked during a lull in the calls. 'If only we'd known earlier about the different clothes and the entry in her diary, we could have alerted the media straight away, but as it is . . .' The phone in front of him rang again and he grabbed the receiver. 'Crimewatch . . . yes, that's right, please go ahead.' Sukey watched his expression change as he listened, made notes and after a few moments said, 'You're absolutely sure of the date, Madam? Yes, I quite understand, there's no need to apologize. Excellent. One of our officers will call on you as soon as possible. Thank you very much for your help.' He turned to his colleagues. 'A Mrs

Follett, who lives along the Upper Keynsham Road close to the point where the field path joins it, happened to be at her front door taking in the milk shortly after half past eight on the morning Daisy disappeared. She remembers seeing a white van go past her house. It was going quite slowly and she thought at the time the driver was probably looking for an address. She didn't attach any particular significance to it until she saw this evening's programme. If you remember, viewers were asked if they remembered seeing a vehicle either parked or going slowly, as if the driver was on the lookout for someone he'd arranged to pick up.'

'Surely that was one of the questions put during the house to house enquiries, sir,' said Rathbone.

'It seems the lady went on holiday the next day and was away for nearly three weeks, so she was never interviewed. She was most apologetic about it. She'd forgotten about it until tonight's programme jogged her memory.'

'I take it she didn't spot any pedestrian who might have been Daisy, sir?' said Sukey.

'No, but it occurs to me that the driver might have been going slowly because he'd already picked her up and was moving off rather than slowing down. One thing that could be significant is that the van had some words painted on the side and Mrs Follett thinks one of them was "services".'

There was an audible intake of breath among the group of detectives. 'That was probably Bennett's van – Bennett's Computer Services, sir!' said DC Penny Osborne excitedly. 'He killed Daisy as well as Sharon – it all adds up!'

'Bennett's name is Josh and Daisy was going to meet someone called Jake,' Sukey pointed out.

'But if he was grooming her on a chat line he quite likely called himself something different,' said Penny.

'It's certainly a possible lead,' said Leach, 'but let's not jump to conclusions. There are probably a dozen white vans in this neck of the woods offering all kinds of services from domestic cleaning to pizza delivery. Just the same, we'll start with the premise that it was Bennett's van and see what he's got to say for himself. It'll be interesting to find out what he does on his computer apart from his legitimate business.'

'As Daisy goes to Over Hampton Comprehensive, sir, couldn't Bennett have made contact with her there, like he did with Sharon, instead of on a chat line?' suggested DC Tim Pringle.

'That doesn't tie in with the entry in Daisy's diary, suggesting that she was on her way to meet Jake for the first time,' DC Mike Haskins objected.

'If their contact was on a chat line it wouldn't have occurred to her that Jake was the man who services the school computers,' said Penny. Sukey had a feeling that in her mind the hunt for Daisy's killer was as good as over. 'Suppose he spotted her in class and took a fancy to her like he did to Sharon, but instead of going after her openly he made contact through a chat line. He could call himself anything – that way she wouldn't know his true identity. It would have to be on her home computer, of course, not one of the machines at school.'

'Maybe he went to the house one day to do a repair job, found out which chat line she used and decided to contact her that way,' she appealed to DCI Leach. 'Don't you think we should check this out, sir?'

'Dating two girls from the same class would have been a pretty stupid thing to do, and Bennett is certainly not stupid,' said Leach. 'No, I'm more inclined to think the relationship was conducted on a chat line from the start. Her Facebook friends knew her real identity, but if she subscribed to a different one as well, she may have indulged in a little fanta-sizing, projected herself as a bit older and maybe a bit sexy. In that case, when they came face to face for the first time, there would have been immediate mutual recognition and he'd have realized that he'd landed himself in a dangerous situ-ation, especially if he'd already killed Sharon. And if Daisy had tried to run away, or worse, threatened to report him, his only option would have been to kill her as well.' He thought for a moment. 'On reflection, though, we can't afford to over-look even the smallest detail. Penny, have a word with the Hewitt's housekeeper and find out if they've had any computer problems recently and if so who they called in to fix them.'

'Yes, sir,' said Penny with a little smile of triumph in Mike's direction.

'We've already handed Bennett's computer to our expert for checking over,' Leach continued. 'He's had to leave work on Daisy's for a bit – one of his team is off sick and another job has taken priority – but he's hoping to get back to it within the next couple of days. It should be easier to check if there's been contact between Bennett and Daisy now he has the two of them to work from. Being an expert himself, Bennett probably has the latest hi-tech software protection against hackers, but young Nick is pretty hi-tech too.'

He checked the time; it was well past midnight and the phones had fallen silent. 'I'm off home. Get some rest, everyone. You're going to be busy tomorrow.'

'There are still plenty of callers from last night to follow up,' said Rathbone when the team assembled the following morning. 'Mike, Tim and Penny – you three will divide them up between yourselves. If you come across anything you think I should know, send me a text immediately and I'll get back to you. Sukey, you and Vicky will join me while I have another crack at Bennett. He's opted for a duty solicitor, by the way, and it so happens he's got Rafferty, who advised Brian Gordon.'

The three of them settled down in the interview room where Joshua Bennett was sitting with Malcolm Rafferty at his side. He sat staring at the table with an expressionless face while the recording was set up.

'Right Josh,' said Rathbone, 'let's continue our conversation, shall we?'

'Before we go any further, Sergeant,' Rafferty began, 'I should like to point out that my client has answered all your questions concerning the death of Sharon Swann to the best of his ability and has nothing to add to what he said yesterday.'

'Understood,' said Rathbone blandly. 'It so happens that I'm not going to talk about Sharon this morning. Not at first, anyway.' He paused for a moment as if to gauge the effect of this statement on Bennett, but seeing no reaction he continued, 'Let's talk about computer chat lines, Josh. How much time do you spend on Facebook, for example?'

Bennett frowned. 'Is this some kind of joke?' he said warily. 'What makes you think I'm interested in chat room gossip?'

'Plenty of chaps your age – and older – enjoy making contact with other computer users . . . especially nubile young women,' he added provocatively.

'I thought I'd made it clear that my wife is the only woman I'm interested in.'

'Ah yes, of course, the lovely Holly. Or she would be lovely if it wasn't for the black eye. How did you say she came by that, Josh?'

'She walked into a door.'

'Oh yes, so she did.' Rathbone made a pretence of checking the file on the table in front of him. 'That's the usual story when a wife doesn't want to admit her husband knocks her about, isn't it?'

'Really, Sergeant,' Rafferty protested, 'my client has already answered these questions and I think you'll find he's given exactly the same answers on both occasions.'

'All right, let's leave that for the time being. Let's leave your wife's bruises and the dead schoolgirl Sharon Swann for the moment and talk about another case, that of another school-girl, Daisy Hewitt.'

'Daisy who?'

'Oh come on, Josh, let's not get silly. We know you keep up with the media. When DC Reynolds and I came to your house you admitted knowing about the discovery of the body that turned out to be Sharon's so you can't pretend you don't know that we thought at first it was Daisy Hewitt's.'

Bennett shrugged. 'I suppose I did at the time. What of it?'

'Two girls, roughly the same age, both students at the school where you have a contract to service computers – and yet the fact that one was murdered and the other still missing after disappearing several weeks ago was of so little interest to you that we had to jog your memory. That's rather strange, don't you think?'

'You might think so – murder and stuff are your business. I've got better things to think about.'

Rathbone took a sheet from the file on his desk. 'Let me remind you of something you said during the same conver-sation. When I mentioned the name "Sharon Swann" you said "Sharon who?" and when I said, "The girl whose body was found in a lay-by not far from here, you said, "Oh, that one. Yes, I heard about that".'

'If you've got it written down there, I suppose it's what I said. What of it?'

'So you admit that at this point you were obviously uncer-tain which girl I was alluding to?'

'I'm not admitting anything,' said Bennett. 'So there were

two girls and you were talking about the other one. I'm not saying any more. You're trying to stitch me up.' He cast a despairing glance at his solicitor, who quickly intervened.

'Sergeant, the expression, "Oh, that one" is hardly an admission of anything except possibly a lapse of memory,' said Rafferty. 'My client has already made it clear that he has not been paying particular attention to either of the cases you mention.'

'All right, we'll leave that for the moment. Excuse me,' Rathbone added as a signal from his mobile indicated the arrival of a text message. He left the room and was absent for several minutes. When he returned he said, 'OK, Josh, let's talk about the other one. Daisy Hewitt, that is, in case you're still not quite clear. We know from your appointments book that some weeks ago you called at the Hewitt's residence in Over Hampton to repair a computer.'

'If you say so. I can't remember every call I make.'

'Quite. However, I have just had a call from one of our detectives, who has spoken to the Hewitt's housekeeper. She remembers you well. It seems that some weeks ago Daisy's computer needed attention. An appointment was made with Bennett's Computer Services and you visited the house and carried out the necessary repair. After you left, Daisy told the housekeeper in some surprise that the man who fixed it was the same man who services the equipment at her school. Perhaps you remember it now?'

Sukey thought she detected the same flicker of unease she had noticed when Rathbone was questioning him about possible contacts with the students at school. His voice, however, was steady enough as he replied, 'Yes, I remember that job now. There was a problem with the modem.'

'And of course, as you were in Daisy's house . . . in fact, in her room . . . there was nothing to stop you talking to her?' Bennett's mouth set, but he made no reply.

'What did you talk about, Josh? Chat rooms, perhaps? Facebook, for example? Girls of that age are often into that sort of thing, aren't they? And they aren't always careful how much they give away to strangers with a smooth line in chat.' Rathbone leaned forward and his voice dropped a tone. Bennett lowered his eyes rather than meet the detective's penetrating gaze. 'She was an unusually beautiful girl,' he said. 'You really fancied her, didn't you? You didn't dare make a pass at her openly because you were already having it off with another girl in her class, so you went into the same chat line as the one she was using, created a false identity for yourself and started grooming her. You gained her confidence and after a while she agreed to meet you, probably thinking you were someone about her own age or maybe a little older . . . and exciting. She was walking to the place where you promised to meet her and you pulled up beside her. She recognized you of course but you managed to persuade her to get into your van, perhaps on the pretext of giving her a lift to where she said she was going. You took her somewhere for sex but she wouldn't have it, tried to fight you off . . . and you knew that if you let her go and she reported you, you'd not only be charged with attempted rape but also lose a substantial part of your livelihood . . .'

'No!' Bennett almost shrieked. He had been sitting as if transfixed until the word 'rape' seemed to prod him into life. 'You're making all this up!' He turned desperately to Rafferty. 'I swear I had nothing to do with that one except to fix her computer!'

'Unless you have some evidence to substantiate this accusation, Sergeant,' said the solicitor, 'I shall advise my client to make no further comment.'

'All right, let's see what your client has to say about this.' Rathbone turned back to Bennett. 'We have a witness who reported seeing a van, identical to yours and with similar wording painted on the side, cruising along the Upper Keynsham Road close to the footpath we believe Daisy took on the morning she disappeared. I put it to you that it was your van, that you were driving and that you had just picked up Daisy as she was on her way to meet someone she thought was a friend she'd met in a chat room.'

Bennett leapt to his feet and for a moment he appeared to be about to attack Rathbone, but Rafferty put a restraining hand on his arm. 'It's all lies, I tell you. It wasn't me . . . I never touched her, not that one . . .'

'So what about the other one?' Rathbone, seeing he was on the verge of cracking, pressed home his advantage. 'I'm talking about Sharon Swann, the one you killed and dumped in a lay-by with a load of bricks on top of her. Two prints on the trailer that held the bricks were unaccounted for, Josh. One was yours, but you'd have needed an accomplice – your brother Max, perhaps? We know the two of you are pretty close and we're checking on him. We'll know for certain once we've got his prints.'

'Stop it, for God's sake!' Bennett almost sobbed. 'Sharon was a lovely kid and I never meant to hurt her . . . but she kept on screaming . . . and I swear I never harmed Daisy . . . I never touched her . . . I only ever saw her that once apart from at school . . . and I've never used a chat room.' His voice trailed to nothing and he listened in silence as Rathbone formally charged him with the murder of Sharon Swann.

THIRTY

'Congratulations everyone. At least we got a result in the Sharon Swann case.' A smile flitted briefly across Superintendent Baird's freckled face as he surveyed his team, assembled later that day in the incident room in Over Hampton Police Station. 'Or perhaps I should say a result of sorts,' he continued. 'We're not out of the wood by a long way. I can at least confirm that the hitherto unidentified prints on Wally Horner's trailer are those of Joshua Bennett's brother Maxwell,' he went on. 'We've pulled him in for questioning and it'll be interesting to compare his explanation with the one already given by his brother. We have Josh's implied admission that he killed Sharon, but you don't need me to tell you that on its own such an admission isn't enough to secure a conviction. From the advice he subsequently received from his brief it's clear that he'll claim this was made while he was in an emotionally distressed state induced by an unacceptably intimidating style of interviewing. Any questions?'

'What about Josh's DNA test, sir?' asked DC Mike Haskins.

'I was coming to that.' Baird referred to a sheet of paper. 'I've just had this email from the lab: initial tests indicate a match between the foetal sample and Josh's DNA. I'll be receiving a full report in a few days, but it looks pretty conclusive.'

'If Sharon was putting pressure on him to marry her – or threatening to tell his wife if she knew he was married – that

would be a pretty strong motive for killing her, wouldn't
it sir?'

'It's a motive, certainly,' Baird agreed, 'but we need to back
it up with some hard evidence. We can assume that the entry
in Sharon's diary to her intention to "sort things out with
Gordie" was to demand support for her and the child, but it
might refer to something completely different. In any case we
can't prove Gordie and Bennett are the same person.'

'So where does that leave us, sir?' asked another member
of the team.

'With a great deal more work to do,' said Baird. 'As I've
already said, there's an urgent need for hard evidence in the
Sharon Swann case. For a start, we need to check the registers of every class at the school for a student with either the
forename or surname of Gordon. Let's hope we don't find
any – or if we do, then hope they can be quickly eliminated.
Then there's a little matter of Daisy Hewitt's disappearance
– and almost certainly her murder. The Crimewatch programme
triggered a lot of calls that will have to be followed up. If
we could get Bennett in the frame for her killing it would
really strengthen our position.' His gaze singled out DS
Rathbone. 'I see from your report, Sergeant, that you believed
him to be speaking the truth when he denied having had any
improper contact with Daisy.'

'That was my impression, sir, and,' Rathbone glanced briefly
at Sukey and Vicky who were seated beside him, 'that of DCs
Reynolds and Armstrong, who were present at the interview.
In fact,' he added as the two nodded in agreement, 'we believe
it was the prospect of being nailed for a second murder that
he *didn't* commit that made him crack and as good as admit
he'd killed Sharon . . . because, as he said, she wouldn't stop
screaming.'

'Well, we'll wait and see what our techies find on his
computer before we eliminate him from the Hewitt case,' said
Baird in a tone suggesting that he was by no means convinced
by Josh's denial. 'If we can prove he's been lying when he
claims never to use chat rooms, that could have been a clever
bit of acting. Yes, Reynolds?' he said as Sukey raised a hand.

'Sir, if Daisy has been murdered, which seems the most
likely reason for her disappearance, has anyone any theory as
to how her killer might have disposed of her body?'

'Good question, Reynolds, and one which has been put by the media more than once. The answer we've given them every time is that the officers engaged on the case have combed the verges on dozens of roads, investigated every place where ground appears to have been disturbed, examined every empty building, looked under every likely-looking heap of stones, dragged every pond and stream and responded to every report from the public of so-called suspicious behaviour. So far without any positive result,' he concluded a trifle gloomily, running his fingers through his mop of sandy hair. 'We've had to scale down the number of uniformed engaged on these searches, but they will of course continue and extend over an increasingly wide area. Meanwhile we in the CID will focus on two essentials: first, to gather hard evidence against Bennett in the Sharon Swann case, and secondly, to find out what's happened to Daisy Hewitt and nail her killer. For the time being, Josh is still in the frame. Any more questions? No? Right, that's all for now. DCI Leach will brief you individually.' He gathered up the papers he had brought to the meeting and left.

'Greg, I'm leaving your team to deal with the Crimewatch callers,' said DCI Leach. 'It so happens that two of them besides Mrs Follett noticed a white commercial van, but these sightings were on the road leading out of Over Hampton village – the one known as Hampton Lane, not the Upper Keynsham Road.'

'That would be the road going past Parson's Acre,' Sukey observed thoughtfully. 'The house where Adelaide Minchin died, sir,' she added as Leach looked at her with a raised eyebrow.

'Ah yes, you spoke to me about that a while ago. The local GP raised some doubt about the verdict – he suspected foul play. I take it you've found nothing to confirm that?'

'No sir, but I've had no time to think about it up to now.'

'You aren't suggesting a connection, surely?'

'No, of course not sir. I was simply fixing the location in my head.'

'I see. Here are the addresses, Greg.' He handed a list to Rathbone. 'You'll notice there are a number of people who claim to have seen Daisy at the crucial time, besides the woman who noticed how happy she looked. It's up to you how you allocate them. When you've briefed your team, you and I will question Maxwell Bennett.'

Rathbone took the list and handed it to DC Haskins. 'Share that lot out between you, Mike. Try and organize the transport as economically as possible. Text me if you come up with anything significant,' he added over his shoulder as he followed Leach from the room.

'We'll each need a copy of this.' Mike made photocopies, which he distributed to the others. 'Do any of these look familiar?' he asked as five pairs of eyes scanned the list.

'Here's one!' Sukey exclaimed. 'Jerry Hubbard – he and his father are builders and Vicky and I interviewed them once when we were trying to track down the bricks that Josh and his brother dumped over Sharon's body.' She scanned the brief details of the call. 'He says he drove past a girl he thinks might have been Daisy on account of the clothes she was wearing. He didn't recognize her as he only saw her back.'

'You'd better take that one to start with, then.' Mike made a note against his list.

'I seem to have heard the name Atwood in some other context,' said Vicky as she scanned the list. 'Does it ring a bell with anyone else?'

'Yes!' Sukey exclaimed after a moment's thought. 'It was a Joe Atwood who discovered Adelaide Minchin's body. I wonder if it's the same person.'

'According to this it was Mrs Atwood who called Crimewatch,' Vicky pointed out, 'but it could of course be Joe's wife.'

'We'll take her as well if no one objects,' said Sukey. There was no objection and after some discussion the remaining addresses were divided up and the five members of the team set off on their respective assignments.

'I have a feeling,' said Vicky, as she and Sukey went to their car, 'that it's more than simple coincidence that makes you so keen to talk to Joe Atwood. It was the interest you showed in a sighting of Daisy on the road to Parson's Acre,' she went on as Sukey made no reply, 'I know you assured DCI Leach that you weren't thinking of a connection between Adelaide's death and Daisy's disappearance, but now I'm beginning to wonder.'

'I've got absolutely no reason for thinking there's a connection,' said Sukey. 'I mean . . . what possible common factor could there be between an elderly woman having a fatal accident in her bathroom and a teenager missing on the way to meet a so far unidentified friend? And yet . . .'

'You feel a hunch coming on!' said Vicky flippantly.

'You could say that. I know our job is to get as many details of Joe's sighting of Daisy as possible, but having done that it wouldn't do any harm to ask him about his discovery of Adelaide's body, would it? At least that would be a sop to offer Doctor Hogan.'

The woman who answered their knock was young, simply but neatly dressed, with a fresh complexion and candid light brown eyes. A toddler with a thumb in her mouth looked solemnly up at the two detectives as they showed their IDs. 'Ah yes, do come in,' she said. 'I'm Jenny Atwood. Actually, it was my husband Joe who saw the programme. Evie was restless last night – she's had a nasty cold – and I was upstairs with her for most of the programme, trying to get her to sleep.'

'So how come it was you who made the call?' asked Vicky.

Jenny appeared slightly embarrassed. 'Actually, he was all for keeping quiet,' she said. 'It's not that he isn't public spirited or anything like that,' she hurried on, 'it's just that the last time he had to talk to the police it was on account of a very upsetting experience.'

'You mean, when he discovered Adelaide Minchin's body?' said Sukey.

'You know about that? Yes, of course you do. The police were called at the time.'

'I remember the officer who attended the scene said he was in a very distressed state,' said Sukey.

'The thing is,' Jenny explained, 'Joe was invalided out of the army with post-traumatic stress disorder and anything to do with death just takes him back to all the terrible things he saw. I do hope you understand.' There were unshed tears in her eyes.

'Of course we do,' Vicky assured her. 'All we want him to do is tell us exactly where he saw Daisy, what time it was, if there was anyone else around at the time and so on. I promise you there won't be any gory details,' she added and received a weak smile in return.

'He's in the living room.' Jenny opened the door and showed them into a bright, comfortably furnished room with a stone fireplace and windows at both ends. Joe Atwood was on his feet, staring out at a small, rather untidy garden littered with toys. 'Joe,' his wife said quietly, 'these ladies are detectives and they want to ask you one or two questions about last night's programme.'

He turned round and nodded. 'Would you like to sit down?' he said tonelessly. He was, Sukey judged, in his mid to late thirties; his clean-shaven face was unlined and his skin had the light healthy tan of someone who spends a lot of time in the open. A weary, resigned expression and a twitching muscle at the corner of his mouth suggested an underlying tension.

When they were all seated, Sukey said, 'Mr Atwood, we understand that you believe you saw Daisy Hewitt, the missing girl who was featured in last night's Crimewatch programme.' He nodded. 'Can you tell us exactly when and where you saw her?'

'I was out on my milk round,' he began hesitantly.

'What day was this?'

'I can't recall the exact day – it was some weeks ago.'

'And about what time would it have been?'

'Around half past eight, I suppose.'

As the interview proceeded he gradually relaxed. It was when they were trying to establish the exact point where Joe's milk float overtook the girl they all believed to be Daisy, a question from Vicky, who was referring to a map of the village, produced an unexpected reaction.

'You say she was walking along the narrow lane that leads out of the village in an easterly direction?'

'That's right – Hampton Lane.'

'The one that goes past Parson's Acre? The house where Miss Adelaide Minchin used to live,' she added as he hesitated.

He put his hands over his eyes. For a moment Sukey was afraid the reference had reawakened distressing memories, but after a moment he lowered his hands and said quietly, 'That's right. Poor Miss Adelaide. I found her, you know.'

'You used to deliver her milk. I think?' said Sukey.

'That's right. Three times a week. I called for the money

every Saturday and that's when I found her.' He sighed and
shook his head. 'She was a lovely lady.'

'How well did you know her? I mean,' Sukey added hastily
as he appeared faintly startled by the question, 'I'm told she
was friendly and outgoing. Unlike her cousin who was a very
private person, she chatted away quite openly about all sorts
of things. For example, everyone knew where she kept her
spare key because she had a phobia about getting locked out
of her house.'

'Yes, that's right,' Atwood agreed. 'That's how I was able
to get in.'

'Did she tell you herself, or did you hear it from someone
else?'

'I can't be sure. Is it important?'

'Not necessarily. Do you happen to remember anything
else about her? Anything unusual?'

He thought for a moment. 'I do remember one Saturday
when she was in a right state when she answered the door.
She said there was a spider in her bath – I had to go in and
get rid of it before she could use the bath.' He gave a sad
little smile at the recollection. 'Real scared of spiders, she
was. I said, "Keep the plug in and they can't come up the
drainpipe". She was ever so grateful for that advice.' A sudden
look of concern appeared on his face. 'Why are you asking
all these questions about Miss Adelaide? I thought . . .'

'We're here officially about your wife's call to Crimewatch
yesterday,' Sukey agreed hastily, 'but it so happens that
someone in the village doesn't believe Miss Adelaide's death
was accidental.'

'Ah, now I remember,' said Atwood. 'It was all round the
village at the time that your lot had been asking questions,
but we thought it had all blown over. Is there anything else
you want to know?'

'I think that's all we need from you for now,' said Vicky
firmly, 'and thank you very much for your help in our enquiries
into Daisy Hewitt's disappearance.'

'No problem. I hope you find her.'

'We're not giving up until we do.'

As they returned to the car, Vicky said, 'Well, you've got
something to tell Doctor Hogan. Adelaide must have forgotten
about leaving the plug in the drain. A spider got in and scared

the pants off her; she staggered back in horror and fell heavily against the washbasin causing a fatal injury. Mystery solved. Accidental death, like the coroner said.'

Sukey nodded. 'You're probably right.'

THIRTY-ONE

'**S**hall we talk to Jerry Hubbard next?' said Sukey. 'It's getting on for six o'clock; with luck he and his Dad will be heading for the Red Lion about now. I haven't got Jerry's mobile number so I'll give Tom a call.' She punched in the number and after a brief conversation she said, 'Thank you very much, Mr Hubbard. We'll be with you shortly. They're already in the Red Lion,' she told Vicky after ending the call. 'We're going to rendezvous with Jerry in the car park so we can talk privately.'

'That makes sense,' said Vicky, 'and perhaps we can go into the bar after we've talked to Jerry. There might be some people there who saw the programme and maybe saw Daisy but never took the trouble to call in. We've been there several times – someone might recognize us and have a twinge of conscience.'

'Good point,' Sukey agreed. 'We can buy the boys a drink after we've taken Jerry's statement.'

As they turned into the Red Lion car park they saw the Hubbards' pick-up truck waiting at the far end. Jerry was leaning with his back against the driver's door, smoking a cigarette. He strolled over to meet them. 'Not sure I can be much help, but I'll do my best,' he said.

'That's the most anyone can do, and we're very grateful for your call,' said Sukey.

After the two detectives had asked him a very similar series of questions to those they had put to Joe Atwood and carefully noted his replies, Sukey said, 'Thank you so much, Jerry, we really appreciate your help. Just one more question: did you happen to notice a white van with a name that included the word "Services" painted on it?'

Jerry frowned and thought for a moment. 'Now you come

to mention it . . . I do remember a white van, but I can't . . .'
He thought some more, while Sukey and Vicky held their
breath. Then he shook his head in evident regret. 'I don't
recall seeing a name. It was just a white van. Sorry.'

'Never mind,' said Sukey. 'Well, I think that's all. Now,
how about us buying you and your Dad a drink?'

'No thanks, we've just popped in for a quick one on our
way home. We've got to get back, we've got people coming.'
Jerry threw down his cigarette and hurried back indoors.

'What do you think – shall we go in anyway?' said Sukey.

Vicky consulted their list. 'We still have several people to
see and time's getting on. People won't appreciate having
their evening interrupted. We can come back another time if
need be.'

By the time they had called on the last witness on their list
and written and emailed their reports to DC Rathbone, it was
after eight o'clock. Sukey stifled a yawn as she shut down
her computer. 'I wonder if DCI Leach and the Sarge got any
joy out of Bennett,' she said.

'There's nothing in my in-box,' said Vicky.

'Nor mine. We'll find out in the morning. We'll be expected
to turn up on the dot regardless of the overtime we've put
in,' Sukey added resignedly. 'Have a good evening – what's
left of it.'

When Sukey arrived home she found a message from Harry.
'I know you said you'd probably be late, so I'm not worrying
. . . not much anyway, but a goodnight call or a text would
be nice, just to let me know you're safely home.' The familiar
glow spread through her as she sent a brief text reading, 'All
OK, sleep well, talk soon, love S.' As she settled down in bed
after a convenience meal from the local supermarket, followed
by a hot drink and a shower, she fell asleep comforted by the
reassurance that he cared enough to worry about her.

The following morning Rathbone assembled his team for
a debriefing. It quickly emerged that the last sighting of Daisy
was at approximately the same point where Joe Atwood and
Jerry Hubbard had seen her within a few minutes of each
other.

'Right, you all have copies of the reports,' said Rathbone.
'Let's take Atwood's evidence first. He was on his milk round
on Hampton Lane – that's the lane leading out of Over

Hampton village – when he saw her. It's quite narrow in
places. He thinks she heard him coming because she glanced
over her shoulder and stepped into one of the passing spaces
– presumably, he thought, to get out of his way. He didn't
recognize her, of course. He recalls idly wondering who she
was and what she was doing there, but otherwise he thought
no more about her. Yes, Penny?' he said as DC Osborne raised
a hand.

'Did he say why he was on that part of the lane, Sarge? I
mean, there's only one house from that point on and that's
Parson's Acre. I seem to recall he only delivered there on
Tuesdays, Thursdays and Saturdays, but Daisy disappeared
on Wednesday.'

'Good question,' said Rathbone. He looked at Vicky and
Sukey. 'Anything to say about that?'

'Sorry Sarge, we should have mentioned it,' said Sukey.
'There are some farm buildings that have recently been
converted to dwellings, just before the junction with the Upper
Keynsham Road. The new owners have all moved in; he's
been calling there for several weeks now.'

'Right.' Rathbone turned back to the report. 'Atwood also
mentioned that a light truck he spotted in his rear view mirror
was the only other vehicle he noticed after seeing Daisy. It
was some distance behind him and he didn't recognize it, but
the report of the interview with Jerry Hubbard indicates that
this was almost certainly his pick-up. Jerry clearly remembers seeing Daisy – or a girl answering the description of the
girl in the reconstruction – but he couldn't be sure exactly at
what point along the lane he pulled out to pass her.'

'At what point along the lane is the path across the field?'
asked DC Mike Haskins, who was studying a map of the
village.

'About here.' Vicky showed him on her map. 'Both Joe
and Jerry must have passed Daisy before she got that far
because she was still on the opposite side of the road.'

Mike nodded. 'I see what you mean – if she intended to
take that path she'd have had to cross over.'

'But if she had arranged with Jake to pick her up in the
lane there'd have been no need to . . .' Penny began, but Mike
was quick to point out that there was no way of telling which
direction Jake was coming from.

'Does Jerry remember seeing Atwood's milk float?' asked DC Tim Pringle.

'He saw it ahead of him in the distance,' said Sukey, 'but by the time he passed Daisy he thinks it must have disappeared because he doesn't remember overtaking it.'

'Presumably by that time he'd turned off to deliver to the barns,' said Rathbone, 'and Jerry could have been going quite slowly as that part of the lane is quite narrow and twisty with poor visibility. Now, about the other sightings. As you've probably gathered there's very little traffic along Hampton Lane at this time in the morning, but two drivers heading towards the village saw a girl answering to Daisy's description walking towards them. Their sightings were both closer to the point where she would have turned into Hampton Lane after leaving her house, which is close to the centre of the village. They put the time at a little before half past eight – they can be reasonably sure because they both had their radios on and the announcer gave the time as eight thirty as they were heading out of the village.'

'OK,' said Rathbone, 'now let's consider the other callers. I'll deal with them collectively as none of them adds anything to what we've already dealt with. Unless Jake drove totally unobserved along Hampton Lane in the direction of Parson's Acre after the last recorded sightings, which is possible but seems unlikely, we're left with the probability that Daisy did use the footpath and he was waiting for her among the trees. The whole area has been gone over with a toothcomb and there was absolutely no sign of a struggle. In other words, if that was where they'd arranged to meet she went willingly with him to his vehicle. In that case he then took her somewhere, presumably for sex, and killed her when she tried to fight him off.'

'That would suggest he had a vehicle parked somewhere off the road, near the end of the path, wouldn't it Sarge?' said Mike.

'That possibility has been considered already, and nothing found to substantiate it,' said Rathbone. 'Added to which,' he went on gloomily, 'we have two witnesses who were exercising their dogs in the field about that time, and neither of them saw anyone using the path. On the face of it,' he went on, 'it looks as if Jake was driving an invisible vehicle.'

'Or one that no one would think worth mentioning,' said
Penny.

Rathbone looked at her enquiringly. 'For example?'

'Well, how many people mentioned Joe's milk float? Or
Jerry's pickup truck?'

'That's a point,' said Rathbone. 'It was only because Joe
and Jerry called in to report seeing Daisy that we know they
drove along the lane at the crucial time. Because people
assumed we were looking for a strange vehicle they didn't
think of mentioning obvious, familiar ones that use the lane
regularly. Maybe you've hit on something, Penny.' He made
a note before gathering up the reports and putting them in a
folder. 'I'll be reporting to DCI Leach in half an hour and my
guess is he'll be issuing a further appeal for witnesses in the
light of what we've uncovered so far. Meanwhile, more people
have called in response to last night's TV programme.' He
handed a list to Mike Haskins. 'Sort that lot out between you.'

After a brief consultation it was agreed that the list would
be split into five, which meant that Sukey's last calls were to
houses a short distance from the Red Lion. On being asked
what vehicles, including local ones, they had seen around the
crucial time, two householders – one living next to the dairy
and the other a few doors away – confirmed having seen Joe's
milk float leave at about eight o'clock. One also recalled
seeing Jerry's pickup shortly before half past eight. A number
of other vehicles had used that road but almost all had been
heading out of the village and were presumably commuters
on their way to Keynsham or Bath.

By mid-afternoon, having completed their interviews, the team
reassembled and compared notes. Little or nothing of any significance appeared to have emerged and after completing their reports
they went in search of refreshment at the Red Lion. Sukey, on
impulse, decided not to join them. 'I'll pick up a drink and a
snack in the village shop and join you later,' she said to Vicky.

Vicky looked at her curiously. 'What's up? Was it something I said?'

'Don't be daft. I've just remembered . . . the first time I was
here I got a lot of background information from the woman
who runs the shop, a Mrs Appleby. She's a very chatty soul
and I just thought . . .'

'Still on the trail of Adelaide's phantom killer?'

'Among other things,' Sukey admitted with a slightly apologetic smile.

'Well I'm starving and I want something more substantial than a bag of crisps,' said Vicky. 'See you later.'

Although Sukey had spoken to her only once, and that over two weeks previously, Mrs Appleby gave her a smile of recognition the moment she entered the shop. 'Ah, Constable Reynolds, I wondered if we'd be seeing you. We saw last night's programme but we never phoned in . . . never saw anything suspicious like, only a few locals like Joe the milkman and young Jerry and a few regulars stopping off to pick up their papers . . .'

'Was one of your regulars driving a white van with "services" painted on the side?' Sukey interposed.

Mrs Appleby shook her head. 'Could have been, I suppose. I don't take much note of what they're driving. Sorry.' She broke off to greet a woman of about sixty, clad in a long black skirt and a shapeless flowered top under a baggy cardigan, who had just entered. 'Afternoon, Mrs Clutterbuck. Lovely day!'

'Afternoon, Mrs Appleby,' the woman responded. 'Yes, nice and sunny so far, but Ben Bridges thinks we're going to have rain later.'

'Well, we can do with it,' said Mrs Appleby. 'What can I get you?'

'Just a bottle of milk and a small loaf.' Mrs Clutterbuck put the items in a carrier bag and handed over the money. 'See you tomorrow,' she said and turned to leave, but Sukey said quickly, 'Mrs Clutterbuck, I believe you used to work for Miss Adelaide Minchin.'

The woman looked at her suspiciously. 'Who wants to know?'

'This lady's a detective,' Mrs Appleby said before Sukey had time to show her ID. 'She was here asking questions after Miss Adelaide died – remember, I told you?'

Mrs Clutterbuck's eyes, set in a rosy and wrinkled face that reminded Sukey irresistibly of an overripe apple, lit up. 'Oh aye, that I do!' she exclaimed. 'You're here about that again? Good. I always said Miss Adelaide's death weren't natural but no one took no notice.'

'Actually, I'm part of the team making enquiries into Daisy Hewitt's disappearance,' Sukey explained.

'Ah yes, poor little Daisy.' Mrs Clutterbuck gave a sorrowful shake of the head. 'Well, I must be getting along.'

'Just a moment,' said Sukey quickly. 'What makes you think Miss Adelaide's death wasn't natural?'

The woman's voice dropped to a sepulchral whisper. 'She were warned not to disturb the dead, but she wouldn't listen.'

'How do you mean, she was warned?'

'It were the dead crow! A dead crow means another death!'

'What dead crow?'

'It lay on the patio outside her garden door. She just picked it up and put it in her dustbin like it was any old bit of rubbish. I told her it were an omen and she should treat it respectful . . . and be on the lookout for any other bad signs . . . but she only laughed. "A dead crow means another death, so be very careful," I said. "Oh Nellie, that's a load of nonsense!" she said . . . and look what happened to her!' Mrs Clutterbuck finished with an air almost of triumph. On her way to the door, she stopped and turned back. 'It's my solemn belief that there's a curse on that house,' she intoned. Remember what happened to poor Mr Cox and then Miss Muriel Minchin after him. That new young lady had better watch out for herself,' she added darkly.

'I heard about Mr Cox,' said Sukey, turning back to Mrs Appleby as Mrs Clutterbuck disappeared, muttering to herself. 'There wasn't anything suspicious about his death, was there?'

Mrs Appleby chuckled. 'Oh bless you, no! He was drunk as a skunk, so I heard, and fell into the lily pond and drowned. You don't want to take what she says seriously,' she confided, tapping her head with a forefinger.

'I heard he'd tripped over some builders' rubble.'

'I think it was material that hadn't been cleared away after some alterations to the house,' said Mrs Appleby. 'It was before we came here. Now, did you want anything?'

'Oh, yes.' Sukey hastily brought her mind back from the vague idea that was germinating in her mind. 'A bottle of water, please, and a packet of cheese and tomato sandwiches.' She paid for her purchases and went and sat down in the shade of an oak tree that bore a plaque to say it had been planted to celebrate Queen Victoria's Diamond Jubilee. While she was eating her sandwiches she tried to decide whether the idea was worth pursuing. One thing was certain: DS Rathbone would pay scant attention to it.

THIRTY-TWO

When Sukey reached home that evening there was a brief message from Harry. 'Any chance of seeing you this evening? It's been far too long.'

She grabbed the phone and keyed in his number. 'Hi there, I just picked up your message,' she said when he answered, trying not to reveal by her tone how much pleasure it had given her. 'For once I'm home at a reasonable time. Where are you?'

'I just got in. Shall I pop round – say in half an hour?'

'That'll be fine. I'd love to see you.'

She threw off her clothes and stepped into the shower. By the time Harry arrived she had dried herself and put on clean jeans and a loose top, but her hair was still damp. He went into the kitchen and put a bottle of wine on the kitchen table. She followed him, still towelling her hair. He turned, took the towel from her, threw it aside, pulled her towards him and kissed her on the mouth.

'You smell divine,' he said softly when he paused for breath.

'It's some fancy shower gel Gus gave me for my birthday,' she said. 'I've had it for ages – this is the first time I've used it.'

'Attar of roses,' he said, sniffing her neck. 'It suits you perfectly. Use it some more.' He drew her closer, sliding his hands down her back. With an effort she pulled away from him and picked up the towel. 'How about letting me finish drying my hair while you open that interesting looking bottle?' she said. She kept her tone light in a determined effort to hold back the surge of excitement that threatened to overwhelm her. *Careful, you keep saying you don't want to rush things,* said a warning voice inside her head. But as she slipped back into the bathroom and brushed her short brown curls into place another voice was saying, *You know it's going to happen some time, you both want it, so why not now?* Her pulse rate began to rise as she returned to the kitchen.

'That's nice,' she said after her first mouthful of wine.

'Australian Merlot,' he said, showing her the label. 'It's quite a mild evening; shall we sit on the terrace?'

'Why not?'

For a while they sat sipping their wine and idly chatting about the events of the day before lapsing into a companionable silence as they contemplated the view of the city spread out before them. The rays of the setting sun struck gold from the River Avon; in the distance, a flight of herons followed its course towards the Bristol Channel. Sukey gave a deep, contented sigh. Harry took the hand nearest to him and gave it a squeeze. She turned to smile at him as she squeezed back.

After a while, when their glasses were empty and the temperature had dropped a little, they went back indoors, still holding hands.

Sukey was awakened by Harry gently shaking her shoulder and his voice in her ear saying, 'Is there anything to eat in this flat?'

'Huh?' She rolled over in the crook of his arm and lifted herself on her elbow to look at the clock on her bedside table. 'It's nearly dark. What time is it?'

'Half past nine.' He pushed her back and brought his face close to hers. 'Happy?'

'Oh yes,' she whispered. 'You?'

'Very,' he whispered back. 'Hungry, though.'

'I'm hungry too, now you come to mention it,' she admitted, after a kiss that lasted a long time.

'Then we'd better get dressed.'

'I suppose so.' Reluctantly, she pushed back the duvet and sat up. 'What happened to my clothes?'

'They're on the floor with mine. What about some light?'

She switched on her bedside lamp. Together they sorted out their scattered garments and put them on, giggling like a pair of teenagers. 'I'll go and raid the freezer,' she said.

She defrosted and cooked a pack of Bolognese sauce, cooked some pasta and grated Parmesan cheese. Harry rummaged among her collection of CDs and put on a recording of a piano concerto. 'It seems we both love Mozart,' he said.

'He's one of my favourite composers.'

'Mine too. Do you think a shared taste in music is important?'

'I don't think there'd be much future for us if you were into heavy metal,' she said after due consideration.

A ping from the microwave signalled that the sauce was ready. She drained the pasta, took heated plates from the oven and served out the food. Harry poured more wine; as they sat down he raised his glass and said, 'Thank you for,' he hesitated, apparently groping for words, before continuing, 'something very special . . . and very lovely.'

She clinked her glass against his and said softly, 'It was lovely for me too.'

'So what sort of a day have you had?' he asked between forkfuls of pasta.

'We've spent most of the time following up the calls that came in after the TV programme.'

'Any new leads?'

'All I can say at the moment is that tomorrow we'll be issuing another appeal for information about Daisy Hewitt's last known movements.'

Harry sighed and shook his head in mock despair. '*All I can say at the moment . . .*' he mocked. 'And there was I, thinking you'd taken off your detective's hat along with the rest of your clothes.'

'I never mix business with pleasure,' she said teasingly. 'More pasta?' He held up his plate and she ladled out a second generous helping. 'There was something I wanted to tell you, though. Nothing to do with the Daisy Hewitt case.'

'Oh, what was that?'

'I met nutty old Mrs Clutterbuck and she told me there's a curse on Parson's Acre and that dead crows are harbingers of doom. She doesn't believe Adelaide Minchin died a natural death and hinted darkly about a malign supernatural influence.' She gave him a graphic account of the conversation with the eccentric old woman.

He laughed uproariously. 'I'll pass that nugget on to Leonora next time I see her. She'll love it,' he said.

'When are you seeing her again?'

'I've no idea. She can't move into Parson's Acre until probate on Adelaide's will has been granted, but as the relatives aren't going to contest it, it shouldn't take too long. She said something about calling me once she's ready to move in. She wants to talk to me about this building project she's very keen on.'

'You mean this garden room that Adelaide asked Tom Hubbard to give an estimate for?'

'I suppose so. I can't imagine why she thinks my opinion might be worth having.' He gave Sukey a keen glance. 'You've thought of something?'

'I'm not sure if it's worth mentioning,' she said slowly, 'but yesterday, after talking to Mrs Clutterbuck and then Flo Appleby who was telling me about the death of the man who owned Parson's Acre before Muriel bought it . . . I began to wonder. Harry, when you've got a moment, will you do a bit more research for me?'

'Tell me.'

He listened carefully and made a few notes. 'Leave it with me and I'll see what I can turn up. It may take a week or two before I have any time,' he added, 'I have to cover a trial starting on Monday at the Old Bailey.'

'That's OK. There's no rush.'

At the time, as she told DS Rathbone later, she had no reason to think otherwise.

Two weeks passed without any progress in the enquiry into the disappearance of Daisy Hewitt. A further appeal for witnesses produced no fresh leads and while Superintendent Baird gave the Hewitts his personal assurance that the case was still being actively investigated, pressure of other work meant that the team assigned to it had to be scaled down. Meanwhile, media attention focused on the trial of a notorious con-man charged with swindling a wealthy Somerset woman out of enormous sums of money. While reporting on the trial, Harry stayed with a relative in London during the week. He called Sukey each evening, first to tell her he missed seeing her, then to enquire about her day, and finally to tell he loved her. By the end of the second week of the trial the accused had been found guilty, remanded in custody and was awaiting sentence.

'I reckon his victim will more than recoup her losses from what she'll be offered for her exclusive story,' Harry told Sukey when he returned to Bristol on Friday evening. 'It was one of the juiciest cases I've had to report on by a long way. The red tops will be falling over themselves to get their hands on it. By the way,' he added while holding her close, 'I told Dad I might not be home till some time tomorrow.'

'Did you now?' she murmured as she nestled against him, 'So where were you planning to spend tonight?'

They were enjoying a leisurely breakfast the following morning and listening to the radio when an item of news caught their attention. 'Concern is growing for the safety of a woman who has not been seen since she left the Red Lion Hotel in Over Hampton three days ago to keep an appointment with a local builder. Her red sports car was outside the house where they had arranged to meet, but when he arrived there was no sign of her.' There followed a brief description.

'That sounds like Leonora!' Harry exclaimed, 'and the builder is probably Tom Hubbard. I know she's been after him to do a job for her. Do you know anything about it?'

Sukey shook her head. 'So far as I know she hasn't been reported as a missing person. Perhaps someone took it into their head to alert the local radio station and left it to them to inform the police.'

'I'll call my editor.' Harry took out his mobile and after a brief conversation he said, 'it was news to him as well. He wants me to go to Over Hampton right away. Coming?'

'Try and stop me.'

To their surprise there was no sign of media activity when they reached the Red Lion. The bar had not yet opened to the public, but as Harry drove into the car park a police car was already there. A uniformed officer got out and with an exclamation of surprise Sukey went over to greet him.

'Constable Gleed!' she said. 'Are you here about the lady who's gone missing?

'DC Reynolds!' He appeared equally surprised. 'Don't tell me the CID have been called in already. The lady isn't officially a missing person yet. My sergeant heard the item on the news and suggested I call round at the Red Lion to find out exactly what happened.'

'I'm not here officially, but from the description we – that is my friend and I – think we know who she is.'

Gleed gave Harry a keen glance. 'And you are, sir . . .?'

'My name's Matthews – I'm on the staff of the *Echo*.'

'Well, maybe you and DC Reynolds can shed some light on the situation. Let's go and have a word with Ben Bridges.' Gleed went to the main door and rang the bell. After a few

moments Bridges appeared in his shirtsleeves. He looked at
the three in some surprise, but on hearing the reason for their
call he invited them into the bar, closing and relocking the
door behind them.

'I can guess why you're here,' he said. 'That item on this
morning's news . . . you probably realize it's Miss Farrell
who's done a disappearing trick. The artist lady who's moving
into Parson's Acre,' he told Gleed.

The constable nodded. 'We thought it might be her. Can
you tell us exactly what happened, Ben?'

'She telephoned on Tuesday to say she was hoping to move
into Parson's Acre on Monday of next week, so she booked
a room here from Tuesday to Sunday. She'd arranged for
curtains and carpets to be fitted on Wednesday and it seems
that was all done to plan. According to what Jerry Hubbard
said, he was supposed to meet her at the house some time
after six o'clock that evening to talk about some plans she
has for an extension. Her car was there, but there was no sign
of her. He hung around for a while, thinking she'd maybe
gone for a walk and forgotten about him, and then he gave
up.'

'And no one's seen or heard from her since?' asked Gleed.

'That's right.'

The constable wrote in his notebook. 'It begins to look as
if we have to consider this lady a missing person,' he
commented.

'This extension,' said Sukey, 'I take it you mean the one
that Adelaide Minchin intended to have built . . . the one an
architect drew some plans for before she died?'

Bridges nodded. 'It seems Tom had a look at the job and told
her he had his doubts about whether it could be done the way
she wanted – something to do with a problem with the foundations – but she was definite she wanted it done to the plans
Miss Adelaide had left. She said if the Hubbards wouldn't do
it she'd give the job to another builder.'

'I remember her saying she'd have to get two estimates
anyway, but she'd rather give the job to the Hubbards,' said
Harry.

'Have you any idea if she's been in touch with another
builder?' asked Sukey.

Bridges shook his head. 'To be honest, from what little I

know it all sounds a bit vague. Miss Farrell is always going on about her plans for the house to anyone who'll listen. Tom and Jerry do first-class work and they're highly thought of, but they do tend to be a bit . . .' He broke off, searching for the right word.

'Unreliable?' suggested Sukey.

'Well, you know what builders are like.' Bridges grinned. 'Not so much unreliable, more a bit disorganized. Bessie has her hands full keeping tabs on them.'

'Do you know who reported that item to the local radio station?' asked Harry.

Bridges shook his head. 'There's been a lot of talk in the bar, of course, and it could be that someone who works for them picked it up and passed it on to the news editor.' He glanced at his watch. 'Look it'll soon be opening time and I've got jobs to see to, so . . .'

'That's all for now, and thank you for your time, Ben,' said Gleed. Back in the car park he said to Sukey, 'Maybe we'll be meeting again before long, Constable Reynolds. You too, Mr Matthews,' he added with a wry smile.'

THIRTY-THREE

'**W**hat d'you reckon?' said Harry as they went back to the car. 'Another woman in Over Hampton disappears without trace. That makes three, including Valerie Deacon, but not counting Sharon Swann because her body's been found. Surely there's a pattern here.'

Sukey shook her head doubtfully. 'On the face of it, yes – but there are discrepancies. A pervert who goes for teenage girls isn't necessarily turned on by a middle-aged woman, even one as glamorous as Leonora. Josh Bennett has been charged with Sharon's murder and he's still in the frame for Daisy's disappearance, but he's in custody so he obviously has nothing to do with Leonora's. It's more than likely that the same man is responsible for the disappearance of both Valerie Deacon and Daisy Hewitt, but Josh Bennett was a child when Valerie disappeared.'

'You're saying there's not necessarily a link between any of these cases?'

'I'm suggesting we should do a bit of lateral thinking. For example,' she went on as Harry raised his eyebrows, 'if we forget the girls for a moment and concentrate on Leonora, there could be more than one explanation for her disappearance. She might be suffering from amnesia and have wandered off somewhere and got lost. It does happen – people sometimes turn up miles away with no idea how they got there.'

'From what I've seen of Leonora so far, she's too much on the ball under that airy-fairy exterior to be liable to attacks of amnesia,' said Harry. 'You heard what Ben Bridges said about the Hubbards – maybe it was Jerry who mistook the time he was supposed to meet her. Supposing she wasn't expecting him until later, went for a walk and was attacked by a total stranger.'

'That's another possibility,' said Sukey. 'Anyway, if she doesn't turn up soon she'll officially become a missing person and we'll have another case on our hands.'

'Meanwhile, I'll get on with that bit of research you asked me to do.'

'Thanks Harry, that'd be great.'

'I suppose there's no use asking you exactly what you're expecting to learn from it?'

'To be honest, I'm not sure myself. Maybe when you give me some answers things will become a little clearer in my mind.'

'OK, I'll see what I can do. Now let's decide how we're going to spend the rest of the day.'

On Monday morning DCI Leach drove out to Over Hampton, where Rathbone and his team were already assembled in the incident room.

'Leonora Farrell is now officially a missing person,' he informed them. 'As you all know, Josh Bennett is in custody awaiting trial for Sharon's murder and as far as we're concerned he's still in the frame for Daisy's disappearance. Obviously he can't be responsible for anything that's happened to Leonora, so we're discounting any possible links for the time being. Superintendent Baird has assumed full control of the Daisy and Sharon cases and put me in charge of the inquiry into Leonora's disappearance. I'll be liaising with the man in charge here, Inspector Watson, about sending out search parties – the usual stuff, concentrating at first on the fields and woodland around the missing woman's house. Greg,' he turned to DS Rathbone, 'I understand one of your officers has had some contact with the missing lady.'

'That's right, sir. DC Reynolds has met her several times.'

'Good, we'll start there. Sukey, tell us what you know.'

'I've only met her a couple of times, sir, but she has a very interesting history. She recently inherited a house in the village under rather unusual circumstances – so unusual, in fact, that she herself couldn't understand why the previous owner bequeathed it to her. In anticipation of this becoming an official missing person case, I've written a brief report. I have it here, sir.'

'Excellent. Read it so we can all hear,' said Leach. When she had finished he said, 'Thank you, that give us a good starting point. Any questions?'

'When and how did it become apparent that she had disappeared?' asked DC Haskins.

'Good question, Mike. According to Ben Bridges, the owner of the Red Lion – that's the pub where she's been staying from time to time during her visits to the village pending taking possession of the house – she didn't come down for breakfast on Thursday. It so happens that all their rooms were booked from Tuesday night until Friday morning. That meant the staff were pretty busy and it seems no one noticed Leonora wasn't there until later in the day when they found her bed hadn't been slept in. You'll have gathered from Sukey's report that she was a somewhat unconventional lady and they assumed she'd stayed the night somewhere else and hadn't troubled to let them know. It wasn't until Friday that they began to grow concerned and asked if anyone had seen her, and it was then that Jerry Hubbard mentioned the broken appointment. He and his father hadn't paid much attention to it – you know what builders are like. They just thought she'd found something else to do and would get in touch again.'

'What about her next of kin – have they been contacted?' asked Tim Pringle.

'Not so far,' said Leach. 'Inspector Watson tells me that Ben Bridges has tried calling her London number but gets no

reply. Obviously, we'll be in touch with the local police to
see what they can find out. Do you know anything about next
of kin, Sukey?'

'All I know is that her mother died when she was a child,
sir. She never mentioned any other relative in my hearing.'

'Perhaps this chap Matthews from the *Echo*, who you say
has been digging into the history of the Minchin family on
her behalf, might be able to help. Have a word with him, will
you?'

'Will do, sir.'

'Right, that's all for now. I'll be back at HQ if you need
me, Greg.'

'Right, sir,' said Rathbone. 'OK folks, here's what we're
going to do,' he went on after Leach left. 'Sukey, you and I
will speak to the Hubbards. Vicky, get a detailed statement from
Ben Bridges and at the same time see what you can pick up
from the rest of his staff and any of the regulars in the Red
Lion. Someone check with the carpet fitters as it appears they
were the last people to see Leonora. The rest of you start with
local residents; Leonora has stayed at the Red Lion several
times and is bound to have spoken to some of them during her
visits. We hear she's a chatty soul so someone may have picked
up something useful. Any suggestions, anyone?' he added.

'Well Sarge,' said Sukey, 'Flo Appleby, who keeps the
village shop and post office, is a bit of a gossip who doesn't
miss much that goes on, and there's also a rather eccentric
woman called Mrs Clutterbuck who has done cleaning at
Parson's Acre for a number of years for a succession of owners.
She believes there's a curse on the place; I know she's issued
dark warnings to Leonora more than once and she said something about a dead crow being an evil omen. I doubt if Leonora
took her seriously, though. Incidentally, she doesn't believe
Adelaide Minchin's death was accidental.'

Rathbone looked sceptical. 'What in the world have dead
crows got to do with anything?' When Sukey explained he
gave a dismissive snort. 'Obviously a fruitcake, but someone
had better get a statement from her. Any other suggestions?'

'Leonora's solicitor, Mr Walker, has obviously had a lot of
contact with her about the legal side of her inheritance. He may
have the address of her next of kin.'

Rathbone made a note. 'I'll pass that on to DCI Leach.

He might want to follow that up himself. Right, if there are no more questions, let's get on with it. Report back here at five thirty, or call me immediately if there's anything urgent. OK Sukey, call the Hubbards and find out where they're working.'

'Sarge.' Receiving no reply from Tom Hubbard's mobile, Sukey rang the office number and spoke to Bessie. 'It's about Miss Farrell,' she explained. 'We need to ask Jerry a few questions so can you tell me . . .'

'Oh dear, I'm afraid he isn't too well, he's not working today,' said Bessie hurriedly. 'I think he's picked up a virus or something so I've kept him at home. Perhaps you could leave it for a day or two.'

'It is rather important that we see him without delay,' said Sukey after a brief consultation with Rathbone. 'It shouldn't take too long.'

'Oh, all right,' said Bessie reluctantly. 'I'll tell him you're coming.'

'Thank you. We'll be along shortly.'

'How old is this bloke?' he asked as they got into Sukey's car.

'I'm not sure, Sarge . . . mid thirties, at a guess.'

'Sounds a real mummy's boy,' he said contemptuously.

The Hubbards' house was called "The Old Forge" and was – as Bessie, in response to a comment by Rathbone, proudly informed them – the original village forge that they had bought as a virtual ruin and converted into a modern dwelling. 'It was Tom's intention to put it on the market,' she informed them. 'He reckoned it would have made a tidy profit, but when it was done we just fell in love with it and we've been living here ever since.'

'So was that the end of your dream of being property developers?' asked Sukey.

Bessie shook her head. 'Oh no, from time to time something comes on the market that looks interesting and we go for it. Nothing's turned up lately, though.'

She entered a room leading off the entrance hall and beckoned them to follow. 'He's in here. Here's two officers to see you again, Jerry,' she called as they entered, adding in a stage whisper, 'I'll leave you to ask your questions, but do please remember he's a bit under the weather.'

'Oh, Mum!' her son said impatiently as the door closed. He was seated in an armchair by the fireplace with a rug draped over his knees; although the day was mild, an electric radiator in the grate was switched on. He said an awkward 'Good morning,' as they entered. Sukey had the impression that he was embarrassed by his mother's solicitude.

'Good morning, Jerry,' said Rathbone. 'Mind if we sit down?' Without waiting for a reply he and Sukey pulled up a couple of upright chairs. 'I'm Detective Sergeant Rathbone and this is Detective Constable Reynolds, who I understand you've already met.' Jerry nodded. 'We're enquiring into the disappearance of Miss Leonora Farrell. We understand you had an appointment to meet her at her house, Parson's Acre, on Wednesday last week? Is that correct?'

'That's right. I turned up at the time she said she'd be there . . .'

'Which was?' Rathbone interrupted.

'About six o'clock, she said.'

'So what happened?'

'Like I told Dick – Constable Gleed, that is – she wasn't there. I thought, that's funny . . . her car's there but she's not answering my knock. Then I thought maybe she's gone for a walk or summat and forgot about me. I hung around a bit and she didn't show, so I left.'

'Did you see anyone else while you were waiting?'

Jerry shook his head. 'It's quiet about then, you see . . . folks are either home or in the Red Lion. That's where I went when I gave up waiting. Dad was there already and I told him what had happened.'

'What did he say?'

Jerry shrugged. 'Can't remember exactly. Something like maybe she'd decided not to bother.'

'About this meeting,' said Sukey. 'We understand that Miss Farrell asked your father to quote for an extension to her house. Is that what it was about?'

Jerry nodded. 'That's right.'

'Exactly what was involved?'

'She wanted what she called a garden room built over her patio,' said Jerry. 'She had some plans that someone had done for Miss Adelaide. She wanted us to work from them. Dad had a look at it; he said it would be a difficult job because it'd need extra strong foundations and cost a lot more than she bargained for.'

'So then what happened?

'She called us again and said she'd asked another firm to look at the job. They'd told her foundations weren't a problem and gave her a better quote. She asked us to have another look at it as she really wanted us to have the job. She's a very persuasive lady; said she thought Dad was being a bit too fussy.'

'Why did you go to meet her instead of your Dad?' asked Sukey.

Jerry shrugged. 'Dad told me to, so I did. He said to tell her the same as what he'd said.'

'Do you happen to know the other builders – the ones who'd given her a lower quote and said they could do the job?' asked Rathbone.

'It was Don and Dave Keegan. Everyone round here knows them. They're in Keynsham.'

'That's right,' Sukey told Rathbone. 'I've met them.'

'One more question, Jerry,' said Rathbone. 'How can you be so sure there'd be a problem with Miss Farrell's garden room?'

'Like I said, it was to do with foundations. The soil's not firm enough.'

'The Keegans are local people so they should be familiar with soil conditions in this area.'

'They don't know everything.'

'So what do you know that they don't?'

Jerry's sly smile reminded Sukey of a child who knows the answer to a riddle. 'This is our territory. We just know.'

'I see.' Rathbone stood up. 'Well, thank you Jerry, that's all for now.'

'I hope you feel better soon,' said Sukey.

Back in the car, Rathbone said, 'It's obvious the Hubbards didn't want the job so they quoted an extortionate price. It's a fairly common practice.'

'I can't say I blame them,' said Sukey. 'Leonora's an artist, possibly with a temperament to match. They probably thought she'd be difficult to deal with.'

'Maybe that's it. By the way, when did you meet the Keegans?'

'It was when Vicky and I were looking for the source of the bricks that Sharon was buried under. We called in at a house they were working on.'

Rathbone nodded. 'That's right, I remember now.'

'They're in very much the same line as the Hubbards. As well as general building jobs they buy run-down properties, usually at auction, do them up and either sell them on at a profit or rent them out.'

Rathbone made a note. 'They seem as keen to get Leonora's job as the Hubbards are to keep out of it,' he remarked. 'Maybe we should find out a bit more about them.'

THIRTY-FOUR

When the team reassembled soon after five thirty there was little progress to report. Several people who had driven along Hampton Lane during Wednesday afternoon and early evening recalled seeing Leonora's car parked outside Parson's Acre and a few mentioned seeing the carpet fitters' van, but no one had noticed anything unusual or seen anyone hanging about or in any way acting suspiciously. And there were no reported sightings of Leonora herself.

The only person in the village who had actually seen and spoken to Leonora during Wednesday appeared to be Flo Appleby, who told Mike Haskins that she had called at the shop that morning to pick up some milk, bread and biscuits. 'Flo said she was in high spirits and looking forward to moving in,' said Mike. 'She was also full of plans for the extension and mentioned she was hoping she could persuade the Hubbards to do it, but Flo didn't recall any mention of a particular time for a meeting with them.'

'Any idea who the carpet fitters are?' asked DS Rathbone.

'Yes, Sarge. It's this outfit,' Mike produced a card bearing the legend Kwiklay Karpets in characters surrounded by what appeared to be a simulated carpet pile, which amused everyone except Rathbone. 'I checked with them and managed to speak to the men who had done the work. They said they arrived about eight thirty and finished the job in the day. They said Leonora was very pleased with their work; she paid the bill with a debit card and gave them a generous tip in cash.'

'Was she there with the fitters all day?'

'No, she popped out as soon as they arrived to get some milk and a few groceries and then had a quick breakfast in the kitchen while they took up the old carpet. Then she told them she had things to do and went out after showing them where they could find tea and sugar and telling them to help themselves. She got back a little after four o'clock. They'd nearly finished and by the time they'd cleared up and put the old carpet in the van it was almost five.'

'Did she say anything about expecting a visitor?'

'Yes, Sarge, she mentioned she was expecting someone about some building work she wanted done. She was "rabbiting on" as one of the men put it about how she'd asked for two quotes and the builders she wanted for the job were too expensive and she was hoping to get them to lower their price. Reading between the lines, I think they thought she was hoping to turn on the charm. They agreed she was "a bit of a sex kitten".'

Sukey nodded. 'I can confirm that. I've seen her in action.'

'So we know she was alive and well at five o'clock on Wednesday,' said Rathbone, 'and there's nothing to suggest she was expecting anyone before her six o'clock appointment with Jerry. We know she wasn't in the house. The SIO contacted her solicitor this morning; he still holds a set of keys and they've been there and looked in every room – and the garage as well – and there was no sign of her. We're working on the theory that she went for a walk and never returned, but we're keeping an open mind about the reason. I've spoken to Inspector Watson and there's been no report so far from the search party. Vicky, any joy from the Red Lion?'

'Not really, Sarge. I spoke to Ben Bridges and he gave me the names and addresses of the kitchen staff and the chambermaids, but they had nothing to add to what we already knew.'

'Meanwhile, Sukey and I managed to track down the other firm that Leonora had asked to quote for her building job,' said Rathbone. 'They said they were quite sure they could do it at the price they'd quoted. When we told them what the

Hubbards had said they laughed and said the tale about the
foundations was a load of eyewash and they obviously didn't
want the job so they'd loaded their price, which is what we'd
already figured.'

'Did they have any idea why, Sarge?' asked Tim Pringle.

'They said they thought Leonora might be a bit of a nuisance,
possibly the sort of customer who'd hang around getting in
the way while they were working, wanting to make changes
halfway through and so on, but they reckoned they could
handle it.'

'Well, at the moment it looks as though neither of them
will get the job,' said Rathbone gloomily. 'Right, an hour's
break everyone. After I've reported to DCI Leach I'm going
for a pint at the Red Lion.'

'I'll join you there in a while, Sarge,' said Sukey. 'I've tried
to contact Harry Matthews, but his phone was switched off
so I left a message. This is him now,' she added, as her own
phone rang. 'Hi Harry, where are you?'

'In the Red Lion and I've got something to tell you,' he
said. 'Can you join me there?'

'I'm on my way.'

It was a little after six and as usual the bar was busy, with
a number of people sitting at tables or standing in groups with
drinks in their hands. Through the open door at the back Sukey
glimpsed more people in the garden enjoying the sunshine.
Among several customers waiting to be served she spotted
Harry. She went up to him and put a hand on his arm. 'Hi!'
she said. 'What's new?'

'I'm not sure how it helps,' he said, 'but I'm pretty sure
someone's been trying to frighten Leonora – probably the
same person who tried to frighten Adelaide Minchin.'

Sukey stared at him. 'Frighten them – how, and more import-
antly, why?'

'Let's take the "how" question first. I've had another talk
with Mrs Clutterbuck, Yes, I know she's a dotty old duck,'
he said, seeing her sceptical expression, 'but there's nothing
wrong with her powers of observation. She was quite definite that shortly before Adelaide's death there was a dead crow
on her patio, and the same thing happened last Tuesday afternoon when she was at Parson's Acre. Leonora had asked her
to clean some windows for her.'

'Look, I've already heard about the dead crows,' said Sukey impatiently.

'Ah, but did you hear about the blood?'

'What blood.'

'Each time when the bird was picked up and thrown in the bin there was blood on the patio.'

'So?'

'Have you never had a bird kill itself by crashing into a window?' Sukey shook her head. 'Well, it sometimes happens when there's a window at each end of a room and there are no curtains, giving the impression there's nothing in between.'

'You mean the bird thinks it can fly straight through and knocks itself out against the glass?'

Harry nodded. 'Right. I remember once it happened when I was quite small. It made a hell of a bump and scared the pants off me. And of course, the poor bird was dead, probably of a broken neck. Anyway, as far as I remember, there was no blood. Think about it.' He turned away as Ben Bridges approached.

'You're suggesting somebody shot these crows and left them on the patio as a kind of sick joke on Adelaide and then Leonora?' said Sukey doubtfully when Harry had ordered their drinks. 'That would account for the blood, of course.'

'Maybe it wasn't a joke,' said Harry soberly. 'Maybe someone was trying to warn them off making alterations to Parson's Acre. And that brings us to the "why" question. You asked me to do a bit more research and I've been delving into some old records and chatting to a few locals. The man who owned Parson's Acre before Muriel Minchin bought it was called Cox.'

'The man who drowned in the fish pond after tripping over some material the builders left lying around?' said Sukey.

Harry nodded. 'That's right. He bought the house from a couple of brothers called Don and Dave Keegan, builders and property developers, who bought it at auction and did an extensive renovation job before selling it on. I can see that name rings a bell,' he added, seeing the change in Sukey's expression. He listened intently as she told him of the conversation she and DS Rathbone had about the Keegans that afternoon. 'Did they tell you they'd worked at Parson's Acre before?'

'Not exactly – that is, they said they knew the property but they didn't go into details.'

'And maybe they were the ones who laid the patio. Maybe they'd rather it wasn't disturbed . . . at least, not by anyone else but them. Maybe that's why their quote was so competitive.'

Sukey felt a sick chill in the pit of her stomach. 'Harry, are you suggesting . . .?'

'I haven't been able to establish precise dates,' he said, 'but supposing that patio was put down at the same time as Valeria Deacon disappeared? Does that say anything to you?'

Sukey shuddered. She took a mouthful from her drink to steady her nerves. 'When word got around that Muriel Minchin was planning to sell Parson's Acre,' she said slowly, 'someone claiming to be a property developer tried to con her into selling it cheaply. We've guessed how word might have got around – it could easily have been one of the Keegans. Then the property passed to Adelaide. If she hadn't died no doubt she'd have gone ahead with her plans and . . .' She broke off as a thought struck her. 'Did Mrs Clutterbuck say what Leonora did with her dead crow?' she asked.

'The same as Adelaide – threw it in the bin.'

'When did you say this was?'

'Last Tuesday – the day before Leonora disappeared.'

'Today's Monday, and the bins are emptied on Tuesday mornings so it will still be there. If the thing was shot and the slug is still in the corpse, there's a chance we might find the gun for ballistics to check. Here, look after this, will you.' She gave Harry her glass. 'I'm going to Parson's Acre to collect it. It won't take more than ten minutes or so. Ah, here's Vicky. She'll keep you company till I get back.'

At about the same time as Sukey got in her car to go to Parson's Acre, DS Rathbone received an urgent call from DCI Leach. 'Greg, our IT whizz kid has identified the man Daisy Hewitt was chatting to on her computer,' he said. 'Guess who?'

'The artful bastard!' Rathbone exploded. 'Under our noses all this time . . . stringing us along . . . kidding us he's being helpful. At least I'm pretty sure I know where he is – it'll be one of two possible places.'

'Cover them both. And don't hang about!' ordered Leach.

Within minutes Rathbone had issued a series of instructions before heading for the Red Lion. He burst into the bar

followed by half a dozen uniformed officers. The chatter in
the bar died away and heads turned in alarm. Rathbone strode
over to Ben Bridges. 'I want a word with Jeremy Hubbard,'
he said. 'Is he here?'

'Jerry? Sure – at least, he was here a few moments ago,
waiting to be served. Come to think about it,' Bridges added,
glancing around, 'that's odd. I don't remember serving him
and he doesn't seem to be here now. Is something wrong?'

'What's up Sarge?' said Vicky, appearing at Rathbone's
elbow.

Rathbone swung round. 'Where's Sukey?'

'She popped out just as I arrived, said she'd be back in a
few minutes.'

'Where did she go?'

'I don't know.' She turned to Harry Matthews, who had
followed her. 'Did Sukey tell you where she was going?'

'Parson's Acre,' said Harry.

'What for?'

'To pick up a dead crow. She thinks it might be evidence.
Is something wrong?'

Ignoring the question, Rathbone charged out through the
door, shouting into his mobile phone and waving to the
uniformed officers to follow him.

'Any idea what that was about?' asked Vicky, but she spoke
to empty air, for Harry had rushed out after them.

THIRTY-FIVE

Sukey parked her car on the drive at Parson's Acre, took
a large plastic sample bag from the glove pocket and
walked along the path leading to the back of the house.
It was obvious that Leonora had not so far bothered to have
any work done on the garden. It appeared sadly neglected,
with a patch of weed-infested grass in the centre and late-
flowering dahlias struggling to make a colourful display in
an overgrown herbaceous border. But the early evening sun
drew a pleasant glow from the red brick wall that surrounded
it on three sides and a weeping willow cast a dappled shade

over the area outside the living room, where a table and a few chairs were arranged on a paved patio. *That's got to be where Adelaide wanted her garden room built . . . and now Leonora . . .* Remembering Harry's ominous speculations, she shuddered and turned away.

It took only a few moments to locate the waste bin in a covered recess beside the back door. Flies were buzzing around it and a sickening stench greeted her when she removed the lid. With one hand inside the plastic bag and the other covering her nose and mouth she reached down into the bin and gingerly rummaged among the few items of household rubbish until her hands closed over something with the feel of feathers and bone. She almost gagged as she lifted out the decaying remains of the crow and sealed the bag before hastily replacing the lid on the bin.

As she rounded the corner of the house on her way back to her car she found her way blocked by Jerry Hubbard. She stopped in surprise, but before she had a chance to speak he pointed to the plastic bag with its putrid contents and said in a strange, almost infantile voice, 'What you doing with Jerry's crow?'

Sukey stared at him. He wore an expression she had never seen before. His narrowed eyes gave him a crafty look but a smile that was almost playful hovered round his mouth. In that instant the sickening, terrifying truth dawned on her; it was not, as Harry had surmised, one of the Keegan brothers who had killed Valerie, Daisy, probably Leonora and who knew how many other women, but the man who was standing before her. Her throat tightened and her voice was barely a croak as she replied, 'This is your crow, Jerry?'

'Course it is – I shot him, didn't I?' His smile became triumphant. 'And the other one as well. I'm a good shot . . . I don't often miss.'

'Why did you shoot them, Jerry?'

'To scare them.'

'Scare who, Jerry?'

'The ladies who wanted us to dig up the patio, of course,' said Jerry. 'First there was Miss Adelaide. The crow didn't scare her, but the spider did.'

'What spider?'

'The one in her bath. Really scared her to death, that one did!' He gave a hoarse cackle.

'You put a spider in Miss Adelaide's bath?'

'That's right. Not a real one, of course. A great big one.' He held up his hands like an angler boasting of a catch. 'I bought it in a joke shop, see. She fell over in fright when she saw it and died. Saved me the trouble.'

'You mean, if she hadn't died in the fall you'd have had to kill her.'

He shrugged. 'S'pose so. She were that set on us digging up the patio.'

'Why didn't you want to dig up the patio, Jerry?' Sukey was perfectly sure she knew the answer, but her instinct told her that her one hope was to play for time by keeping him talking. If she didn't return soon, someone – probably Harry because he knew where she was – would come looking for her. She said a silent prayer that he wouldn't be too late.

'Never you mind,' said Jerry. He held out a hand. 'Give Jerry his crow.'

'I'll give it to you in a minute. Was this one for Miss Leonora?'

'That's right. She wouldn't scare either. Then she asked to meet me here. Made out it was to talk about the extension. We tried to explain it couldn't be the way she wanted it and maybe a nice conservatory would do the job, but no, she was going to have it done her way come hell or high water. And then she started rolling those big eyes and saying nice things . . . and I said to myself, Jerry you're all right there . . . she wants a real man and she fancies you.' He drew himself up to his full height, raised his chin and flexed his muscles. Their outline showed beneath the sleeves of his rough working shirt and there was hidden strength in his closed fists. Despite the danger, Sukey could not help but admire his physique and his undoubted sex appeal. His hands fell to his sides and his expression changed again, this time to anger bordering on hatred. 'She was just like the others . . . a bit older, but real pretty . . . but just another prick-teaser. So I taught her a lesson.'

Sukey's heart was pounding in her chest but she strove to appear calm. 'Where is she now, Jerry?'

'Never mind her.' He eyed her up and down and a new fear flooded over her. 'You're a bit old too, but you're real pretty. Maybe not a prick-teaser like the others?'

'No Jerry, I'm not . . . and I already have a boyfriend, so if you don't mind . . .'

'That's all right . . . there'll be others.' His smile was almost gentle. Relief at the change in his manner turned to alarm as he moved a step closer and held out a hand. 'Give Jerry his crow now.'

'In a minute, Jerry. What about Daisy Hewitt? Was she a prick-teaser too?'

His expression hardened again. 'That little tart! Wearing all that sexy stuff, waggling her backside in that short skirt instead of her nice school things.' His expression of disgust would have been comic had the situation not been so terrifying.

'She was expecting a stranger, Jerry . . . someone she only knew as Jake but probably someone about her own age. How come she went with you?'

The crafty grin returned. 'Sent a different picture, didn't I?'

'So what happened when she saw you?'

'I pulled up and offered her a lift to where she wanted to go. It was that easy . . . ever so grateful she was . . . hopped into the cab and started chatting about this chap she was meeting . . . sitting there showing her legs up to her bottom . . . she was asking for it wasn't she?' His expression darkened again. 'Just another prick-teaser, like the others.'

'Where is she now, Jerry?'

'Never you mind. Jerry wants his crow now.'

'All right, here it is.' She swung her arm back in an arc and with all her strength flung the bag across the garden. It was too light to carry far but the ruse was sufficient to distract Jerry's attention from her. Without hesitation he ran to retrieve it, opening her escape route. Seconds later she heard a shout of rage as he realized he had been tricked. She heard his footsteps pounding up the path behind her. She was still ahead of him when she reached the car and yanked open the door, but before she could scramble in he caught up with her, grabbed her by the arm and swung her round. His powerful hands closed round her throat. She raised her knee and caught him in the groin. He gave a yelp of pain but his grip did not slacken. The pressure increased; she could no longer draw breath. Lights flashed before her eyes. She had almost passed out when the throttling hands were torn away and she drew a long, shuddering breath before collapsing, semi-conscious, into a pair of waiting arms.

Some time later, after she had been examined by a doctor and given DCI Leach and DS Rathbone details of her encounter with Jerry Hubbard up to the moment when he attacked her, she sank with a sigh of relief into an armchair in her living room while Harry, after pouring two stiff gin and tonics with the remark, 'I think we need something a bit stronger than wine,' sat beside her and held her hand.

'That was a close call,' he muttered, half to himself. 'Another couple of minutes and . . .' She gave him a grateful smile and squeezed his hand. 'I don't suppose,' he went on, 'there's any chance you might find a less dangerous job?'

'It does get a bit hairy at times,' she admitted, 'but I'd get terribly bored sitting behind a desk.'

The following day the police announced that two men and a woman had been arrested and were being questioned in connection with the disappearance of Valerie Deacon and Daisy Hewitt and the murder of Leonora Farrell, whose body had been discovered in a shed on land owned by Hubbard and Son, builders. Meanwhile, Superintendent Baird congratulated his officers on their work on two long-standing unsolved cases in addition to a very recent one. 'We're confident that Jerry Hubbard is the killer and it's almost certain his parents have been protecting him. As you're doubtless aware,' he went on, 'there's a great deal of work ahead before we can bring charges. A team is already digging up the patio in the grounds of Parson's Acre; a check in the Hubbards' records shows that it was laid at the same time as Valerie Deacon disappeared and we expect to find her remains there. Another patio was being laid when Daisy Hewitt went missing and that site is being examined as well. Understandably the householders, a Mr and Mrs Wilson, are considerably distressed at the thought that there might be the remains of a murder victim in their garden, but they are being very cooperative. And of course Daisy's parents have been warned of what to expect.'

'Do we know yet how Daisy made contact with Jerry, sir?' asked Vicky.

'It seems he spent most of his free time on his computer and he picked her up on a chat line. She'd been asking for friends. Her father confirms that the Hubbards did some work for him and Jerry probably recognized her from the picture she put up on her Facebook page. We'll know more when our technician has tracked down all the exchanges that passed between them.'

On Wednesday, Jeremy Hubbard appeared before a magistrate charged with the attempted murder of a police officer and was remanded in custody. His parents were released on police bail, pending further enquiries. Meanwhile, Leonora's solicitor, Mr Walker, was trying to contact her next of kin, a distant cousin last heard of in Australia. 'Not the happiest of legacies,' Harry remarked to Sukey as they shared a meal a few evenings later.

'I wouldn't want a house with that history,' she agreed.

EPILOGUE

During the ensuing weeks, following a detailed examination of Hubbard and Son's records and Jerry Hubbard's computer, enquiries were reopened into two cold cases where young women had vanished without trace. In each case, both of which had taken place in neighbouring counties, police found that the Hubbards had been working on contracts in the neighbourhood. An investigation into Jerry's early life revealed that he had been in trouble at school for what was euphemistically described as 'inappropriate behaviour of a sexual nature' towards female students.

'Long before the Violent and Sexual Offender Register was set up, of course,' commented Vicky as she and Sukey discussed the latest developments over lunch in the canteen. 'His parents knew – or at least suspected – that he had a problem; to be fair to them they made sure he stayed at home where they could keep an eye on him. Fortunately, from their point of view, he took to the building trade and once he'd served his apprenticeship they set up the family firm of Hubbard and Son.'

'Which is how he came to be what the Sarge described as a mummy's boy,' said Sukey. 'I wonder if he was ever seen by a psychiatrist.'

'He will be now for sure,' said Vicky. 'It wouldn't surprise me if they found he had some personality disorder. They may even decide he's unfit to plead.'

'It must have been pretty devastating for the parents when they realized their son was a killer,' said Sukey. 'It was wrong, of course, to cover up what he'd done, but in a way you can sympathize with their predicament. Apart from the pain, they were facing potential ruin. Tom isn't a hundred per cent fit and without Jerry his business would probably fold.'

'But if he'd turned him in the first time, at least four of the victims would still be alive,' Vicky pointed out.

'Yes, of course,' Sukey agreed sadly. 'It was obvious Leonora was determined to have the extension the way she wanted it, so their only option was to kill her. They couldn't risk her giving the job to the Keegans – or anyone else. And being the kind of woman she was, it was odds on she'd be constantly popping in and out to see how they were getting on, so there was no way they could conceal what lay underneath. We know that Muriel had the patio laid about five years after she bought Parson's Acre,' she went on after a few minutes' thought. 'Enquiries show that she was away on holiday while the work was being done.'

'Which was mighty convenient for the Hubbards,' Vicky commented.

At that moment there was a series of beeps from Sukey's mobile phone. 'It's a text from Gus,' she told Vicky. 'They've just landed in Berlin.'

'They?'

'Gus and his girlfriend. They're spending a couple of months of the vacation bumming round Europe.'

'All right for some,' Vicky commented.

'Some do have it easier than others,' Sukey admitted. She offered a silent prayer of thankfulness for all the joy her son brought her. 'And yes, I do feel sorry for Tom and Bessie Hubbard. I wouldn't like to have their burden to carry.'

'I doubt if Doctor Hogan will share your sympathy,' Vicky remarked dryly.

Sukey grinned. 'Tell me about it! He was on the phone to me as soon as he saw the press release. DCI Leach gave me permission to tell him that in the light of recent developments there's likely to be a review of the verdict on Adelaide Minchin's death. Needless to say he wanted chapter and verse but I insisted that was all I could tell him. He muttered something about knowing all along that it was suspicious and threatened to take it up with his friend the Chief Constable.'

'Any word of appreciation of your efforts on his behalf?'

'What do you think?'